J.R.R. Tolkien .

J.R.R. TOLKIEN

THE LORD OF THE RINGS

comprising:

BOOK ONE
THE RING SETS OUT

BOOK TWO
THE RING GOES SOUTH

BOOK THREE
THE TREASON OF ISENGARD

BOOK FOUR
THE RING GOES EAST

BOOK FIVE
THE WAR OF THE RING

BOOK SIX
THE END OF THE THIRD AGE

and

APPENDICES

THE RING
SETS OUT

BEING THE FIRST BOOK OF
THE LORD OF THE RINGS

BY

J.R.R. TOLKIEN

HarperCollins*Publishers*

HarperCollins*Publishers*
77–85 Fulham Palace Road,
Hammersmith, London W6 8JB
www.**fire**and**water**.com

Seven-volume edition 1999
1 3 5 7 9 8 6 4 2

First published in Great Britain by
George Allen & Unwin 1954
Second edition 1966
This new reset edition published
by HarperCollins*Publishers* 1994

Copyright © George Allen & Unwin (Publishers) Ltd 1966

 ® is a registered trademark of
The J.R.R. Tolkien Estate Limited

ISBN 0 261 10393 8

Set in Post Script Monotype Plantin Light by
Rowland Phototypesetting Ltd,
Bury St Edmunds, Suffolk

Printed and bound in Great Britain by
Clays Ltd, St Ives plc

Three Rings for the Elven-kings under the sky,
  Seven for the Dwarf-lords in their halls of stone,
Nine for Mortal Men doomed to die,
  One for the Dark Lord on his dark throne
In the Land of Mordor where the Shadows lie.
  One Ring to rule them all, One Ring to find them,
  One Ring to bring them all and in the darkness bind them
In the Land of Mordor where the Shadows lie.

CONTENTS

NOTE ON THE TEXT

The Lord of the Rings is often erroneously called a trilogy, when it is in fact a single novel, consisting of six books plus appendices, sometimes published in three volumes.

The first volume, *The Fellowship of the Ring*, was published in Great Britain by the London firm George Allen & Unwin on 29 July 1954; an American edition followed on 21 October of the same year, published by Houghton Mifflin Company of Boston. In the production of this first volume, Tolkien experienced what became for him a continual problem: printer's errors and compositor's mistakes, including well-intentioned 'corrections' of his sometimes idiosyncratic usage. These 'corrections' include the altering of *dwarves* to *dwarfs*, *elvish* to *elfish*, *further* to *farther*, *nasturtians* to *nasturtiums*, *try and say* to *try to say* and ('worst of all' to Tolkien) *elven* to *elfin*. In a work such as *The Lord of the Rings*, containing invented languages and delicately constructed nomenclatures, errors and inconsistencies impede both the understanding and the appreciation of serious readers – and Tolkien had many such readers from very early on. Even before the publication of the third volume, which contained much hitherto unrevealed information on the invented languages and writing systems, Tolkien received many letters from readers written in these systems, in addition to numerous enquiries on the finer points of their usage.

The second volume, *The Two Towers*, was published in England on 11 November 1954 and in the United States on 21 April 1955. Meanwhile Tolkien worked to keep a promise he had made in the foreword to volume one: that 'an index of names and strange words' would appear in the third volume. As originally planned, this index would contain much etymological information on the languages, particularly on the elven tongues, with a large vocabulary. It proved the chief cause of the delay in publishing volume three, which in the end contained no index at all, only an apology from the publisher for its absence. For Tolkien had abandoned work on it after indexing volumes one and two, believing its size and therefore its cost to be ruinous.

Volume three, *The Return of the King*, finally appeared in England on 20 October 1955 and in the United States on 5 January 1956. With the appearance of the third volume, *The Lord of the Rings* was published in its entirety, and its first edition text remained virtually unchanged for a decade. (Tolkien made a few small corrections, but further errors entered *The Fellowship of the Ring* in its second impression when the printer, having distributed the type after the first printing, reset the book without informing the author or publisher.)

In 1965, stemming from what then appeared to be copyright problems in the United States, an American paperback firm published an unauthorized and non-royalty-paying edition of *The Lord of the Rings*. For this new edition by Ace Books the text of the narrative was reset, thus introducing new typographical errors; the appendices, however, were reproduced photographically from the hardcover edition, and remain consistent with it.

Tolkien set to work on his first version of the text so that a newly revised and authorized edition could successfully compete on the American market. This first revision of the text was published in America in paperback by Ballantine Books in October 1965. In addition to revisions within the text itself, Tolkien replaced his original foreword with a new one. He was pleased to remove the original foreword; in his check copy, he wrote of it: 'confusing (as it does) real personal matters with the "machinery" of the Tale, is a serious mistake'. Tolkien also added an extension to the prologue and an index – not the detailed index of names promised in the first edition, but, rather, a bald index with only names and page references. Additionally, at this time the appendices were greatly revised.

Tolkien received his copies of the Ballantine edition in late

January 1966, and in early February he recorded in his diary that he had 'worked for some hours on the Appendices in Ballantine version & found more errors than I at first expected'. Soon after this he sent a small number of further revisions to Ballantine for the appendices, including the now well-known addition of 'Estella Bolger' as wife of Meriadoc in the family trees in Appendix C. Most of these revisions, which entered variously in the third and fourth impressions (June and August 1966) of volume three, and which were not always inserted correctly (thereby causing further confusion in the text), somehow never made it into the main sequence of revision in the three-volume British hardcover edition, and for long remained an anomaly. Tolkien once wrote, concerning the revising of *The Lord of the Rings*, that perhaps he had failed to keep his notes in order; this errant branch of revision seems likely to be an example of that disorder.

The revised text first appeared in Great Britain in a three-volume hardcover 'Second Edition' from Allen & Unwin on 27 October 1966. But again there were problems. Although the revisions Tolkien sent to America of the text itself were available to be utilized in the new British edition, his extensive revisions to the appendices were lost after being entered into the Ballantine edition. Allen & Unwin were forced to reset the appendices using the copy as published in the first Ballantine edition. This did not include Tolkien's second, small set of revisions sent to Ballantine; but, more significantly, it did include a great number of errors and omissions, many of which were not discovered until long afterwards. Thus, in the appendices, a close scrutiny of the first edition text and of the much later corrected impressions of the second edition is necessary to discern whether any particular change in this edition is authorial or erroneous.

In America, the revised text appeared in hardcover in the three-volume edition published by Houghton Mifflin on 27 February 1967. This text was evidently photo-offset from the 1966 Allen & Unwin three-volume hardcover, and is thus

consistent with it. Aside from the first printing of this second
Houghton Mifflin edition, which has a 1967 date on the title
page, none of the many reprintings is dated. After the initial
printings of this edition, which bore a 1966 copyright notice,
the date of copyright was changed in 1965 to match the
statement in the Ballantine edition. This change has caused
a great deal of confusion for librarians and other researchers
who have tried to sort out the sequence of publications of
these editions.

Meanwhile, Tolkien spent much of the summer of 1966
further revising the text. In June he learned that any more
revisions were too late for inclusion in the 1966 Allen &
Unwin second edition, and he recorded in his diary: 'But I
am attempting to complete my work [on the revisions] – I
cannot leave it while it is all in my mind. So much time has
been wasted in all my work by this constant breaking of
threads.' This was the last major set of revisions Tolkien
himself made to the text during his lifetime. (Some small
alterations were made by Tolkien in the 1969 one-volume
India paper edition.) They were added to the second impression (1967) of the three-volume hardcover Allen & Unwin
second edition. The revisions themselves mostly include corrections of nomenclature and attempts at consistency of
usage throughout the three volumes.

J.R.R. Tolkien died in 1973. His third son and literary
executor, Christopher Tolkien, sent a large set of further
corrections of misprints, mainly in the appendices and index,
to Allen & Unwin for use in their editions in 1974. Most of
these corrections were typographical, and in line with his
father's expressed intent in his own check copies.

Since 1974, Christopher Tolkien has sent additional corrections, as errors have been discovered, to the British publishers of *The Lord of the Rings* (Allen & Unwin, later Unwin
Hyman, and now HarperCollins), who have tried to be con-
scientious in the impossible task of maintaining a textual
integrity in whichever editions of *The Lord of the Rings* they
have published. However, every time the text has been reset

for publication in a new format (e.g. the various paperback editions published in England in the 1970s and 1980s), huge numbers of new misprints have crept in, though at times some of these errors have been observed and corrected in later printings. Still, throughout these years the three-volume British hardcover edition has retained the highest textual integrity.

In the United States, the text of the Ballantine paperback has remained unchanged since Tolkien added his few revisions in 1966. The text in all of the Houghton Mifflin editions remained unchanged from 1967 until 1987, when Houghton Mifflin photo-offset the then current three-volume British hardcover edition in order to update the text used in their editions. In those new reprintings a number of further corrections (overseen by Christopher Tolkien) were added, and the errant Ballantine branch of revision (including the 'Estella Bolger' addition) was integrated into the main branch of textual descent. Beginning in 1987, the Houghton Mifflin editions also included an earlier version of this 'Note on the Text', which contains some slight errors and simplifications based upon what I then understood to be true. This revision of the 'Note on the Text', undertaken for a new reset edition of *The Lord of the Rings* (to be published in various formats), replaces and supersedes the earlier version.

This new edition also contains a number of new corrections (again supervised by Christopher Tolkien), as well as a reconfigured index of names and page references. For this 'best possible' version, the text of *The Lord of the Rings* is being entered into computers, which should allow for a greater uniformity of text in future editions. Rayner Unwin, for much of his life Tolkien's publisher, has reminisced that as a child he was told, as an incentive to improve his religious knowledge, 'that the University Presses would pay five pounds to anyone who detected a printer's error in one of their authorized Bibles. I never heard of anyone who earned this small fortune, but I have often imagined an equivalent reward being offered three centuries after the first publication of *The Lord of the Rings*. It would take at least that long to achieve typographical perfection.'

It may indeed, but this new edition makes a significant stride towards such perfection, as well as achieving a desirable conformity of the text in the various formats in which it is published.

The textual history of *The Lord of the Rings*, merely in its published form, is a vast and complex web. In this brief note I have given only a glimpse of the overall sequence and structure. Further details on the revisions and corrections made over the years to the published text of *The Lord of the Rings*, and a fuller account of its publishing history, may be found in *J.R.R. Tolkien: A Descriptive Bibliography*, by Wayne G. Hammond, with the assistance of Douglas A. Anderson (1993).

For those interested in observing the gradual evolving of *The Lord of the Rings* from its earliest drafts to its published form, I highly recommend Christopher Tolkien's account in volumes six to nine of his series *The History of Middle-earth*: *The Return of the Shadow* (1988); *The Treason of Isengard* (1989); *The War of the Ring* (1990); and *Sauron Defeated* (1992). These volumes contain an engrossing over-the-shoulder look at the growth and unfolding of a masterpiece-in-progress, unparalleled in literature.

Last, I must acknowledge with great pleasure the friendly assistance and cooperation over many years of Christopher Tolkien and Wayne G. Hammond.

Douglas A. Anderson
Ithaca, New York
April 1993

FOREWORD TO
THE SECOND EDITION

This tale grew in the telling, until it became a history of the Great War of the Ring and included many glimpses of the yet more ancient history that preceded it. It was begun soon after *The Hobbit* was written and before its publication in 1937; but I did not go on with this sequel, for I wished first to complete and set in order the mythology and legends of the Elder Days, which had then been taking shape for some years. I desired to do this for my own satisfaction, and I had little hope that other people would be interested in this work, especially since it was primarily linguistic in inspiration and was begun in order to provide the necessary background of 'history' for Elvish tongues.

When those whose advice and opinion I sought corrected *little hope* to *no hope*, I went back to the sequel, encouraged by requests from readers for more information concerning hobbits and their adventures. But the story was drawn irresistibly towards the older world, and became an account, as it were, of its end and passing away before its beginning and middle had been told. The process had begun in the writing of *The Hobbit*, in which there were already some references to the older matter: Elrond, Gondolin, the High-elves, and the orcs, as well as glimpses that had arisen unbidden of things higher or deeper or darker than its surface: Durin, Moria, Gandalf, the Necromancer, the Ring. The discovery of the significance of these glimpses and of their relation to the ancient histories revealed the Third Age and its culmination in the War of the Ring.

Those who had asked for more information about hobbits eventually got it, but they had to wait a long time; for the composition of *The Lord of the Rings* went on at intervals during the years 1936 to 1949, a period in which I had many

duties that I did not neglect, and many other interests as a
learner and teacher that often absorbed me. The delay was,
of course, also increased by the outbreak of war in 1939, by
the end of which year the tale had not yet reached the end
of Book One. In spite of the darkness of the next five years
I found that the story could not now be wholly abandoned,
and I plodded on, mostly by night, till I stood by Balin's
tomb in Moria. There I halted for a long while. It was almost
a year later when I went on and so came to Lothlórien and
the Great River late in 1941. In the next year I wrote the
first drafts of the matter that now stands as Book Three, and
the beginnings of chapters I and III of Book Five; and there
as the beacons flared in Anórien and Théoden came to Har-
rowdale I stopped. Foresight had failed and there was no
time for thought.

It was during 1944 that, leaving the loose ends and perplex-
ities of a war which it was my task to conduct, or at least to
report, I forced myself to tackle the journey of Frodo to
Mordor. These chapters, eventually to become Book Four,
were written and sent out as a serial to my son, Christopher,
then in South Africa with the RAF. Nonetheless it took
another five years before the tale was brought to its present
end; in that time I changed my house, my chair, and my
college, and the days though less dark were no less laborious.
Then when the 'end' had at last been reached the whole story
had to be revised, and indeed largely re-written backwards.
And it had to be typed, and re-typed: by me; the cost of
professional typing by the ten-fingered was beyond my
means.

The Lord of the Rings has been read by many people since
it finally appeared in print; and I should like to say something
here with reference to the many opinions or guesses that I
have received or have read concerning the motives and meaning of the tale. The prime motive was the desire of a tale-teller
to try his hand at a really long story that would hold the
attention of readers, amuse them, delight them, and at times
maybe excite them or deeply move them. As a guide I had

only my own feelings for what is appealing or moving, and for many the guide was inevitably often at fault. Some who have read the book, or at any rate have reviewed it, have found it boring, absurd, or contemptible; and I have no cause to complain, since I have similar opinions of their works, or of the kinds of writing that they evidently prefer. But even from the points of view of many who have enjoyed my story there is much that fails to please. It is perhaps not possible in a long tale to please everybody at all points, nor to displease everybody at the same points; for I find from the letters that I have received that the passages or chapters that are to some a blemish are all by others specially approved. The most critical reader of all, myself, now finds many defects, minor and major, but being fortunately under no obligation either to review the book or to write it again, he will pass over these in silence, except one that has been noted by others: the book is too short.

As for any inner meaning or 'message', it has in the intention of the author none. It is neither allegorical nor topical. As the story grew it put down roots (into the past) and threw out unexpected branches: but its main theme was settled from the outset by the inevitable choice of the Ring as the link between it and *The Hobbit*. The crucial chapter, 'The Shadow of the Past', is one of the oldest parts of the tale. It was written long before the foreshadow of 1939 had yet become a threat of inevitable disaster, and from that point the story would have developed along essentially the same lines, if that disaster had been averted. Its sources are things long before in mind, or in some cases already written, and little or nothing in it was modified by the war that began in 1939 or its sequels.

The real war does not resemble the legendary war in its process or its conclusion. If it had inspired or directed the development of the legend, then certainly the Ring would have been seized and used against Sauron; he would not have been annihilated but enslaved, and Barad-dûr would not have been destroyed but occupied. Saruman, failing to get possession of the Ring, would in the confusion and treacheries of the time have found in Mordor the missing links in his own researches into Ring-lore, and before long he would have made a Great Ring of his own with which to challenge the self-styled Ruler of Middle-earth. In that conflict both sides would have held hobbits in hatred and contempt: they would not long have survived even as slaves.

Other arrangements could be devised according to the tastes or views of those who like allegory or topical reference. But I cordially dislike allegory in all its manifestations, and always have done so since I grew old and wary enough to detect its presence. I much prefer history, true or feigned, with its varied applicability to the thought and experience of readers. I think that many confuse 'applicability' with 'allegory'; but the one resides in the freedom of the reader, and the other in the purposed domination of the author.

An author cannot of course remain wholly unaffected by his experience, but the ways in which a story-germ uses the soil of experience are extremely complex, and attempts to define the process are at best guesses from evidence that is inadequate and ambiguous. It is also false, though naturally attractive, when the lives of an author and critic have overlapped, to suppose that the movements of thought or the events of times common to both were necessarily the most powerful influences. One has indeed personally to come under the shadow of war to feel fully its oppression; but as the years go by it seems now often forgotten that to be caught in youth by 1914 was no less hideous an experience than to be involved in 1939 and the following years. By 1918 all but one of my close friends were dead. Or to take a less grievous matter: it has been supposed by some that 'The Scouring of the Shire' reflects the situation in England at the time when I was finishing my tale. It does not. It is an essential part of the plot, foreseen from the outset, though in the event modified by the character of Saruman as developed in the story without, need I say, any allegorical significance or contemporary political reference whatsoever. It has indeed some basis in experience, though slender (for the economic situation was entirely different), and much further back. The country in which I lived in childhood was being shabbily destroyed before I was ten, in days when motor-cars were rare objects (I had never seen one) and men were still building suburban railways. Recently I saw in a paper a picture of the last decrepitude of the once thriving corn-mill beside its pool that long ago seemed to me so important. I never liked the looks of the Young miller, but his father, the Old miller, had a black beard, and he was not named Sandyman.

The Lord of the Rings is now issued in a new edition, and the opportunity has been taken of revising it. A number of errors and inconsistencies that still remained in the text have been corrected, and an attempt has been made to provide information on a few points which attentive readers have raised. I have considered all their comments and enquiries, and if some seem to have been passed over that may be because I have failed to keep my notes in order; but many enquiries could only be answered by additional appendices, or indeed by the production of an accessory volume containing much of the material that I did not include in the original edition, in particular more detailed linguistic information. In the meantime this edition offers this Foreword, an addition to the Prologue, some notes, and an index of the names of persons and places. This index is in intention complete in items but not in references, since for the present purpose it has been necessary to reduce its bulk. A complete index, making full use of the material prepared for me by Mrs. N. Smith, belongs rather to the accessory volume.

J.R.R. TOLKIEN
1966

PROLOGUE

1
Concerning Hobbits

This book is largely concerned with Hobbits, and from its pages a reader may discover much of their character and a little of their history. Further information will also be found in the selection from the Red Book of Westmarch that has already been published, under the title of *The Hobbit*. That story was derived from the earlier chapters of the Red Book, composed by Bilbo himself, the first Hobbit to become famous in the world at large, and called by him *There and Back Again*, since they told of his journey into the East and his return: an adventure which later involved all the Hobbits in the great events of that Age that are here related.

Many, however, may wish to know more about this remarkable people from the outset, while some may not possess the earlier book. For such readers a few notes on the more important points are here collected from Hobbit-lore, and the first adventure is briefly recalled.

Hobbits are an unobtrusive but very ancient people, more numerous formerly than they are today; for they love peace and quiet and good tilled earth: a well-ordered and well-farmed countryside was their favourite haunt. They do not and did not understand or like machines more complicated than a forge-bellows, a water-mill, or a hand-loom, though they were skilful with tools. Even in ancient days they were, as a rule, shy of 'the Big Folk', as they call us, and now they avoid us with dismay and are becoming hard to find. They are quick of hearing and sharp-eyed, and though they are inclined to be fat and do not hurry unnecessarily, they are nonetheless nimble and deft in their movements. They possessed from the first the art of disappearing swiftly and silently, when large folk whom they do not wish to meet come blundering by; and this art they have developed until to Men it may seem magical. But Hobbits have never, in fact, studied magic of any kind, and their elusiveness is due solely to a professional skill that heredity and practice, and a close friendship with the earth, have rendered inimitable by bigger and clumsier races.

For they are a little people, smaller than Dwarves: less stout and stocky, that is, even when they are not actually much shorter. Their height is variable, ranging between two and four feet of our measure. They seldom now reach three feet; but they have dwindled, they say, and in ancient days they were taller. According to the Red Book, Bandobras Took (Bullroarer), son of Isengrim the Second, was four foot five and able to ride a horse. He was surpassed in all Hobbit records only by two famous characters of old; but that curious matter is dealt with in this book.

As for the Hobbits of the Shire, with whom these tales are concerned, in the days of their peace and prosperity they were a merry folk. They dressed in bright colours, being notably fond of yellow and green; but they seldom wore shoes, since their feet had tough leathery soles and were clad in a thick curling hair, much like the hair of their heads, which was commonly brown. Thus, the only craft little practised among them was shoe-making; but they had long and skilful fingers and could make many other useful and comely things. Their faces were as a rule good-natured rather than beautiful, broad, bright-eyed, red-cheeked, with mouths apt to laughter, and to eating and drinking. And laugh they did, and eat, and drink, often and heartily, being fond of simple jests at all times, and of six meals a day (when they could get them). They were hospitable and delighted in parties, and in presents, which they gave away freely and eagerly accepted.

It is plain indeed that in spite of later estrangement Hobbits are relatives of ours: far nearer to us than Elves, or even than

Dwarves. Of old they spoke the languages of Men, after their own fashion, and liked and disliked much the same things as Men did. But what exactly our relationship is can no longer be discovered. The beginning of Hobbits lies far back in the Elder Days that are now lost and forgotten. Only the Elves still preserve any records of that vanished time, and their traditions are concerned almost entirely with their own history, in which Men appear seldom and Hobbits are not mentioned at all. Yet it is clear that Hobbits had, in fact, lived quietly in Middle-earth for many long years before other folk became even aware of them. And the world being after all full of strange creatures beyond count, these little people seemed of very little importance. But in the days of Bilbo, and of Frodo his heir, they suddenly became, by no wish of their own, both important and renowned, and troubled the counsels of the Wise and the Great.

Those days, the Third Age of Middle-earth, are now long past, and the shape of all lands has been changed; but the regions in which Hobbits then lived were doubtless the same as those in which they still linger: the North-West of the Old World, east of the Sea. Of their original home the Hobbits in Bilbo's time preserved no knowledge. A love of learning (other than genealogical lore) was far from general among them, but there remained still a few in the older families who studied their own books, and even gathered reports of old times and distant lands from Elves, Dwarves, and Men. Their own records began only after the settlement of the Shire, and their most ancient legends hardly looked further back than their Wandering Days. It is clear, nonetheless, from these legends, and from the evidence of their peculiar words and customs, that like many other folk Hobbits had in the distant past moved westward. Their earliest tales seem to glimpse a time when they dwelt in the upper vales of Anduin, between the eaves of Greenwood the Great and the Misty Mountains. Why they later undertook the hard and perilous crossing of the mountains into Eriador is no longer certain. Their own accounts speak of the multiplying of Men in the land, and of a shadow that fell on the forest, so that it became darkened and its new name was Mirkwood.

Before the crossing of the mountains the Hobbits had already become divided into three somewhat different breeds: Harfoots, Stoors, and Fallohides. The Harfoots were browner of skin, smaller, and shorter, and they were beardless and bootless; their hands and feet were neat and nimble; and they preferred highlands and hillsides. The Stoors were broader, heavier in build; their feet and hands were larger, and they preferred flat lands and riversides. The Fallohides were fairer of skin and also of hair, and they were taller and slimmer than the others; they were lovers of trees and of woodlands.

The Harfoots had much to do with Dwarves in ancient times, and long lived in the foothills of the mountains. They moved westward early, and roamed over Eriador as far as Weathertop while the others were still in the Wilderland. They were the most normal and representative variety of Hobbit, and far the most numerous. They were the most inclined to settle in one place, and longest preserved their ancestral habit of living in tunnels and holes.

The Stoors lingered long by the banks of the Great River Anduin, and were less shy of Men. They came west after the Harfoots and followed the course of the Loudwater south-wards; and there many of them long dwelt between Tharbad and the borders of Dunland before they moved north again.

The Fallohides, the least numerous, were a northerly branch. They were more friendly with Elves than the other Hobbits were, and had more skill in language and song than in handicrafts; and of old they preferred hunting to tilling. They crossed the mountains north of Rivendell and came down the River Hoarwell. In Eriador they soon mingled with the other kinds that had preceded them, but being somewhat bolder and more adventurous, they were often found as leaders or chieftains among clans of Harfoots or Stoors. Even in Bilbo's time the strong Fallohidish strain could still be noted among the greater families, such as the Tooks and the Masters of Buckland.

In the westlands of Eriador, between the Misty Mountains and the Mountains of Lune, the Hobbits found both Men and Elves. Indeed, a remnant still dwelt there of the Dúnedain, the kings of Men that came over the Sea out of Westernesse; but they were dwindling fast and the lands of their North Kingdom were falling far and wide into waste. There was room and to spare for incomers, and ere long the Hobbits began to settle in ordered communities. Most of their earlier settlements had long disappeared and been forgotten in Bilbo's time; but one of the first to become important still endured, though reduced in size; this was at Bree and in the Chetwood that lay round about, some forty miles east of the Shire.

It was in these early days, doubtless, that the Hobbits learned their letters and began to write after the manner of the Dúnedain, who had in their turn long before learned the art from the Elves. And in those days also they forgot whatever languages they had used before, and spoke ever after the Common Speech, the Westron as it was named, that was current through all the lands of the kings from Arnor to Gondor, and about all the coasts of the Sea from Belfalas to Lune. Yet they kept a few words of their own, as well as their own names of months and days, and a great store of personal names out of the past.

About this time legend among the Hobbits first becomes history with a reckoning of years. For it was in the one thousand six hundred and first year of the Third Age that the Fallohide brothers, Marcho and Blanco, set out from Bree; and having obtained permission from the high king at Fornost,* they crossed the brown river Baranduin with a great following of Hobbits. They passed over the Bridge of Stonebows, that had been built in the days of the power of

---

* As the records of Gondor relate this was Argeleb II, the twentieth of the Northern line, which came to an end with Arvedui three hundred years later.

the North Kingdom, and they took all the land beyond to dwell in, between the river and the Far Downs. All that was demanded of them was that 'they should keep the Great Bridge in repair, and all other bridges and roads, speed the king's messengers, and acknowledge his lordship.

Thus began the *Shire-reckoning*, for the year of the crossing of the Brandywine (as the Hobbits turned the name) became Year One of the Shire, and all later dates were reckoned from it.* At once the western Hobbits fell in love with their new land, and they remained there, and soon passed once more out of the history of Men and of Elves. While there was still a king they were in name his subjects, but they were, in fact, ruled by their own chieftains and meddled not at all with events in the world outside. To the last battle at Fornost with the Witch-lord of Angmar they sent some bowmen to the aid of the king, or so they maintained, though no tales of Men record it. But in that war the North Kingdom ended; and then the Hobbits took the land for their own, and they chose from their own chiefs a Thain to hold the authority of the king that was gone. There for a thousand years they were little troubled by wars, and they prospered and multiplied after the Dark Plague (S.R. 37) until the disaster of the Long Winter and the famine that followed it. Many thousands then perished, but the Days of Dearth (1158–60) were at the time of this tale long past and the Hobbits had again become accustomed to plenty. The land was rich and kindly, and though it had long been deserted when they entered it, it had before been well tilled, and there the king had once had many farms, cornlands, vineyards, and woods.

Forty leagues it stretched from the Far Downs to the Brandywine Bridge, and fifty from the northern moors to the marshes in the south. The Hobbits named it the Shire, as the region of the authority of their Thain, and a district of

* Thus, the years of the Third Age in the reckoning of the Elves and the Dúnedain may be found by adding 1600 to the dates of Shire-reckoning.

well-ordered business; and there in that pleasant corner of the world they plied their well-ordered business of living, and they heeded less and less the world outside where dark things moved, until they came to think that peace and plenty were the rule in Middle-earth and the right of all sensible folk. They forgot or ignored what little they had ever known of the Guardians, and of the labours of those that made possible the long peace of the Shire. They were, in fact, sheltered, but they had ceased to remember it.

At no time had Hobbits of any kind been warlike, and they had never fought among themselves. In olden days they had, of course, been often obliged to fight to maintain themselves in a hard world; but in Bilbo's time that was very ancient history. The last battle, before this story opens, and indeed the only one that had ever been fought within the borders of the Shire, was beyond living memory: the Battle of Greenfields, S.R. 1147, in which Bandobras Took routed an invasion of Orcs. Even the weathers had grown milder, and the wolves that had once come ravening out of the North in bitter white winters were now only a grandfather's tale. So, though there was still some store of weapons in the Shire, these were used mostly as trophies, hanging above hearths or on walls, or gathered into the museum at Michel Delving. The Mathom-house it was called; for anything that Hobbits had no immediate use for, but were unwilling to throw away, they called a *mathom*. Their dwellings were apt to become rather crowded with mathoms, and many of the presents that passed from hand to hand were of that sort.

Nonetheless, ease and peace had left this people still curiously tough. They were, if it came to it, difficult to daunt or to kill; and they were, perhaps, so unwearyingly fond of good things not least because they could, when put to it, do without them, and could survive rough handling by grief, foe, or weather in a way that astonished those who did not know them well and looked no further than their bellies and their well-fed faces. Though slow to quarrel, and for sport killing nothing that lived, they were doughty at bay, and at need could still handle arms. They shot well with the bow, for they were keen-eyed and sure at the mark. Not only with bows and arrows. If any Hobbit stooped for a stone, it was well to get quickly under cover, as all trespassing beasts knew very well.

All Hobbits had originally lived in holes in the ground, or so they believed, and in such dwellings they still felt most at home; but in the course of time they had been obliged to adopt other forms of abode. Actually in the Shire in Bilbo's days it was, as a rule, only the richest and the poorest Hobbits that maintained the old custom. The poorest went on living in burrows of the most primitive kind, mere holes indeed, with only one window or none; while the well-to-do still constructed more luxurious versions of the simple diggings of old. But suitable sites for these large and ramifying tunnels (or *smials* as they called them) were not everywhere to be found; and in the flats and the low-lying districts the Hobbits, as they multiplied, began to build above ground. Indeed, even in the hilly regions and the older villages, such as Hobbiton or Tuckborough, or in the chief township of the Shire, Michel Delving on the White Downs, there were now many houses of wood, brick, or stone. These were specially favoured by millers, smiths, ropers, and cartwrights, and others of that sort; for even when they had holes to live in, Hobbits had long been accustomed to build sheds and workshops.

The habit of building farmhouses and barns was said to have begun among the inhabitants of the Marish down by the Brandywine. The Hobbits of that quarter, the Eastfarthing, were rather large and heavy-legged, and they wore dwarf-boots in muddy weather. But they were well known to be Stoors in a large part of their blood, as indeed was shown by the down that many grew on their chins. No Harfoot or Fallohide had any trace of a beard. Indeed, the folk of the Marish, and of Buckland, east of the River, which they afterwards occupied, came for the most part later into the Shire up from south-away; and they still had many peculiar names and strange words not found elsewhere in the Shire.

It is probable that the craft of building, as many other crafts beside, was derived from the Dúnedain. But the Hobbits may have learned it direct from the Elves, the teachers of Men in their youth. For the Elves of the High Kindred had not yet forsaken Middle-earth, and they dwelt still at that time at the Grey Havens away to the west, and in other places within reach of the Shire. Three Elf-towers of immemorial age were still to be seen on the Tower Hills beyond the western marches. They shone far off in the moonlight. The tallest was furthest away, standing alone upon a green mound. The Hobbits of the Westfarthing said that one could see the Sea from the top of that tower; but no Hobbit had ever been known to climb it. Indeed, few Hobbits had ever seen or sailed upon the Sea, and fewer still had ever returned to report it. Most Hobbits regarded even rivers and small boats with deep misgivings, and not many of them could swim. And as the days of the Shire lengthened they spoke less and less with the Elves, and grew afraid of them, and distrustful of those that had dealings with them; and the Sea became a word of fear among them, and a token of death, and they turned their faces away from the hills in the west.

The craft of building may have come from Elves or Men, but the Hobbits used it in their own fashion. They did not go in for towers. Their houses were usually long, low, and comfortable. The oldest kind were, indeed, no more than built imitations of *smials*, thatched with dry grass or straw, or roofed with turves, and having walls somewhat bulged. That stage, however, belonged to the early days of the Shire, and hobbit-building had long since been altered, improved by devices, learned from Dwarves, or discovered by themselves. A preference for round windows, and even round doors, was the chief remaining peculiarity of hobbit-architecture.

The houses and the holes of Shire-hobbits were often large, and inhabited by large families. (Bilbo and Frodo Baggins were as bachelors very exceptional, as they were also in many other ways, such as their friendship with the Elves.) Sometimes, as in the case of the Tooks of Great Smials, or the Brandybucks of Brandy Hall, many generations of relatives lived in (comparative) peace together in one ancestral and many-tunnelled mansion. All Hobbits were, in any case, clannish and reckoned up their relationships with great care. They drew long and elaborate family-trees with innumerable branches. In dealing with Hobbits it is important to remember who is related to whom, and in what degree. It would be impossible in this book to set out a family-tree that included even the more important members of the more important families at the time which these tales tell of. The genealogical trees at the end of the Red Book of Westmarch are a small book in themselves, and all but Hobbits would find them exceedingly dull. Hobbits delighted in such things, if they were accurate: they liked to have books filled with things that they already knew, set out fair and square with no contradictions.

2
Concerning Pipe-weed

There is another astonishing thing about Hobbits of old that must be mentioned, an astonishing habit: they imbibed or inhaled, through pipes of clay or wood, the smoke of the burning leaves of a herb, which they called *pipe-weed* or *leaf*, a variety probably of *Nicotiana*. A great deal of mystery surrounds the origin of this peculiar custom, or 'art' as the Hobbits preferred to call it. All that could be discovered about it in antiquity was put together by Meriadoc Brandybuck (later Master of Buckland), and since he and the tobacco of the Southfarthing play a part in the history that follows, his remarks in the introduction to his *Herblore of the Shire* may be quoted.

'This,' he says, 'is the one art that we can certainly claim to be our own invention. When Hobbits first began to smoke is not known, all the legends and family histories take it for

granted; for ages folk in the Shire smoked various herbs, some
fouler, some sweeter. But all accounts agree that Tobold
Hornblower of Longbottom in the Southfarthing first grew
the true pipe-weed in his gardens in the days of Isengrim the
Second, about the year 1070 of Shire-reckoning. The best
home-grown still comes from that district, especially the var-
ieties now known as Longbottom Leaf, Old Toby, and
Southern Star.

'How Old Toby came by the plant is not recorded, for to
his dying day he would not tell. He knew much about herbs,
but he was no traveller. It is said that in his youth he went
often to Bree, though he certainly never went further from
the Shire than that. It is thus quite possible that he learned
of this plant in Bree, where now, at any rate, it grows well
on the south slopes of the hill. The Bree-hobbits claim to
have been the first actual smokers of the pipe-weed. They
claim, of course, to have done everything before the people
of the Shire, whom they refer to as "colonists"; but in this
case their claim is, I think, likely to be true. And certainly it
was from Bree that the art of smoking the genuine weed
spread in the recent centuries among Dwarves and such other
folk, Rangers, Wizards, or wanderers, as still passed to and
fro through that ancient road-meeting. The home and centre
of the art is thus to be found in the old inn of Bree, *The
Prancing Pony*, that has been kept by the family of Butterbur
from time beyond record.

'All the same, observations that I have made on my own
many journeys south have convinced me that the weed itself
is not native to our parts of the world, but came northward
from the lower Anduin, whither it was, I suspect, originally
brought over Sea by the Men of Westernesse. It grows abun-
dantly in Gondor, and there is richer and larger than in the
North, where it is never found wild, and flourishes only in
warm sheltered places like Longbottom. The Men of Gondor
call it *sweet galenas*, and esteem it only for the fragrance of
its flowers. From that land it must have been carried up the
Greenway during the long centuries between the coming of

Elendil and our own days. But even the Dúnedain of Gondor allow us this credit: Hobbits first put it into pipes. Not even the Wizards first thought of that before we did. Though one Wizard that I knew took up the art long ago, and became as skilful in it as in all other things that he put his mind to.'

3

Of the Ordering of the Shire

The Shire was divided into four quarters, the Farthings already referred to, North, South, East, and West; and these again each into a number of folklands, which still bore the names of some of the old leading families, although by the time of this history these names were no longer found only in their proper folklands. Nearly all Tooks still lived in the Tookland, but that was not true of many other families, such as the Bagginses or the Boffins. Outside the Farthings were the East and West Marches: the Buckland (p. 130); and the Westmarch added to the Shire in S.R. 1462.

The Shire at this time had hardly any 'government'. Families for the most part managed their own affairs. Growing food and eating it occupied most of their time. In other matters they were, as a rule, generous and not greedy, but contented and moderate, so that estates, farms, workshops, and small trades tended to remain unchanged for generations.

There remained, of course, the ancient tradition concerning the high king at Fornost, or Norbury as they called it, away north of the Shire. But there had been no king for nearly a thousand years, and even the ruins of Kings' Norbury were covered with grass. Yet the Hobbits still said of wild folk and wicked things (such as trolls) that they had not heard of the king. For they attributed to the king of old all their essential laws; and usually they kept the laws of free will, because they were The Rules (as they said), both ancient and just.

It is true that the Took family had long been pre-eminent; for the office of Thain had passed to them (from the Old-bucks) some centuries before, and the chief Took had borne that title ever since. The Thain was the master of the Shire-moot, and captain of the Shire-muster and the Hobbitry-in-arms, but as muster and moot were only held in times of emergency, which no longer occurred, the Thainship had ceased to be more than a nominal dignity. The Took family was still, indeed, accorded a special respect, for it remained both numerous and exceedingly wealthy, and was liable to produce in every generation strong characters of peculiar habits and even adventurous temperament. The latter qualities, however, were now rather tolerated (in the rich) than generally approved. The custom endured, nonetheless, of referring to the head of the family as The Took, and of adding to his name, if required, a number: such as Isengrim the Second, for instance.

The only real official in the Shire at this date was the Mayor of Michel Delving (or of the Shire), who was elected every seven years at the Free Fair on the White Downs at the Lithe, that is at Midsummer. As mayor almost his only duty was to preside at banquets, given on the Shire-holidays, which occurred at frequent intervals. But the offices of Postmaster and First Shirriff were attached to the mayoralty, so that he managed both the Messenger Service and the Watch. These were the only Shire-services, and the Messengers were the most numerous, and much the busier of the two. By no means all Hobbits were lettered, but those who were wrote constantly to all their friends (and a selection of their relations) who lived further off than an afternoon's walk.

The Shirriffs was the name that the Hobbits gave to their police, or the nearest equivalent that they possessed. They had, of course, no uniforms (such things being quite unknown), only a feather in their caps; and they were in practice rather haywards than policemen, more concerned with the strayings of beasts than of people. There were in all the Shire only twelve of them, three in each Farthing, for Inside Work. A rather larger body, varying at need, was employed to 'beat the bounds', and to see that Outsiders of any kind, great or small, did not make themselves a nuisance.

At the time when this story begins the Bounders, as they were called, had been greatly increased. There were many reports and complaints of strange persons and creatures prowling about the borders, or over them: the first sign that all was not quite as it should be, and always had been except in tales and legends of long ago. Few heeded the sign, and not even Bilbo yet had any notion of what it portended. Sixty years had passed since he set out on his memorable journey, and he was old even for Hobbits, who reached a hundred as often as not; but much evidently still remained of the considerable wealth that he had brought back. How much or how little he revealed to no one, not even to Frodo his favourite 'nephew'. And he still kept secret the ring that he had found.

4

Of the Finding of the Ring

As is told in *The Hobbit*, there came one day to Bilbo's door the great Wizard, Gandalf the Grey, and thirteen dwarves with him: none other, indeed, than Thorin Oakenshield, descendant of kings, and his twelve companions in exile. With them he set out, to his own lasting astonishment, on a morning of April, it being then the year 1341 Shire-reckoning, on a quest of great treasure, the dwarf-hoards of the Kings under the Mountain, beneath Erebor in Dale, far off in the East. The quest was successful, and the Dragon that guarded the hoard was destroyed. Yet, though before all was won the Battle of Five Armies was fought, and Thorin was slain, and many deeds of renown were done, the matter would scarcely have concerned later history, or earned more than a note in the long annals of the Third Age, but for an 'accident' by the way. The party was assailed by Orcs in a high pass of the Misty Mountains as they went towards Wilderland; and so it happened that Bilbo was lost for a while in the black orc-mines deep under the mountains, and there, as he groped in vain in the dark, he put his hand on a ring, lying on the floor of a tunnel. He put it in his pocket. It seemed then like mere luck.

Trying to find his way out, Bilbo went on down to the roots of the mountains, until he could go no further. At the bottom of the tunnel lay a cold lake far from the light, and on an island of rock in the water lived Gollum. He was a loathsome little creature: he paddled a small boat with his large flat feet, peering with pale luminous eyes and catching blind fish with his long fingers, and eating them raw. He ate any living thing, even orc, if he could catch it and strangle it without a struggle. He possessed a secret treasure that had come to him long ages ago, when he still lived in the light: a ring of gold that made its wearer invisible. It was the one thing he loved, his 'precious', and he talked to it, even when it was not with him. For he kept it hidden safe in a hole on his island, except when he was hunting or spying on the orcs of the mines.

Maybe he would have attacked Bilbo at once, if the ring had been on him when they met; but it was not, and the hobbit held in his hand an Elvish knife, which served him as a sword. So to gain time Gollum challenged Bilbo to the Riddle-game, saying that if he asked a riddle which Bilbo could not guess, then he would kill him and eat him; but if Bilbo defeated him, then he would do as Bilbo wished: he would lead him to a way out of the tunnels.

Since he was lost in the dark without hope, and could neither go on nor back, Bilbo accepted the challenge; and they asked one another many riddles. In the end Bilbo won the game, more by luck (as it seemed) than by wits; for he was stumped at last for a riddle to ask, and cried out, as his hand came upon the ring he had picked up and forgotten: *What have I got in my pocket?* This Gollum failed to answer, though he demanded three guesses.

The Authorities, it is true, differ whether this last question was a mere 'question' and not a 'riddle' according to the strict rules of the Game; but all agree that, after accepting it and trying to guess the answer, Gollum was bound by his promise. And Bilbo pressed him to keep his word; for the thought came to him that this slimy creature might prove false, even though such promises were held sacred, and of old all but the wickedest things feared to break them. But after ages alone in the dark Gollum's heart was black, and treachery was in it. He slipped away, and returned to his island, of which Bilbo knew nothing, not far off in the dark water. There, he thought, lay his ring. He was hungry now, and angry, and once his 'precious' was with him he would not fear any weapon at all.

But the ring was not on the island; he had lost it, it was gone. His screech sent a shiver down Bilbo's back, though he did not yet understand what had happened. But Gollum had at last leaped to a guess, too late. *What has it got in its pocketses?* he cried. The light in his eyes was like a green flame as he sped back to murder the hobbit and recover his 'precious'. Just in time Bilbo saw his peril, and he fled blindly up the passage away from the water; and once more he was saved by his luck. For just as he ran he put his hand in his pocket, and the ring slipped quietly on to his finger. So it was that Gollum passed him without seeing him, and went to guard the way out, lest the 'thief' should escape. Warily Bilbo followed him, as he went along, cursing, and talking to himself about his 'precious'; from which talk at last even Bilbo guessed the truth, and hope came to him in the darkness: he himself had found the marvellous ring and a chance of escape from the orcs and from Gollum.

At length they came to a halt before an unseen opening that led to the lower gates of the mines, on the eastward side of the mountains. There Gollum crouched at bay, smelling and listening; and Bilbo was tempted to slay him with his sword. But pity stayed him, and though he kept the ring, in which his only hope lay, he would not use it to help him kill the wretched creature at a disadvantage. In the end, gathering his courage, he leaped over Gollum in the dark, and fled

away down the passage, pursued by his enemy's cries of hate
and despair: *Thief, thief! Baggins! We hates it for ever!*

Now it is a curious fact that this is not the story as Bilbo
first told it to his companions. To them his account was that
Gollum had promised to give him a *present*, if he won the
game; but when Gollum went to fetch it from his island he
found the treasure was gone: a magic ring, which had been
given to him long ago on his birthday. Bilbo guessed that
this was the very ring that he had found, and as he had won
the game, it was already his by right. But being in a tight
place, he said nothing about it, and made Gollum show him
the way out, as a reward instead of a present. This account
Bilbo set down in his memoirs, and he seems never to have
altered it himself, not even after the Council of Elrond. Evidently it still appeared in the original Red Book, as it did in
several of the copies and abstracts. But many copies contain
the true account (as an alternative), derived no doubt from
notes by Frodo or Samwise, both of whom learned the truth,
though they seem to have been unwilling to delete anything
actually written by the old hobbit himself.

Gandalf, however, disbelieved Bilbo's first story, as soon
as he heard it, and he continued to be very curious about
the ring. Eventually he got the true tale out of Bilbo after
much questioning, which for a while strained their friendship;
but the wizard seemed to think the truth important. Though
he did not say so to Bilbo, he also thought it important, and
disturbing, to find that the good hobbit had not told the truth
from the first: quite contrary to his habit. The idea of a
'present' was not mere hobbitlike invention, all the same. It
was suggested to Bilbo, as he confessed, by Gollum's talk
that he overheard; for Gollum did, in fact, call the ring
his 'birthday present', many times. That also Gandalf
thought strange and suspicious; but he did not discover the
truth in this point for many more years, as will be seen in
this book.

                    *   *   *

Of Bilbo's later adventures little more need be said here. With the help of the ring he escaped from the orc-guards at the gate and rejoined his companions. He used the ring many times on his quest, chiefly for the help of his friends; but he kept it secret from them as long as he could. After his return to his home he never spoke of it again to anyone, save Gandalf and Frodo; and no one else in the Shire knew of its existence, or so he believed. Only to Frodo did he show the account of his Journey that he was writing.

His sword, Sting, Bilbo hung over his fireplace, and his coat of marvellous mail, the gift of the Dwarves from the Dragon-hoard, he lent to a museum, to the Michel Delving Mathom-house in fact. But he kept in a drawer at Bag End the old cloak and hood that he had worn on his travels; and the ring, secured by a fine chain, remained in his pocket.

He returned to his home at Bag End on June the 22nd in his fifty-second year (S.R. 1342), and nothing very notable occurred in the Shire until Mr. Baggins began the preparations for the celebration of his hundred-and-eleventh birthday (S.R. 1401). At this point this History begins.

NOTE ON THE SHIRE RECORDS

At the end of the Third Age the part played by the Hobbits in the great events that led to the inclusion of the Shire in the Reunited Kingdom awakened among them a more widespread interest in their own history; and many of their traditions, up to that time still mainly oral, were collected and written down. The greater families were also concerned with events in the Kingdom at large, and many of their members studied its ancient histories and legends. By the end of the first century of the Fourth Age there were already to be found in the Shire several libraries that contained many historical books and records.

The largest of these collections were probably at Undertowers, at Great Smials, and at Brandy Hall. This account of the end of the Third Age is drawn mainly from the Red Book of Westmarch. That most important source for the history of the War of the Ring was so called because it was long preserved at Undertowers, the home of the Fairbairns, Wardens of the Westmarch.* It was in origin Bilbo's private diary, which he took with him to Rivendell. Frodo brought it back to the Shire, together with many loose leaves of notes, and during S.R. 1420–1 he nearly filled its pages with his account of the War. But annexed to it and preserved with it, probably in a single red case, were the three large volumes, bound in red leather, that Bilbo gave to him as a parting gift. To these four volumes there was added in Westmarch a fifth containing commentaries, genealogies, and various other matter concerning the hobbit members of the Fellowship.

The original Red Book has not been preserved, but many copies were made, especially of the first volume, for the use

* See Appendix B: annals 1451, 1462, 1482; and note at end of Appendix C.

of the descendants of the children of Master Samwise. The
most important copy, however, has a different history. It was
kept at Great Smials, but it was written in Gondor, probably
at the request of the great-grandson of Peregrin, and com-
pleted in S.R. 1592 (F.A. 172). Its southern scribe appended
this note: Findegil, King's Writer, finished this work in IV
172. It is an exact copy in all details of the Thain's Book in
Minas Tirith. That book was a copy, made at the request of
King Elessar, of the Red Book of the Periannath, and was
brought to him by the Thain Peregrin when he retired to
Gondor in IV 64.

The Thain's Book was thus the first copy made of the Red
Book and contained much that was later omitted or lost. In
Minas Tirith it received much annotation, and many corrections, especially of names, words, and quotations in the Elvish
languages; and there was added to it an abbreviated version
of those parts of *The Tale of Aragorn and Arwen* which lie
outside the account of the War. The full tale is stated to have
been written by Barahir, grandson of the Steward Faramir,
some time after the passing of the King. But the chief importance of Findegil's copy is that it alone contains the whole of
Bilbo's 'Translations from the Elvish'. These three volumes
were found to be a work of great skill and learning in which,
between 1403 and 1418, he had used all the sources available
to him in Rivendell, both living and written. But since they
were little used by Frodo, being almost entirely concerned
with the Elder Days, no more is said of them here.

Since Meriadoc and Peregrin became the heads of their
great families, and at the same time kept up their connexions
with Rohan and Gondor, the libraries at Bucklebury and
Tuckborough contained much that did not appear in the Red
Book. In Brandy Hall there were many works dealing with
Eriador and the history of Rohan. Some of these were
composed or begun by Meriadoc himself, though in the Shire
he was chiefly remembered for his *Herblore of the Shire*, and
for his *Reckoning of Years* in which he discussed the relation
of the calendars of the Shire and Bree to those of Rivendell,

Gondor, and Rohan. He also wrote a short treatise on *Old Words and Names in the Shire*, showing special interest in discovering the kinship with the language of the Rohirrim of such 'shire-words' as *mathom* and old elements in place names.

At Great Smials the books were of less interest to Shire-folk, though more important for larger history. None of them was written by Peregrin, but he and his successors collected many manuscripts written by scribes of Gondor: mainly copies or summaries of histories or legends relating to Elendil and his heirs. Only here in the Shire were to be found extensive materials for the history of Númenor and the arising of Sauron. It was probably at Great Smials that *The Tale of Years** was put together, with the assistance of material collected by Meriadoc. Though the dates given are often conjectural, especially for the Second Age, they deserve attention. It is probable that Meriadoc obtained assistance and information from Rivendell, which he visited more than once. There, though Elrond had departed, his sons long remained, together with some of the High-elven folk. It is said that Celeborn went to dwell there after the departure of Galadriel; but there is no record of the day when at last he sought the Grey Havens, and with him went the last living memory of the Elder Days in Middle-earth.

* Represented in much reduced form in Appendix B as far as the end of the Third Age.

The Lord of the Rings

A PART of the SHIRE

To Bree

The HEDGE

River Brandywine [Baranduin]

CLOUD LAND

Bucklebury

Crickhollow
Brandy Hall

Newbury
Haysend

Brandywine Bridge

Buckland

To Bree

Overbourn Marshes

Girdley Island

BRIDGEFIELDS

Budge Ford

STOCK

The Marish

Rushey

Deephallow

Willowbottom

QUARRY

Whitfurrows

The Yale

Scary

Frogmorton

Stockbrook

Woodhall

WOODY END

Thistle Brook

River Shirebourn

Brockenborings

To Dwaling

EAST FARTHING

The Water

To Oatbarton

NORTH FARTHING

Bywater Pool

BYWATER

Three Farthing Stone

TUCKBOROUGH

Pincup

GREEN-HILL COUNTRY

SOUTH FARTHING

overhill

HOBBITON

The Hill

The East Road

Bindbole Wood

Needlehole

The Water

WEST FARTHING

Waymoot

Tookbank

Longbottom

To Sarn Ford

Rushock Bog

FARTHING

Nobottle

To Little Delving

TO DELVING

MICHEL DELVING on the White Downs

CHAPTER I

A LONG-EXPECTED PARTY

When Mr. Bilbo Baggins of Bag End announced that he would shortly be celebrating his eleventy-first birthday with a party of special magnificence, there was much talk and excitement in Hobbiton.

Bilbo was very rich and very peculiar, and had been the wonder of the Shire for sixty years, ever since his remarkable disappearance and unexpected return. The riches he had brought back from his travels had now become a local legend, and it was popularly believed, whatever the old folk might say, that the Hill at Bag End was full of tunnels stuffed with treasure. And if that was not enough for fame, there was also his prolonged vigour to marvel at. Time wore on, but it seemed to have little effect on Mr. Baggins. At ninety he was much the same as at fifty. At ninety-nine they began to call him *well-preserved*; but *unchanged* would have been nearer the mark. There were some that shook their heads and thought this was too much of a good thing; it seemed unfair that anyone should possess (apparently) perpetual youth as well as (reputedly) inexhaustible wealth.

'It will have to be paid for,' they said. 'It isn't natural, and trouble will come of it!'

But so far trouble had not come; and as Mr. Baggins was generous with his money, most people were willing to forgive him his oddities and his good fortune. He remained on visiting terms with his relatives (except, of course, the Sackville-Bagginses), and he had many devoted admirers among the hobbits of poor and unimportant families. But he had no close friends, until some of his younger cousins began to grow up.

The eldest of these, and Bilbo's favourite, was young Frodo
Baggins. When Bilbo was ninety-nine he adopted Frodo as
his heir, and brought him to live at Bag End; and the hopes of
the Sackville-Bagginses were finally dashed. Bilbo and Frodo
happened to have the same birthday, September 22nd. 'You
had better come and live here, Frodo my lad,' said Bilbo
one day; 'and then we can celebrate our birthday-parties
comfortably together.' At that time Frodo was still in his
tweens, as the hobbits called the irresponsible twenties
between childhood and coming of age at thirty-three.

Twelve more years passed. Each year the Bagginses had
given very lively combined birthday-parties at Bag End; but
now it was understood that something quite exceptional was
being planned for that autumn. Bilbo was going to be
eleventy-one, 111, a rather curious number, and a very
respectable age for a hobbit (the Old Took himself had only
reached 130); and Frodo was going to be *thirty-three*, 33, an
important number: the date of his 'coming of age'.

Tongues began to wag in Hobbiton and Bywater; and
rumour of the coming event travelled all over the Shire. The
history and character of Mr. Bilbo Baggins became once
again the chief topic of conversation; and the older folk suddenly found their reminiscences in welcome demand.

No one had a more attentive audience than old Ham
Gamgee, commonly known as the Gaffer. He held forth at
The Ivy Bush, a small inn on the Bywater road; and he spoke
with some authority, for he had tended the garden at Bag
End for forty years, and had helped old Holman in the same
job before that. Now that he was himself growing old and
stiff in the joints, the job was mainly carried on by his youngest son, Sam Gamgee. Both father and son were on very
friendly terms with Bilbo and Frodo. They lived on the Hill
itself, in Number 3 Bagshot Row just below Bag End.

'A very nice well-spoken gentlehobbit is Mr. Bilbo, as I've
always said,' the Gaffer declared. With perfect truth: for Bilbo
was very polite to him, calling him 'Master Hamfast', and

consulting him constantly upon the growing of vegetables – in the matter of 'roots', especially potatoes, the Gaffer was recognized as the leading authority by all in the neighbourhood (including himself).

'But what about this Frodo that lives with him?' asked Old Noakes of Bywater. 'Baggins is his name, but he's more than half a Brandybuck, they say. It beats me why any Baggins of Hobbiton should go looking for a wife away there in Buckland, where folks are so queer.'

'And no wonder they're queer,' put in Daddy Twofoot (the Gaffer's next-door neighbour), 'if they live on the wrong side of the Brandywine River, and right agin the Old Forest. That's a dark bad place, if half the tales be true.'

'You're right, Dad!' said the Gaffer. 'Not that the Brandybucks of Buckland live *in* the Old Forest; but they're a queer breed, seemingly. They fool about with boats on that big river – and that isn't natural. Small wonder that trouble came of it, I say. But be that as it may, Mr. Frodo is as nice a young hobbit as you could wish to meet. Very much like Mr. Bilbo, and in more than looks. After all his father was a Baggins. A decent respectable hobbit was Mr. Drogo Baggins; there was never much to tell of him, till he was drownded.'

'Drownded?' said several voices. They had heard this and other darker rumours before, of course; but hobbits have a passion for family history, and they were ready to hear it again.

'Well, so they say,' said the Gaffer. 'You see: Mr. Drogo, he married poor Miss Primula Brandybuck. She was our Mr. Bilbo's first cousin on the mother's side (her mother being the youngest of the Old Took's daughters); and Mr. Drogo was his second cousin. So Mr. Frodo is his first *and* second cousin, once removed either way, as the saying is, if you follow me. And Mr. Drogo was staying at Brandy Hall with his father-in-law, old Master Gorbadoc, as he often did after his marriage (him being partial to his vittles, and old Gorbadoc keeping a mighty generous table); and he went out *boat-*

ing on the Brandywine River; and he and his wife were drownded, and poor Mr. Frodo only a child and all.'

'I've heard they went on the water after dinner in the moonlight,' said Old Noakes; 'and it was Drogo's weight as sunk the boat.'

'And *I* heard she pushed him in, and he pulled her in after him,' said Sandyman, the Hobbiton miller.

'You shouldn't listen to all you hear, Sandyman,' said the Gaffer, who did not much like the miller. 'There isn't no call to go talking of pushing and pulling. Boats are quite tricky enough for those that sit still without looking further for the cause of trouble. Anyway: there was this Mr. Frodo left an orphan and stranded, as you might say, among those queer Bucklanders, being brought up anyhow in Brandy Hall. A regular warren, by all accounts. Old Master Gorbadoc never had fewer than a couple of hundred relations in the place. Mr. Bilbo never did a kinder deed than when he brought the lad back to live among decent folk.

'But I reckon it was a nasty shock for those Sackville-Bagginses. They thought they were going to get Bag End, that time when he went off and was thought to be dead. And then he comes back and orders them off; and he goes on living and living, and never looking a day older, bless him! And suddenly he produces an heir, and has all the papers made out proper. The Sackville-Bagginses won't never see the inside of Bag End now, or it is to be hoped not.'

'There's a tidy bit of money tucked away up there, I hear tell,' said a stranger, a visitor on business from Michel Delving in the Westfarthing. 'All the top of your hill is full of tunnels packed with chests of gold and silver, *and* jools, by what I've heard.'

'Then you've heard more than I can speak to,' answered the Gaffer. 'I know nothing about *jools*. Mr. Bilbo is free with his money, and there seems no lack of it; but I know of no tunnel-making. I saw Mr. Bilbo when he came back, a matter of sixty years ago, when I was a lad. I'd not long come prentice to old Holman (him being my dad's cousin), but he

had me up at Bag End helping him to keep folks from tram-
pling and trapessing all over the garden while the sale was
on. And in the middle of it all Mr. Bilbo comes up the Hill
with a pony and some mighty big bags and a couple of chests.
I don't doubt they were mostly full of treasure he had picked
up in foreign parts, where there be mountains of gold, they
say; but there wasn't enough to fill tunnels. But my lad Sam
will know more about that. He's in and out of Bag End.
Crazy about stories of the old days he is, and he listens to
all Mr. Bilbo's tales. Mr. Bilbo has learned him his letters –
meaning no harm, mark you, and I hope no harm will come
of it.

  '*Elves and Dragons!* I says to him. *Cabbages and potatoes
are better for me and you. Don't go getting mixed up in the
business of your betters, or you'll land in trouble too big for you*,
I says to him. And I might say it to others,' he added with
a look at the stranger and the miller.

  But the Gaffer did not convince his audience. The legend
of Bilbo's wealth was now too firmly fixed in the minds of
the younger generation of hobbits.

  'Ah, but he has likely enough been adding to what he
brought at first,' argued the miller, voicing common opinion.
'He's often away from home. And look at the outlandish folk
that visit him: dwarves coming at night, and that old wandering
conjuror, Gandalf, and all. You can say what you like, Gaffer,
but Bag End's a queer place, and its folk are queerer.'

  'And you can say what *you* like, about what you know no
more of than you do of boating, Mr. Sandyman,' retorted
the Gaffer, disliking the miller even more than usual. 'If that's
being queer, then we could do with a bit more queerness in
these parts. There's some not far away that wouldn't offer a
pint of beer to a friend, if they lived in a hole with golden
walls. But they do things proper at Bag End. Our Sam says
that *everyone's* going to be invited to the party, and there's
going to be presents, mark you, presents for all – this very
month as is.'

*   *   *

That very month was September, and as fine as you could ask. A day or two later a rumour (probably started by the knowledgeable Sam) was spread about that there were going to be fireworks – fireworks, what is more, such as had not been seen in the Shire for nigh on a century, not indeed since the Old Took died.

Days passed and The Day drew nearer. An odd-looking waggon laden with odd-looking packages rolled into Hobbiton one evening and toiled up the Hill to Bag End. The startled hobbits peered out of lamplit doors to gape at it. It was driven by outlandish folk, singing strange songs: dwarves with long beards and deep hoods. A few of them remained at Bag End. At the end of the second week in September a cart came in through Bywater from the direction of the Brandywine Bridge in broad daylight. An old man was driving it all alone. He wore a tall pointed blue hat, a long grey cloak, and a silver scarf. He had a long white beard and bushy eyebrows that stuck out beyond the brim of his hat. Small hobbit-children ran after the cart all through Hobbiton and right up the hill. It had a cargo of fireworks, as they rightly guessed. At Bilbo's front door the old man began to unload: there were great bundles of fireworks of all sorts and shapes, each labelled with a large red G ᚷ and the elf-rune, ᚹ.

That was Gandalf's mark, of course, and the old man was Gandalf the Wizard, whose fame in the Shire was due mainly to his skill with fires, smokes, and lights. His real business was far more difficult and dangerous, but the Shire-folk knew nothing about it. To them he was just one of the 'attractions' at the Party. Hence the excitement of the hobbit-children. 'G for Grand!' they shouted, and the old man smiled. They knew him by sight, though he only appeared in Hobbiton occasionally and never stopped long; but neither they nor any but the oldest of their elders had seen one of his firework displays – they now belonged to the legendary past.

When the old man, helped by Bilbo and some dwarves, had finished unloading, Bilbo gave a few pennies away; but

not a single squib or cracker was forthcoming, to the dis-
appointment of the onlookers.

'Run away now!' said Gandalf. 'You will get plenty when
the time comes.' Then he disappeared inside with Bilbo, and
the door was shut. The young hobbits stared at the door in
vain for a while, and then made off, feeling that the day of
the party would never come.

Inside Bag End, Bilbo and Gandalf were sitting at the open
window of a small room looking out west on to the garden.
The late afternoon was bright and peaceful. The flowers
glowed red and golden: snap-dragons and sunflowers, and
nasturtians trailing all over the turf walls and peeping in at
the round windows.

'How bright your garden looks!' said Gandalf.

'Yes,' said Bilbo. 'I am very fond indeed of it, and of all
the dear old Shire; but I think I need a holiday.'

'You mean to go on with your plan then?'

'I do. I made up my mind months ago, and I haven't
changed it.'

'Very well. It is no good saying any more. Stick to your
plan – your whole plan, mind – and I hope it will turn out
for the best, for you, and for all of us.'

'I hope so. Anyway I mean to enjoy myself on Thursday,
and have my little joke.'

'Who will laugh, I wonder?' said Gandalf, shaking his head.

'We shall see,' said Bilbo.

The next day more carts rolled up the Hill, and still more
carts. There might have been some grumbling about 'dealing
locally', but that very week orders began to pour out of Bag
End for every kind of provision, commodity, or luxury that
could be obtained in Hobbiton or Bywater or anywhere in
the neighbourhood. People became enthusiastic; and they
began to tick off the days on the calendar; and they watched
eagerly for the postman, hoping for invitations.

Before long the invitations began pouring out, and the

Hobbiton post-office was blocked, and the Bywater post-office was snowed under, and voluntary assistant postmen were called for. There was a constant stream of them going up the Hill, carrying hundreds of polite variations on *Thank you, I shall certainly come.*

A notice appeared on the gate at Bag End: NO ADMITTANCE EXCEPT ON PARTY BUSINESS. Even those who had, or pretended to have Party Business were seldom allowed inside. Bilbo was busy: writing invitations, ticking off answers, packing up presents, and making some private preparations of his own. From the time of Gandalf's arrival he remained hidden from view.

One morning the hobbits woke to find the large field, south of Bilbo's front door, covered with ropes and poles for tents and pavilions. A special entrance was cut into the bank leading to the road, and wide steps and a large white gate were built there. The three hobbit-families of Bagshot Row, adjoining the field, were intensely interested and generally envied. Old Gaffer Gamgee stopped even pretending to work in his garden.

The tents began to go up. There was a specially large pavilion, so big that the tree that grew in the field was right inside it, and stood proudly near one end, at the head of the chief table. Lanterns were hung on all its branches. More promising still (to the hobbits' mind): an enormous open-air kitchen was erected in the north corner of the field. A draught of cooks, from every inn and eating-house for miles around, arrived to supplement the dwarves and other odd folk that were quartered at Bag End. Excitement rose to its height.

Then the weather clouded over. That was on Wednesday the eve of the Party. Anxiety was intense. Then Thursday, September the 22nd, actually dawned. The sun got up, the clouds vanished, flags were unfurled and the fun began.

Bilbo Baggins called it a *party*, but it was really a variety of entertainments rolled into one. Practically everybody living near was invited. A very few were overlooked by accident, but as they turned up all the same, that did not matter. Many

people from other parts of the Shire were also asked; and
there were even a few from outside the borders. Bilbo met
the guests (and additions) at the new white gate in person.
He gave away presents to all and sundry – the latter were
those who went out again by a back way and came in again
by the gate. Hobbits give presents to other people on their
own birthdays. Not very expensive ones, as a rule, and not
so lavishly as on this occasion; but it was not a bad system.
Actually in Hobbiton and Bywater every day in the year it
was somebody's birthday, so that every hobbit in those parts
had a fair chance of at least one present at least once a week.
But they never got tired of them.

On this occasion the presents were unusually good. The
hobbit-children were so excited that for a while they almost
forgot about eating. There were toys the like of which they
had never seen before, all beautiful and some obviously
magical. Many of them had indeed been ordered a year
before, and had come all the way from the Mountain and
from Dale, and were of real dwarf-make.

When every guest had been welcomed and was finally
inside the gate, there were songs, dances, music, games, and,
of course, food and drink. There were three official meals:
lunch, tea, and dinner (or supper). But lunch and tea were
marked chiefly by the fact that at those times all the guests
were sitting down and eating together. At other times there
were merely lots of people eating and drinking – continuously
from elevenses until six-thirty, when the fireworks started.

The fireworks were by Gandalf: they were not only brought
by him, but designed and made by him; and the special
effects, set pieces, and flights of rockets were let off by him.
But there was also a generous distribution of squibs, crackers,
backarappers, sparklers, torches, dwarf-candles, elf-
fountains, goblin-barkers and thunder-claps. They were all
superb. The art of Gandalf improved with age.

There were rockets like a flight of scintillating birds singing
with sweet voices. There were green trees with trunks of dark
smoke: their leaves opened like a whole spring unfolding in a

moment, and their shining branches dropped glowing flowers
down upon the astonished hobbits, disappearing with a sweet
scent just before they touched their upturned faces. There
were fountains of butterflies that flew glittering into the trees;
there were pillars of coloured fires that rose and turned into
eagles, or sailing ships, or a phalanx of flying swans; there
was a red thunderstorm and a shower of yellow rain; there
was a forest of silver spears that sprang suddenly into the air
with a yell like an embattled army, and came down again
into the Water with a hiss like a hundred hot snakes. And
there was also one last surprise, in honour of Bilbo, and it
startled the hobbits exceedingly, as Gandalf intended. The
lights went out. A great smoke went up. It shaped itself like
a mountain seen in the distance, and began to glow at the
summit. It spouted green and scarlet flames. Out flew a red-
golden dragon – not life-size, but terribly life-like: fire came
from his jaws, his eyes glared down; there was a roar, and
he whizzed three times over the heads of the crowd. They
all ducked, and many fell flat on their faces. The dragon
passed like an express train, turned a somersault, and burst
over Bywater with a deafening explosion.

'That is the signal for supper!' said Bilbo. The pain and
alarm vanished at once, and the prostrate hobbits leaped to
their feet. There was a splendid supper for everyone; for
everyone, that is, except those invited to the special family
dinner-party. This was held in the great pavilion with the
tree. The invitations were limited to twelve dozen (a number
also called by the hobbits one Gross, though the word was
not considered proper to use of people); and the guests were
selected from all the families to which Bilbo and Frodo were
related, with the addition of a few special unrelated friends
(such as Gandalf). Many young hobbits were included, and
present by parental permission; for hobbits were easy-going
with their children in the matter of sitting up late, especially
when there was a chance of getting them a free meal. Bringing
up young hobbits took a lot of provender.

There were many Bagginses and Boffins, and also many

Tooks and Brandybucks; there were various Grubbs (relations of Bilbo Baggins' grandmother), and various Chubbs (connexions of his Took grandfather); and a selection of Burrowses, Bolgers, Bracegirdles, Brockhouses, Goodbodies, Hornblowers and Proudfoots. Some of these were only very distantly connected with Bilbo, and some of them had hardly ever been in Hobbiton before, as they lived in remote corners of the Shire. The Sackville-Bagginses were not forgotten. Otho and his wife Lobelia were present. They disliked Bilbo and detested Frodo, but so magnificent was the invitation card, written in golden ink, that they had felt it was impossible to refuse. Besides, their cousin, Bilbo, had been specializing in food for many years and his table had a high reputation.

All the one hundred and forty-four guests expected a pleasant feast; though they rather dreaded the after-dinner speech of their host (an inevitable item). He was liable to drag in bits of what he called poetry; and sometimes, after a glass or two, would allude to the absurd adventures of his mysterious journey. The guests were not disappointed: they had a *very* pleasant feast, in fact an engrossing entertainment: rich, abundant, varied, and prolonged. The purchase of provisions fell almost to nothing throughout the district in the ensuing weeks; but as Bilbo's catering had depleted the stocks of most stores, cellars and warehouses for miles around, that did not matter much.

After the feast (more or less) came the Speech. Most of the company were, however, now in a tolerant mood, at that delightful stage which they called 'filling up the corners'. They were sipping their favourite drinks, and nibbling at their favourite dainties, and their fears were forgotten. They were prepared to listen to anything, and to cheer at every full stop.

My dear People, began Bilbo, rising in his place. 'Hear! Hear! Hear!' they shouted, and kept on repeating it in chorus, seeming reluctant to follow their own advice. Bilbo left his place and went and stood on a chair under the illuminated tree. The light of the lanterns fell on his beaming face; the golden buttons shone on his embroidered silk waistcoat. They could all see him standing, waving one hand in the air, the other was in his trouser-pocket.

My dear Bagginses and Boffins, he began again; *and my dear Tooks and Brandybucks, and Grubbs, and Chubbs, and Burrowses, and Hornblowers, and Bolgers, Bracegirdles, Good- bodies, Brockhouses and Proudfoots.* 'ProudFEET!' shouted an elderly hobbit from the back of the pavilion. His name, of course, was Proudfoot, and well merited; his feet were large, exceptionally furry, and both were on the table.

Proudfoots, repeated Bilbo. *Also my good Sackville-Bagginses that I welcome back at last to Bag End. Today is my one hundred and eleventh birthday: I am eleventy-one today!* 'Hurray! Hur- ray! Many Happy Returns!' they shouted, and they ham- mered joyously on the tables. Bilbo was doing splendidly. This was the sort of stuff they liked: short and obvious.

I hope you are all enjoying yourselves as much as I am. Deaf- ening cheers. Cries of *Yes* (and *No*). Noises of trumpets and horns, pipes and flutes, and other musical instruments. There were, as has been said, many young hobbits present. Hun- dreds of musical crackers had been pulled. Most of them bore the mark DALE on them; which did not convey much to most of the hobbits, but they all agreed they were marvellous crackers. They contained instruments, small, but of perfect make and enchanting tones. Indeed, in one corner some of the young Tooks and Brandybucks, supposing Uncle Bilbo to have finished (since he had plainly said all that was neces- sary), now got up an impromptu orchestra, and began a merry dance-tune. Master Everard Took and Miss Melilot Brandybuck got on a table and with bells in their hands began to dance the Springle-ring: a pretty dance, but rather vigorous.

But Bilbo had not finished. Seizing a horn from a youngster near by, he blew three loud hoots. The noise subsided. *I shall not keep you long,* he cried. Cheers from all the assembly. *I have called you all together for a Purpose.* Something in the way that he said this made an impression. There was almost silence, and one or two of the Tooks pricked up their ears.

Indeed, for Three Purposes! First of all, to tell you that I am immensely fond of you all, and that eleventy-one years is too short a time to live among such excellent and admirable hobbits. Tremendous outburst of approval.

I don't know half of you half as well as I should like; and I like less than half of you half as well as you deserve. This was unexpected and rather difficult. There was some scattered clapping, but most of them were trying to work it out and see if it came to a compliment.

Secondly, to celebrate my birthday. Cheers again. *I should say: OUR birthday. For it is, of course, also the birthday of my heir and nephew, Frodo. He comes of age and into his inheritance today.* Some perfunctory clapping by the elders; and some loud shouts of 'Frodo! Frodo! Jolly old Frodo,' from the juniors. The Sackville-Bagginses scowled, and wondered what was meant by 'coming into his inheritance'.

Together we score one hundred and forty-four. Your numbers were chosen to fit this remarkable total: One Gross, if I may use the expression. No cheers. This was ridiculous. Many of his guests, and especially the Sackville-Bagginses, were insulted, feeling sure they had only been asked to fill up the required number, like goods in a package. 'One Gross, indeed! Vulgar expression.'

It is also, if I may be allowed to refer to ancient history, the anniversary of my arrival by barrel at Esgaroth on the Long Lake; though the fact that it was my birthday slipped my memory on that occasion. I was only fifty-one then, and birthdays did not seem so important. The banquet was very splendid, however, though I had a bad cold at the time, I remember, and could only say 'thag you very buch'. I now repeat it more correctly: Thank you very much for coming to my little party. Obstinate silence. They all feared that a song or some poetry was now imminent; and they were getting bored. Why couldn't he stop talking and let them drink his health? But Bilbo did not sing or recite. He paused for a moment.

Thirdly and finally, he said, *I wish to make an ANNOUNCEMENT.* He spoke this last word so loudly and suddenly that everyone sat up who still could. *I regret to announce that – though, as I said, eleventy-one years is far too short a time to spend among you – this is the END. I am going. I am leaving NOW. GOOD-BYE!*

He stepped down and vanished. There was a blinding flash of light, and the guests all blinked. When they opened their eyes Bilbo was nowhere to be seen. One hundred and forty-four flabbergasted hobbits sat back speechless. Old Odo Proudfoot removed his feet from the table and stamped. Then there was a dead silence, until suddenly, after several deep breaths, every Baggins, Boffin, Took, Brandybuck, Grubb, Chubb, Burrows, Bolger, Bracegirdle, Brockhouse, Goodbody, Hornblower, and Proudfoot began to talk at once.

It was generally agreed that the joke was in very bad taste, and more food and drink were needed to cure the guests of shock and annoyance. 'He's mad. I always said so,' was probably the most popular comment. Even the Tooks (with a few exceptions) thought Bilbo's behaviour was absurd. For the moment most of them took it for granted that his disappearance was nothing more than a ridiculous prank.

But old Rory Brandybuck was not so sure. Neither age nor an enormous dinner had clouded his wits, and he said to his daughter-in-law, Esmeralda: 'There's something fishy in this, my dear! I believe that mad Baggins is off again. Silly old fool. But why worry? He hasn't taken the vittles with him.' He called loudly to Frodo to send the wine round again.

Frodo was the only one present who had said nothing. For some time he had sat silent beside Bilbo's empty chair, and ignored all remarks and questions. He had enjoyed the joke, of course, even though he had been in the know. He had difficulty in keeping from laughter at the indignant surprise of the guests. But at the same time he felt deeply troubled: he realized suddenly that he loved the old hobbit dearly. Most of the guests went on eating and drinking and discussing

Bilbo Baggins' oddities, past and present; but the Sackville-Bagginses had already departed in wrath. Frodo did not want to have any more to do with the party. He gave orders for more wine to be served; then he got up and drained his own glass silently to the health of Bilbo, and slipped out of the pavilion.

As for Bilbo Baggins, even while he was making his speech, he had been fingering the golden ring in his pocket: his magic ring that he had kept secret for so many years. As he stepped down he slipped it on his finger, and he was never seen by any hobbit in Hobbiton again.

He walked briskly back to his hole, and stood for a moment listening with a smile to the din in the pavilion and to the sounds of merrymaking in other parts of the field. Then he went in. He took off his party clothes, folded up and wrapped in tissue-paper his embroidered silk waistcoat, and put it away. Then he put on quickly some old untidy garments, and fastened round his waist a worn leather belt. On it he hung a short sword in a battered black-leather scabbard. From a locked drawer, smelling of moth-balls, he took out an old cloak and hood. They had been locked up as if they were very precious, but they were so patched and weatherstained that their original colour could hardly be guessed: it might have been dark green. They were rather too large for him. He then went into his study, and from a large strong-box took out a bundle wrapped in old cloths, and a leather-bound manuscript; and also a large bulky envelope. The book and bundle he stuffed into the top of a heavy bag that was standing there, already nearly full. Into the envelope he slipped his golden ring, and its fine chain, and then sealed it, and addressed it to Frodo. At first he put it on the mantelpiece, but suddenly he removed it and stuck it in his pocket. At that moment the door opened and Gandalf came quickly in.

'Hullo!' said Bilbo. 'I wondered if you would turn up.'

'I am glad to find you visible,' replied the wizard, sitting down in a chair, 'I wanted to catch you and have a few final words. I suppose you feel that everything has gone off splendidly and according to plan?'

'Yes, I do,' said Bilbo. 'Though that flash was surprising: it quite startled me, let alone the others. A little addition of your own, I suppose?'

'It was. You have wisely kept that ring secret all these years, and it seemed to me necessary to give your guests something else that would seem to explain your sudden vanishment.'

'And would spoil my joke. You are an interfering old busybody,' laughed Bilbo, 'but I expect you know best, as usual.'

'I do – when I know anything. But I don't feel too sure about this whole affair. It has now come to the final point. You have had your joke, and alarmed or offended most of your relations, and given the whole Shire something to talk about for nine days, or ninety-nine more likely. Are you going any further?'

'Yes, I am. I feel I need a holiday, a very long holiday, as I have told you before. Probably a permanent holiday: I don't expect I shall return. In fact, I don't mean to, and I have made all arrangements.

'I am old, Gandalf. I don't look it, but I am beginning to feel it in my heart of hearts. *Well-preserved* indeed!' he snorted. 'Why, I feel all thin, sort of *stretched*, if you know what I mean: like butter that has been scraped over too much bread. That can't be right. I need a change, or something.'

Gandalf looked curiously and closely at him. 'No, it does not seem right,' he said thoughtfully. 'No, after all I believe your plan is probably the best.'

'Well, I've made up my mind, anyway. I want to see mountains again, Gandalf – *mountains*; and then find somewhere where I can *rest*. In peace and quiet, without a lot of relatives prying around, and a string of confounded visitors hanging on the bell. I might find somewhere where I can finish my book. I have thought of a nice ending for it: *and he lived happily ever after to the end of his days*.'

Gandalf laughed. 'I hope he will. But nobody will read the book, however it ends.'

'Oh, they may, in years to come. Frodo has read some already, as far as it has gone. You'll keep an eye on Frodo, won't you?'

'Yes, I will – two eyes, as often as I can spare them.'

'He would come with me, of course, if I asked him. In fact he offered to once, just before the party. But he does not really want to, yet. I want to see the wild country again before I die, and the Mountains; but he is still in love with the Shire, with woods and fields and little rivers. He ought to be comfortable here. I am leaving everything to him, of course, except a few oddments. I hope he will be happy, when he gets used to being on his own. It's time he was his own master now.'

'Everything?' said Gandalf. 'The ring as well? You agreed to that, you remember.'

'Well, er, yes, I suppose so,' stammered Bilbo.

'Where is it?'

'In an envelope, if you must know,' said Bilbo impatiently. 'There on the mantelpiece. Well, no! Here it is in my pocket!' He hesitated. 'Isn't that odd now?' he said softly to himself. 'Yet after all, why not? Why shouldn't it stay there?'

Gandalf looked again very hard at Bilbo, and there was a gleam in his eyes. 'I think, Bilbo,' he said quietly, 'I should leave it behind. Don't you want to?'

'Well yes – and no. Now it comes to it, I don't like parting with it at all, I may say. And I don't really see why I should. Why do you want me to?' he asked, and a curious change came over his voice. It was sharp with suspicion and annoyance. 'You are always badgering me about my ring; but you have never bothered me about the other things that I got on my journey.'

'No, but I had to badger you,' said Gandalf. 'I wanted the truth. It was important. Magic rings are – well, magical; and they are rare and curious. I was professionally interested in your ring, you may say; and I still am. I should like to know where it is, if you go wandering again. Also I think *you* have had it quite long enough. You won't need it any more, Bilbo, unless I am quite mistaken.'

Bilbo flushed, and there was an angry light in his eyes. His kindly face grew hard. 'Why not?' he cried. 'And what business is it of yours, anyway, to know what I do with my own things? It is my own. I found it. It came to me.'

'Yes, yes,' said Gandalf. 'But there is no need to get angry.'

'If I am it is your fault,' said Bilbo. 'It is mine, I tell you. My own. My precious. Yes, my precious.'

The wizard's face remained grave and attentive, and only a flicker in his deep eyes showed that he was startled and indeed alarmed. 'It has been called that before,' he said, 'but not by you.'

'But I say it now. And why not? Even if Gollum said the same once. It's not his now, but mine. And I shall keep it, I say.'

Gandalf stood up. He spoke sternly. 'You will be a fool if you do, Bilbo,' he said. 'You make that clearer with every word you say. It has got far too much hold on you. Let it go! And then you can go yourself, and be free.'

'I'll do as I choose and go as I please,' said Bilbo obstinately.

'Now, now, my dear hobbit!' said Gandalf. 'All your long life we have been friends, and you owe me something. Come! Do as you promised: give it up!'

'Well, if you want my ring yourself, say so!' cried Bilbo. 'But you won't get it. I won't give my precious away, I tell you.' His hand strayed to the hilt of his small sword.

Gandalf's eyes flashed. 'It will be my turn to get angry soon,' he said. 'If you say that again, I shall. Then you will see Gandalf the Grey uncloaked.' He took a step towards the hobbit, and he seemed to grow tall and menacing; his shadow filled the little room.

Bilbo backed away to the wall, breathing hard, his hand clutching at his pocket. They stood for a while facing one another, and the air of the room tingled. Gandalf's eyes remained bent on the hobbit. Slowly his hands relaxed, and he began to tremble.

'I don't know what has come over you, Gandalf,' he said. 'You have never been like this before. What is it all about? It is mine isn't it? I found it, and Gollum would have killed me, if I hadn't kept it. I'm not a thief, whatever he said.'

'I have never called you one,' Gandalf answered. 'And I am not one either. I am not trying to rob you, but to help you. I wish you would trust me, as you used.' He turned away, and the shadow passed. He seemed to dwindle again to an old grey man, bent and troubled.

Bilbo drew his hand over his eyes. 'I am sorry,' he said. 'But I felt so queer. And yet it would be a relief in a way not to be bothered with it any more. It has been so growing on my mind lately. Sometimes I have felt it was like an eye looking at me. And I am always wanting to put it on and disappear, don't you know; or wondering if it is safe, and pulling it out to make sure. I tried locking it up, but I found I couldn't rest without it in my pocket. I don't know why. And I don't seem able to make up my mind.'

'Then trust mine,' said Gandalf. 'It is quite made up. Go away and leave it behind. Stop possessing it. Give it to Frodo, and I will look after him.'

Bilbo stood for a moment tense and undecided. Presently he sighed. 'All right,' he said with an effort. 'I will.' Then he shrugged his shoulders, and smiled rather ruefully. 'After all that's what this party business was all about, really: to give away lots of birthday presents, and somehow make it easier to give it away at the same time. It hasn't made it any easier in the end, but it would be a pity to waste all my preparations. It would quite spoil the joke.'

'Indeed it would take away the only point I ever saw in the affair,' said Gandalf.

'Very well,' said Bilbo, 'it goes to Frodo with all the rest.' He drew a deep breath. 'And now I really must be starting, or somebody else will catch me. I have said good-bye, and I

couldn't bear to do it all over again.' He picked up his bag
and moved to the door.

'You have still got the ring in your pocket,' said the wizard.

'Well, so I have!' cried Bilbo. 'And my will and all the
other documents too. You had better take it and deliver it
for me. That will be safest.'

'No, don't give the ring to me,' said Gandalf. 'Put it on
the mantelpiece. It will be safe enough there, till Frodo comes.
I shall wait for him.'

Bilbo took out the envelope, but just as he was about to
set it by the clock, his hand jerked back, and the packet fell
on the floor. Before he could pick it up, the wizard stooped
and seized it and set it in its place. A spasm of anger passed
swiftly over the hobbit's face again. Suddenly it gave way to
a look of relief and a laugh.

'Well, that's that,' he said. 'Now I'm off!'

They went out into the hall. Bilbo chose his favourite stick
from the stand; then he whistled. Three dwarves came out
of different rooms where they had been busy.

'Is everything ready?' asked Bilbo. 'Everything packed and
labelled?'

'Everything,' they answered.

'Well, let's start then!' He stepped out of the front-door.

It was a fine night, and the black sky was dotted with stars.
He looked up, sniffing the air. 'What fun! What fun to be
off again, off on the Road with dwarves! This is what I have
really been longing for, for years! Good-bye!' he said, looking
at his old home and bowing to the door. 'Good-bye,
Gandalf!'

'Good-bye, for the present, Bilbo. Take care of yourself!
You are old enough, and perhaps wise enough.'

'Take care! I don't care. Don't you worry about me! I am
as happy now as I have ever been, and that is saying a great
deal. But the time has come. I am being swept off my feet
at last,' he added, and then in a low voice, as if to himself,
he sang softly in the dark:

The Road goes ever on and on
  Down from the door where it began.
Now far ahead the Road has gone,
  And I must follow, if I can,
Pursuing it with eager feet,
  Until it joins some larger way
Where many paths and errands meet.
And whither then? I cannot say.

He paused, silent for a moment. Then without another word he turned away from the lights and voices in the fields and tents, and followed by his three companions went round into his garden, and trotted down the long sloping path. He jumped over a low place in the hedge at the bottom, and took to the meadows, passing into the night like a rustle of wind in the grass.

Gandalf remained for a while staring after him into the darkness. 'Good-bye, my dear Bilbo – until our next meeting!' he said softly and went back indoors.

Frodo came in soon afterwards, and found him sitting in the dark, deep in thought. 'Has he gone?' he asked.

'Yes,' answered Gandalf, 'he has gone at last.'

'I wish – I mean, I hoped until this evening that it was only a joke,' said Frodo. 'But I knew in my heart that he really meant to go. He always used to joke about serious things. I wish I had come back sooner, just to see him off.'

'I think really he preferred slipping off quietly in the end,' said Gandalf. 'Don't be too troubled. He'll be all right – now. He left a packet for you. There it is!'

Frodo took the envelope from the mantelpiece, and glanced at it, but did not open it.

'You'll find his will and all the other documents in there, I think,' said the wizard. 'You are the master of Bag End now. And also, I fancy, you'll find a golden ring.'

'The ring!' exclaimed Frodo. 'Has he left me that? I wonder why. Still, it may be useful.'

'It may, and it may not,' said Gandalf. 'I should not make use of it, if I were you. But keep it secret, and keep it safe! Now I am going to bed.'

As master of Bag End Frodo felt it his painful duty to say good-bye to the guests. Rumours of strange events had by now spread all over the field, but Frodo would only say *no doubt everything will be cleared up in the morning*. About midnight carriages came for the important folk. One by one they rolled away, filled with full but very unsatisfied hobbits. Gardeners came by arrangement, and removed in wheelbarrows those that had inadvertently remained behind.

Night slowly passed. The sun rose. The hobbits rose rather later. Morning went on. People came and began (by orders) to clear away the pavilions and the tables and the chairs, and the spoons and knives and bottles and plates, and the lanterns, and the flowering shrubs in boxes, and the crumbs and cracker-paper, the forgotten bags and gloves and handkerchiefs, and the uneaten food (a very small item). Then a number of other people came (without orders): Bagginses, and Boffins, and Bolgers, and Tooks, and other guests that lived or were staying near. By mid-day, when even the best-fed were out and about again, there was a large crowd at Bag End, uninvited but not unexpected.

Frodo was waiting on the step, smiling, but looking rather tired and worried. He welcomed all the callers, but he had not much more to say than before. His reply to all inquiries was simply this: 'Mr. Bilbo Baggins has gone away; as far as I know, for good.' Some of the visitors he invited to come inside, as Bilbo had left 'messages' for them.

Inside in the hall there was piled a large assortment of packages and parcels and small articles of furniture. On every item there was a label tied. There were several labels of this sort:

For ADELARD TOOK, for his VERY OWN, from Bilbo; on an umbrella. Adelard had carried off many unlabelled ones.

For DORA BAGGINS in memory of a LONG correspond-ence, with love from Bilbo; on a large waste-paper basket. Dora was Drogo's sister and the eldest surviving female relative of Bilbo and Frodo; she was ninety-nine, and had written reams of good advice for more than half a century.

For MILO BURROWS, hoping it will be useful, from B.B.; on a gold pen and ink-bottle. Milo never answered letters.

For ANGELICA'S use, from Uncle Bilbo; on a round convex mirror. She was a young Baggins, and too obviously con-sidered her face shapely.

For the collection of HUGO BRACEGIRDLE, from a con-tributor; on an (empty) book-case. Hugo was a great borrower of books, and worse than usual at returning them.

For LOBELIA SACKVILLE-BAGGINS, as a PRESENT; on a case of silver spoons. Bilbo believed that she had acquired a good many of his spoons, while he was away on his former journey. Lobelia knew that quite well. When she arrived later in the day, she took the point at once, but she also took the spoons.

This is only a small selection of the assembled presents. Bilbo's residence had got rather cluttered up with things in the course of his long life. It was a tendency of hobbit-holes to get cluttered up: for which the custom of giving so many birthday-presents was largely responsible. Not, of course, that the birthday-presents were always *new*; there were one or two old *mathoms* of forgotten uses that had circulated all around the district; but Bilbo had usually given new presents, and kept those that he received. The old hole was now being cleared a little.

Every one of the various parting gifts had labels, written out personally by Bilbo, and several had some point, or some joke. But, of course, most of the things were given where they would be wanted and welcome. The poorer hobbits, and especially those of Bagshot Row, did very well. Old Gaffer Gamgee got two sacks of potatoes, a new spade, a woollen waistcoat, and a bottle of ointment for creaking joints. Old Rory Brandybuck, in return for much hospitality, got a dozen bottles of Old Winyards: a strong red wine from the Southfarthing, and now quite mature, as it had been laid down by Bilbo's father. Rory quite forgave Bilbo, and voted him a capital fellow after the first bottle.

There was plenty of everything left for Frodo. And, of course, all the chief treasures, as well as the books, pictures, and more than enough furniture, were left in his possession. There was, however, no sign nor mention of money or jewellery: not a penny-piece or a glass bead was given away.

Frodo had a very trying time that afternoon. A false rumour that the whole household was being distributed free spread like wildfire; and before long the place was packed with people who had no business there, but could not be kept out. Labels got torn off and mixed, and quarrels broke out. Some people tried to do swaps and deals in the hall; and others tried to make off with minor items not addressed to them, or with anything that seemed unwanted or unwatched. The road to the gate was blocked with barrows and handcarts.

In the middle of the commotion the Sackville-Bagginses arrived. Frodo had retired for a while and left his friend Merry Brandybuck to keep an eye on things. When Otho loudly demanded to see Frodo, Merry bowed politely.

'He is indisposed,' he said. 'He is resting.'

'Hiding, you mean,' said Lobelia. 'Anyway we want to see him and we mean to see him. Just go and tell him so!'

Merry left them a long while in the hall, and they had time to discover their parting gift of spoons. It did not improve their tempers. Eventually they were shown into the study. Frodo was sitting at a table with a lot of papers in front of him. He looked indisposed – to see Sackville-Bagginses at any rate; and he stood up, fidgeting with something in his pocket. But he spoke quite politely.

The Sackville-Bagginses were rather offensive. They began by offering him bad bargain-prices (as between friends) for various valuable and unlabelled things. When Frodo replied that only the things specially directed by Bilbo were being given away, they said the whole affair was very fishy.

'Only one thing is clear to me,' said Otho, 'and that is that you are doing exceedingly well out of it. I insist on seeing the will.'

Otho would have been Bilbo's heir, but for the adoption of Frodo. He read the will carefully and snorted. It was, unfortunately, very clear and correct (according to the legal customs of hobbits, which demand among other things seven signatures of witnesses in red ink).

'Foiled again!' he said to his wife. 'And after waiting *sixty* years. Spoons? Fiddlesticks!' He snapped his fingers under Frodo's nose and stumped off. But Lobelia was not so easily got rid of. A little later Frodo came out of the study to see how things were going on and found her still about the place, investigating nooks and corners and tapping the floors. He escorted her firmly off the premises, after he had relieved her of several small (but rather valuable) articles that had somehow fallen inside her umbrella. Her face looked as if she was in the throes of thinking out a really crushing parting remark; but all she found to say, turning round on the step, was:

'You'll live to regret it, young fellow! Why didn't you go too? You don't belong here; you're no Baggins – you – you're a Brandybuck!'

'Did you hear that, Merry? That was an insult, if you like,' said Frodo as he shut the door on her.

'It was a compliment,' said Merry Brandybuck, 'and so, of course, not true.'

Then they went round the hole, and evicted three young hobbits (two Boffins and a Bolger) who were knocking holes in the walls of one of the cellars. Frodo also had a tussle with young Sancho Proudfoot (old Odo Proudfoot's grandson), who had begun an excavation in the larger pantry, where he thought there was an echo. The legend of Bilbo's gold excited both curiosity and hope; for legendary gold (mysteriously obtained, if not positively ill-gotten), is, as every one knows, any one's for the finding – unless the search is interrupted.

When he had overcome Sancho and pushed him out, Frodo collapsed on a chair in the hall. 'It's time to close the shop, Merry,' he said. 'Lock the door, and don't open it to anyone today, not even if they bring a battering ram.' Then he went to revive himself with a belated cup of tea.

He had hardly sat down, when there came a soft knock at the front-door. 'Lobelia again most likely,' he thought. 'She must have thought of something really nasty, and have come back again to say it. It can wait.'

He went on with his tea. The knock was repeated, much louder, but he took no notice. Suddenly the wizard's head appeared at the window.

'If you don't let me in, Frodo, I shall blow your door right down your hole and out through the hill,' he said.

'My dear Gandalf! Half a minute!' cried Frodo, running out of the room to the door. 'Come in! Come in! I thought it was Lobelia.'

'Then I forgive you. But I saw her some time ago, driving a pony-trap towards Bywater with a face that would have curdled new milk.'

'She had already nearly curdled me. Honestly, I nearly tried on Bilbo's ring. I longed to disappear.'

'Don't do that!' said Gandalf, sitting down. 'Do be careful of that ring, Frodo! In fact, it is partly about that that I have come to say a last word.'

'Well, what about it?'

'What do you know already?'

'Only what Bilbo told me. I have heard his story: how he found it, and how he used it: on his journey, I mean.'

'Which story, I wonder,' said Gandalf.

'Oh, not what he told the dwarves and put in his book,' said Frodo. 'He told me the true story soon after I came to live here. He said you had pestered him till he told you, so I had better know too. "No secrets between us, Frodo," he said; "but they are not to go any further. It's mine anyway."'

'That's interesting,' said Gandalf. 'Well, what did you think of it all?'

'If you mean, inventing all that about a "present", well, I thought the true story much more likely, and I couldn't see the point of altering it at all. It was very unlike Bilbo to do so, anyway; and I thought it rather odd.'

'So did I. But odd things may happen to people that have such treasures – if they use them. Let it be a warning to you to be very careful with it. It may have other powers than just making you vanish when you wish to.'

'I don't understand,' said Frodo.

'Neither do I,' answered the wizard. 'I have merely begun to wonder about the ring, especially since last night. No need to worry. But if you take my advice you will use it very seldom, or not at all. At least I beg you not to use it in any way that will cause talk or rouse suspicion. I say again: keep it safe, and keep it secret!'

'You are very mysterious! What are you afraid of?'

'I am not certain, so I will say no more. I may be able to tell you something when I come back. I am going off at once: so this is good-bye for the present.' He got up.

'At once!' cried Frodo. 'Why, I thought you were staying on for at least a week. I was looking forward to your help.'

'I did mean to – but I have had to change my mind. I may be away for a good while; but I'll come and see you again, as soon as I can. Expect me when you see me! I shall slip in quietly. I shan't often be visiting the Shire openly again. I find that I have become rather unpopular. They say I am a nuisance and a disturber of the peace. Some people are actually accusing me of spiriting Bilbo away, or worse. If you want to know, there is supposed to be a plot between you and me to get hold of his wealth.'

'Some people!' exclaimed Frodo. 'You mean Otho and Lobelia. How abominable! I would give them Bag End and everything else, if I could get Bilbo back and go off tramping in the country with him. I love the Shire. But I begin to wish,

somehow, that I had gone too. I wonder if I shall ever see
him again.'

'So do I,' said Gandalf. 'And I wonder many other things.
Good-bye now! Take care of yourself! Look out for me,
especially at unlikely times! Good-bye!'

Frodo saw him to the door. He gave a final wave of his
hand, and walked off at a surprising pace; but Frodo thought
the old wizard looked unusually bent, almost as if he was
carrying a great weight. The evening was closing in, and his
cloaked figure quickly vanished into the twilight. Frodo did
not see him again for a long time.

CHAPTER II

THE SHADOW OF THE PAST

The talk did not die down in nine or even ninety-nine days.
The second disappearance of Mr. Bilbo Baggins was discussed in Hobbiton, and indeed all over the Shire, for a year
and a day, and was remembered much longer than that. It
became a fireside-story for young hobbits; and eventually
Mad Baggins, who used to vanish with a bang and a flash
and reappear with bags of jewels and gold, became a favourite
character of legend and lived on long after all the true events
were forgotten.

But in the meantime, the general opinion in the neighbourhood was that Bilbo, who had always been rather cracked,
had at last gone quite mad, and had run off into the Blue.
There he had undoubtedly fallen into a pool or a river and
come to a tragic, but hardly an untimely, end. The blame
was mostly laid on Gandalf.

'If only that dratted wizard will leave young Frodo alone,
perhaps he'll settle down and grow some hobbit-sense,' they
said. And to all appearance the wizard did leave Frodo alone,
and he did settle down, but the growth of hobbit-sense was
not very noticeable. Indeed, he at once began to carry on
Bilbo's reputation for oddity. He refused to go into mourning;
and the next year he gave a party in honour of Bilbo's
hundred-and-twelfth birthday, which he called a Hundred-
weight Feast. But that was short of the mark, for twenty
guests were invited and there were several meals at which it
snowed food and rained drink, as hobbits say.

Some people were rather shocked; but Frodo kept up the
custom of giving Bilbo's Birthday Party year after year until
they got used to it. He said that he did not think Bilbo was

dead. When they asked: 'Where is he then?' he shrugged his shoulders.

He lived alone, as Bilbo had done; but he had a good many friends, especially among the younger hobbits (mostly descendants of the Old Took) who had as children been fond of Bilbo and often in and out of Bag End. Folco Boffin and Fredegar Bolger were two of these; but his closest friends were Peregrin Took (usually called Pippin), and Merry Brandybuck (his real name was Meriadoc, but that was seldom remembered). Frodo went tramping all over the Shire with them; but more often he wandered by himself, and to the amazement of sensible folk he was sometimes seen far from home walking in the hills and woods under the starlight. Merry and Pippin suspected that he visited the Elves at times, as Bilbo had done.

As time went on, people began to notice that Frodo also showed signs of good 'preservation': outwardly he retained the appearance of a robust and energetic hobbit just out of his tweens. 'Some folk have all the luck,' they said; but it was not until Frodo approached the usually more sober age of fifty that they began to think it queer.

Frodo himself, after the first shock, found that being his own master and *the* Mr. Baggins of Bag End was rather pleasant. For some years he was quite happy and did not worry much about the future. But half unknown to himself the regret that he had not gone with Bilbo was steadily growing. He found himself wondering at times, especially in the autumn, about the wild lands, and strange visions of mountains that he had never seen came into his dreams. He began to say to himself: 'Perhaps I shall cross the River myself one day.' To which the other half of his mind always replied: 'Not yet.'

So it went on, until his forties were running out, and his fiftieth birthday was drawing near: fifty was a number that he felt was somehow significant (or ominous); it was at any rate at that age that adventure had suddenly befallen Bilbo.

Frodo began to feel restless, and the old paths seemed too well-trodden. He looked at maps, and wondered what lay beyond their edges: maps made in the Shire showed mostly white spaces beyond its borders. He took to wandering further afield and more often by himself; and Merry and his other friends watched him anxiously. Often he was seen walking and talking with the strange wayfarers that began at this time to appear in the Shire.

There were rumours of strange things happening in the world outside; and as Gandalf had not at that time appeared or sent any message for several years, Frodo gathered all the news he could. Elves, who seldom walked in the Shire, could now be seen passing westward through the woods in the evening, passing and not returning; but they were leaving Middle-earth and were no longer concerned with its troubles. There were, however, dwarves on the road in unusual numbers. The ancient East–West Road ran through the Shire to its end at the Grey Havens, and dwarves had always used it on their way to their mines in the Blue Mountains. They were the hobbits' chief source of news from distant parts – if they wanted any: as a rule dwarves said little and hobbits asked no more. But now Frodo often met strange dwarves of far countries, seeking refuge in the West. They were troubled, and some spoke in whispers of the Enemy and of the Land of Mordor.

That name the hobbits only knew in legends of the dark past, like a shadow in the background of their memories; but it was ominous and disquieting. It seemed that the evil power in Mirkwood had been driven out by the White Council only to reappear in greater strength in the old strongholds of Mordor. The Dark Tower had been rebuilt, it was said. From there the power was spreading far and wide, and away far east and south there were wars and growing fear. Orcs were multiplying again in the mountains. Trolls were abroad, no longer dull-witted, but cunning and armed with dreadful weapons. And there were murmured hints of creatures more terrible than all these, but they had no name.

Little of all this, of course, reached the ears of ordinary hobbits. But even the deafest and most stay-at-home began to hear queer tales; and those whose business took them to the borders saw strange things. The conversation in *The Green Dragon* at Bywater, one evening in the spring of Frodo's fiftieth year, showed that even in the comfortable heart of the Shire rumours had been heard, though most hobbits still laughed at them.

Sam Gamgee was sitting in one corner near the fire, and opposite him was Ted Sandyman, the miller's son; and there were various other rustic hobbits listening to their talk.

'Queer things you do hear these days, to be sure,' said Sam.

'Ah,' said Ted, 'you do, if you listen. But I can hear fire-side-tales and children's stories at home, if I want to.'

'No doubt you can,' retorted Sam, 'and I daresay there's more truth in some of them than you reckon. Who invented the stories anyway? Take dragons now.'

'No thank 'ee,' said Ted, 'I won't. I heard tell of them when I was a youngster, but there's no call to believe in them now. There's only one Dragon in Bywater, and that's Green,' he said, getting a general laugh.

'All right,' said Sam, laughing with the rest. 'But what about these Tree-men, these giants, as you might call them? They do say that one bigger than a tree was seen up away beyond the North Moors not long back.'

'Who's *they*?'

'My cousin Hal for one. He works for Mr. Boffin at Overhill and goes up to the Northfarthing for the hunting. He *saw* one.'

'Says he did, perhaps. Your Hal's always saying he's seen things; and maybe he sees things that ain't there.'

'But this one was as big as an elm tree, and walking – walking seven yards to a stride, if it was an inch.'

'Then I bet it wasn't an inch. What he saw *was* an elm tree, as like as not.'

'But this one was *walking*, I tell you; and there ain't no elm tree on the North Moors.'

'Then Hal can't have seen one,' said Ted. There was some laughing and clapping: the audience seemed to think that Ted had scored a point.

'All the same,' said Sam, 'you can't deny that others besides our Halfast have seen queer folk crossing the Shire – crossing it, mind you: there are more that are turned back at the borders. The Bounders have never been so busy before.

'And I've heard tell that Elves are moving west. They do say they are going to the harbours, out away beyond the White Towers.' Sam waved his arm vaguely: neither he nor any of them knew how far it was to the Sea, past the old towers beyond the western borders of the Shire. But it was an old tradition that away over there stood the Grey Havens, from which at times elven-ships set sail, never to return.

'They are sailing, sailing, sailing over the Sea, they are going into the West and leaving us,' said Sam, half chanting the words, shaking his head sadly and solemnly. But Ted laughed.

'Well, that isn't anything new, if you believe the old tales. And I don't see what it matters to me or you. Let them sail! But I warrant you haven't seen them doing it; nor any one else in the Shire.'

'Well I don't know,' said Sam thoughtfully. He believed he had once seen an Elf in the woods, and still hoped to see more one day. Of all the legends that he had heard in his early years such fragments of tales and half-remembered stories about the Elves as the hobbits knew, had always moved him most deeply. 'There are some, even in these parts, as know the Fair Folk and get news of them,' he said. 'There's Mr. Baggins now, that I work for. He told me that they were sailing and he knows a bit about Elves. And old Mr. Bilbo knew more: many's the talk I had with him when I was a little lad.'

'Oh, they're both cracked,' said Ted. 'Leastways old Bilbo was cracked, and Frodo's cracking. If that's where you get your news from, you'll never want for moonshine. Well, friends, I'm off home. Your good health!' He drained his mug and went out noisily.

Sam sat silent and said no more. He had a good deal to think about. For one thing, there was a lot to do up in the Bag End garden, and he would have a busy day tomorrow, if the weather cleared. The grass was growing fast. But Sam had more on his mind than gardening. After a while he sighed, and got up and went out.

It was early April and the sky was now clearing after heavy rain. The sun was down, and a cool pale evening was quietly fading into night. He walked home under the early stars through Hobbiton and up the Hill, whistling softly and thoughtfully.

It was just at this time that Gandalf reappeared after his long absence. For three years after the Party he had been away. Then he paid Frodo a brief visit, and after taking a good look at him he went off again. During the next year or two he had turned up fairly often, coming unexpectedly after dusk, and going off without warning before sunrise. He would not discuss his own business and journeys, and seemed chiefly interested in small news about Frodo's health and doings.

Then suddenly his visits had ceased. It was over nine years since Frodo had seen or heard of him, and he had begun to think that the wizard would never return and had given up all interest in hobbits. But that evening, as Sam was walking home and twilight was fading, there came the once familiar tap on the study window.

Frodo welcomed his old friend with surprise and great delight. They looked hard at one another.

'Ah well eh?' said Gandalf. 'You look the same as ever, Frodo!'

'So do you,' Frodo replied; but secretly he thought that

Gandalf looked older and more careworn. He pressed him for news of himself and of the wide world, and soon they were deep in talk, and they stayed up far into the night.

Next morning after a late breakfast, the wizard was sitting with Frodo by the open window of the study. A bright fire was on the hearth, but the sun was warm, and the wind was in the South. Everything looked fresh, and the new green of Spring was shimmering in the fields and on the tips of the trees' fingers.

Gandalf was thinking of a spring, nearly eighty years before, when Bilbo had run out of Bag End without a hand-kerchief. His hair was perhaps whiter than it had been then, and his beard and eyebrows were perhaps longer, and his face more lined with care and wisdom; but his eyes were as bright as ever, and he smoked and blew smoke-rings with the same vigour and delight.

He was smoking now in silence, for Frodo was sitting still, deep in thought. Even in the light of morning he felt the dark shadow of the tidings that Gandalf had brought. At last he broke the silence.

'Last night you began to tell me strange things about my ring, Gandalf,' he said. 'And then you stopped, because you said that such matters were best left until daylight. Don't you think you had better finish now? You say the ring is danger-ous, far more dangerous than I guess. In what way?'

'In many ways,' answered the wizard. 'It is far more power-ful than I ever dared to think at first, so powerful that in the end it would utterly overcome anyone of mortal race who possessed it. It would possess him.

'In Eregion long ago many Elven-rings were made, magic rings as you call them, and they were, of course, of various kinds: some more potent and some less. The lesser rings were only essays in the craft before it was full-grown, and to the Elven-smiths they were but trifles – yet still to my mind dangerous for mortals. But the Great Rings, the Rings of Power, they were perilous.

'A mortal, Frodo, who keeps one of the Great Rings, does not die, but he does not grow or obtain more life, he merely continues, until at last every minute is a weariness. And if he often uses the Ring to make himself invisible, he *fades*: he becomes in the end invisible permanently, and walks in the twilight under the eye of the dark power that rules the Rings. Yes, sooner or later – later, if he is strong or well-meaning to begin with, but neither strength nor good purpose will last – sooner or later the dark power will devour him.'

'How terrifying!' said Frodo. There was another long silence. The sound of Sam Gamgee cutting the lawn came in from the garden.

'How long have you known this?' asked Frodo at length. 'And how much did Bilbo know?'

'Bilbo knew no more than he told you, I am sure,' said Gandalf. 'He would certainly never have passed on to you anything that he thought would be a danger, even though I promised to look after you. He thought the ring was very beautiful, and very useful at need; and if anything was wrong or queer, it was himself. He said that it was "growing on his mind", and he was always worrying about it; but he did not suspect that the ring itself was to blame. Though he had found out that the thing needed looking after; it did not seem always of the same size or weight; it shrank or expanded in an odd way, and might suddenly slip off a finger where it had been tight.'

'Yes, he warned me of that in his last letter,' said Frodo, 'so I have always kept it on its chain.'

'Very wise,' said Gandalf. 'But as for his long life, Bilbo never connected it with the ring at all. He took all the credit for that to himself, and he was very proud of it. Though he was getting restless and uneasy. *Thin and stretched* he said. A sign that the ring was getting control.'

'How long have you known all this?' asked Frodo again.

'Known?' said Gandalf. 'I have known much that only the Wise know, Frodo. But if you mean "known about *this* ring", well, I still do not *know*, one might say. There is a last test to make. But I no longer doubt my guess.

'When did I first begin to guess?' he mused, searching back in memory. 'Let me see – it was in the year that the White Council drove the dark power from Mirkwood, just before the Battle of Five Armies, that Bilbo found his ring. A shadow fell on my heart then, though I did not know yet what I feared. I wondered often how Gollum came by a Great Ring, as plainly it was – that at least was clear from the first. Then I heard Bilbo's strange story of how he had "won" it, and I could not believe it. When I at last got the truth out of him, I saw at once that he had been trying to put his claim to the ring beyond doubt. Much like Gollum with his "birthday present". The lies were too much alike for my comfort. Clearly the ring had an unwholesome power that set to work on its keeper at once. That was the first real warning I had that all was not well. I told Bilbo often that such rings were better left unused; but he resented it, and soon got angry. There was little else that I could do. I could not take it from him without doing greater harm; and I had no right to do so anyway. I could only watch and wait. I might perhaps have consulted Saruman the White, but something always held me back.'

'Who is he?' asked Frodo. 'I have never heard of him before.'

'Maybe not,' answered Gandalf. 'Hobbits are, or were, no concern of his. Yet he is great among the Wise. He is the chief of my order and the head of the Council. His knowledge is deep, but his pride has grown with it, and he takes ill any meddling. The lore of the Elven-rings, great and small, is his province. He has long studied it, seeking the lost secrets of their making; but when the Rings were debated in the Council, all that he would reveal to us of his ring-lore told against my fears. So my doubt slept – but uneasily. Still I watched and I waited.

'And all seemed well with Bilbo. And the years passed. Yes, they passed, and they seemed not to touch him. He showed no signs of age. The shadow fell on me again. But I said to myself: "After all he comes of a long-lived family on his mother's side. There is time yet. Wait!"

'And I waited. Until that night when he left this house. He said and did things then that filled me with a fear that no words of Saruman could allay. I knew at last that something dark and deadly was at work. And I have spent most of the years since then in finding out the truth of it.'

'There wasn't any permanent harm done, was there?' asked Frodo anxiously. 'He would get all right in time, wouldn't he? Be able to rest in peace, I mean?'

'He felt better at once,' said Gandalf. 'But there is only one Power in this world that knows all about the Rings and their effects; and as far as I know there is no Power in the world that knows all about hobbits. Among the Wise I am the only one that goes in for hobbit-lore: an obscure branch of knowledge, but full of surprises. Soft as butter they can be, and yet sometimes as tough as old tree-roots. I think it likely that some would resist the Rings far longer than most of the Wise would believe. I don't think you need worry about Bilbo.

'Of course, he possessed the ring for many years, and used it, so it might take a long while for the influence to wear off – before it was safe for him to see it again, for instance. Otherwise, he might live on for years, quite happily: just stop as he was when he parted with it. For he gave it up in the end of his own accord: an important point. No, I was not troubled about dear Bilbo any more, once he had let the thing go. It is for *you* that I feel responsible.

'Ever since Bilbo left I have been deeply concerned about you, and about all these charming, absurd, helpless hobbits. It would be a grievous blow to the world, if the Dark Power overcame the Shire; if all your kind, jolly, stupid Bolgers, Hornblowers, Boffins, Bracegirdles, and the rest, not to mention the ridiculous Bagginses, became enslaved.'

Frodo shuddered. 'But why should we be?' he asked. 'And why should he want such slaves?'

'To tell you the truth,' replied Gandalf, 'I believe that hitherto – *hitherto*, mark you – he has entirely overlooked the existence of hobbits. You should be thankful. But your safety has passed. He does not need you – he has many more useful servants – but he won't forget you again. And hobbits as miserable slaves would please him far more than hobbits happy and free. There is such a thing as malice and revenge.'

'Revenge?' said Frodo. 'Revenge for what? I still don't understand what all this has to do with Bilbo and myself, and our ring.'

'It has everything to do with it,' said Gandalf. 'You do not know the real peril yet; but you shall. I was not sure of it myself when I was last here; but the time has come to speak. Give me the ring for a moment.'

Frodo took it from his breeches-pocket, where it was clasped to a chain that hung from his belt. He unfastened it and handed it slowly to the wizard. It felt suddenly very heavy, as if either it or Frodo himself was in some way reluctant for Gandalf to touch it.

Gandalf held it up. It looked to be made of pure and solid gold. 'Can you see any markings on it?' he asked.

'No,' said Frodo. 'There are none. It is quite plain, and it never shows a scratch or sign of wear.'

'Well then, look!' To Frodo's astonishment and distress the wizard threw it suddenly into the middle of a glowing corner of the fire. Frodo gave a cry and groped for the tongs; but Gandalf held him back.

'Wait!' he said in a commanding voice, giving Frodo a quick look from under his bristling brows.

No apparent change came over the ring. After a while Gandalf got up, closed the shutters outside the window, and drew the curtains. The room became dark and silent, though the clack of Sam's shears, now nearer to the windows, could still be heard faintly from the garden. For a moment the wizard stood looking at the fire; then he stooped and removed the ring to the hearth with the tongs, and at once picked it up. Frodo gasped.

'It is quite cool,' said Gandalf. 'Take it!' Frodo received it on his shrinking palm: it seemed to have become thicker and heavier than ever.

'Hold it up!' said Gandalf. 'And look closely!'

As Frodo did so, he now saw fine lines, finer than the finest pen-strokes, running along the ring, outside and inside: lines of fire that seemed to form the letters of a flowing script. They shone piercingly bright, and yet remote, as if out of a great depth.

'I cannot read the fiery letters,' said Frodo in a quavering voice.

'No,' said Gandalf, 'but I can. The letters are Elvish, of an ancient mode, but the language is that of Mordor, which I will not utter here. But this in the Common Tongue is what is said, close enough:

> *One Ring to rule them all, One Ring to find them,*
> *One Ring to bring them all and in the darkness bind them.*

It is only two lines of a verse long known in Elven-lore:

> *Three Rings for the Elven-kings under the sky,*
> *Seven for the Dwarf-lords in their halls of stone,*
> *Nine for Mortal Men doomed to die,*
> *One for the Dark Lord on his dark throne*
> *In the Land of Mordor where the Shadows lie.*
> *One Ring to rule them all, One Ring to find them,*

One Ring to bring them all and in the darkness bind
   them
In the Land of Mordor where the Shadows lie.'

He paused, and then said slowly in a deep voice: 'This is the Master-ring, the One Ring to rule them all. This is the One Ring that he lost many ages ago, to the great weakening of his power. He greatly desires it – but he must *not* get it.'

Frodo sat silent and motionless. Fear seemed to stretch out a vast hand, like a dark cloud rising in the East and looming up to engulf him. 'This ring!' he stammered. 'How, how on earth did it come to me?'

'Ah!' said Gandalf. 'That is a very long story. The beginnings lie back in the Black Years, which only the lore-masters now remember. If I were to tell you all that tale, we should still be sitting here when Spring had passed into Winter.

'But last night I told you of Sauron the Great, the Dark Lord. The rumours that you have heard are true: he has indeed arisen again and left his hold in Mirkwood and returned to his ancient fastness in the Dark Tower of Mordor. That name even you hobbits have heard of, like a shadow on the borders of old stories. Always after a defeat and a respite, the Shadow takes another shape and grows again.'

'I wish it need not have happened in my time,' said Frodo.

'So do I,' said Gandalf, 'and so do all who live to see such times. But that is not for them to decide. All we have to decide is what to do with the time that is given us. And already, Frodo, our time is beginning to look black. The Enemy is fast becoming very strong. His plans are far from ripe, I think, but they are ripening. We shall be hard put to it. We should be very hard put to it, even if it were not for this dreadful chance.

'The Enemy still lacks one thing to give him strength and knowledge to beat down all resistance, break the last defences, and cover all the lands in a second darkness. He lacks the One Ring.

'The Three, fairest of all, the Elf-lords hid from him, and his hand never touched them or sullied them. Seven the Dwarf-kings possessed, but three he has recovered, and the others the dragons have consumed. Nine he gave to Mortal Men, proud and great, and so ensnared them. Long ago they fell under the dominion of the One, and they became Ringwraiths, shadows under his great Shadow, his most terrible servants. Long ago. It is many a year since the Nine walked abroad. Yet who knows? As the Shadow grows once more, they too may walk again. But come! We will not speak of such things even in the morning of the Shire.

'So it is now: the Nine he has gathered to himself; the Seven also, or else they are destroyed. The Three are hidden still. But that no longer troubles him. He only needs the One; for he made that Ring himself, it is his, and he let a great part of his own former power pass into it, so that he could rule all the others. If he recovers it, then he will command them all again, wherever they be, even the Three, and all that has been wrought with them will be laid bare, and he will be stronger than ever.

'And this is the dreadful chance, Frodo. He believed that the One had perished; that the Elves had destroyed it, as should have been done. But he knows now that it has *not* perished, that it has been found. So he is seeking it, seeking it, and all his thought is bent on it. It is his great hope and our great fear.'

'Why, why wasn't it destroyed?' cried Frodo. 'And how did the Enemy ever come to lose it, if he was so strong, and it was so precious to him?' He clutched the Ring in his hand, as if he saw already dark fingers stretching out to seize it.

'It was taken from him,' said Gandalf. 'The strength of the Elves to resist him was greater long ago; and not all Men were estranged from them. The Men of Westernesse came to their aid. That is a chapter of ancient history which it might be good to recall; for there was sorrow then too, and gathering dark, but great valour, and great deeds that were not wholly vain. One day, perhaps, I will tell you all the tale, or you shall hear it told in full by one who knows it best.

'But for the moment, since most of all you need to know how this thing came to you, and that will be tale enough, this is all that I will say. It was Gil-galad, Elven-king and Elendil of Westernesse who overthrew Sauron, though they themselves perished in the deed; and Isildur Elendil's son cut the Ring from Sauron's hand and took it for his own. Then Sauron was vanquished and his spirit fled and was hidden for long years, until his shadow took shape again in Mirkwood.

'But the Ring was lost. It fell into the Great River, Anduin, and vanished. For Isildur was marching north along the east banks of the River, and near the Gladden Fields he was waylaid by the Orcs of the Mountains, and almost all his folk were slain. He leaped into the waters, but the Ring slipped from his finger as he swam, and then the Orcs saw him and killed him with arrows.'

Gandalf paused. 'And there in the dark pools amid the Gladden Fields,' he said, 'the Ring passed out of knowledge and legend; and even so much of its history is known now only to a few, and the Council of the Wise could discover no more. But at last I can carry on the story, I think.

'Long after, but still very long ago, there lived by the banks of the Great River on the edge of Wilderland a clever-handed and quiet-footed little people. I guess they were of hobbit-kind; akin to the fathers of the fathers of the Stoors, for they loved the River, and often swam in it, or made little boats of reeds. There was among them a family of high repute, for it was large and wealthier than most, and it was ruled by a grandmother of the folk, stern and wise in old lore, such as they had. The most inquisitive and curious-minded of that family was called Sméagol. He was interested in roots and beginnings; he dived into deep pools; he burrowed under trees and growing plants; he tunnelled into green mounds; and he ceased to look up at the hill-tops, or the leaves on trees, or the flowers opening in the air: his head and his eyes were downward.

'He had a friend called Déagol, of similar sort, sharper-eyed but not so quick and strong. On a time they took a boat and went down to the Gladden Fields, where there were great beds of iris and flowering reeds. There Sméagol got out and went nosing about the banks but Déagol sat in the boat and fished. Suddenly a great fish took his hook, and before he knew where he was, he was dragged out and down into the water, to the bottom. Then he let go of his line, for he thought he saw something shining in the river-bed; and holding his breath he grabbed at it.

'Then up he came spluttering, with weeds in his hair and a handful of mud; and he swam to the bank. And behold! when he washed the mud away, there in his hand lay a beautiful golden ring; and it shone and glittered in the sun, so that his heart was glad. But Sméagol had been watching him from behind a tree, and as Déagol gloated over the ring, Sméagol came softly up behind.

' "Give us that, Déagol, my love," said Sméagol, over his friend's shoulder.

' "Why?" said Déagol.

' "Because it's my birthday, my love, and I wants it," said Sméagol.

' "I don't care," said Déagol. "I have given you a present already, more than I could afford. I found this, and I'm going to keep it."

' "Oh, are you indeed, my love," said Sméagol; and he caught Déagol by the throat and strangled him, because the gold looked so bright and beautiful. Then he put the ring on his finger.

'No one ever found out what had become of Déagol; he was murdered far from home, and his body was cunningly hidden. But Sméagol returned alone; and he found that none of his family could see him, when he was wearing the ring. He was very pleased with his discovery and he concealed it; and he used it to find out secrets, and he put his knowledge to crooked and malicious uses. He became sharp-eyed and keen-eared for all that was hurtful. The ring had given him power according to his stature. It is not to be wondered at that he became very unpopular and was shunned (when visible) by all his relations. They kicked him, and he bit their feet. He took to thieving, and going about muttering to himself, and gurgling in his throat. So they called him *Gollum*, and cursed him, and told him to go far away; and his grandmother, desiring peace, expelled him from the family and turned him out of her hole.

'He wandered in loneliness, weeping a little for the hardness of the world, and he journeyed up the River, till he came to a stream that flowed down from the mountains, and he went that way. He caught fish in deep pools with invisible fingers and ate them raw. One day it was very hot, and as he was bending over a pool, he felt a burning on the back of his head, and a dazzling light from the water pained his wet eyes. He wondered at it, for he had almost forgotten about the Sun. Then for the last time he looked up and shook his fist at her.

'But as he lowered his eyes, he saw far above the tops of the Misty Mountains, out of which the stream came. And he thought suddenly: "It would be cool and shady under those mountains. The Sun could not watch me there. The roots of those mountains must be roots indeed; there must be great secrets buried there which have not been discovered since the beginning."

'So he journeyed by night up into the highlands, and he found a little cave out of which the dark stream ran; and he wormed his way like a maggot into the heart of the hills, and vanished out of all knowledge. The Ring went into the shadows with him, and even the maker, when his power had begun to grow again, could learn nothing of it.'

'Gollum!' cried Frodo. 'Gollum? Do you mean that this is the very Gollum-creature that Bilbo met? How loathsome!'

'I think it is a sad story,' said the wizard, 'and it might have happened to others, even to some hobbits that I have known.'

'I can't believe that Gollum was connected with hobbits, however distantly,' said Frodo with some heat. 'What an abominable notion!'

'It is true all the same,' replied Gandalf. 'About their origins, at any rate, I know more than hobbits do themselves. And even Bilbo's story suggests the kinship. There was a great deal in the background of their minds and memories that was very similar. They understood one another remarkably well, very much better than a hobbit would understand, say, a Dwarf, or an Orc, or even an Elf. Think of the riddles they both knew, for one thing.'

'Yes,' said Frodo. 'Though other folks besides hobbits ask riddles, and of much the same sort. And hobbits don't cheat. Gollum meant to cheat all the time. He was just trying to put poor Bilbo off his guard. And I daresay it amused his wickedness to start a game which might end in providing him with an easy victim, but if he lost would not hurt him.'

'Only too true, I fear,' said Gandalf. 'But there was something else in it, I think, which you don't see yet. Even Gollum was not wholly ruined. He had proved tougher than even one of the Wise would have guessed – as a hobbit might. There was a little corner of his mind that was still his own, and light came through it, as through a chink in the dark: light out of the past. It was actually pleasant, I think, to hear a kindly voice again, bringing up memories of wind, and trees, and sun on the grass, and such forgotten things.

'But that, of course, would only make the evil part of him angrier in the end – unless it could be conquered. Unless it could be cured.' Gandalf sighed. 'Alas! there is little hope of that for him. Yet not no hope. No, not though he possessed the Ring so long, almost as far back as he can remember. For it was long since he had worn it much: in the black darkness it was seldom needed. Certainly he had never "faded". He is thin and tough still. But the thing was eating up his mind, of course, and the torment had become almost unbearable.

'All the "great secrets" under the mountains had turned out to be just empty night: there was nothing more to find out, nothing worth doing, only nasty furtive eating and resentful remembering. He was altogether wretched. He hated the dark, and he hated light more: he hated everything, and the Ring most of all.'

'What do you mean?' said Frodo. 'Surely the Ring was his precious and the only thing he cared for? But if he hated it, why didn't he get rid of it, or go away and leave it?'

'You ought to begin to understand, Frodo, after all you have heard,' said Gandalf. 'He hated it and loved it, as he hated and loved himself. He could not get rid of it. He had no will left in the matter.

'A Ring of Power looks after itself, Frodo. *It* may slip off treacherously, but its keeper never abandons it. At most he plays with the idea of handing it on to someone else's care – and that only at an early stage, when it first begins to grip. But as far as I know Bilbo alone in history has ever gone beyond playing, and really done it. He needed all my help, too. And even so he would never have just forsaken it, or cast it aside. It was not Gollum, Frodo, but the Ring itself that decided things. The Ring left *him*.'

'What, just in time to meet Bilbo?' said Frodo. 'Wouldn't an Orc have suited it better?'

'It is no laughing matter,' said Gandalf. 'Not for you. It was the strangest event in the whole history of the Ring so far: Bilbo's arrival just at that time, and putting his hand on it, blindly, in the dark.

'There was more than one power at work, Frodo. The Ring was trying to get back to its master. It had slipped from Isildur's hand and betrayed him; then when a chance came it caught poor Déagol, and he was murdered; and after that Gollum, and it had devoured him. It could make no further use of him: he was too small and mean; and as long as it stayed with him he would never leave his deep pool again. So now, when its master was awake once more and sending out his dark thought from Mirkwood, it abandoned Gollum.

Only to be picked up by the most unlikely person imaginable: Bilbo from the Shire!

'Behind that there was something else at work, beyond any design of the Ring-maker. I can put it no plainer than by saying that Bilbo was *meant* to find the Ring, and *not* by its maker. In which case you also were *meant* to have it. And that may be an encouraging thought.'

'It is not,' said Frodo. 'Though I am not sure that I understand you. But how have you learned all this about the Ring, and about Gollum? Do you really know it all, or are you just guessing still?'

Gandalf looked at Frodo, and his eyes glinted. 'I knew much and I have learned much,' he answered. 'But I am not going to give an account of all my doings to *you*. The history of Elendil and Isildur and the One Ring is known to all the Wise. Your ring is shown to be that One Ring by the fire-writing alone, apart from any other evidence.'

'And when did you discover that?' asked Frodo, interrupting.

'Just now in this room, of course,' answered the wizard sharply. 'But I expected to find it. I have come back from dark journeys and long search to make that final test. It is the last proof, and all is now only too clear. Making out Gollum's part, and fitting it into the gap in the history, required some thought. I may have started with guesses about Gollum, but I am not guessing now. I know. I have seen him.'

'You have seen Gollum?' exclaimed Frodo in amazement.

'Yes. The obvious thing to do, of course, if one could. I tried long ago; but I have managed it at last.'

'Then what happened after Bilbo escaped from him? Do you know that?'

'Not so clearly. What I have told you is what Gollum was willing to tell – though not, of course, in the way I have reported it. Gollum is a liar, and you have to sift his words. For instance, he called the Ring his "birthday present", and he stuck to that. He said it came from his grandmother, who had lots of beautiful things of that kind. A ridiculous story. I have no doubt that Sméagol's grandmother was a matriarch, a great person in her way, but to talk of her possessing many Elven-rings was absurd, and as for giving them away, it was a lie. But a lie with a grain of truth.

'The murder of Déagol haunted Gollum, and he had made up a defence, repeating it to his "precious" over and over again, as he gnawed bones in the dark, until he almost believed it. It *was* his birthday. Déagol ought to have given the ring to him. It had previously turned up just so as to be a present. It *was* his birthday present, and so on, and on.

'I endured him as long as I could, but the truth was desperately important, and in the end I had to be harsh. I put the fear of fire on him, and wrung the true story out of him, bit by bit, together with much snivelling and snarling. He thought he was misunderstood and ill-used. But when he had at last told me his history, as far as the end of the Riddle-game and Bilbo's escape, he would not say any more, except in dark hints. Some other fear was on him greater than mine. He muttered that he was going to get his own back. People would see if he would stand being kicked, and driven into a hole and then *robbed*. Gollum had good friends now, good friends and very strong. They would help him. Baggins would pay for it. That was his chief thought. He hated Bilbo and cursed his name. What is more, he knew where he came from.'

'But how did he find that out?' asked Frodo.

'Well, as for the name, Bilbo very foolishly told Gollum himself; and after that it would not be difficult to discover his country, once Gollum came out. Oh yes, he came out. His longing for the Ring proved stronger than his fear of the Orcs, or even of the light. After a year or two he left the mountains. You see, though still bound by desire of it, the Ring was no longer devouring him; he began to revive a little. He felt old, terribly old, yet less timid, and he was mortally hungry.

'Light, light of Sun and Moon, he still feared and hated, and he always will, I think; but he was cunning. He found he could hide from daylight and moonshine, and make his way swiftly and softly by dead of night with his pale cold eyes, and catch small frightened or unwary things. He grew stronger and bolder with new food and new air. He found his way into Mirkwood, as one would expect.'

'Is that where you found him?' asked Frodo.

'I saw him there,' answered Gandalf, 'but before that he had wandered far, following Bilbo's trail. It was difficult to learn anything from him for certain, for his talk was constantly interrupted by curses and threats. "What had it got in its pocketses?" he said. "It wouldn't say, no precious. Little cheat. Not a fair question. It cheated first, it did. It broke the rules. We ought to have squeezed it, yes precious. And we will, precious!"

'That is a sample of his talk. I don't suppose you want any more. I had weary days of it. But from hints dropped among the snarls I even gathered that his padding feet had taken him at last to Esgaroth, and even to the streets of Dale, listening secretly and peering. Well, the news of the great events went far and wide in Wilderland, and many had heard Bilbo's name and knew where he came from. We had made no secret of our return journey to his home in the West. Gollum's sharp ears would soon learn what he wanted.'

'Then why didn't he track Bilbo further?' asked Frodo. 'Why didn't he come to the Shire?'

'Ah,' said Gandalf, 'now we come to it. I think Gollum tried to. He set out and came back westward, as far as the Great River. But then he turned aside. He was not daunted by the distance, I am sure. No, something else drew him away. So my friends think, those that hunted him for me.

'The Wood-elves tracked him first, an easy task for them, for his trail was still fresh then. Through Mirkwood and back again it led them, though they never caught him. The wood was full of the rumour of him, dreadful tales even among beasts and birds. The Woodmen said that there was some new terror abroad, a ghost that drank blood. It climbed trees to find nests; it crept into holes to find the young; it slipped through windows to find cradles.

'But at the western edge of Mirkwood the trail turned away. It wandered off southwards and passed out of the Wood-elves' ken, and was lost. And then I made a great mistake. Yes, Frodo, and not the first; though I fear it may prove the worst. I let the matter be. I let him go; for I had much else to think of at that time, and I still trusted the lore of Saruman.

'Well, that was years ago. I have paid for it since with many dark and dangerous days. The trail was long cold when I took it up again, after Bilbo left here. And my search would have been in vain, but for the help that I had from a friend: Aragorn, the greatest traveller and huntsman of this age of the world. Together we sought for Gollum down the whole length of Wilderland, without hope, and without success. But at last, when I had given up the chase and turned to other parts, Gollum was found. My friend returned out of great perils bringing the miserable creature with him.

'What he had been doing he would not say. He only wept and called us cruel, with many a *gollum* in his throat; and when we pressed him he whined and cringed, and rubbed his long hands, licking his fingers as if they pained him, as if he remembered some old torture. But I am afraid there is no possible doubt: he had made his slow, sneaking way, step by step, mile by mile, south, down at last to the Land of Mordor.'

A heavy silence fell in the room. Frodo could hear his heart beating. Even outside everything seemed still. No sound of Sam's shears could now be heard.

'Yes, to Mordor,' said Gandalf. 'Alas! Mordor draws all wicked things, and the Dark Power was bending all its will to gather them there. The Ring of the Enemy would leave its mark, too, leave him open to the summons. And all folk were whispering then of the new Shadow in the South, and its hatred of the West. There were his fine new friends, who would help him in his revenge!

'Wretched fool! In that land he would learn much, too much for his comfort. And sooner or later as he lurked and pried on the borders he would be caught, and taken – for examination. That was the way of it, I fear. When he was found he had already been there long, and was on his way back. On some errand of mischief. But that does not matter much now. His worst mischief was done.

'Yes, alas! through him the Enemy has learned that the One has been found again. He knows where Isildur fell. He knows where Gollum found his ring. He knows that it is a Great Ring, for it gave long life. He knows that it is not one of the Three, for they have never been lost, and they endure no evil. He knows that it is not one of the Seven, or the Nine, for they are accounted for. He knows that it is the One. And he has at last heard, I think, of *hobbits* and the *Shire*.

'The Shire – he may be seeking for it now, if he has not already found out where it lies. Indeed, Frodo, I fear that he may even think that the long-unnoticed name of *Baggins* has become important.'

'But this is terrible!' cried Frodo. 'Far worse than the worst that I imagined from your hints and warnings. O Gandalf, best of friends, what am I to do? For now I am really afraid. What am I to do? What a pity that Bilbo did not stab that vile creature, when he had a chance!'

'Pity? It was Pity that stayed his hand. Pity, and Mercy: not to strike without need. And he has been well rewarded, Frodo. Be sure that he took so little hurt from the evil, and escaped in the end, because he began his ownership of the Ring so. With Pity.'

'I am sorry,' said Frodo. 'But I am frightened; and I do not feel any pity for Gollum.'

'You have not seen him,' Gandalf broke in.

'No, and I don't want to,' said Frodo. 'I can't understand you. Do you mean to say that you, and the Elves, have let him live on after all those horrible deeds? Now at any rate he is as bad as an Orc, and just an enemy. He deserves death.'

'Deserves it! I daresay he does. Many that live deserve death. And some that die deserve life. Can you give it to them? Then do not be too eager to deal out death in judgement. For even the very wise cannot see all ends. I have not much hope that Gollum can be cured before he dies, but there is a chance of it. And he is bound up with the fate of the Ring. My heart tells me that he has some part to play yet, for good or ill, before the end; and when that comes, the pity of Bilbo may rule the fate of many – yours not least. In any case we did not kill him: he is very old and very wretched. The Wood-elves have him in prison, but they treat him with such kindness as they can find in their wise hearts.'

'All the same,' said Frodo, 'even if Bilbo could not kill Gollum, I wish he had not kept the Ring. I wish he had never found it, and that I had not got it! Why did you let me keep it? Why didn't you make me throw it away, or, or destroy it?'

'Let you? Make you?' said the wizard. 'Haven't you been listening to all that I have said? You are not thinking of what you are saying. But as for throwing it away, that was obviously wrong. These Rings have a way of being found. In evil hands it might have done great evil. Worst of all, it might have fallen into the hands of the Enemy. Indeed it certainly would; for this is the One, and he is exerting all his power to find it or draw it to himself.

'Of course, my dear Frodo, it was dangerous for you; and that has troubled me deeply. But there was so much at stake that I had to take some risk – though even when I was far away there has never been a day when the Shire has not been guarded by watchful eyes. As long as you never used it, I did not think that the Ring would have any lasting effect on you, not for evil, not at any rate for a very long time. And you must remember that nine years ago, when I last saw you, I still knew little for certain.'

'But why not destroy it, as you say should have been done

long ago?' cried Frodo again. 'If you had warned me, or even
sent me a message, I would have done away with it.'

'Would you? How would you do that? Have you ever
tried?'

'No. But I suppose one could hammer it or melt it.'

'Try!' said Gandalf. 'Try now!'

Frodo drew the Ring out of his pocket again and looked
at it. It now appeared plain and smooth, without mark or
device that he could see. The gold looked very fair and pure,
and Frodo thought how rich and beautiful was its colour,
how perfect was its roundness. It was an admirable thing and
altogether precious. When he took it out he had intended to
fling it from him into the very hottest part of the fire. But
he found now that he could not do so, not without a great
struggle. He weighed the Ring in his hand, hesitating, and
forcing himself to remember all that Gandalf had told him;
and then with an effort of will he made a movement, as if to
cast it away – but he found that he had put it back in his
pocket.

Gandalf laughed grimly. 'You see? Already you too, Frodo,
cannot easily let it go, nor will to damage it. And I could not
"make" you – except by force, which would break your mind.
But as for breaking the Ring, force is useless. Even if you
took it and struck it with a heavy sledge-hammer, it would
make no dint in it. It cannot be unmade by your hands, or
by mine.

'Your small fire, of course, would not melt even ordinary
gold. This Ring has already passed through it unscathed, and
even unheated. But there is no smith's forge in this Shire
that could change it at all. Not even the anvils and furnaces
of the Dwarves could do that. It has been said that dragon-fire
could melt and consume the Rings of Power, but there is not
now any dragon left on earth in which the old fire is hot
enough; nor was there ever any dragon, not even Ancalagon
the Black, who could have harmed the One Ring, the Ruling
Ring, for that was made by Sauron himself.

'There is only one way: to find the Cracks of Doom in the depths of Orodruin, the Fire-mountain, and cast the Ring in there, if you really wish to destroy it, to put it beyond the grasp of the Enemy for ever.'

'I do really wish to destroy it!' cried Frodo. 'Or, well, to have it destroyed. I am not made for perilous quests. I wish I had never seen the Ring! Why did it come to me? Why was I chosen?'

'Such questions cannot be answered,' said Gandalf. 'You may be sure that it was not for any merit that others do not possess: not for power or wisdom, at any rate. But you have been chosen, and you must therefore use such strength and heart and wits as you have.'

'But I have so little of any of these things! You are wise and powerful. Will you not take the Ring?'

'No!' cried Gandalf, springing to his feet. 'With that power I should have power too great and terrible. And over me the Ring would gain a power still greater and more deadly.' His eyes flashed and his face was lit as by a fire within. 'Do not tempt me! For I do not wish to become like the Dark Lord himself. Yet the way of the Ring to my heart is by pity, pity for weakness and the desire of strength to do good. Do not tempt me! I dare not take it, not even to keep it safe, unused. The wish to wield it would be too great for my strength. I shall have such need of it. Great perils lie before me.'

He went to the window and drew aside the curtains and the shutters. Sunlight streamed back again into the room. Sam passed along the path outside whistling. 'And now,' said the wizard, turning back to Frodo, 'the decision lies with you. But I will always help you.' He laid his hand on Frodo's shoulder. 'I will help you bear this burden, as long as it is yours to bear. But we must do something, soon. The Enemy is moving.'

There was a long silence. Gandalf sat down again and puffed at his pipe, as if lost in thought. His eyes seemed closed, but under the lids he was watching Frodo intently.

Frodo gazed fixedly at the red embers on the hearth, until they filled all his vision, and he seemed to be looking down into profound wells of fire. He was thinking of the fabled Cracks of Doom and the terror of the Fiery Mountain.

'Well!' said Gandalf at last. 'What are you thinking about? Have you decided what to do?'

'No!' answered Frodo, coming back to himself out of darkness, and finding to his surprise that it was not dark, and that out of the window he could see the sunlit garden. 'Or perhaps, yes. As far as I understand what you have said, I suppose I must keep the Ring and guard it, at least for the present, whatever it may do to me.'

'Whatever it may do, it will be slow, slow to evil, if you keep it with that purpose,' said Gandalf.

'I hope so,' said Frodo. 'But I hope that you may find some other better keeper soon. But in the meanwhile it seems that I am a danger, a danger to all that live near me. I cannot keep the Ring and stay here. I ought to leave Bag End, leave the Shire, leave everything and go away.' He sighed.

'I should like to save the Shire, if I could – though there have been times when I thought the inhabitants too stupid and dull for words, and have felt that an earthquake or an invasion of dragons might be good for them. But I don't feel like that now. I feel that as long as the Shire lies behind, safe and comfortable, I shall find wandering more bearable: I shall know that somewhere there is a firm foothold, even if my feet cannot stand there again.

'Of course, I have sometimes thought of going away, but I imagined that as a kind of holiday, a series of adventures like Bilbo's or better, ending in peace. But this would mean exile, a flight from danger into danger, drawing it after me. And I suppose I must go alone, if I am to do that and save the Shire. But I feel very small, and very uprooted, and well – desperate. The Enemy is so strong and terrible.'

He did not tell Gandalf, but as he was speaking a great desire to follow Bilbo flamed up in his heart – to follow Bilbo, and even perhaps to find him again. It was so strong that it overcame his fear: he could almost have run out there and then down the road without his hat, as Bilbo had done on a similar morning long ago.

'My dear Frodo!' exclaimed Gandalf. 'Hobbits really are amazing creatures, as I have said before. You can learn all that there is to know about their ways in a month, and yet after a hundred years they can still surprise you at a pinch. I hardly expected to get such an answer, not even from you. But Bilbo made no mistake in choosing his heir, though he little thought how important it would prove. I am afraid you are right. The Ring will not be able to stay hidden in the Shire much longer; and for your own sake, as well as for others, you will have to go, and leave the name of Baggins behind you. That name will not be safe to have, outside the Shire or in the Wild. I will give you a travelling name now. When you go, go as Mr. Underhill.

'But I don't think you need go alone. Not if you know of anyone you can trust, and who would be willing to go by your side – and that you would be willing to take into unknown perils. But if you look for a companion, be careful in choosing! And be careful of what you say, even to your closest friends! The enemy has many spies and many ways of hearing.'

Suddenly he stopped as if listening. Frodo became aware that all was very quiet, inside and outside. Gandalf crept to one side of the window. Then with a dart he sprang to the sill, and thrust a long arm out and downwards. There was a squawk, and up came Sam Gamgee's curly head hauled by one ear.

'Well, well, bless my beard!' said Gandalf. 'Sam Gamgee is it? Now what may you be doing?'

'Lor bless you, Mr. Gandalf, sir!' said Sam. 'Nothing! Leastways I was just trimming the grass-border under the window, if you follow me.' He picked up his shears and exhibited them as evidence.

'I don't,' said Gandalf grimly. 'It is some time since I last heard the sound of your shears. How long have you been eavesdropping?'

'Eavesdropping, sir? I don't follow you, begging your pardon. There ain't no eaves at Bag End, and that's a fact.'

'Don't be a fool! What have you heard, and why did you listen?' Gandalf's eyes flashed and his brows stuck out like bristles.

'Mr. Frodo, sir!' cried Sam quaking. 'Don't let him hurt me, sir! Don't let him turn me into anything unnatural! My old dad would take on so. I meant no harm, on my honour, sir!'

'He won't hurt you,' said Frodo, hardly able to keep from laughing, although he was himself startled and rather puzzled. 'He knows, as well as I do, that you mean no harm. But just you up and answer his questions straight away!'

'Well, sir,' said Sam dithering a little. 'I heard a deal that I didn't rightly understand, about an enemy, and rings, and Mr. Bilbo, sir, and dragons, and a fiery mountain, and – and Elves, sir. I listened because I couldn't help myself, if you know what I mean. Lor bless me, sir, but I do love tales of that sort. And I believe them too, whatever Ted may say. Elves, sir! I would dearly love to see *them*. Couldn't you take me to see Elves, sir, when you go?'

Suddenly Gandalf laughed. 'Come inside!' he shouted, and putting out both his arms he lifted the astonished Sam, shears, grass-clippings and all, right through the window and stood him on the floor. 'Take you to see Elves, eh?' he said, eyeing Sam closely, but with a smile flickering on his face. 'So you heard that Mr. Frodo is going away?'

'I did, sir. And that's why I choked: which you heard seemingly. I tried not to, sir, but it burst out of me: I was so upset.'

'It can't be helped, Sam,' said Frodo sadly. He had suddenly realized that flying from the Shire would mean more painful partings than merely saying farewell to the familiar comforts of Bag End. 'I shall have to go. But' – and here he looked hard at Sam – 'if you really care about me, you will keep that *dead* secret. See? If you don't, if you even breathe a word of what you've heard here, then I hope Gandalf will turn you into a spotted toad and fill the garden full of grass-snakes.'

Sam fell on his knees, trembling. 'Get up, Sam!' said Gandalf. 'I have thought of something better than that. Something to shut your mouth, and punish you properly for listening. You shall go away with Mr. Frodo!'

'Me, sir!' cried Sam, springing up like a dog invited for a walk. 'Me go and see Elves and all! Hooray!' he shouted, and then burst into tears.

CHAPTER III

THREE IS COMPANY

'You ought to go quietly, and you ought to go soon,' said Gandalf. Two or three weeks had passed, and still Frodo made no sign of getting ready to go.

'I know. But it is difficult to do both,' he objected. 'If I just vanish like Bilbo, the tale will be all over the Shire in no time.'

'Of course you mustn't vanish!' said Gandalf. 'That wouldn't do at all! I said *soon*, not *instantly*. If you can think of any way of slipping out of the Shire without its being generally known, it will be worth a little delay. But you must not delay too long.'

'What about the autumn, on or after Our Birthday?' asked Frodo. 'I think I could probably make some arrangements by then.'

To tell the truth, he was very reluctant to start, now that it had come to the point. Bag End seemed a more desirable residence than it had for years, and he wanted to savour as much as he could of his last summer in the Shire. When autumn came, he knew that part at least of his heart would think more kindly of journeying, as it always did at that season. He had indeed privately made up his mind to leave on his fiftieth birthday: Bilbo's one hundred and twenty-eighth. It seemed somehow the proper day on which to set out and follow him. Following Bilbo was uppermost in his mind, and the one thing that made the thought of leaving bearable. He thought as little as possible about the Ring, and where it might lead him in the end. But he did not tell all his thoughts to Gandalf. What the wizard guessed was always difficult to tell.

He looked at Frodo and smiled. 'Very well,' he said. 'I

think that will do – but it must not be any later. I am getting
very anxious. In the meanwhile, do take care, and don't let
out any hint of where you are going! And see that Sam
Gamgee does not talk. If he does, I really shall turn him into
a toad.'

'As for *where* I am going,' said Frodo, 'it would be difficult
to give that away, for I have no clear idea myself, yet.'

'Don't be absurd!' said Gandalf. 'I am not warning you
against leaving an address at the post-office! But you are
leaving the Shire – and that should not be known, until you
are far away. And you must go, or at least set out, either
North, South, West or East – and the direction should certainly not be known.'

'I have been so taken up with the thoughts of leaving Bag
End, and of saying farewell, that I have never even considered
the direction,' said Frodo. 'For where am I to go? And by
what shall I steer? What is to be my quest? Bilbo went to
find a treasure, there and back again; but I go to lose one,
and not return, as far as I can see.'

'But you cannot see very far,' said Gandalf. 'Neither can
I. It may be your task to find the Cracks of Doom; but that
quest may be for others: I do not know. At any rate you are
not ready for that long road yet.'

'No indeed!' said Frodo. 'But in the meantime what course
am I to take?'

'Towards danger; but not too rashly, nor too straight,'
answered the wizard. 'If you want my advice, make for Rivendell. That journey should not prove too perilous, though the
Road is less easy than it was, and it will grow worse as the
year fails.'

'Rivendell!' said Frodo. 'Very good: I will go east, and I
will make for Rivendell. I will take Sam to visit the Elves; he
will be delighted.' He spoke lightly; but his heart was moved
suddenly with a desire to see the house of Elrond Halfelven,
and breathe the air of that deep valley where many of the
Fair Folk still dwelt in peace.

*   *   *

One summer's evening an astonishing piece of news reached the *Ivy Bush* and *Green Dragon*. Giants and other portents on the borders of the Shire were forgotten for more important matters: Mr. Frodo was selling Bag End, indeed he had already sold it – to the Sackville-Bagginses!

'For a nice bit, too,' said some. 'At a bargain price,' said others, 'and that's more likely when Mistress Lobelia's the buyer.' (Otho had died some years before, at the ripe but disappointed age of 102.)

Just why Mr. Frodo was selling his beautiful hole was even more debatable than the price. A few held the theory – supported by the nods and hints of Mr. Baggins himself – that Frodo's money was running out: he was going to leave Hobbiton and live in a quiet way on the proceeds of the sale down in Buckland among his Brandybuck relations. 'As far from the Sackville-Bagginses as may be,' some added. But so firmly fixed had the notion of the immeasurable wealth of the Bagginses of Bag End become that most found this hard to believe, harder than any other reason or unreason that their fancy could suggest: to most it suggested a dark and yet unrevealed plot by Gandalf. Though he kept himself very quiet and did not go about by day, it was well known that he was 'hiding up in the Bag End'. But however a removal might fit in with the designs of his wizardry, there was no doubt about the fact: Frodo Baggins was going back to Buckland.

'Yes, I shall be moving this autumn,' he said. 'Merry Brandybuck is looking out for a nice little hole for me, or perhaps a small house.'

As a matter of fact with Merry's help he had already chosen and bought a little house at Crickhollow in the country beyond Bucklebury. To all but Sam he pretended he was going to settle down there permanently. The decision to set out eastwards had suggested the idea to him; for Buckland was on the eastern borders of the Shire, and as he had lived there in childhood his going back would at least seem credible.

*   *   *

Gandalf stayed in the Shire for over two months. Then one evening, at the end of June, soon after Frodo's plan had been finally arranged, he suddenly announced that he was going off again next morning. 'Only for a short while, I hope,' he said. 'But I am going down beyond the southern borders to get some news, if I can. I have been idle longer than I should.'

He spoke lightly, but it seemed to Frodo that he looked rather worried. 'Has anything happened?' he asked.

'Well no; but I have heard something that has made me anxious and needs looking into. If I think it necessary after all for you to get off at once, I shall come back immediately, or at least send word. In the meanwhile stick to your plan; but be more careful than ever, especially of the Ring. Let me impress on you once more: *don't use it!*'

He went off at dawn. 'I may be back any day,' he said. 'At the very latest I shall come back for the farewell party. I think after all you may need my company on the Road.'

At first Frodo was a good deal disturbed, and wondered often what Gandalf could have heard; but his uneasiness wore off, and in the fine weather he forgot his troubles for a while. The Shire had seldom seen so fair a summer, or so rich an autumn: the trees were laden with apples, honey was dripping in the combs, and the corn was tall and full.

Autumn was well under way before Frodo began to worry about Gandalf again. September was passing and there was still no news of him. The Birthday, and the removal, drew nearer, and still he did not come, or send word. Bag End began to be busy. Some of Frodo's friends came to stay and help him with the packing: there was Fredegar Bolger and Folco Boffin, and of course his special friends Pippin Took and Merry Brandybuck. Between them they turned the whole place upside-down.

On September 20th two covered carts went off laden to Buckland, conveying the furniture and goods that Frodo had not sold to his new home, by way of the Brandywine Bridge.

The next day Frodo became really anxious, and kept a constant look-out for Gandalf. Thursday, his birthday morning,
dawned as fair and clear as it had long ago for Bilbo's great
party. Still Gandalf did not appear. In the evening Frodo
gave his farewell feast: it was quite small, just a dinner for
himself and his four helpers; but he was troubled and felt in
no mood for it. The thought that he would so soon have to
part with his young friends weighed on his heart. He wondered how he would break it to them.

The four younger hobbits were, however, in high spirits,
and the party soon became very cheerful in spite of Gandalf's
absence. The dining-room was bare except for a table and
chairs, but the food was good, and there was good wine:
Frodo's wine had not been included in the sale to the
Sackville-Bagginses.

'Whatever happens to the rest of my stuff, when the S.-B.s
get their claws on it, at any rate I have found a good home
for this!' said Frodo, as he drained his glass. It was the last
drop of Old Winyards.

When they had sung many songs, and talked of many
things they had done together, they toasted Bilbo's birthday,
and they drank his health and Frodo's together according to
Frodo's custom. Then they went out for a sniff of air, and
glimpse of the stars, and then they went to bed. Frodo's party
was over, and Gandalf had not come.

The next morning they were busy packing another cart
with the remainder of the luggage. Merry took charge of this,
and drove off with Fatty (that is Fredegar Bolger). 'Someone
must get there and warm the house before you arrive,' said
Merry. 'Well, see you later – the day after tomorrow, if you
don't go to sleep on the way!'

Folco went home after lunch, but Pippin remained behind.
Frodo was restless and anxious, listening in vain for a sound
of Gandalf. He decided to wait until nightfall. After that, if
Gandalf wanted him urgently, he would go to Crickhollow,
and might even get there first. For Frodo was going on foot.

His plan – for pleasure and a last look at the Shire as much as any other reason – was to walk from Hobbiton to Bucklebury Ferry, taking it fairly easy.

'I shall get myself a bit into training, too,' he said, looking at himself in a dusty mirror in the half-empty hall. He had not done any strenuous walking for a long time, and the reflection looked rather flabby, he thought.

After lunch, the Sackville-Bagginses, Lobelia and her sandy-haired son, Lotho, turned up, much to Frodo's annoyance. 'Ours at last!' said Lobelia, as she stepped inside. It was not polite; nor strictly true, for the sale of Bag End did not take effect until midnight. But Lobelia can perhaps be forgiven: she had been obliged to wait about seventy-seven years longer for Bag End than she once hoped, and she was now a hundred years old. Anyway, she had come to see that nothing she had paid for had been carried off; and she wanted the keys. It took a long while to satisfy her, as she had brought a complete inventory with her and went right through it. In the end she departed with Lotho and the spare key and the promise that the other key would be left at the Gamgees' in Bagshot Row. She snorted, and showed plainly that she thought the Gamgees capable of plundering the hole during the night. Frodo did not offer her any tea.

He took his own tea with Pippin and Sam Gamgee in the kitchen. It had been officially announced that Sam was coming to Buckland 'to do for Mr. Frodo and look after his bit of garden'; an arrangement that was approved by the Gaffer, though it did not console him for the prospect of having Lobelia as a neighbour.

'Our last meal at Bag End!' said Frodo, pushing back his chair. They left the washing up for Lobelia. Pippin and Sam strapped up their three packs and piled them in the porch. Pippin went out for a last stroll in the garden. Sam disappeared.

The sun went down. Bag End seemed sad and gloomy and dishevelled. Frodo wandered round the familiar rooms,

and saw the light of the sunset fade on the walls, and shadows
creep out of the corners. It grew slowly dark indoors. He
went out and walked down to the gate at the bottom of the
path, and then on a short way down the Hill Road. He
half expected to see Gandalf come striding up through
the dusk.

The sky was clear and the stars were growing bright. 'It's
going to be a fine night,' he said aloud. 'That's good for a
beginning. I feel like walking. I can't bear any more hanging
about. I am going to start, and Gandalf must follow me.' He
turned to go back, and then stopped, for he heard voices,
just round the corner by the end of Bagshot Row. One voice
was certainly the old Gaffer's; the other was strange, and
somehow unpleasant. He could not make out what it said,
but he heard the Gaffer's answers, which were rather shrill.
The old man seemed put out.

'No, Mr. Baggins has gone away. Went this morning, and
my Sam went with him: anyway all his stuff went. Yes, sold
out and gone, I tell'ee. Why? Why's none of my business,
or yours. Where to? That ain't no secret. He's moved to
Bucklebury or some such place, away down yonder. Yes it
is – a tidy way. I've never been so far myself; they're queer
folks in Buckland. No, I can't give no message. Good night
to you!'

Footsteps went away down the Hill. Frodo wondered
vaguely why the fact that they did not come on up the Hill
seemed a great relief. 'I am sick of questions and curiosity
about my doings, I suppose,' he thought. 'What an inquisitive
lot they all are!' He had half a mind to go and ask the Gaffer
who the inquirer was; but he thought better (or worse) of it,
and turned and walked quickly back to Bag End.

Pippin was sitting on his pack in the porch. Sam was not
there. Frodo stepped inside the dark door. 'Sam!' he called.
'Sam! Time!'

'Coming, sir!' came the answer from far within, followed
soon by Sam himself, wiping his mouth. He had been saying
farewell to the beer-barrel in the cellar.

'All aboard, Sam?' said Frodo.

'Yes, sir. I'll last for a bit now, sir.'

Frodo shut and locked the round door, and gave the key to Sam. 'Run down with this to your home, Sam!' he said. 'Then cut along the Row and meet us as quick as you can at the gate in the lane beyond the meadows. We are not going through the village tonight. Too many ears pricking and eyes prying.' Sam ran off at full speed.

'Well, now we're off at last!' said Frodo. They shouldered their packs and took up their sticks, and walked round the corner to the west side of Bag End. 'Good-bye!' said Frodo, looking at the dark blank windows. He waved his hand, and then turned and (following Bilbo, if he had known it) hurried after Peregrin down the garden-path. They jumped over the low place in the hedge at the bottom and took to the fields, passing into the darkness like a rustle in the grasses.

At the bottom of the Hill on its western side they came to the gate opening on to a narrow lane. There they halted and adjusted the straps of their packs. Presently Sam appeared, trotting quickly and breathing hard; his heavy pack was hoisted high on his shoulders, and he had put on his head a tall shapeless felt bag, which he called a hat. In the gloom he looked very much like a dwarf.

'I am sure you have given me all the heaviest stuff,' said Frodo. 'I pity snails, and all that carry their homes on their backs.'

'I could take a lot more yet, sir. My packet is quite light,' said Sam stoutly and untruthfully.

'No, you don't, Sam!' said Pippin. 'It is good for him. He's got nothing except what he ordered us to pack. He's been slack lately, and he'll feel the weight less when he's walked off some of his own.'

'Be kind to a poor old hobbit!' laughed Frodo. 'I shall be as thin as a willow-wand, I'm sure, before I get to Buckland. But I was talking nonsense. I suspect you have taken more than your share, Sam, and I shall look into it at our next packing.' He picked up his stick again. 'Well, we all like walking in the dark,' he said, 'so let's put some miles behind us before bed.'

For a short way they followed the lane westwards. Then leaving it they turned left and took quietly to the fields again. They went in single file along hedgerows and the borders of coppices, and night fell dark about them. In their dark cloaks they were as invisible as if they all had magic rings. Since they were all hobbits, and were trying to be silent, they made no noise that even hobbits would hear. Even the wild things in the fields and woods hardly noticed their passing.

After some time they crossed the Water, west of Hobbiton, by a narrow plank-bridge. The stream was there no more than a winding black ribbon, bordered with leaning alder-trees. A mile or two further south they hastily crossed the great road from the Brandywine Bridge; they were now in the Tookland and bending south-eastwards they made for the Green Hill Country. As they began to climb its first slopes they looked back and saw the lamps in Hobbiton far off twinkling in the gentle valley of the Water. Soon it disappeared in the folds of the darkened land, and was followed by Bywater beside its grey pool. When the light of the last farm was far behind, peeping among the trees, Frodo turned and waved a hand in farewell.

'I wonder if I shall ever look down into that valley again,' he said quietly.

When they had walked for about three hours they rested. The night was clear, cool, and starry, but smoke-like wisps of mist were creeping up the hill-sides from the streams and deep meadows. Thin-clad birches, swaying in a light wind above their heads, made a black net against the pale sky. They ate a very frugal supper (for hobbits), and then went on again. Soon they struck a narrow road, that went rolling up and down, fading grey into the darkness ahead: the road to Woodhall, and Stock, and the Bucklebury Ferry. It climbed away from the main road in the Water-valley, and wound over the skirts of the Green Hills towards Woody-End, a wild corner of the Eastfarthing.

After a while they plunged into a deeply cloven track between tall trees that rustled their dry leaves in the night. It was very dark. At first they talked, or hummed a tune softly together, being now far away from inquisitive ears. Then they marched on in silence, and Pippin began to lag behind. At last, as they began to climb a steep slope, he stopped and yawned.

'I am so sleepy,' he said, 'that soon I shall fall down on the road. Are you going to sleep on your legs? It is nearly midnight.'

'I thought you liked walking in the dark,' said Frodo. 'But there is no great hurry. Merry expects us some time the day after tomorrow; but that leaves us nearly two days more. We'll halt at the first likely spot.'

'The wind's in the West,' said Sam. 'If we get to the other side of this hill, we shall find a spot that is sheltered and snug enough, sir. There is a dry fir-wood just ahead, if I remember rightly.' Sam knew the land well within twenty miles of Hobbiton, but that was the limit of his geography.

Just over the top of the hill they came on the patch of fir-wood. Leaving the road they went into the deep resin-scented darkness of the trees, and gathered dead sticks and cones to make a fire. Soon they had a merry crackle of flame at the foot of a large fir-tree and they sat round it for a while, until they began to nod. Then, each in an angle of the great tree's roots, they curled up in their cloaks and blankets, and were soon fast asleep. They set no watch; even Frodo feared no danger yet, for they were still in the heart of the Shire. A few creatures came and looked at them when the fire had died away. A fox passing through the wood on business of his own stopped several minutes and sniffed.

'Hobbits!' he thought. 'Well, what next? I have heard of strange doings in this land, but I have seldom heard of a hobbit sleeping out of doors under a tree. Three of them! There's something mighty queer behind this.' He was quite right, but he never found out any more about it.

The morning came, pale and clammy. Frodo woke up first, and found that a tree-root had made a hole in his back, and that his neck was stiff. 'Walking for pleasure! Why didn't I drive?' he thought, as he usually did at the beginning of an expedition. 'And all my beautiful feather beds are sold to the Sackville-Bagginses! These tree-roots would do them good.' He stretched. 'Wake up, hobbits!' he cried. 'It's a beautiful morning.'

'What's beautiful about it?' said Pippin, peering over the edge of his blanket with one eye. 'Sam! Get breakfast ready for half-past nine! Have you got the bath-water hot?'

Sam jumped up, looking rather bleary. 'No, sir, I haven't, sir!' he said.

Frodo stripped the blankets from Pippin and rolled him over, and then walked off to the edge of the wood. Away eastward the sun was rising red out of the mists that lay thick on the world. Touched with gold and red the autumn trees seemed to be sailing rootless in a shadowy sea. A little below him to the left the road ran down steeply into a hollow and disappeared.

When he returned Sam and Pippin had got a good fire going. 'Water!' shouted Pippin. 'Where's the water?'

'I don't keep water in my pockets,' said Frodo.

'We thought you had gone to find some,' said Pippin, busy setting out the food, and cups. 'You had better go now.'

'You can come too,' said Frodo, 'and bring all the water-bottles.' There was a stream at the foot of the hill. They filled their bottles and the small camping kettle at a little fall where the water fell a few feet over an outcrop of grey stone. It was icy cold; and they spluttered and puffed as they bathed their faces and hands.

When their breakfast was over, and their packs all trussed

up again, it was after ten o'clock, and the day was beginning
to turn fine and hot. They went down the slope, and across
the stream where it dived under the road, and up the next
slope, and up and down another shoulder of the hills; and
by that time their cloaks, blankets, water, food, and other
gear already seemed a heavy burden.

The day's march promised to be warm and tiring work.
After some miles, however, the road ceased to roll up and
down: it climbed to the top of a steep bank in a weary zig-
zagging sort of way, and then prepared to go down for the
last time. In front of them they saw the lower lands dotted
with small clumps of trees that melted away in the distance
to a brown woodland haze. They were looking across the
Woody End towards the Brandywine River. The road wound
away before them like a piece of string.

'The road goes on for ever,' said Pippin; 'but I can't without a rest. It is high time for lunch.' He sat down on the
bank at the side of the road and looked away east into the
haze, beyond which lay the River, and the end of the Shire
in which he had spent all his life. Sam stood by him. His
round eyes were wide open – for he was looking across lands
he had never seen to a new horizon.

'Do Elves live in those woods?' he asked.

'Not that I ever heard,' said Pippin. Frodo was silent. He
too was gazing eastward along the road, as if he had never
seen it before. Suddenly he spoke, aloud but as if to himself,
saying slowly:

> The Road goes ever on and on
>   Down from the door where it began.
> Now far ahead the Road has gone,
>   And I must follow, if I can,
> Pursuing it with weary feet,
>   Until it joins some larger way,
> Where many paths and errands meet.
>   And whither then? I cannot say.

'That sounds like a bit of old Bilbo's rhyming,' said Pippin. 'Or is it one of your imitations? It does not sound altogether encouraging.'

'I don't know,' said Frodo. 'It came to me then, as if I was making it up; but I may have heard it long ago. Certainly it reminds me very much of Bilbo in the last years, before he went away. He used often to say there was only one Road; that it was like a great river: its springs were at every doorstep, and every path was its tributary. "It's a dangerous business, Frodo, going out of your door," he used to say. "You step into the Road, and if you don't keep your feet, there is no knowing where you might be swept off to. Do you realize that this is the very path that goes through Mirkwood, and that if you let it, it might take you to the Lonely Mountain or even further and to worse places?" He used to say that on the path outside the front door at Bag End, especially after he had been out for a long walk.'

'Well, the Road won't sweep me anywhere for an hour at least,' said Pippin, unslinging his pack. The others followed his example, putting their packs against the bank and their legs out into the road. After a rest they had a good lunch, and then more rest.

The sun was beginning to get low and the light of afternoon was on the land as they went down the hill. So far they had not met a soul on the road. This way was not much used, being hardly fit for carts, and there was little traffic to the Woody End. They had been jogging along again for an hour or more when Sam stopped a moment as if listening. They were now on level ground, and the road after much winding lay straight ahead through grass-land sprinkled with tall trees, outliers of the approaching woods.

'I can hear a pony or a horse coming along the road behind,' said Sam.

They looked back, but the turn of the road prevented them from seeing far. 'I wonder if that is Gandalf coming after us,' said Frodo; but even as he said it, he had a feeling that

it was not so, and a sudden desire to hide from the view of
the rider came over him.

'It may not matter much,' he said apologetically, 'but I
would rather not be seen on the road – by anyone. I am sick
of my doings being noticed and discussed. And if it is Gandalf,' he added as an afterthought, 'we can give him a little
surprise, to pay him out for being so late. Let's get out of
sight!'

The other two ran quickly to the left and down into a little
hollow not far from the road. There they lay flat. Frodo
hesitated for a second: curiosity or some other feeling was
struggling with his desire to hide. The sound of hoofs drew
nearer. Just in time he threw himself down in a patch of long
grass behind a tree that overshadowed the road. Then he
lifted his head and peered cautiously above one of the great
roots.

Round the corner came a black horse, no hobbit-pony but
a full-sized horse; and on it sat a large man, who seemed to
crouch in the saddle, wrapped in a great black cloak and
hood, so that only his boots in the high stirrups showed
below; his face was shadowed and invisible.

When it reached the tree and was level with Frodo the
horse stopped. The riding figure sat quite still with its head
bowed, as if listening. From inside the hood came a noise as
of someone sniffing to catch an elusive scent; the head turned
from side to side of the road.

A sudden unreasoning fear of discovery laid hold of Frodo,
and he thought of his Ring. He hardly dared to breathe, and
yet the desire to get it out of his pocket became so strong
that he began slowly to move his hand. He felt that he had
only to slip it on, and then he would be safe. The advice of
Gandalf seemed absurd. Bilbo had used the Ring. 'And I am
still in the Shire,' he thought, as his hand touched the chain
on which it hung. At that moment the rider sat up, and shook
the reins. The horse stepped forward, walking slowly at first,
and then breaking into a quick trot.

Frodo crawled to the edge of the road and watched the

rider, until he dwindled into the distance. He could not be quite sure, but it seemed to him that suddenly, before it passed out of sight, the horse turned aside and went into the trees on the right.

'Well, I call that very queer, and indeed disturbing,' said Frodo to himself, as he walked towards his companions. Pippin and Sam had remained flat in the grass, and had seen nothing; so Frodo described the rider and his strange behaviour.

'I can't say why, but I felt certain he was looking or *smelling* for me; and also I felt certain that I did not want him to discover me. I've never seen or felt anything like it in the Shire before.'

'But what has one of the Big People got to do with us?' said Pippin. 'And what is he doing in this part of the world?'

'There are some Men about,' said Frodo. 'Down in the Southfarthing they have had trouble with Big People, I believe. But I have never heard of anything like this rider. I wonder where he comes from.'

'Begging your pardon,' put in Sam suddenly, 'I know where he comes from. It's from Hobbiton that this here black rider comes, unless there's more than one. And I know where he's going to.'

'What do you mean?' said Frodo sharply, looking at him in astonishment. 'Why didn't you speak up before?'

'I have only just remembered, sir. It was like this: when I got back to our hole yesterday evening with the key, my dad, he says to me: *Hallo, Sam!* he says. *I thought you were away with Mr. Frodo this morning. There's been a strange customer asking for Mr. Baggins of Bag End, and he's only just gone. I've sent him on to Bucklebury. Not that I liked the sound of him. He seemed mighty put out, when I told him Mr. Baggins had left his old home for good. Hissed at me, he did. It gave me quite a shudder. What sort of a fellow was he? says I to the Gaffer. I don't know, says he; but he wasn't a hobbit. He was tall and black-like, and he stooped over me. I reckon it was one of the Big Folk from foreign parts. He spoke funny.*

'I couldn't stay to hear more, sir, since you were waiting; and I didn't give much heed to it myself. The Gaffer is getting old, and more than a bit blind, and it must have been near dark when this fellow come up the Hill and found him taking the air at the end of our Row. I hope he hasn't done no harm, sir, nor me.'

'The Gaffer can't be blamed anyway,' said Frodo. 'As a matter of fact I heard him talking to a stranger, who seemed to be inquiring for me, and I nearly went and asked him who it was. I wish I had, or you had told me about it before. I might have been more careful on the road.'

'Still, there may be no connexion between this rider and the Gaffer's stranger,' said Pippin. 'We left Hobbiton secretly enough, and I don't see how he could have followed us.'

'What about the *smelling*, sir?' said Sam. 'And the Gaffer said he was a black chap.'

'I wish I had waited for Gandalf,' Frodo muttered. 'But perhaps it would only have made matters worse.'

'Then you know or guess something about this rider?' said Pippin, who had caught the muttered words.

'I don't know, and I would rather not guess,' said Frodo.

'All right, cousin Frodo! You can keep your secret for the present, if you want to be mysterious. In the meanwhile what are we to do? I should like a bite and a sup, but somehow I think we had better move on from here. Your talk of sniffing riders with invisible noses has unsettled me.'

'Yes, I think we will move on now,' said Frodo; 'but not on the road – in case that rider comes back, or another follows him. We ought to do a good step more today. Buckland is still miles away.'

The shadows of the trees were long and thin on the grass, as they started off again. They now kept a stone's throw to the left of the road, and kept out of sight of it as much as they could. But this hindered them; for the grass was thick and tussocky, and the ground uneven, and the trees began to draw together into thickets.

The sun had gone down red behind the hills at their backs, and evening was coming on before they came back to the road at the end of the long level over which it had run straight for some miles. At that point it bent left and went down into the lowlands of the Yale making for Stock; but a lane branched right, winding through a wood of ancient oak-trees on its way to Woodhall. 'That is the way for us,' said Frodo.

Not far from the road-meeting they came on the huge hulk of a tree: it was still alive and had leaves on the small branches that it had put out round the broken stumps of its long-fallen limbs; but it was hollow, and could be entered by a great crack on the side away from the road. The hobbits crept inside, and sat there upon a floor of old leaves and decayed wood. They rested and had a light meal, talking quietly and listening from time to time.

Twilight was about them as they crept back to the lane. The West wind was sighing in the branches. Leaves were whispering. Soon the road began to fall gently but steadily into the dusk. A star came out above the trees in the darkening East before them. They went abreast and in step, to keep up their spirits. After a time, as the stars grew thicker and brighter, the feeling of disquiet left them, and they no longer listened for the sound of hoofs. They began to hum softly, as hobbits have a way of doing as they walk along, especially when they are drawing near to home at night. With most hobbits it is a supper-song or a bed-song; but these hobbits hummed a walking-song (though not, of course, without any mention of supper and bed). Bilbo Baggins had made the words, to a tune that was as old as the hills, and taught it to Frodo as they walked in the lanes of the Water-valley and talked about Adventure.

> *Upon the hearth the fire is red,*
> *Beneath the roof there is a bed;*
> *But not yet weary are our feet,*
> *Still round the corner we may meet*

A sudden tree or standing stone
That none have seen but we alone.
    Tree and flower and leaf and grass,
    Let them pass! Let them pass!
    Hill and water under sky,
    Pass them by! Pass them by!

Still round the corner there may wait
A new road or a secret gate,
And though we pass them by today,
Tomorrow we may come this way
And take the hidden paths that run
Towards the Moon or to the Sun.
    Apple, thorn, and nut and sloe,
    Let them go! Let them go!
    Sand and stone and pool and dell,
    Fare you well! Fare you well!

Home is behind, the world ahead,
And there are many paths to tread
Through shadows to the edge of night,
Until the stars are all alight.
Then world behind and home ahead,
We'll wander back to home and bed.
    Mist and twilight, cloud and shade,
    Away shall fade! Away shall fade!
    Fire and lamp, and meat and bread,
    And then to bed! And then to bed!

The song ended. 'And *now* to bed! And *now* to bed!' sang Pippin in a high voice.

'Hush!' said Frodo. 'I think I hear hoofs again.'

They stopped suddenly and stood as silent as tree-shadows, listening. There was a sound of hoofs in the lane, some way behind, but coming slow and clear down the wind. Quickly and quietly they slipped off the path, and ran into the deeper shade under the oak-trees.

'Don't let us go too far!' said Frodo. 'I don't want to be seen, but I want to see if it is another Black Rider.'

'Very well!' said Pippin. 'But don't forget the sniffing!'

The hoofs drew nearer. They had no time to find any hiding-place better than the general darkness under the trees; Sam and Pippin crouched behind a large tree-bole, while Frodo crept back a few yards towards the lane. It showed grey and pale, a line of fading light through the wood. Above it the stars were thick in the dim sky, but there was no moon.

The sound of hoofs stopped. As Frodo watched he saw something dark pass across the lighter space between two trees, and then halt. It looked like the black shade of a horse led by a smaller black shadow. The black shadow stood close to the point where they had left the path, and it swayed from side to side. Frodo thought he heard the sound of snuffling. The shadow bent to the ground, and then began to crawl towards him.

Once more the desire to slip on the Ring came over Frodo; but this time it was stronger than before. So strong that, almost before he realized what he was doing, his hand was groping in his pocket. But at that moment there came a sound like mingled song and laughter. Clear voices rose and fell in the starlit air. The black shadow straightened up and retreated. It climbed on to the shadowy horse and seemed to vanish across the lane into the darkness on the other side. Frodo breathed again.

'Elves!' exclaimed Sam in a hoarse whisper. 'Elves, sir!' He would have burst out of the trees and dashed off towards the voices, if they had not pulled him back.

'Yes, it is Elves,' said Frodo. 'One can meet them sometimes in the Woody End. They don't live in the Shire, but they wander into it in Spring and Autumn, out of their own lands away beyond the Tower Hills. I am thankful that they do! You did not see, but that Black Rider stopped just here and was actually crawling towards us when the song began. As soon as he heard the voices he slipped away.'

'What about the Elves?' said Sam, too excited to trouble about the rider. 'Can't we go and see them?'

'Listen! They are coming this way,' said Frodo. 'We have only to wait.'

The singing drew nearer. One clear voice rose now above the others. It was singing in the fair elven-tongue, of which Frodo knew only a little, and the others knew nothing. Yet the sound blending with the melody seemed to shape itself in their thought into words which they only partly understood. This was the song as Frodo heard it:

> Snow-white! Snow-white! O Lady clear!
>   O Queen beyond the Western Seas!
> O Light to us that wander here
>   Amid the world of woven trees!
>
> Gilthoniel! O Elbereth!
>   Clear are thy eyes and bright thy breath!
> Snow-white! Snow-white! We sing to thee
>   In a far land beyond the Sea.
>
> O stars that in the Sunless Year
>   With shining hand by her were sown,
> In windy fields now bright and clear
>   We see your silver blossom blown!
>
> O Elbereth! Gilthoniel!
>   We still remember, we who dwell
> In this far land beneath the trees,
>   Thy starlight on the Western Seas.

The song ended. 'These are High Elves! They spoke the name of Elbereth!' said Frodo in amazement. 'Few of that fairest folk are ever seen in the Shire. Not many now remain in Middle-earth, east of the Great Sea. This is indeed a strange chance!'

The hobbits sat in shadow by the wayside. Before long the

Elves came down the lane towards the valley. They passed slowly, and the hobbits could see the starlight glimmering on their hair and in their eyes. They bore no lights, yet as they walked a shimmer, like the light of the moon above the rim of the hills before it rises, seemed to fall about their feet. They were now silent, and as the last Elf passed he turned and looked towards the hobbits and laughed.

'Hail, Frodo!' he cried. 'You are abroad late. Or are you perhaps lost?' Then he called aloud to the others, and all the company stopped and gathered round.

'This is indeed wonderful!' they said. 'Three hobbits in a wood at night! We have not seen such a thing since Bilbo went away. What is the meaning of it?'

'The meaning of it, fair people,' said Frodo, 'is simply that we seem to be going the same way as you are. I like walking under the stars. But I would welcome your company.'

'But we have no need of other company, and hobbits are so dull,' they laughed. 'And how do you know that we go the same way as you, for you do not know whither we are going?'

'And how do you know my name?' asked Frodo in return.

'We know many things,' they said. 'We have seen you often before with Bilbo, though you may not have seen us.'

'Who are you, and who is your lord?' asked Frodo.

'I am Gildor,' answered their leader, the Elf who had first hailed him. 'Gildor Inglorion of the House of Finrod. We are Exiles, and most of our kindred have long ago departed and we too are now only tarrying here a while, ere we return over the Great Sea. But some of our kinsfolk dwell still in peace in Rivendell. Come now, Frodo, tell us what you are doing? For we see that there is some shadow of fear upon you.'

'O Wise People!' interrupted Pippin eagerly. 'Tell us about the Black Riders!'

'Black Riders?' they said in low voices. 'Why do you ask about Black Riders?'

'Because two Black Riders have overtaken us today, or one

has done so twice,' said Pippin; 'only a little while ago he slipped away as you drew near.'

The Elves did not answer at once, but spoke together softly in their own tongue. At length Gildor turned to the hobbits. 'We will not speak of this here,' he said. 'We think you had best come now with us. It is not our custom, but for this time we will take you on our road, and you shall lodge with us tonight, if you will.'

'O Fair Folk! This is good fortune beyond my hope,' said Pippin. Sam was speechless. 'I thank you indeed, Gildor Inglorion,' said Frodo bowing. '*Elen síla lúmenn' omentielvo*, a star shines on the hour of our meeting,' he added in the high-elven speech.

'Be careful, friends!' cried Gildor laughing. 'Speak no secrets! Here is a scholar in the Ancient Tongue. Bilbo was a good master. Hail, Elf-friend!' he said, bowing to Frodo. 'Come now with your friends and join our company! You had best walk in the middle so that you may not stray. You may be weary before we halt.'

'Why? Where are you going?' asked Frodo.

'For tonight we go to the woods on the hills above Wood-hall. It is some miles, but you shall have rest at the end of it, and it will shorten your journey tomorrow.'

They now marched on again in silence, and passed like shadows and faint lights: for Elves (even more than hobbits) could walk when they wished without sound or footfall. Pippin soon began to feel sleepy, and staggered once or twice; but each time a tall Elf at his side put out his arm and saved him from a fall. Sam walked along at Frodo's side, as if in a dream, with an expression on his face half of fear and half of astonished joy.

The woods on either side became denser; the trees were now younger and thicker; and as the lane went lower, running down into a fold of the hills, there were many deep brakes of hazel on the rising slopes at either hand. At last the Elves turned aside from the path. A green ride lay almost unseen through the thickets on the right; and this they followed as it wound away back up the wooded slopes on to the top of a shoulder of the hills that stood out into the lower land of the river-valley. Suddenly they came out of the shadow of the trees, and before them lay a wide space of grass, grey under the night. On three sides the woods pressed upon it; but eastward the ground fell steeply and the tops of the dark trees, growing at the bottom of the slope, were below their feet. Beyond, the low lands lay dim and flat under the stars. Nearer at hand a few lights twinkled in the village of Woodhall.

The Elves sat on the grass and spoke together in soft voices; they seemed to take no further notice of the hobbits. Frodo and his companions wrapped themselves in cloaks and blankets, and drowsiness stole over them. The night grew on, and the lights in the valley went out. Pippin fell asleep, pillowed on a green hillock.

Away high in the East swung Remmirath, the Netted Stars, and slowly above the mists red Borgil rose, glowing like a jewel of fire. Then by some shift of airs all the mist was drawn away like a veil, and there leaned up, as he climbed over the rim of the world, the Swordsman of the Sky, Menelvagor with his shining belt. The Elves all burst into song. Suddenly under the trees a fire sprang up with a red light.

'Come!' the Elves called to the hobbits. 'Come! Now is the time for speech and merriment!'

Pippin sat up and rubbed his eyes. He shivered. 'There is a fire in the hall, and food for hungry guests,' said an Elf standing before him.

At the south end of the greensward there was an opening. There the green floor ran on into the wood, and formed a wide space like a hall, roofed by the boughs of trees. Their great trunks ran like pillars down each side. In the middle there was a wood-fire blazing, and upon the tree-pillars torches with lights of gold and silver were burning steadily. The Elves sat round the fire upon the grass or upon the sawn rings of old trunks. Some went to and fro bearing cups and pouring drink; others brought food on heaped plates and dishes.

'This is poor fare,' they said to the hobbits; 'for we are lodging in the greenwood far from our halls. If ever you are our guests at home, we will treat you better.'

'It seems to me good enough for a birthday-party,' said Frodo.

Pippin afterwards recalled little of either food or drink, for his mind was filled with the light upon the elf-faces, and the sound of voices so various and so beautiful that he felt in a waking dream. But he remembered that there was bread, surpassing the savour of a fair white loaf to one who is starving; and fruits sweet as wildberries and richer than the tended fruits of gardens; he drained a cup that was filled with a fragrant draught, cool as a clear fountain, golden as a summer afternoon.

Sam could never describe in words, nor picture clearly to himself, what he felt or thought that night, though it remained in his memory as one of the chief events of his life. The nearest he ever got was to say: 'Well, sir, if I could grow apples like that, I would call myself a gardener. But it was the singing that went to my heart, if you know what I mean.'

Frodo sat, eating, drinking, and talking with delight; but his mind was chiefly on the words spoken. He knew a little of the elf-speech and listened eagerly. Now and again he spoke to those that served him and thanked them in their own language. They smiled at him and said laughing: 'Here is a jewel among hobbits!'

After a while Pippin fell fast asleep, and was lifted up and borne away to a bower under the trees; there he was laid upon a soft bed and slept the rest of the night away. Sam refused to leave his master. When Pippin had gone, he came and sat curled up at Frodo's feet, where at last he nodded and closed his eyes. Frodo remained long awake, talking with Gildor.

They spoke of many things, old and new, and Frodo questioned Gildor much about happenings in the wide world outside the Shire. The tidings were mostly sad and ominous: of gathering darkness, the wars of Men, and the flight of the Elves. At last Frodo asked the question that was nearest to his heart:

'Tell me, Gildor, have you ever seen Bilbo since he left us?'

Gildor smiled. 'Yes,' he answered. 'Twice. He said farewell to us on this very spot. But I saw him once again, far from here.' He would say no more about Bilbo, and Frodo fell silent.

'You do not ask me or tell me much that concerns yourself, Frodo,' said Gildor. 'But I already know a little, and I can read more in your face and in the thought behind your questions. You are leaving the Shire, and yet you doubt that you will find what you seek, or accomplish what you intend, or that you will ever return. Is not that so?'

'It is,' said Frodo; 'but I thought my going was a secret known only to Gandalf and my faithful Sam.' He looked down at Sam, who was snoring gently.

'The secret will not reach the Enemy from us,' said Gildor.

'The Enemy?' said Frodo. 'Then you know why I am leaving the Shire?'

'I do not know for what reason the Enemy is pursuing you,' answered Gildor; 'but I perceive that he is – strange indeed though that seems to me. And I warn you that peril is now both before you and behind you, and upon either side.'

'You mean the Riders? I feared that they were servants of the Enemy. What *are* the Black Riders?'

'Has Gandalf told you nothing?'

'Nothing about such creatures.'

'Then I think it is not for me to say more – lest terror should keep you from your journey. For it seems to me that you have set out only just in time, if indeed you are in time. You must now make haste, and neither stay nor turn back; for the Shire is no longer any protection to you.'

'I cannot imagine what information could be more terrifying than your hints and warnings,' exclaimed Frodo. 'I knew that danger lay ahead, of course; but I did not expect to meet it in our own Shire. Can't a hobbit walk from the Water to the River in peace?'

'But it is not your own Shire,' said Gildor. 'Others dwelt here before hobbits were; and others will dwell here again when hobbits are no more. The wide world is all about you: you can fence yourselves in, but you cannot for ever fence it out.'

'I know – and yet it has always seemed so safe and familiar. What can I do now? My plan was to leave the Shire secretly, and make my way to Rivendell; but now my footsteps are dogged, before ever I get to Buckland.'

'I think you should still follow that plan,' said Gildor. 'I do not think the Road will prove too hard for your courage. But if you desire clearer counsel, you should ask Gandalf. I do not know the reason for your flight, and therefore I do not know by what means your pursuers will assail you. These things Gandalf must know. I suppose that you will see him before you leave the Shire?'

'I hope so. But that is another thing that makes me anxious. I have been expecting Gandalf for many days. He was to have come to Hobbiton at the latest two nights ago; but he has never appeared. Now I am wondering what can have happened. Should I wait for him?'

Gildor was silent for a moment. 'I do not like this news,' he said at last. 'That Gandalf should be late, does not bode well. But it is said: *Do not meddle in the affairs of Wizards, for they are subtle and quick to anger.* The choice is yours: to go or wait.'

'And it is also said,' answered Frodo: '*Go not to the Elves for counsel, for they will say both no and yes.*'

'Is it indeed?' laughed Gildor. 'Elves seldom give unguarded advice, for advice is a dangerous gift, even from the wise to the wise, and all courses may run ill. But what would you? You have not told me all concerning yourself;

and how then shall I choose better than you? But if you demand advice, I will for friendship's sake give it. I think you should now go at once, without delay; and if Gandalf does not come before you set out, then I also advise this: do not go alone. Take such friends as are trusty and willing. Now you should be grateful, for I do not give this counsel gladly. The Elves have their own labours and their own sorrows, and they are little concerned with the ways of hobbits, or of any other creatures upon earth. Our paths cross theirs seldom, by chance or purpose. In this meeting there may be more than chance; but the purpose is not clear to me, and I fear to say too much.'

'I am deeply grateful,' said Frodo; 'but I wish you would tell me plainly what the Black Riders are. If I take your advice I may not see Gandalf for a long while, and I ought to know what is the danger that pursues me.'

'Is it not enough to know that they are servants of the Enemy?' answered Gildor. 'Flee them! Speak no words to them! They are deadly. Ask no more of me! But my heart forbodes that, ere all is ended, you, Frodo son of Drogo, will know more of these fell things than Gildor Inglorion. May Elbereth protect you!'

'But where shall I find courage?' asked Frodo. 'That is what I chiefly need.'

'Courage is found in unlikely places,' said Gildor. 'Be of good hope! Sleep now! In the morning we shall have gone; but we will send our messages through the lands. The Wandering Companies shall know of your journey, and those that have power for good shall be on the watch. I name you Elf-friend; and may the stars shine upon the end of your road! Seldom have we had such delight in strangers, and it is fair to hear words of the Ancient Speech from the lips of other wanderers in the world.'

Frodo felt sleep coming upon him, even as Gildor finished speaking. 'I will sleep now,' he said; and the Elf led him to a bower beside Pippin, and he threw himself upon a bed and fell at once into a dreamless slumber.

CHAPTER IV

A SHORT CUT TO MUSHROOMS

In the morning Frodo woke refreshed. He was lying in a bower made by a living tree with branches laced and drooping to the ground; his bed was of fern and grass, deep and soft and strangely fragrant. The sun was shining through the fluttering leaves, which were still green upon the tree. He jumped up and went out.

Sam was sitting on the grass near the edge of the wood. Pippin was standing studying the sky and weather. There was no sign of the Elves.

'They have left us fruit and drink, and bread,' said Pippin. 'Come and have your breakfast. The bread tastes almost as good as it did last night. I did not want to leave you any, but Sam insisted.'

Frodo sat down beside Sam and began to eat. 'What is the plan for today?' asked Pippin.

'To walk to Bucklebury as quickly as possible,' answered Frodo, and gave his attention to the food.

'Do you think we shall see anything of those Riders?' asked Pippin cheerfully. Under the morning sun the prospect of seeing a whole troop of them did not seem very alarming to him.

'Yes, probably,' said Frodo, not liking the reminder. 'But I hope to get across the river without their seeing us.'

'Did you find out anything about them from Gildor?'

'Not much – only hints and riddles,' said Frodo evasively.

'Did you ask about the sniffing?'

'We didn't discuss it,' said Frodo with his mouth full.

'You should have. I am sure it is very important.'

'In that case I am sure Gildor would have refused to explain it,' said Frodo sharply. 'And now leave me in peace for a bit!

I don't want to answer a string of questions while I am eating. I want to think!'

'Good heavens!' said Pippin. 'At breakfast?' He walked away towards the edge of the green.

From Frodo's mind the bright morning – treacherously bright, he thought – had not banished the fear of pursuit; and he pondered the words of Gildor. The merry voice of Pippin came to him. He was running on the green turf and singing.

'No! I could not!' he said to himself. 'It is one thing to take my young friends walking over the Shire with me, until we are hungry and weary, and food and bed are sweet. To take them into exile, where hunger and weariness may have no cure, is quite another – even if they are willing to come. The inheritance is mine alone. I don't think I ought even to take Sam.' He looked at Sam Gamgee, and discovered that Sam was watching him.

'Well, Sam!' he said. 'What about it? I am leaving the Shire as soon as ever I can – in fact I have made up my mind now not even to wait a day at Crickhollow, if it can be helped.'

'Very good, sir!'

'You still mean to come with me?'

'I do.'

'It is going to be very dangerous, Sam. It is already dangerous. Most likely neither of us will come back.'

'If you don't come back, sir, then I shan't, that's certain,' said Sam. '*Don't you leave him!* they said to me. *Leave him!* I said. *I never mean to. I am going with him, if he climbs to the Moon, and if any of those Black Riders try to stop him, they'll have Sam Gamgee to reckon with,* I said. They laughed.'

'Who are *they*, and what are you talking about?'

'The Elves, sir. We had some talk last night; and they seemed to know you were going away, so I didn't see the use of denying it. Wonderful folk, Elves, sir! Wonderful!'

'They are,' said Frodo. 'Do you like them still, now you have had a closer view?'

'They seem a bit above my likes and dislikes, so to speak,'

answered Sam slowly. 'It don't seem to matter what I think about them. They are quite different from what I expected – so old and young, and so gay and sad, as it were.'

Frodo looked at Sam rather startled, half expecting to see some outward sign of the odd change that seemed to have come over him. It did not sound like the voice of the old Sam Gamgee that he thought he knew. But it looked like the old Sam Gamgee sitting there, except that his face was unusually thoughtful.

'Do you feel any need to leave the Shire now – now that your wish to see them has come true already?' he asked.

'Yes, sir. I don't know how to say it, but after last night I feel different. I seem to see ahead, in a kind of way. I know we are going to take a very long road, into darkness; but I know I can't turn back. It isn't to see Elves now, nor dragons, nor mountains, that I want – I don't rightly know what I want: but I have something to do before the end, and it lies ahead, not in the Shire. I must see it through, sir, if you understand me.'

'I don't altogether. But I understand that Gandalf chose me a good companion. I am content. We will go together.'

Frodo finished his breakfast in silence. Then standing up he looked over the land ahead, and called to Pippin.

'All ready to start?' he said as Pippin ran up. 'We must be getting off at once. We slept late; and there are a good many miles to go.'

'*You* slept late, you mean,' said Pippin. 'I was up long before; and we are only waiting for you to finish eating and thinking.'

'I have finished both now. And I am going to make for Bucklebury Ferry as quickly as possible. I am not going out of the way, back to the road we left last night: I am going to cut straight across country from here.'

'Then you are going to fly,' said Pippin. 'You won't cut straight on foot anywhere in this country.'

'We can cut straighter than the road anyway,' answered Frodo. 'The Ferry is east from Woodhall; but the hard road

curves away to the left – you can see a bend of it away north
over there. It goes round the north end of the Marish so as
to strike the causeway from the Bridge above Stock. But that
is miles out of the way. We could save a quarter of the
distance if we made a line for the Ferry from where we stand.'

'*Short cuts make long delays*,' argued Pippin. 'The country
is rough round here, and there are bogs and all kinds of
difficulties down in the Marish – I know the land in these
parts. And if you are worrying about Black Riders, I can't
see that it is any worse meeting them on a road than in a
wood or a field.'

'It is less easy to find people in the woods and fields,'
answered Frodo. 'And if you are supposed to be on the road,
there is some chance that you will be looked for on the road
and not off it.'

'All right!' said Pippin. 'I will follow you into every bog
and ditch. But it is hard! I had counted on passing the *Golden
Perch* at Stock before sundown. The best beer in the Eastfarthing, or used to be: it is a long time since I tasted it.'

'That settles it!' said Frodo. 'Short cuts make delays, but
inns make longer ones. At all costs we must keep you away
from the *Golden Perch*. We want to get to Bucklebury before
dark. What do you say, Sam?'

'I will go along with you, Mr. Frodo,' said Sam (in spite
of private misgiving and a deep regret for the best beer in
the Eastfarthing).

'Then if we are going to toil through bog and briar, let's
go now!' said Pippin.

It was already nearly as hot as it had been the day before;
but clouds were beginning to come up from the West. It
looked likely to turn to rain. The hobbits scrambled down a
steep green bank and plunged into the thick trees below.
Their course had been chosen to leave Woodhall to their left,
and to cut slanting through the woods that clustered along
the eastern side of the hills, until they reached the flats
beyond. Then they could make straight for the Ferry over

country that was open, except for a few ditches and fences.
Frodo reckoned they had eighteen miles to go in a straight
line.

He soon found that the thicket was closer and more tangled
than it had appeared. There were no paths in the undergrowth, and they did not get on very fast. When they had
struggled to the bottom of the bank, they found a stream
running down from the hills behind in a deeply dug bed with
steep slippery sides overhung with brambles. Most incon-
veniently it cut across the line they had chosen. They could
not jump over it, nor indeed get across it at all without getting
wet, scratched, and muddy. They halted, wondering what to
do. 'First check!' said Pippin, smiling grimly.

Sam Gamgee looked back. Through an opening in the
trees he caught a glimpse of the top of the green bank from
which they had climbed down.

'Look!' he said, clutching Frodo by the arm. They all
looked, and on the edge high above them they saw against
the sky a horse standing. Beside it stooped a black figure.

They at once gave up any idea of going back. Frodo led
the way, and plunged quickly into the thick bushes beside
the stream. 'Whew!' he said to Pippin. 'We were both right!
The short cut has gone crooked already; but we got under
cover only just in time. You've got sharp ears, Sam: can you
hear anything coming?'

They stood still, almost holding their breath as they
listened; but there was no sound of pursuit. 'I don't fancy
he would try bringing his horse down that bank,' said Sam.
'But I guess he knows we came down it. We had better be
going on.'

Going on was not altogether easy. They had packs to carry,
and the bushes and brambles were reluctant to let them
through. They were cut off from the wind by the ridge
behind, and the air was still and stuffy. When they forced
their way at last into more open ground, they were hot and
tired and very scratched, and they were also no longer certain
of the direction in which they were going. The banks of the

stream sank, as it reached the levels and became broader and shallower, wandering off towards the Marish and the River.

'Why, this is the Stock-brook!' said Pippin. 'If we are going to try and get back on to our course, we must cross at once and bear right.'

They waded the stream, and hurried over a wide open space, rush-grown and treeless, on the further side. Beyond that they came again to a belt of trees: tall oaks, for the most part, with here and there an elm tree or an ash. The ground was fairly level, and there was little undergrowth; but the trees were too close for them to see far ahead. The leaves blew upwards in sudden gusts of wind, and spots of rain began to fall from the overcast sky. Then the wind died away and the rain came streaming down. They trudged along as fast as they could, over patches of grass, and through thick drifts of old leaves; and all about them the rain pattered and trickled. They did not talk, but kept glancing back, and from side to side.

After half an hour Pippin said: 'I hope we have not turned too much towards the south, and are not walking longwise through this wood! It is not a very broad belt – I should have said no more than a mile at the widest – and we ought to have been through it by now.'

'It is no good our starting to go in zig-zags,' said Frodo. 'That won't mend matters. Let us keep on as we are going! I am not sure that I want to come out into the open yet.'

They went on for perhaps another couple of miles. Then the sun gleamed out of ragged clouds again and the rain lessened. It was now past mid-day, and they felt it was high time for lunch. They halted under an elm tree: its leaves though fast turning yellow were still thick, and the ground at its feet was fairly dry and sheltered. When they came to make their meal, they found that the Elves had filled their bottles with a clear drink, pale golden in colour: it had the scent of a honey made of many flowers, and was wonderfully refreshing. Very soon they were laughing, and snapping their

fingers at rain, and at Black Riders. The last few miles, they
felt, would soon be behind them.

Frodo propped his back against the tree-trunk, and closed
his eyes. Sam and Pippin sat near, and they began to hum,
and then to sing softly:

> Ho! Ho! Ho! to the bottle I go
> To heal my heart and drown my woe.
> Rain may fall and wind may blow,
> And many miles be still to go,
> But under a tall tree I will lie,
> And let the clouds go sailing by.

Ho! Ho! Ho! they began again louder. They stopped short
suddenly. Frodo sprang to his feet. A long-drawn wail came
down the wind, like the cry of some evil and lonely creature.
It rose and fell, and ended on a high piercing note. Even as
they sat and stood, as if suddenly frozen, it was answered by
another cry, fainter and further off, but no less chilling to
the blood. There was then a silence, broken only by the sound
of the wind in the leaves.

'And what do you think that was?' Pippin asked at last,
trying to speak lightly, but quavering a little. 'If it was a bird,
it was one that I never heard in the Shire before.'

'It was not bird or beast,' said Frodo. 'It was a call, or a
signal – there were words in that cry, though I could not
catch them. But no hobbit has such a voice.'

No more was said about it. They were all thinking of the
Riders, but no one spoke of them. They were now reluctant
either to stay or go on; but sooner or later they had got to
get across the open country to the Ferry, and it was best to
go sooner and in daylight. In a few moments they had shouldered their packs again and were off.

Before long the wood came to a sudden end. Wide grass-
lands stretched before them. They now saw that they had,
in fact, turned too much to the south. Away over the flats

they could glimpse the low hill of Bucklebury across the River, but it was now to their left. Creeping cautiously out from the edge of the trees, they set off across the open as quickly as they could.

At first they felt afraid, away from the shelter of the wood. Far back behind them stood the high place where they had breakfasted. Frodo half expected to see the small distant figure of a horseman on the ridge dark against the sky; but there was no sign of one. The sun escaping from the breaking clouds, as it sank towards the hills they had left, was now shining brightly again. Their fear left them, though they still felt uneasy. But the land became steadily more tame and well-ordered. Soon they came into well-tended fields and meadows: there were hedges and gates and dikes for drainage. Everything seemed quiet and peaceful, just an ordinary corner of the Shire. Their spirits rose with every step. The line of the River grew nearer; and the Black Riders began to seem like phantoms of the woods now left far behind.

They passed along the edge of a huge turnip-field, and came to a stout gate. Beyond it a rutted lane ran between low well-laid hedges towards a distant clump of trees. Pippin stopped.

'I know these fields and this gate!' he said. 'This is Bam-furlong, old Farmer Maggot's land. That's his farm away there in the trees.'

'One trouble after another!' said Frodo, looking nearly as much alarmed as if Pippin had declared the lane was the slot leading to a dragon's den. The others looked at him in surprise.

'What's wrong with old Maggot?' asked Pippin. 'He's a good friend to all the Brandybucks. Of course he's a terror to trespassers, and keeps ferocious dogs – but after all, folk down here are near the border and have to be more on their guard.'

'I know,' said Frodo. 'But all the same,' he added with a shamefaced laugh, 'I am terrified of him and his dogs. I have avoided his farm for years and years. He caught me several times trespassing after mushrooms, when I was a youngster at Brandy Hall. On the last occasion he beat me, and then took me and showed me to his dogs. "See, lads," he said, "next time this young varmint sets foot on my land, you can eat him. Now see him off!" They chased me all the way to the Ferry. I have never got over the fright – though I daresay the beasts knew their business and would not really have touched me.'

Pippin laughed. 'Well, it's time you made it up. Especially if you are coming back to live in Buckland. Old Maggot is really a stout fellow – if you leave his mushrooms alone. Let's get into the lane and then we shan't be trespassing. If we meet him, I'll do the talking. He is a friend of Merry's, and I used to come here with him a good deal at one time.'

They went along the lane, until they saw the thatched roofs of a large house and farm-buildings peeping out among the trees ahead. The Maggots, and the Puddifoots of Stock, and most of the inhabitants of the Marish, were house-dwellers; and this farm was stoutly built of brick and had a high wall all round it. There was a wide wooden gate opening out of the wall into the lane.

Suddenly as they drew nearer a terrific baying and barking broke out, and a loud voice was heard shouting: 'Grip! Fang! Wolf! Come on, lads!'

Frodo and Sam stopped dead, but Pippin walked on a few paces. The gate opened and three huge dogs came pelting out into the lane, and dashed towards the travellers, barking fiercely. They took no notice of Pippin; but Sam shrank against the wall, while two wolvish-looking dogs sniffed at him suspiciously, and snarled if he moved. The largest and most ferocious of the three halted in front of Frodo, bristling and growling.

Through the gate there now appeared a broad thick-set hobbit with a round red face. 'Hallo! Hallo! And who may you be, and what may you be wanting?' he asked.

'Good afternoon, Mr. Maggot!' said Pippin.

The farmer looked at him closely. 'Well, if it isn't Master Pippin – Mr. Peregrin Took, I should say!' he cried, changing from a scowl to a grin. 'It's a long time since I saw you round here. It's lucky for you that I know you. I was just going out to set my dogs on any strangers. There are some funny things going on today. Of course, we do get queer folk wandering in these parts at times. Too near the River,' he said, shaking his head. 'But this fellow was the most outlandish I have ever set eyes on. He won't cross my land without leave a second time, not if I can stop it.'

'What fellow do you mean?' asked Pippin.

'Then you haven't seen him?' said the farmer. 'He went up the lane towards the causeway not a long while back. He was a funny customer and asking funny questions. But perhaps you'll come along inside, and we'll pass the news more comfortable. I've a drop of good ale on tap, if you and your friends are willing, Mr. Took.'

It seemed plain that the farmer would tell them more, if allowed to do it in his own time and fashion, so they all accepted the invitation. 'What about the dogs?' asked Frodo anxiously.

The farmer laughed. 'They won't harm you – not unless I tell 'em to. Here, Grip! Fang! Heel!' he cried. 'Heel, Wolf!' To the relief of Frodo and Sam, the dogs walked away and let them go free.

Pippin introduced the other two to the farmer. 'Mr. Frodo Baggins,' he said. 'You may not remember him, but he used to live at Brandy Hall.' At the name Baggins the farmer started, and gave Frodo a sharp glance. For a moment Frodo thought that the memory of stolen mushrooms had been aroused, and that the dogs would be told to see him off. But Farmer Maggot took him by the arm.

'Well, if that isn't queerer than ever?' he exclaimed. 'Mr. Baggins is it? Come inside! We must have a talk.'

They went into the farmer's kitchen, and sat by the wide fire-place. Mrs. Maggot brought out beer in a huge jug, and filled four large mugs. It was a good brew, and Pippin found himself more than compensated for missing the *Golden Perch*. Sam sipped his beer suspiciously. He had a natural mistrust of the inhabitants of other parts of the Shire; and also he was not disposed to be quick friends with anyone who had beaten his master, however long ago.

After a few remarks about the weather and the agricultural prospects (which were no worse than usual), Farmer Maggot put down his mug and looked at them all in turn.

'Now, Mr. Peregrin,' he said, 'where might you be coming from, and where might you be going to? Were you coming to visit me? For, if so, you had gone past my gate without my seeing you.'

'Well, no,' answered Pippin. 'To tell you the truth, since you have guessed it, we got into the lane from the other end: we had come over your fields. But that was quite by accident. We lost our way in the woods, back near Woodhall, trying to take a short cut to the Ferry.'

'If you were in a hurry, the road would have served you better,' said the farmer. 'But I wasn't worrying about that. You have leave to walk over my land, if you have a mind, Mr. Peregrin. And you, Mr. Baggins – though I daresay you still like mushrooms.' He laughed. 'Ah yes, I recognized the name. I recollect the time when young Frodo Baggins was one of the worst young rascals of Buckland. But it wasn't mushrooms I was thinking of. I had just heard the name Baggins before you turned up. What do you think that funny customer asked me?'

They waited anxiously for him to go on. 'Well,' the farmer continued, approaching his point with slow relish, 'he came riding on a big black horse in at the gate, which happened to be open, and right up to my door. All black he was himself, too, and cloaked and hooded up, as if he did not want to be known. "Now what in the Shire can he want?" I thought to myself. We don't see many of the Big Folk over the border; and anyway I had never heard of any like this black fellow.

' "Good-day to you!" I says, going out to him. "This lane don't lead anywhere, and wherever you may be going, your

quickest way will be back to the road." I didn't like the looks
of him; and when Grip came out, he took one sniff and let
out a yelp as if he had been stung: he put down his tail and
bolted off howling. The black fellow sat quite still.

'"I come from yonder," he said, slow and stiff-like,
pointing back west, over *my* fields, if you please. "Have you
seen *Baggins*?" he asked in a queer voice, and bent down
towards me. I could not see any face, for his hood fell
down so low; and I felt a sort of shiver down my back. But
I did not see why he should come riding over my land so
bold.

'"Be off!" I said. "There are no Bagginses here. You're
in the wrong part of the Shire. You had better go back west
to Hobbiton – but you can go by road this time."

'"Baggins has left," he answered in a whisper. "He is
coming. He is not far away. I wish to find him. If he passes
will you tell me? I will come back with gold."

'"No you won't," I said. "You'll go back where you
belong, double quick. I give you one minute before I call all
my dogs."

'He gave a sort of hiss. It might have been laughing, and
it might not. Then he spurred his great horse right at me,
and I jumped out of the way only just in time. I called the
dogs, but he swung off, and rode through the gate and up
the lane towards the causeway like a bolt of thunder. What
do you think of that?'

Frodo sat for a moment looking at the fire, but his only
thought was how on earth would they reach the Ferry. 'I
don't know what to think,' he said at last.

'Then I'll tell you what to think,' said Maggot. 'You should
never have gone mixing yourself up with Hobbiton folk, Mr.
Frodo. Folk are queer up there.' Sam stirred in his chair, and
looked at the farmer with an unfriendly eye. 'But you were
always a reckless lad. When I heard you had left the Brandybucks and gone off to that old Mr. Bilbo, I said that you
were going to find trouble. Mark my words, this all comes
of those strange doings of Mr. Bilbo's. His money was got

in some strange fashion in foreign parts, they say. Maybe there is some that want to know what has become of the gold and jewels that he buried in the hill of Hobbiton, as I hear?'

Frodo said nothing: the shrewd guesses of the farmer were rather disconcerting.

'Well, Mr. Frodo,' Maggot went on, 'I'm glad that you've had the sense to come back to Buckland. My advice is: stay there! And don't get mixed up with these outlandish folk. You'll have friends in these parts. If any of these black fellows come after you again, I'll deal with them. I'll say you're dead, or have left the Shire, or anything you like. And that might be true enough; for as like as not it is old Mr. Bilbo they want news of.'

'Maybe you're right,' said Frodo, avoiding the farmer's eye and staring at the fire.

Maggot looked at him thoughtfully. 'Well, I see you have ideas of your own,' he said. 'It is as plain as my nose that no accident brought you and that rider here on the same afternoon; and maybe my news was no great news to you, after all. I am not asking you to tell me anything you have a mind to keep to yourself; but I see you are in some kind of trouble. Perhaps you are thinking it won't be too easy to get to the Ferry without being caught?'

'I was thinking so,' said Frodo. 'But we have got to try and get there; and it won't be done by sitting and thinking. So I am afraid we must be going. Thank you very much indeed for your kindness! I've been in terror of you and your dogs for over thirty years, Farmer Maggot, though you may laugh to hear it. It's a pity: for I've missed a good friend. And now I'm sorry to leave so soon. But I'll come back, perhaps, one day – if I get a chance.'

'You'll be welcome when you come,' said Maggot. 'But now I've a notion. It's near sundown already, and we are going to have our supper; for we mostly go to bed soon after the Sun. If you and Mr. Peregrin and all could stay and have a bite with us, we would be pleased!'

'And so should we!' said Frodo. 'But we must be going at once, I'm afraid. Even now it will be dark before we can reach the Ferry.'

'Ah! but wait a minute! I was going to say: after a bit of supper, I'll get out a small waggon, and I'll drive you all to the Ferry. That will save you a good step, and it might also save you trouble of another sort.'

Frodo now accepted the invitation gratefully, to the relief of Pippin and Sam. The sun was already behind the western hills, and the light was failing. Two of Maggot's sons and his three daughters came in, and a generous supper was laid on the large table. The kitchen was lit with candles and the fire was mended. Mrs. Maggot bustled in and out. One or two other hobbits belonging to the farm-household came in. In a short while fourteen sat down to eat. There was beer in plenty, and a mighty dish of mushrooms and bacon, besides much other solid farmhouse fare. The dogs lay by the fire and gnawed rinds and cracked bones.

When they had finished, the farmer and his sons went out with a lantern and got the waggon ready. It was dark in the yard, when the guests came out. They threw their packs on board and climbed in. The farmer sat in the driving-seat, and whipped up his two stout ponies. His wife stood in the light of the open door.

'You be careful of yourself, Maggot!' she called. 'Don't go arguing with any foreigners, and come straight back!'

'I will!' said he, and drove out of the gate. There was now no breath of wind stirring; the night was still and quiet, and a chill was in the air. They went without lights and took it slowly. After a mile or two the lane came to an end, crossing a deep dike, and climbing a short slope up on to the high-banked causeway.

Maggot got down and took a good look either way, north and south, but nothing could be seen in the darkness, and there was not a sound in the still air. Thin strands of river-mist were hanging above the dikes, and crawling over the fields.

'It's going to be thick,' said Maggot; 'but I'll not light my lantern till I turn for home. We'll hear anything on the road long before we meet it tonight.'

It was five miles or more from Maggot's lane to the Ferry. The hobbits wrapped themselves up, but their ears were strained for any sound above the creak of the wheels and the slow *clop* of the ponies' hoofs. The waggon seemed slower than a snail to Frodo. Beside him Pippin was nodding towards sleep; but Sam was staring forwards into the rising fog.

They reached the entrance to the Ferry lane at last. It was marked by two tall white posts that suddenly loomed up on their right. Farmer Maggot drew in his ponies and the waggon creaked to a halt. They were just beginning to scramble out, when suddenly they heard what they had all been dreading: hoofs on the road ahead. The sound was coming towards them.

Maggot jumped down and stood holding the ponies' heads, and peering forward into the gloom. *Clip-clop*, *clip-clop* came the approaching rider. The fall of the hoofs sounded loud in the still, foggy air.

'You'd better be hidden, Mr. Frodo,' said Sam anxiously. 'You get down in the waggon and cover up with blankets, and we'll send this rider to the rightabouts!' He climbed out and went to the farmer's side. Black Riders would have to ride over him to get near the waggon.

Clop-clop, clop-clop. The rider was nearly on them.

'Hallo there!' called Farmer Maggot. The advancing hoofs stopped short. They thought they could dimly guess a dark cloaked shape in the mist, a yard or two ahead.

'Now then!' said the farmer, throwing the reins to Sam and striding forward. 'Don't you come a step nearer! What do you want, and where are you going?'

'I want Mr. Baggins. Have you seen him?' said a muffled voice – but the voice was the voice of Merry Brandybuck. A dark lantern was uncovered, and its light fell on the astonished face of the farmer.

'Mr. Merry!' he cried.

'Yes, of course! Who did you think it was?' said Merry coming forward. As he came out of the mist and their fears subsided, he seemed suddenly to diminish to ordinary hobbit-size. He was riding a pony, and a scarf was swathed round his neck and over his chin to keep out the fog.

Frodo sprang out of the waggon to greet him. 'So there you are at last!' said Merry. 'I was beginning to wonder if you would turn up at all today, and I was just going back to supper. When it grew foggy I came across and rode up towards Stock to see if you had fallen in any ditches. But I'm blest if I know which way you have come. Where did you find them, Mr. Maggot? In your duck-pond?'

'No, I caught 'em trespassing,' said the farmer, 'and nearly set my dogs on 'em; but they'll tell you all the story, I've no doubt. Now, if you'll excuse me, Mr. Merry and Mr. Frodo and all, I'd best be turning for home. Mrs. Maggot will be worriting with the night getting thick.'

He backed the waggon into the lane and turned it. 'Well, good night to you all,' he said. 'It's been a queer day, and no mistake. But all's well as ends well; though perhaps we should not say that until we reach our own doors. I'll not deny that I'll be glad now when I do.' He lit his lanterns, and got up. Suddenly he produced a large basket from under the seat. 'I was nearly forgetting,' he said. 'Mrs. Maggot put this up for Mr. Baggins, with her compliments.' He handed it down and moved off, followed by a chorus of thanks and good-nights.

They watched the pale rings of light round his lanterns as they dwindled into the foggy night. Suddenly Frodo laughed: from the covered basket he held, the scent of mushrooms was rising.

CHAPTER V

A CONSPIRACY UNMASKED

'Now we had better get home ourselves,' said Merry. 'There's something funny about all this, I see; but it must wait till we get in.'

They turned down the Ferry lane, which was straight and well-kept and edged with large white-washed stones. In a hundred yards or so it brought them to the river-bank, where there was a broad wooden landing-stage. A large flat ferry-boat was moored beside it. The white bollards near the water's edge glimmered in the light of two lamps on high posts. Behind them the mists in the flat fields were now above the hedges; but the water before them was dark, with only a few curling wisps like steam among the reeds by the bank. There seemed to be less fog on the further side.

Merry led the pony over a gangway on to the ferry, and the others followed. Merry then pushed slowly off with a long pole. The Brandywine flowed slow and broad before them. On the other side the bank was steep, and up it a winding path climbed from the further landing. Lamps were twinkling there. Behind loomed up the Buck Hill; and out of it, through stray shrouds of mist, shone many round windows, yellow and red. They were the windows of Brandy Hall, the ancient home of the Brandybucks.

Long ago Gorhendad Oldbuck, head of the Oldbuck family, one of the oldest in the Marish or indeed in the Shire, had crossed the river, which was the original boundary of the land eastwards. He built (and excavated) Brandy Hall, changed his name to Brandybuck, and settled down to become master of what was virtually a small independent country. His family grew and grew, and after his days continued to grow, until Brandy Hall occupied the whole of the low hill, and had three large front-doors, many side-doors, and about a hundred windows. The Brandybucks and their numerous dependants then began to burrow, and later to build, all round about. That was the origin of Buckland, a thickly inhabited strip between the river and the Old Forest, a sort of colony from the Shire. Its chief village was Bucklebury, clustering in the banks and slopes behind Brandy Hall.

The people in the Marish were friendly with the Bucklanders, and the authority of the Master of the Hall (as the head of the Brandybuck family was called) was still acknowledged by the farmers between Stock and Rushey. But most of the folk of the old Shire regarded the Bucklanders as peculiar, half foreigners as it were. Though, as a matter of fact, they were not very different from the other hobbits of the Four Farthings. Except in one point: they were fond of boats, and some of them could swim.

Their land was originally unprotected from the East; but on that side they had built a hedge: the High Hay. It had been planted many generations ago, and was now thick and tall, for it was constantly tended. It ran all the way from Brandywine Bridge, in a big loop curving away from the river, to Haysend (where the Withywindle flowed out of the Forest into the Brandywine): well over twenty miles from end to end. But, of course, it was not a complete protection. The Forest drew close to the hedge in many places. The Bucklanders kept their doors locked after dark, and that also was not usual in the Shire.

The ferry-boat moved slowly across the water. The Buckland shore drew nearer. Sam was the only member of the party who had not been over the river before. He had a strange feeling as the slow gurgling stream slipped by: his old life lay behind in the mists, dark adventure lay in front. He scratched his head, and for a moment had a passing wish that Mr. Frodo could have gone on living quietly at Bag End.

The four hobbits stepped off the ferry. Merry was tying it up, and Pippin was already leading the pony up the path, when Sam (who had been looking back, as if to take farewell of the Shire) said in a hoarse whisper:

'Look back, Mr. Frodo! Do you see anything?'

On the far stage, under the distant lamps, they could just make out a figure: it looked like a dark black bundle left behind. But as they looked it seemed to move and sway this way and that, as if searching the ground. It then crawled, or went crouching, back into the gloom beyond the lamps.

'What in the Shire is that?' exclaimed Merry.

'Something that is following us,' said Frodo. 'But don't ask any more now! Let's get away at once!' They hurried up the path to the top of the bank, but when they looked back the far shore was shrouded in mist, and nothing could be seen.

'Thank goodness you don't keep any boats on the west-bank!' said Frodo. 'Can horses cross the river?'

'They can go twenty miles north to Brandywine Bridge – or they might swim,' answered Merry. 'Though I never heard of any horse swimming the Brandywine. But what have horses to do with it?'

'I'll tell you later. Let's get indoors and then we can talk.'

'All right! You and Pippin know your way; so I'll just ride on and tell Fatty Bolger that you are coming. We'll see about supper and things.'

'We had our supper early with Farmer Maggot,' said Frodo; 'but we could do with another.'

'You shall have it! Give me that basket!' said Merry, and rode ahead into the darkness.

It was some distance from the Brandywine to Frodo's new house at Crickhollow. They passed Buck Hill and Brandy Hall on their left, and on the outskirts of Bucklebury struck the main road of Buckland that ran south from the Bridge. Half a mile northward along this they came to a lane opening on their right. This they followed for a couple of miles as it climbed up and down into the country.

At last they came to a narrow gate in a thick hedge. Nothing could be seen of the house in the dark: it stood back from the lane in the middle of a wide circle of lawn surrounded by a belt of low trees inside the outer hedge. Frodo had chosen it, because it stood in an out-of-the-way corner of the country, and there were no other dwellings close by. You could get in and out without being noticed. It had been built a long while before by the Brandybucks, for the use of guests, or members of the family that wished to escape from the crowded life of Brandy Hall for a time. It was an old-fashioned countrified house, as much like a hobbit-hole as possible: it was long and low, with no upper storey; and it had a roof of turf, round windows, and a large round door.

As they walked up the green path from the gate no light was visible; the windows were dark and shuttered. Frodo knocked on the door, and Fatty Bolger opened it. A friendly light streamed out. They slipped in quickly and shut themselves and the light inside. They were in a wide hall with doors on either side; in front of them a passage ran back down the middle of the house.

'Well, what do you think of it?' asked Merry coming up the passage. 'We have done our best in a short time to make it look like home. After all Fatty and I only got here with the last cart-load yesterday.'

Frodo looked round. It did look like home. Many of his own favourite things – or Bilbo's things (they reminded him sharply of him in their new setting) – were arranged as nearly as possible as they had been at Bag End. It was a pleasant, comfortable, welcoming place; and he found himself wishing that he was really coming here to settle down in quiet retirement. It seemed unfair to have put his friends to all this trouble; and he wondered again how he was going to break the news to them that he must leave them so soon, indeed at once. Yet that would have to be done that very night, before they all went to bed.

'It's delightful!' he said with an effort. 'I hardly feel that I have moved at all.'

The travellers hung up their cloaks, and piled their packs on the floor. Merry led them down the passage and threw open a door at the far end. Firelight came out, and a puff of steam.

'A bath!' cried Pippin. 'O blessed Meriadoc!'

'Which order shall we go in?' said Frodo. 'Eldest first, or quickest first? You'll be last either way, Master Peregrin.'

'Trust me to arrange things better than that!' said Merry. 'We can't begin life at Crickhollow with a quarrel over baths. In that room there are *three* tubs, and a copper full of boiling water. There are also towels, mats and soap. Get inside, and be quick!'

Merry and Fatty went into the kitchen on the other side of the passage, and busied themselves with the final preparations for a late supper. Snatches of competing songs came from the bathroom mixed with the sound of splashing and wallowing. The voice of Pippin was suddenly lifted up above the others in one of Bilbo's favourite bath-songs.

> *Sing hey! for the bath at close of day*
> *that washes the weary mud away!*
> *A loon is he that will not sing:*
> *O! Water Hot is a noble thing!*
>
> *O! Sweet is the sound of falling rain,*
> *and the brook that leaps from hill to plain;*
> *but better than rain or rippling streams*
> *is Water Hot that smokes and steams.*
>
> *O! Water cold we may pour at need*
> *down a thirsty throat and be glad indeed;*
> *but better is Beer, if drink we lack,*
> *and Water Hot poured down the back.*

O! Water is fair that leaps on high
in a fountain white beneath the sky;
but never did fountain sound so sweet
as splashing Hot Water with my feet!

There was a terrific splash, and a shout of *Whoa!* from
Frodo. It appeared that a lot of Pippin's bath had imitated
a fountain and leaped on high.

Merry went to the door: 'What about supper and beer in
the throat?' he called. Frodo came out drying his hair.

'There's so much water in the air that I'm coming into the
kitchen to finish,' he said.

'Lawks!' said Merry, looking in. The stone floor was swimming. 'You ought to mop all that up before you get anything
to eat, Peregrin,' he said. 'Hurry up, or we shan't wait for
you.'

They had supper in the kitchen on a table near the fire. 'I
suppose you three won't want mushrooms again?' said Fredegar without much hope.

'Yes we shall!' cried Pippin.

'They're mine!' said Frodo. 'Given to *me* by Mrs. Maggot,
a queen among farmers' wives. Take your greedy hands
away, and I'll serve them.'

Hobbits have a passion for mushrooms, surpassing even
the greediest likings of Big People. A fact which partly
explains young Frodo's long expeditions to the renowned
fields of the Marish, and the wrath of the injured Maggot.
On this occasion there was plenty for all, even according to
hobbit standards. There were also many other things to follow, and when they had finished even Fatty Bolger heaved
a sigh of content. They pushed back the table, and drew
chairs round the fire.

'We'll clear up later,' said Merry. 'Now tell me all about
it! I guess that you have been having adventures, which was
not quite fair without me. I want a full account; and most of
all I want to know what was the matter with old Maggot, and

why he spoke to me like that. He sounded almost as if he was *scared*, if that is possible.'

'We have all been scared,' said Pippin after a pause, in which Frodo stared at the fire and did not speak. 'You would have been, too, if you had been chased for two days by Black Riders.'

'And what are they?'

'Black figures riding on black horses,' answered Pippin. 'If Frodo won't talk, I will tell you the whole tale from the beginning.' He then gave a full account of their journey from the time when they left Hobbiton. Sam gave various supporting nods and exclamations. Frodo remained silent.

'I should think you were making it all up,' said Merry, 'if I had not seen that black shape on the landing-stage – and heard the queer sound in Maggot's voice. What do you make of it all, Frodo?'

'Cousin Frodo has been very close,' said Pippin. 'But the time has come for him to open out. So far we have been given nothing more to go on than Farmer Maggot's guess that it has something to do with old Bilbo's treasure.'

'That was only a guess,' said Frodo hastily. 'Maggot does not *know* anything.'

'Old Maggot is a shrewd fellow,' said Merry. 'A lot goes on behind his round face that does not come out in his talk. I've heard that he used to go into the Old Forest at one time, and he has the reputation of knowing a good many strange things. But you can at least tell us, Frodo, whether you think his guess good or bad.'

'I *think*,' answered Frodo slowly, 'that it was a good guess, as far as it goes. There *is* a connexion with Bilbo's old adventures, and the Riders are looking, or perhaps one ought to say *searching*, for him or for me. I also fear, if you want to know, that it is no joke at all; and that I am not safe here or anywhere else.' He looked round at the windows and walls, as if he was afraid they would suddenly give way. The others looked at him in silence, and exchanged meaning glances among themselves.

'It's coming out in a minute,' whispered Pippin to Merry. Merry nodded.

'Well!' said Frodo at last, sitting up and straightening his back, as if he had made a decision. 'I can't keep it dark any longer. I have got something to tell you all. But I don't know quite how to begin.'

'I think I could help you,' said Merry quietly, 'by telling you some of it myself.'

'What do you mean?' said Frodo, looking at him anxiously.

'Just this, my dear old Frodo: you are miserable, because you don't know how to say good-bye. You meant to leave the Shire, of course. But danger has come on you sooner than you expected, and now you are making up your mind to go at once. And you don't want to. We are very sorry for you.'

Frodo opened his mouth and shut it again. His look of surprise was so comical that they laughed. 'Dear old Frodo!' said Pippin. 'Did you really think you had thrown dust in all our eyes? You have not been nearly careful or clever enough for that! You have obviously been planning to go and saying farewell to all your haunts all this year since April. We have constantly heard you muttering: "Shall I ever look down into that valley again, I wonder", and things like that. And pretending that you had come to the end of your money, and actually selling your beloved Bag End to those Sackville-Bagginses! And all those close talks with Gandalf.'

'Good heavens!' said Frodo. 'I thought I had been both careful and clever. I don't know what Gandalf would say. Is all the Shire discussing my departure then?'

'Oh no!' said Merry. 'Don't worry about that! The secret won't keep for long, of course; but at present it is, I think, only known to us conspirators. After all, you must remember that we know you well, and are often with you. We can usually guess what you are thinking. I knew Bilbo, too. To tell you the truth, I had been watching you rather closely ever since he left. I thought you would go after him sooner or later; indeed I expected you to go sooner, and lately we have been very anxious. We have been terrified that you might give us the slip, and go off suddenly, all on your own like he did. Ever since this spring we have kept our eyes open, and done a good deal of planning on our own account. You are not going to escape so easily!'

'But I must go,' said Frodo. 'It cannot be helped, dear friends. It is wretched for us all, but it is no use your trying to keep me. Since you have guessed so much, please help me and do not hinder me!'

'You do not understand!' said Pippin. 'You must go – and therefore we must, too. Merry and I are coming with you. Sam is an excellent fellow, and would jump down a dragon's throat to save you, if he did not trip over his own feet; but you will need more than one companion in your dangerous adventure.'

'My dear and most beloved hobbits!' said Frodo deeply moved. 'But I could not allow it. I decided that long ago, too. You speak of danger, but you do not understand. This is no treasure-hunt, no there-and-back journey. I am flying from deadly peril into deadly peril.'

'Of course we understand,' said Merry firmly. 'That is why we have decided to come. We know the Ring is no laughing-matter; but we are going to do our best to help you against the Enemy.'

'The Ring!' said Frodo, now completely amazed.

'Yes, the Ring,' said Merry. 'My dear old hobbit, you don't allow for the inquisitiveness of friends. I have known about the existence of the Ring for years – before Bilbo went away, in fact; but since he obviously regarded it as secret, I kept the knowledge in my head, until we formed our conspiracy. I did not know Bilbo, of course, as well as I know you; I was too young, and he was also more careful – but he was not careful enough. If you want to know how I first found out, I will tell you.'

'Go on!' said Frodo faintly.

'It was the Sackville-Bagginses that were his downfall, as you might expect. One day, a year before the Party, I happened to be walking along the road, when I saw Bilbo ahead. Suddenly in the distance the S.-B.s appeared, coming towards us. Bilbo slowed down, and then hey presto! he vanished. I was so startled that I hardly had the wits to hide myself in a more ordinary fashion; but I got through the hedge and walked along the field inside. I was peeping through into the road, after the S.-B.s had passed, and was looking straight at Bilbo when he suddenly reappeared. I caught a glint of gold as he put something back in his trouser-pocket.

'After that I kept my eyes open. In fact, I confess that I spied. But you must admit that it was very intriguing, and I was only in my teens. I must be the only one in the Shire, besides you Frodo, that has ever seen the old fellow's secret book.'

'You have read his book!' cried Frodo. 'Good heavens above! Is nothing safe?'

'Not too safe, I should say,' said Merry. 'But I have only had one rapid glance, and that was difficult to get. He never left the book about. I wonder what became of it. I should like another look. Have you got it, Frodo?'

'No. It was not at Bag End. He must have taken it away.'

'Well, as I was saying,' Merry proceeded, 'I kept my knowledge to myself, till this Spring when things got serious. Then we formed our conspiracy; and as we were serious, too, and meant business, we have not been too scrupulous. You are not a very easy nut to crack, and Gandalf is worse. But if you want to be introduced to our chief investigator, I can produce him.'

'Where is he?' said Frodo, looking round, as if he expected a masked and sinister figure to come out of a cupboard.

'Step forward, Sam!' said Merry; and Sam stood up with a face scarlet up to the ears. 'Here's our collector of information! And he collected a lot, I can tell you, before he was finally caught. After which, I may say, he seemed to regard himself as on parole, and dried up.'

'Sam!' cried Frodo, feeling that amazement could go no

further, and quite unable to decide whether he felt angry, amused, relieved, or merely foolish.

'Yes, sir!' said Sam. 'Begging your pardon, sir! But I meant no wrong to you, Mr. Frodo, nor to Mr. Gandalf for that matter. *He* has some sense, mind you; and when you said *go alone*, he said *no! take someone as you can trust.*'

'But it does not seem that I can trust anyone,' said Frodo.

Sam looked at him unhappily. 'It all depends on what you want,' put in Merry. 'You can trust us to stick to you through thick and thin – to the bitter end. And you can trust us to keep any secret of yours – closer than you keep it yourself. But you cannot trust us to let you face trouble alone, and go off without a word. We are your friends, Frodo. Anyway: there it is. We know most of what Gandalf has told you. We know a good deal about the Ring. We are horribly afraid – but we are coming with you; or following you like hounds.'

'And after all, sir,' added Sam, 'you did ought to take the Elves' advice. Gildor said you should take them as was willing, and you can't deny it.'

'I don't deny it,' said Frodo, looking at Sam, who was now grinning. 'I don't deny it, but I'll never believe you are sleeping again, whether you snore or not. I shall kick you hard to make sure.

'You are a set of deceitful scoundrels!' he said, turning to the others. 'But bless you!' he laughed, getting up and waving his arms, 'I give in. I will take Gildor's advice. If the danger were not so dark, I should dance for joy. Even so, I cannot help feeling happy; happier than I have felt for a long time. I had dreaded this evening.'

'Good! That's settled. Three cheers for Captain Frodo and company!' they shouted; and they danced round him. Merry and Pippin began a song, which they had apparently got ready for the occasion.

It was made on the model of the dwarf-song that started Bilbo on his adventure long ago, and went to the same tune:

Farewell we call to hearth and hall!
Though wind may blow and rain may fall,
We must away ere break of day
Far over wood and mountain tall.

To Rivendell, where Elves yet dwell
In glades beneath the misty fell,
Through moor and waste we ride in haste,
And whither then we cannot tell.

With foes ahead, behind us dread,
Beneath the sky shall be our bed,
Until at last our toil be passed,
Our journey done, our errand sped.

We must away! We must away!
We ride before the break of day!

'Very good!' said Frodo. 'But in that case there are a lot
of things to do before we go to bed – under a roof, for tonight
at any rate.'

'Oh! That was poetry!' said Pippin. 'Do you really mean
to start before the break of day?'

'I don't know,' answered Frodo. 'I fear those Black Riders,
and I am sure it is unsafe to stay in one place long, especially
in a place to which it is known I was going. Also Gildor
advised me not to wait. But I should very much like to see
Gandalf. I could see that even Gildor was disturbed when
he heard that Gandalf had never appeared. It really depends
on two things. How soon could the Riders get to Bucklebury?
And how soon could we get off? It will take a good deal of
preparation.'

'The answer to the second question,' said Merry, 'is that
we could get off in an hour. I have prepared practically everything. There are six ponies in a stable across the fields; stores
and tackle are all packed, except for a few extra clothes, and
the perishable food.'

'It seems to have been a very efficient conspiracy,' said Frodo. 'But what about the Black Riders? Would it be safe to wait one day for Gandalf?'

'That all depends on what you think the Riders would do, if they found you here,' answered Merry. 'They *could* have reached here by now, of course, if they were not stopped at the North-gate, where the Hedge runs down to the river-bank, just this side of the Bridge. The gate-guards would not let them through by night, though they might break through. Even in the daylight they would try to keep them out, I think, at any rate until they got a message through to the Master of the Hall – for they would not like the look of the Riders, and would certainly be frightened by them. But, of course, Buckland cannot resist a determined attack for long. And it is possible that in the morning even a Black Rider that rode up and asked for Mr. Baggins would be let through. It is pretty generally known that you are coming back to live at Crickhollow.'

Frodo sat for a while in thought. 'I have made up my mind,' he said finally. 'I am starting tomorrow, as soon as it is light. But I am not going by road: it would be safer to wait here than that. If I go through the North-gate my departure from Buckland will be known at once, instead of being secret for several days at least, as it might be. And what is more, the Bridge and the East Road near the borders will certainly be watched, whether any Rider gets into Buckland or not. We don't know how many there are; but there are at least two, and possibly more. The only thing to do is to go off in a quite unexpected direction.'

'But that can only mean going into the Old Forest!' said Fredegar horrified. 'You can't be thinking of doing that. It is quite as dangerous as Black Riders.'

'Not quite,' said Merry. 'It sounds very desperate, but I believe Frodo is right. It is the only way of getting off without being followed at once. With luck we might get a considerable start.'

'But you won't have any luck in the Old Forest,' objected Fredegar. 'No one ever has luck in there. You'll get lost. People don't go in there.'

'Oh yes they do!' said Merry. 'The Brandybucks go in – occasionally when the fit takes them. We have a private entrance. Frodo went in once, long ago. I have been in several times: usually in daylight, of course, when the trees are sleepy and fairly quiet.'

'Well, do as you think best!' said Fredegar. 'I am more afraid of the Old Forest than of anything I know about: the stories about it are a nightmare; but my vote hardly counts, as I am not going on the journey. Still, I am very glad someone is stopping behind, who can tell Gandalf what you have done, when he turns up, as I am sure he will before long.'

Fond as he was of Frodo, Fatty Bolger had no desire to leave the Shire, nor to see what lay outside it. His family came from the Eastfarthing, from Budgeford in Bridgefields in fact, but he had never been over the Brandywine Bridge. His task, according to the original plans of the conspirators, was to stay behind and deal with inquisitive folk, and to keep up as long as possible the pretence that Mr. Baggins was still living at Crickhollow. He had even brought along some old clothes of Frodo's to help him in playing the part. They little thought how dangerous that part might prove.

'Excellent!' said Frodo, when he understood the plan. 'We could not have left any message behind for Gandalf otherwise. I don't know whether these Riders can read or not, of course, but I should not have dared to risk a written message, in case they got in and searched the house. But if Fatty is willing to hold the fort, and I can be sure of Gandalf knowing the way we have gone, that decides me. I am going into the Old Forest first thing tomorrow.'

'Well, that's that,' said Pippin. 'On the whole I would rather have our job than Fatty's – waiting here till Black Riders come.'

'You wait till you are well inside the Forest,' said Fredegar.

'You'll wish you were back here with me before this time tomorrow.'

'It's no good arguing about it any more,' said Merry. 'We have still got to tidy up and put the finishing touches to the packing, before we get to bed. I shall call you all before the break of day.'

When at last he had got to bed, Frodo could not sleep for some time. His legs ached. He was glad that he was riding in the morning. Eventually he fell into a vague dream, in which he seemed to be looking out of a high window over a dark sea of tangled trees. Down below among the roots there was the sound of creatures crawling and snuffling. He felt sure they would smell him out sooner or later.

Then he heard a noise in the distance. At first he thought it was a great wind coming over the leaves of the forest. Then he knew that it was not leaves, but the sound of the Sea far-off; a sound he had never heard in waking life, though it had often troubled his dreams. Suddenly he found he was out in the open. There were no trees after all. He was on a dark heath, and there was a strange salt smell in the air. Looking up he saw before him a tall white tower, standing alone on a high ridge. A great desire came over him to climb the tower and see the Sea. He started to struggle up the ridge towards the tower: but suddenly a light came in the sky, and there was a noise of thunder.

CHAPTER VI

THE OLD FOREST

Frodo woke suddenly. It was still dark in the room. Merry was standing there with a candle in one hand, and banging on the door with the other. 'All right! What is it?' said Frodo, still shaken and bewildered.

'What is it!' cried Merry. 'It is time to get up. It is half past four and very foggy. Come on! Sam is already getting breakfast ready. Even Pippin is up. I am just going to saddle the ponies, and fetch the one that is to be the baggage-carrier. Wake that sluggard Fatty! At least he must get up and see us off.'

Soon after six o'clock the five hobbits were ready to start. Fatty Bolger was still yawning. They stole quietly out of the house. Merry went in front leading a laden pony, and took his way along a path that went through a spinney behind the house, and then cut across several fields. The leaves of trees were glistening, and every twig was dripping; the grass was grey with cold dew. Everything was still, and far-away noises seemed near and clear: fowls chattering in a yard, someone closing a door of a distant house.

In their shed they found the ponies; sturdy little beasts of the kind loved by hobbits, not speedy, but good for a long day's work. They mounted, and soon they were riding off into the mist, which seemed to open reluctantly before them and close forbiddingly behind them. After riding for about an hour, slowly and without talking, they saw the Hedge looming suddenly ahead. It was tall and netted over with silver cobwebs.

'How are you going to get through this?' asked Fredegar.

'Follow me!' said Merry, 'and you will see.' He turned to the left along the Hedge, and soon they came to a point where it bent inwards, running along the lip of a hollow. A cutting had been made, at some distance from the Hedge, and went sloping gently down into the ground. It had walls of brick at the sides, which rose steadily, until suddenly they arched over and formed a tunnel that dived deep under the Hedge and came out in the hollow on the other side.

Here Fatty Bolger halted. 'Good-bye, Frodo!' he said. 'I wish you were not going into the Forest. I only hope you will not need rescuing before the day is out. But good luck to you – today and every day!'

'If there are no worse things ahead than the Old Forest, I shall be lucky,' said Frodo. 'Tell Gandalf to hurry along the East Road: we shall soon be back on it and going as fast as we can.' 'Good-bye!' they cried, and rode down the slope and disappeared from Fredegar's sight into the tunnel.

It was dark and damp. At the far end it was closed by a gate of thick-set iron bars. Merry got down and unlocked the gate, and when they had all passed through he pushed it to again. It shut with a clang, and the lock clicked. The sound was ominous.

'There!' said Merry. 'You have left the Shire, and are now outside, and on the edge of the Old Forest.'

'Are the stories about it true?' asked Pippin.

'I don't know what stories you mean,' Merry answered. 'If you mean the old bogey-stories Fatty's nurses used to tell him, about goblins and wolves and things of that sort, I should say no. At any rate I don't believe them. But the Forest *is* queer. Everything in it is very much more alive, more aware of what is going on, so to speak, than things are in the Shire. And the trees do not like strangers. They watch you. They are usually content merely to watch you, as long as daylight lasts, and don't do much. Occasionally the most unfriendly ones may drop a branch, or stick a root out, or grasp at you with a long trailer. But at night things can be most alarming, or so I am told. I have only once or twice been in here after dark, and then only near the hedge. I thought all the trees were whispering to each other, passing news and plots along in an unintelligible language; and the branches swayed and groped without any wind. They do say the trees do actually move, and can surround strangers and hem them in. In fact long ago they attacked the Hedge: they came and planted themselves right by it, and leaned over it. But the hobbits came and cut down hundreds of trees, and made a great bonfire in the Forest, and burned all the ground in a long strip east of the Hedge. After that the trees gave up the attack, but they became very unfriendly. There is still a wide bare space not far inside where the bonfire was made.'

'Is it only the trees that are dangerous?' asked Pippin.

'There are various queer things living deep in the Forest, and on the far side,' said Merry, 'or at least I have heard so; but I have never seen any of them. But something makes paths. Whenever one comes inside one finds open tracks; but they seem to shift and change from time to time in a queer fashion. Not far from this tunnel there is, or was for a long time, the beginning of quite a broad path leading to the Bonfire Glade, and then on more or less in our direction, east and a little north. That is the path I am going to try and find.'

The hobbits now left the tunnel-gate and rode across the wide hollow. On the far side was a faint path leading up on to the floor of the Forest, a hundred yards and more beyond the Hedge; but it vanished as soon as it brought them under the trees. Looking back they could see the dark line of the Hedge through the stems of trees that were already thick about them. Looking ahead they could see only tree-trunks of innumerable sizes and shapes: straight or bent, twisted, leaning, squat or slender, smooth or gnarled and branched; and all the stems were green or grey with moss and slimy, shaggy growths.

Merry alone seemed fairly cheerful. 'You had better lead on and find that path,' Frodo said to him. 'Don't let us lose one another, or forget which way the Hedge lies!'

They picked a way among the trees, and their ponies plodded along, carefully avoiding the many writhing and interlacing roots. There was no undergrowth. The ground was rising steadily, and as they went forward it seemed that the trees became taller, darker, and thicker. There was no sound, except an occasional drip of moisture falling through the still leaves. For the moment there was no whispering or movement among the branches; but they all got an uncomfortable feeling that they were being watched with disapproval, deepening to dislike and even enmity. The feeling steadily grew, until they found themselves looking up quickly, or glancing back over their shoulders, as if they expected a sudden blow.

There was not as yet any sign of a path, and the trees seemed constantly to bar their way. Pippin suddenly felt that he could not bear it any longer, and without warning let out a shout. 'Oi! Oi!' he cried. 'I am not going to do anything. Just let me pass through, will you!'

The others halted startled; but the cry fell as if muffled by a heavy curtain. There was no echo or answer though the wood seemed to become more crowded and more watchful than before.

'I should not shout, if I were you,' said Merry. 'It does more harm than good.'

Frodo began to wonder if it were possible to find a way through, and if he had been right to make the others come into this abominable wood. Merry was looking from side to side, and seemed already uncertain which way to go. Pippin noticed it. 'It has not taken you long to lose us,' he said. But at that moment Merry gave a whistle of relief and pointed ahead.

'Well, well!' he said. 'These trees *do* shift. There is the Bonfire Glade in front of us (or I hope so), but the path to it seems to have moved away!'

The light grew clearer as they went forward. Suddenly they came out of the trees and found themselves in a wide circular space. There was sky above them, blue and clear to their surprise, for down under the Forest-roof they had not been able to see the rising morning and the lifting of the mist. The sun was not, however, high enough yet to shine down into the clearing, though its light was on the tree-tops. The leaves were all thicker and greener about the edges of the glade, enclosing it with an almost solid wall. No tree grew there, only rough grass and many tall plants: stalky and faded hemlocks and wood-parsley, fire-weed seeding into fluffy ashes, and rampant nettles and thistles. A dreary place: but it seemed a charming and cheerful garden after the close Forest.

The hobbits felt encouraged, and looked up hopefully at the broadening daylight in the sky. At the far side of the glade there was a break in the wall of trees, and a clear path beyond it. They could see it running on into the wood, wide in places and open above, though every now and again the trees drew in and overshadowed it with their dark boughs. Up this path they rode. They were still climbing gently, but they now went much quicker, and with better heart; for it seemed to them that the Forest had relented, and was going to let them pass unhindered after all.

But after a while the air began to get hot and stuffy. The trees drew close again on either side, and they could no longer see far ahead. Now stronger than ever they felt again the ill will of the wood pressing on them. So silent was it that the fall of their ponies' hoofs, rustling on dead leaves and occasionally stumbling on hidden roots, seemed to thud in their ears. Frodo tried to sing a song to encourage them, but his voice sank to a murmur.

> O! Wanderers in the shadowed land
> despair not! For though dark they stand,
> all woods there be must end at last,
> and see the open sun go past:
> the setting sun, the rising sun,
> the day's end, or the day begun.
> For east or west all woods must fail . . .

Fail – even as he said the word his voice faded into silence. The air seemed heavy and the making of words wearisome. Just behind them a large branch fell from an old overhanging tree with a crash into the path. The trees seemed to close in before them.

'They do not like all that about ending and failing,' said Merry. 'I should not sing any more at present. Wait till we do get to the edge, and then we'll turn and give them a rousing chorus!'

He spoke cheerfully, and if he felt any great anxiety, he did not show it. The others did not answer. They were depressed. A heavy weight was settling steadily on Frodo's heart, and he regretted now with every step forward that he had ever thought of challenging the menace of the trees. He was, indeed, just about to stop and propose going back (if that was still possible), when things took a new turn. The path stopped climbing, and became for a while nearly level. The dark trees drew aside, and ahead they could see the path going almost straight forward. Before them, but some distance off, there stood a green hill-top, treeless, rising like a bald head out of the encircling wood. The path seemed to be making directly for it.

They now hurried forward again, delighted with the thought of climbing out for a while above the roof of the Forest. The path dipped, and then again began to climb upwards, leading them at last to the foot of the steep hillside. There it left the trees and faded into the turf. The wood stood all round the hill like thick hair that ended sharply in a circle round a shaven crown.

The hobbits led their ponies up, winding round and round until they reached the top. There they stood and gazed about them. The air was gleaming and sunlit, but hazy; and they could not see to any great distance. Near at hand the mist was now almost gone; though here and there it lay in hollows of the wood, and to the south of them, out of a deep fold cutting right across the Forest, the fog still rose like steam or wisps of white smoke.

'That,' said Merry, pointing with his hand, 'that is the line of the Withywindle. It comes down out of the Downs and flows south-west through the midst of the Forest to join the Brandywine below Haysend. We don't want to go *that* way! The Withywindle valley is said to be the queerest part of the whole wood – the centre from which all the queerness comes, as it were.'

The others looked in the direction that Merry pointed out, but they could see little but mists over the damp and deep-cut valley; and beyond it the southern half of the Forest faded from view.

The sun on the hill-top was now getting hot. It must have been about eleven o'clock; but the autumn haze still prevented them from seeing much in other directions. In the west they could not make out either the line of the Hedge or the valley of the Brandywine beyond it. Northward, where they looked most hopefully, they could see nothing that might be the line of the great East Road, for which they were making. They were on an island in a sea of trees, and the horizon was veiled.

On the south-eastern side the ground fell very steeply, as if the slopes of the hill were continued far down under the trees, like island-shores that really are the sides of a mountain rising out of deep waters. They sat on the green edge and looked out over the woods below them, while they ate their mid-day meal. As the sun rose and passed noon they glimpsed far off in the east the grey-green lines of the Downs that lay beyond the Old Forest on that side. That cheered them greatly; for it was good to see a sight of anything beyond the wood's borders, though they did not mean to go that way, if they could help it: the Barrow-downs had as sinister a reputation in hobbit-legend as the Forest itself.

At length they made up their minds to go on again. The path that had brought them to the hill reappeared on the northward side; but they had not followed it far before they became aware that it was bending steadily to the right. Soon it began to descend rapidly and they guessed that it must actually be heading towards the Withywindle valley: not at all the direction they wished to take. After some discussion they decided to leave this misleading path and strike north-ward; for although they had not been able to see it from the hill-top, the Road must lie that way, and it could not be many miles off. Also northward, and to the left of the path, the land seemed to be drier and more open, climbing up to slopes where the trees were thinner, and pines and firs replaced the oaks and ashes and other strange and nameless trees of the denser wood.

At first their choice seemed to be good: they got along at a fair speed, though whenever they got a glimpse of the sun in an open glade they seemed unaccountably to have veered eastwards. But after a time the trees began to close in again, just where they had appeared from a distance to be thinner and less tangled. Then deep folds in the ground were dis-covered unexpectedly, like the ruts of great giant-wheels or wide moats and sunken roads long disused and choked with brambles. These lay usually right across their line of march, and could only be crossed by scrambling down and out again, which was troublesome and difficult with their ponies. Each time they climbed down they found the hollow filled with thick bushes and matted undergrowth, which somehow would not yield to the left, but only gave way when they turned to the right; and they had to go some distance along the bottom before they could find a way up the further bank. Each time they clambered out, the trees seemed deeper and darker; and always to the left and upwards it was most diffi-cult to find a way, and they were forced to the right and downwards.

After an hour or two they had lost all clear sense of direc-tion, though they knew well enough that they had long ceased to go northward at all. They were being headed off, and were simply following a course chosen for them – eastwards and southwards, into the heart of the Forest and not out of it.

The afternoon was wearing away when they scrambled and stumbled into a fold that was wider and deeper than any they had yet met. It was so steep and overhung that it proved impossible to climb out of it again, either forwards or backwards, without leaving their ponies and their baggage behind. All they could do was to follow the fold – downwards. The ground grew soft, and in places boggy; springs appeared in the banks, and soon they found themselves following a brook that trickled and babbled through a weedy bed. Then the ground began to fall rapidly, and the brook growing strong and noisy, flowed and leaped swiftly downhill. They were in a deep dim-lit gully over-arched by trees high above them.

After stumbling along for some way along the stream, they came quite suddenly out of the gloom. As if through a gate they saw the sunlight before them. Coming to the opening they found that they had made their way down through a cleft in a high steep bank, almost a cliff. At its feet was a wide space of grass and reeds; and in the distance could be glimpsed another bank almost as steep. A golden afternoon of late sunlight lay warm and drowsy upon the hidden land between. In the midst of it there wound lazily a dark river of brown water, bordered with ancient willows, arched over with willows, blocked with fallen willows, and flecked with thousands of faded willow-leaves. The air was thick with them, fluttering yellow from the branches; for there was a warm and gentle breeze blowing softly in the valley, and the reeds were rustling, and the willow-boughs were creaking.

'Well, now I have at least some notion of where we are!' said Merry. 'We have come almost in the opposite direction to which we intended. This is the River Withywindle! I will go on and explore.'

He passed out into the sunshine and disappeared into the long grasses. After a while he reappeared, and reported that there was fairly solid ground between the cliff-foot and the river; in some places firm turf went down to the water's edge. 'What's more,' he said, 'there seems to be something like a footpath winding along on this side of the river. If we turn left and follow it, we shall be bound to come out on the east side of the Forest eventually.'

'I dare say!' said Pippin. 'That is, if the track goes on so far, and does not simply lead us into a bog and leave us there. Who made the track, do you suppose, and why? I am sure it was not for our benefit. I am getting very suspicious of this Forest and everything in it, and I begin to believe all the stories about it. And have you any idea how far eastward we should have to go?'

'No,' said Merry, 'I haven't. I don't know in the least how far down the Withywindle we are, or who could possibly come here often enough to make a path along it. But there is no other way out that I can see or think of.'

There being nothing else for it, they filed out, and Merry led them to the path that he had discovered. Everywhere the reeds and grasses were lush and tall, in places far above their heads; but once found, the path was easy to follow, as it turned and twisted, picking out the sounder ground among the bogs and pools. Here and there it passed over other rills, running down gullies into the Withywindle out of the higher forest-lands, and at these points there were tree-trunks or bundles of brushwood laid carefully across.

The hobbits began to feel very hot. There were armies of flies of all kinds buzzing round their ears, and the afternoon sun was burning on their backs. At last they came suddenly into a thin shade; great grey branches reached across the path. Each step forward became more reluctant than the last. Sleepiness seemed to be creeping out of the ground and up their legs, and falling softly out of the air upon their heads and eyes.

Frodo felt his chin go down and his head nod. Just in front of him Pippin fell forward on to his knees. Frodo halted. 'It's no good,' he heard Merry saying. 'Can't go another step without rest. Must have nap. It's cool under the willows. Less flies!'

Frodo did not like the sound of this. 'Come on!' he cried.

'We can't have a nap yet. We must get clear of the Forest first.' But the others were too far gone to care. Beside them Sam stood yawning and blinking stupidly.

Suddenly Frodo himself felt sleep overwhelming him. His head swam. There now seemed hardly a sound in the air. The flies had stopped buzzing. Only a gentle noise on the edge of hearing, a soft fluttering as of a song half whispered, seemed to stir in the boughs above. He lifted his heavy eyes and saw leaning over him a huge willow-tree, old and hoary. Enormous it looked, its sprawling branches going up like reaching arms with many long-fingered hands, its knotted and twisted trunk gaping in wide fissures that creaked faintly as the boughs moved. The leaves fluttering against the bright sky dazzled him, and he toppled over, lying where he fell upon the grass.

Merry and Pippin dragged themselves forward and lay down with their backs to the willow-trunk. Behind them the great cracks gaped wide to receive them as the tree swayed and creaked. They looked up at the grey and yellow leaves, moving softly against the light, and singing. They shut their eyes, and then it seemed that they could almost hear words, cool words, saying something about water and sleep. They gave themselves up to the spell and fell fast asleep at the foot of the great grey willow.

Frodo lay for a while fighting with the sleep that was over-powering him; then with an effort he struggled to his feet again. He felt a compelling desire for cool water. 'Wait for me, Sam,' he stammered. 'Must bathe feet a minute.'

Half in a dream he wandered forward to the riverward side of the tree, where great winding roots grew out into the stream, like gnarled dragonets straining down to drink. He straddled one of these, and paddled his hot feet in the cool brown water; and there he too suddenly fell asleep with his back against the tree.

Sam sat down and scratched his head, and yawned like a cavern. He was worried. The afternoon was getting late, and he thought this sudden sleepiness uncanny. 'There's more behind this than sun and warm air,' he muttered to himself. 'I don't like this great big tree. I don't trust it. Hark at it singing about sleep now! This won't do at all!'

He pulled himself to his feet, and staggered off to see what had become of the ponies. He found that two had wandered on a good way along the path; and he had just caught them and brought them back towards the others, when he heard two noises; one loud, and the other soft but very clear. One was the splash of something heavy falling into the water; the other was a noise like the snick of a lock when a door quietly closes fast.

He rushed back to the bank. Frodo was in the water close to the edge, and a great tree-root seemed to be over him and holding him down, but he was not struggling. Sam gripped him by the jacket, and dragged him from under the root; and then with difficulty hauled him on to the bank. Almost at once he woke, and coughed and spluttered.

'Do you know, Sam,' he said at length, 'the beastly tree *threw* me in! I felt it. The big root just twisted round and tipped me in!'

'You were dreaming I expect, Mr. Frodo,' said Sam. 'You shouldn't sit in such a place, if you feel sleepy.'

'What about the others?' Frodo asked. 'I wonder what sort of dreams they are having.'

They went round to the other side of the tree, and then Sam understood the click that he had heard. Pippin had vanished. The crack by which he had laid himself had closed together, so that not a chink could be seen. Merry was trapped: another crack had closed about his waist; his legs lay outside, but the rest of him was inside a dark opening, the edges of which gripped like a pair of pincers.

Frodo and Sam beat first upon the tree-trunk where Pippin had lain. They then struggled frantically to pull open the jaws of the crack that held poor Merry. It was quite useless.

'What a foul thing to happen!' cried Frodo wildly. 'Why did we ever come into this dreadful Forest? I wish we were all back at Crickhollow!' He kicked the tree with all his strength, heedless of his own feet. A hardly perceptible shiver ran through the stem and up into the branches; the leaves rustled and whispered, but with a sound now of faint and far-off laughter.

'I suppose we haven't got an axe among our luggage, Mr. Frodo?' asked Sam.

'I brought a little hatchet for chopping firewood,' said Frodo. 'That wouldn't be much use.'

'Wait a minute!' cried Sam, struck by an idea suggested by firewood. 'We might do something with fire!'

'We might,' said Frodo doubtfully. 'We might succeed in roasting Pippin alive inside.'

'We might try to hurt or frighten this tree to begin with,' said Sam fiercely. 'If it don't let them go, I'll have it down, if I have to gnaw it.' He ran to the ponies and before long came back with two tinder-boxes and a hatchet.

Quickly they gathered dry grass and leaves, and bits of bark; and made a pile of broken twigs and chopped sticks. These they heaped against the trunk on the far side of the tree from the prisoners. As soon as Sam had struck a spark into the tinder, it kindled the dry grass and a flurry of flame and smoke went up. The twigs crackled. Little fingers of fire licked against the dry scored rind of the ancient tree and scorched it. A tremor ran through the whole willow. The leaves seemed to hiss above their heads with a sound of pain and anger. A loud scream came from Merry, and from far inside the tree they heard Pippin give a muffled yell.

'Put it out! Put it out!' cried Merry. 'He'll squeeze me in two, if you don't. He says so!'

'Who? What?' shouted Frodo, rushing round to the other side of the tree.

'Put it out! Put it out!' begged Merry. The branches of the willow began to sway violently. There was a sound as of a wind rising and spreading outwards to the branches of all the other trees round about, as though they had dropped a stone into the quiet slumber of the river-valley and set up ripples of anger that ran out over the whole Forest. Sam kicked at the little fire and stamped out the sparks. But Frodo, without any clear idea of why he did so, or what he hoped for, ran along the path crying *help! help! help!* It seemed to him that he could hardly hear the sound of his own shrill voice: it was blown away from him by the willow-wind and drowned in a clamour of leaves, as soon as the words left his mouth. He felt desperate: lost and witless.

Suddenly he stopped. There was an answer, or so he thought; but it seemed to come from behind him, away down the path further back in the Forest. He turned round and listened, and soon there could be no doubt: someone was singing a song; a deep glad voice was singing carelessly and happily, but it was singing nonsense:

> *Hey dol! merry dol! ring a dong dillo!*
> *Ring a dong! hop along! fal lal the willow!*
> *Tom Bom, jolly Tom, Tom Bombadillo!*

Half hopeful and half afraid of some new danger, Frodo and Sam now both stood still. Suddenly out of a long string of nonsense-words (or so they seemed) the voice rose up loud and clear and burst into this song:

> *Hey! Come merry dol! derry dol! My darling!*
> *Light goes the weather-wind and the feathered starling.*
> *Down along under Hill, shining in the sunlight,*
> *Waiting on the doorstep for the cold starlight,*
> *There my pretty lady is, River-woman's daughter,*
> *Slender as the willow-wand, clearer than the water.*
> *Old Tom Bombadil water-lilies bringing*
> *Comes hopping home again. Can you hear him singing?*
> *Hey! Come merry dol! derry dol! and merry-o,*
> *Goldberry, Goldberry, merry yellow berry-o!*
> *Poor old Willow-man, you tuck your roots away!*
> *Tom's in a hurry now. Evening will follow day.*
> *Tom's going home again water-lilies bringing.*
> *Hey! Come derry dol! Can you hear me singing?*

Frodo and Sam stood as if enchanted. The wind puffed out. The leaves hung silently again on stiff branches. There was another burst of song, and then suddenly, hopping and dancing along the path, there appeared above the reeds an old battered hat with a tall crown and a long blue feather stuck in the band. With another hop and a bound there came into view a man, or so it seemed. At any rate he was too large and heavy for a hobbit, if not quite tall enough for one of the Big People, though he made noise enough for one, stumping along with great yellow boots on his thick legs, and charging through grass and rushes like a cow going down to drink. He had a blue coat and a long brown beard; his eyes were blue and bright, and his face was red as a ripe apple, but creased into a hundred wrinkles of laughter. In his hands he carried on a large leaf as on a tray a small pile of white water-lilies.

'Help!' cried Frodo and Sam running towards him with their hands stretched out.

'Whoa! Whoa! steady there!' cried the old man, holding up one hand, and they stopped short, as if they had been struck stiff. 'Now, my little fellows, where be you a-going to, puffing like a bellows? What's the matter here then? Do you know who I am? I'm Tom Bombadil. Tell me what's your trouble! Tom's in a hurry now. Don't you crush my lilies!'

'My friends are caught in the willow-tree,' cried Frodo breathlessly.

'Master Merry's being squeezed in a crack!' cried Sam.

'What?' shouted Tom Bombadil, leaping up in the air. 'Old Man Willow? Naught worse than that, eh? That can soon be mended. I know the tune for him. Old grey Willow-man! I'll freeze his marrow cold, if he don't behave himself. I'll sing his roots off. I'll sing a wind up and blow leaf and branch away. Old Man Willow!'

Setting down his lilies carefully on the grass, he ran to the tree. There he saw Merry's feet still sticking out – the rest had already been drawn further inside. Tom put his mouth to the crack and began singing into it in a low voice. They could not catch the words, but evidently Merry was aroused. His legs began to kick. Tom sprang away, and breaking off a hanging branch smote the side of the willow with it. 'You let them out again, Old Man Willow!' he said. 'What be you a-thinking of? You should not be waking. Eat earth! Dig deep! Drink water! Go to sleep! Bombadil is talking!' He then seized Merry's feet and drew him out of the suddenly widening crack.

There was a tearing creak and the other crack split open, and out of it Pippin sprang, as if he had been kicked. Then with a loud snap both cracks closed fast again. A shudder ran through the tree from root to tip, and complete silence fell.

'Thank you!' said the hobbits, one after the other.

Tom Bombadil burst out laughing. 'Well, my little fellows!' said he, stooping so that he peered into their faces. 'You shall come home with me! The table is all laden with yellow cream, honeycomb, and white bread and butter. Goldberry is waiting. Time enough for questions around the supper table. You follow after me as quick as you are able!' With that he picked up his lilies, and then with a beckoning wave of his hand went hopping and dancing along the path eastward, still singing loudly and nonsensically.

Too surprised and too relieved to talk, the hobbits followed after him as fast as they could. But that was not fast enough. Tom soon disappeared in front of them, and the noise of his singing got fainter and further away. Suddenly his voice came floating back to them in a loud halloo!

> Hop along, my little friends, up the Withywindle!
> Tom's going on ahead candles for to kindle.
> Down west sinks the Sun: soon you will be groping.
> When the night-shadows fall, then the door will open,
> Out of the window-panes light will twinkle yellow.
> Fear no alder black! Heed no hoary willow!
> Fear neither root nor bough! Tom goes on before you.
> Hey now! merry dol! We'll be waiting for you!

After that the hobbits heard no more. Almost at once the sun seemed to sink into the trees behind them. They thought of the slanting light of evening glittering on the Brandywine River, and the windows of Bucklebury beginning to gleam with hundreds of lights. Great shadows fell across them; trunks and branches of trees hung dark and threatening over the path. White mists began to rise and curl on the surface of the river and stray about the roots of the trees upon its borders. Out of the very ground at their feet a shadowy steam arose and mingled with the swiftly falling dusk.

It became difficult to follow the path, and they were very tired. Their legs seemed leaden. Strange furtive noises ran among the bushes and reeds on either side of them; and if they looked up to the pale sky, they caught sight of queer gnarled and knobbly faces that gloomed dark against the twilight, and leered down at them from the high bank and the edges of the wood. They began to feel that all this country was unreal, and that they were stumbling through an ominous dream that led to no awakening.

Just as they felt their feet slowing down to a standstill, they noticed that the ground was gently rising. The water began to murmur. In the darkness they caught the white glimmer of foam, where the river flowed over a short fall. Then suddenly the trees came to an end and the mists were left behind. They stepped out from the Forest, and found a wide sweep of grass welling up before them. The river, now small and swift, was leaping merrily down to meet them, glinting here and there in the light of the stars, which were already shining in the sky.

The grass under their feet was smooth and short, as if it had been mown or shaven. The eaves of the Forest behind were clipped, and trim as a hedge. The path was now plain before them, well-tended and bordered with stone. It wound up on to the top of a grassy knoll, now grey under the pale starry night; and there, still high above them on a further slope, they saw the twinkling lights of a house. Down again the path went, and then up again, up a long smooth hillside of turf, towards the light. Suddenly a wide yellow beam flowed out brightly from a door that was opened. There was Tom Bombadil's house before them, up, down, under hill. Behind it a steep shoulder of the land lay grey and bare, and beyond that the dark shapes of the Barrow-downs stalked away into the eastern night.

They all hurried forward, hobbits and ponies. Already half their weariness and all their fears had fallen from them. *Hey! Come merry dol!* rolled out the song to greet them.

> *Hey! Come derry dol! Hop along, my hearties!*
> *Hobbits! Ponies all! We are fond of parties.*
> *Now let the fun begin! Let us sing together!*

Then another clear voice, as young and as ancient as Spring, like the song of a glad water flowing down into the night from a bright morning in the hills, came falling like silver to meet them:

> *Now let the song begin! Let us sing together*
> *Of sun, stars, moon and mist, rain and cloudy weather,*
> *Light on the budding leaf, dew on the feather,*
> *Wind on the open hill, bells on the heather,*
> *Reeds by the shady pool, lilies on the water:*
> *Old Tom Bombadil and the River-daughter!*

And with that song the hobbits stood upon the threshold, and a golden light was all about them.

CHAPTER VII

IN THE HOUSE OF TOM BOMBADIL

The four hobbits stepped over the wide stone threshold, and stood still, blinking. They were in a long low room, filled with the light of lamps swinging from the beams of the roof; and on the table of dark polished wood stood many candles, tall and yellow, burning brightly.

In a chair, at the far side of the room facing the outer door, sat a woman. Her long yellow hair rippled down her shoulders; her gown was green, green as young reeds, shot with silver like beads of dew; and her belt was of gold, shaped like a chain of flag-lilies set with the pale-blue eyes of forget-me-nots. About her feet in wide vessels of green and brown earthenware, white water-lilies were floating, so that she seemed to be enthroned in the midst of a pool.

'Enter, good guests!' she said, and as she spoke they knew that it was her clear voice they had heard singing. They came a few timid steps further into the room, and began to bow low, feeling strangely surprised and awkward, like folk that, knocking at a cottage door to beg for a drink of water, have been answered by a fair young elf-queen clad in living flowers. But before they could say anything, she sprang lightly up and over the lily-bowls, and ran laughing towards them; and as she ran her gown rustled softly like the wind in the flowering borders of a river.

'Come dear folk!' she said, taking Frodo by the hand. 'Laugh and be merry! I am Goldberry, daughter of the River.' Then lightly she passed them and closing the door she turned her back to it, with her white arms spread out across it. 'Let us shut out the night!' she said. 'For you are still afraid, perhaps, of mist and tree-shadows and deep water, and untame things. Fear nothing! For tonight you are under the roof of Tom Bombadil.'

The hobbits looked at her in wonder; and she looked at each of them and smiled. 'Fair lady Goldberry!' said Frodo at last, feeling his heart moved with a joy that he did not understand. He stood as he had at times stood enchanted by fair elven-voices; but the spell that was now laid upon him was different: less keen and lofty was the delight, but deeper and nearer to mortal heart; marvellous and yet not strange. 'Fair lady Goldberry!' he said again. 'Now the joy that was hidden in the songs we heard is made plain to me.

> O slender as a willow-wand! O clearer than clear water!
> O reed by the living pool! Fair River-daughter!
> O spring-time and summer-time, and spring again after!
> O wind on the waterfall, and the leaves' laughter!

Suddenly he stopped and stammered, overcome with surprise to hear himself saying such things. But Goldberry laughed.

'Welcome!' she said. 'I had not heard that folk of the Shire were so sweet-tongued. But I see you are an elf-friend; the light in your eyes and the ring in your voice tells it. This is a merry meeting! Sit now, and wait for the Master of the house! He will not be long. He is tending your tired beasts.'

The hobbits sat down gladly in low rush-seated chairs, while Goldberry busied herself about the table; and their eyes followed her, for the slender grace of her movement filled them with quiet delight. From somewhere behind the house came the sound of singing. Every now and again they caught, among many a *derry dol* and a *merry dol* and a *ring a ding dillo* the repeated words:

> Old Tom Bombadil is a merry fellow;
> Bright blue his jacket is, and his boots are yellow.

'Fair lady!' said Frodo again after a while. 'Tell me, if my asking does not seem foolish, who is Tom Bombadil?'

'He is,' said Goldberry, staying her swift movements and smiling.

Frodo looked at her questioningly. 'He is, as you have seen him,' she said in answer to his look. 'He is the Master of wood, water, and hill.'

'Then all this strange land belongs to him?'

'No indeed!' she answered, and her smile faded. 'That would indeed be a burden,' she added in a low voice, as if to herself. 'The trees and the grasses and all things growing or living in the land belong each to themselves. Tom Bombadil is the Master. No one has ever caught old Tom walking in the forest, wading in the water, leaping on the hill-tops under light and shadow. He has no fear. Tom Bombadil is master.'

A door opened and in came Tom Bombadil. He had now no hat and his thick brown hair was crowned with autumn leaves. He laughed, and going to Goldberry, took her hand.

'Here's my pretty lady!' he said, bowing to the hobbits. 'Here's my Goldberry clothed all in silver-green with flowers in her girdle! Is the table laden? I see yellow cream and honeycomb, and white bread, and butter; milk, cheese, and green herbs and ripe berries gathered. Is that enough for us? Is the supper ready?'

'It is,' said Goldberry; 'but the guests perhaps are not?'

Tom clapped his hands and cried: 'Tom, Tom! your guests are tired, and you had near forgotten! Come now, my merry friends, and Tom will refresh you! You shall clean grimy hands, and wash your weary faces; cast off your muddy cloaks and comb out your tangles!'

He opened the door, and they followed him down a short passage and round a sharp turn. They came to a low room with a sloping roof (a penthouse, it seemed, built on to the north end of the house). Its walls were of clean stone, but they were mostly covered with green hanging mats and yellow curtains. The floor was flagged, and strewn with fresh green rushes. There were four deep mattresses, each piled with white blankets, laid on the floor along one side. Against the opposite wall was a long bench laden with wide earthenware basins, and beside it stood brown ewers filled with water, some cold, some steaming hot. There were soft green slippers set ready beside each bed.

Before long, washed and refreshed, the hobbits were seated at the table, two on each side, while at either end sat Goldberry and the Master. It was a long and merry meal. Though the hobbits ate, as only famished hobbits can eat, there was no lack. The drink in their drinking-bowls seemed to be clear cold water, yet it went to their hearts like wine and set free their voices. The guests became suddenly aware that they were singing merrily, as if it was easier and more natural than talking.

At last Tom and Goldberry rose and cleared the table swiftly. The guests were commanded to sit quiet, and were set in chairs, each with a footstool to his tired feet. There was a fire in the wide hearth before them, and it was burning with a sweet smell, as if it were built of apple-wood. When everything was set in order, all the lights in the room were put out, except one lamp and a pair of candles at each end of the chimney-shelf. Then Goldberry came and stood before them, holding a candle; and she wished them each a good night and deep sleep.

'Have peace now,' she said, 'until the morning! Heed no nightly noises! For nothing passes door and window here save moonlight and starlight and the wind off the hill-top. Good night!' She passed out of the room with a glimmer and a rustle. The sound of her footsteps was like a stream falling gently away downhill over cool stones in the quiet of night.

Tom sat on a while beside them in silence, while each of them tried to muster the courage to ask one of the many questions he had meant to ask at supper. Sleep gathered on their eyelids. At last Frodo spoke:

'Did you hear me calling, Master, or was it just chance that brought you at that moment?'

Tom stirred like a man shaken out of a pleasant dream. 'Eh, what?' said he. 'Did I hear you calling? Nay, I did not hear: I was busy singing. Just chance brought me then, if chance you call it. It was no plan of mine, though I was waiting for you. We heard news of you, and learned that you were wandering. We guessed you'd come ere long down to the water: all paths lead that way, down to Withywindle. Old grey Willow-man, he's a mighty singer; and it's hard for little folk to escape his cunning mazes. But Tom had an errand there, that he dared not hinder.' Tom nodded as if sleep was taking him again; but he went on in a soft singing voice:

> *I had an errand there: gathering water-lilies,*
> *green leaves and lilies white to please my pretty lady,*
> *the last ere the year's end to keep them from the winter,*
> *to flower by her pretty feet till the snows are melted.*
> *Each year at summer's end I go to find them for her,*
> *in a wide pool, deep and clear, far down Withywindle;*
> *there they open first in spring and there they linger latest.*
> *By that pool long ago I found the River-daughter,*
> *fair young Goldberry sitting in the rushes.*
> *Sweet was her singing then, and her heart was beating!*

He opened his eyes and looked at them with a sudden glint of blue:

> *And that proved well for you — for now I shall no longer*
> *go down deep again along the forest-water,*
> *not while the year is old. Nor shall I be passing*
> *Old Man Willow's house this side of spring-time,*
> *not till the merry spring, when the River-daughter*
> *dances down the withy-path to bathe in the water.*

He fell silent again; but Frodo could not help asking one more question: the one he most desired to have answered.

'Tell us, Master,' he said, 'about the Willow-man. What is he? I have never heard of him before.'

'No, don't!' said Merry and Pippin together, sitting suddenly upright. 'Not now! Not until the morning!'

'That is right!' said the old man. 'Now is the time for resting. Some things are ill to hear when the world's in shadow. Sleep till the morning-light, rest on the pillow! Heed no nightly noise! Fear no grey willow!' And with that he took down the lamp and blew it out, and grasping a candle in either hand he led them out of the room.

Their mattresses and pillows were soft as down, and the blankets were of white wool. They had hardly laid themselves on the deep beds and drawn the light covers over them before they were asleep.

In the dead night, Frodo lay in a dream without light. Then he saw the young moon rising; under its thin light there loomed before him a black wall of rock, pierced by a dark arch like a great gate. It seemed to Frodo that he was lifted up, and passing over he saw that the rock-wall was a circle of hills, and that within it was a plain, and in the midst of the plain stood a pinnacle of stone, like a vast tower but not made by hands. On its top stood the figure of a man. The moon as it rose seemed to hang for a moment above his head and glistened in his white hair as the wind stirred it. Up from the dark plain below came the crying of fell voices, and the howling of many wolves. Suddenly a shadow, like the shape of great wings, passed across the moon. The figure lifted his arms and a light flashed from the staff that he wielded. A mighty eagle swept down and bore him away. The voices wailed and the wolves yammered. There was a noise like a strong wind blowing, and on it was borne the sound of hoofs, galloping, galloping, galloping from the East. 'Black Riders!' thought Frodo as he wakened, with the sound of the hoofs still echoing in his mind. He wondered if he would ever again have the courage to leave the safety of these stone walls. He lay motionless, still listening; but all was now silent, and at last he turned and fell asleep again or wandered into some other unremembered dream.

At his side Pippin lay dreaming pleasantly; but a change came over his dreams and he turned and groaned. Suddenly he woke, or thought he had waked, and yet still heard in the darkness the sound that had disturbed his dream: *tip-tap, squeak*: the noise was like branches fretting in the wind, twig-fingers scraping wall and window: *creak, creak, creak*. He wondered if there were willow-trees close to the house; and then suddenly he had a dreadful feeling that he was not in an ordinary house at all, but inside the willow and listening to that horrible dry creaking voice laughing at him again. He sat up, and felt the soft pillows yield to his hands, and he lay down again relieved. He seemed to hear the echo of words in his ears: 'Fear nothing! Have peace until the morning! Heed no nightly noises!' Then he went to sleep again.

It was the sound of water that Merry heard falling into his quiet sleep: water streaming down gently, and then spreading, spreading irresistibly all round the house into a dark shoreless pool. It gurgled under the walls, and was rising slowly but surely. 'I shall be drowned!' he thought. 'It will find its way in, and then I shall drown.' He felt that he was lying in a soft slimy bog, and springing up he set his foot on the corner of a cold hard flagstone. Then he remembered where he was and lay down again. He seemed to hear or remember hearing: 'Nothing passes doors or windows save moonlight and starlight and the wind off the hill-top.' A little breath of sweet air moved the curtain. He breathed deep and fell asleep again.

As far as he could remember, Sam slept through the night in deep content, if logs are contented.

They woke up, all four at once, in the morning light. Tom was moving about the room whistling like a starling. When he heard them stir he clapped his hands, and cried: 'Hey! Come merry dol! derry dol! My hearties!' He drew back the yellow curtains, and the hobbits saw that these had covered the windows, at either end of the room, one looking east and the other looking west.

They leapt up refreshed. Frodo ran to the eastern window, and found himself looking into a kitchen-garden grey with dew. He had half expected to see turf right up to the walls, turf all pocked with hoof-prints. Actually his view was screened by a tall line of beans on poles; but above and far beyond them the grey top of the hill loomed up against the sunrise. It was a pale morning: in the East, behind long clouds like lines of soiled wool stained red at the edges, lay glimmering deeps of yellow. The sky spoke of rain to come; but the light was broadening quickly, and the red flowers on the beans began to glow against the wet green leaves.

Pippin looked out of the western window, down into a pool of mist. The Forest was hidden under a fog. It was like looking down on to a sloping cloud-roof from above. There was a fold or channel where the mist was broken into many plumes and billows; the valley of the Withywindle. The stream ran down the hill on the left and vanished into the white shadows. Near at hand was a flower-garden and a clipped hedge silver-netted, and beyond that grey shaven grass pale with dew-drops. There was no willow-tree to be seen.

'Good morning, merry friends!' cried Tom, opening the eastern window wide. A cool air flowed in; it had a rainy smell. 'Sun won't show her face much today, I'm thinking. I have been walking wide, leaping on the hill-tops, since the grey dawn began, nosing wind and weather, wet grass underfoot, wet sky above me. I wakened Goldberry singing under window; but nought wakes hobbit-folk in the early morning. In the night little folk wake up in the darkness, and sleep after light has come! Ring a ding dillo! Wake now, my merry friends! Forget the nightly noises! Ring a ding dillo del! derry del, my hearties! If you come soon you'll find breakfast on the table. If you come late you'll get grass and rain-water!'

Needless to say – not that Tom's threat sounded very serious – the hobbits came soon, and left the table late and only when it was beginning to look rather empty. Neither Tom nor Goldberry were there. Tom could be heard about the house, clattering in the kitchen, and up and down the stairs, and singing here and there outside. The room looked westward over the mist-clouded valley, and the window was open. Water dripped down from the thatched eaves above. Before they had finished breakfast the clouds had joined into an unbroken roof, and a straight grey rain came softly and steadily down. Behind its deep curtain the Forest was completely veiled.

As they looked out of the window there came falling gently as if it was flowing down the rain out of the sky, the clear voice of Goldberry singing up above them. They could hear few words, but it seemed plain to them that the song was a rain-song, as sweet as showers on dry hills, that told the tale of a river from the spring in the highlands to the Sea far below. The hobbits listened with delight; and Frodo was glad in his heart, and blessed the kindly weather, because it delayed them from departing. The thought of going had been heavy upon him from the moment he awoke; but he guessed now that they would not go further that day.

The upper wind settled in the West and deeper and wetter clouds rolled up to spill their laden rain on the bare heads of the Downs. Nothing could be seen all round the house but falling water. Frodo stood near the open door and watched the white chalky path turn into a little river of milk and go bubbling away down into the valley. Tom Bombadil came trotting round the corner of the house, waving his arms as if he was warding off the rain – and indeed when he sprang over the threshold he seemed quite dry, except for his boots. These he took off and put in the chimney-corner. Then he sat in the largest chair and called the hobbits to gather round him.

'This is Goldberry's washing day,' he said, 'and her

autumn-cleaning. Too wet for hobbit-folk – let them rest while they are able! It's a good day for long tales, for questions and for answers, so Tom will start the talking.'

He then told them many remarkable stories, sometimes half as if speaking to himself, sometimes looking at them suddenly with a bright blue eye under his deep brows. Often his voice would turn to song, and he would get out of his chair and dance about. He told them tales of bees and flowers, the ways of trees, and the strange creatures of the Forest, about the evil things and good things, things friendly and things unfriendly, cruel things and kind things, and secrets hidden under brambles.

As they listened, they began to understand the lives of the Forest, apart from themselves, indeed to feel themselves as the strangers where all other things were at home. Moving constantly in and out of his talk was Old Man Willow, and Frodo learned now enough to content him, indeed more than enough, for it was not comfortable lore. Tom's words laid bare the hearts of trees and their thoughts, which were often dark and strange, and filled with a hatred of things that go free upon the earth, gnawing, biting, breaking, hacking, burning: destroyers and usurpers. It was not called the Old Forest without reason, for it was indeed ancient, a survivor of vast forgotten woods; and in it there lived yet, ageing no quicker than the hills, the fathers of the fathers of trees, remembering times when they were lords. The countless years had filled them with pride and rooted wisdom, and with malice. But none were more dangerous than the Great Willow: his heart was rotten, but his strength was green; and he was cunning, and a master of winds, and his song and thought ran through the woods on both sides of the river. His grey thirsty spirit drew power out of the earth and spread like fine root-threads in the ground, and invisible twig-fingers in the air, till it had under its dominion nearly all the trees of the Forest from the Hedge to the Downs.

Suddenly Tom's talk left the woods and went leaping up the young stream, over bubbling waterfalls, over pebbles and

worn rocks, and among small flowers in close grass and wet
crannies, wandering at last up on to the Downs. They heard
of the Great Barrows, and the green mounds, and the stone-
rings upon the hills and in the hollows among the hills. Sheep
were bleating in flocks. Green walls and white walls rose.
There were fortresses on the heights. Kings of little kingdoms
fought together, and the young Sun shone like fire on the
red metal of their new and greedy swords. There was victory
and defeat; and towers fell, fortresses were burned, and
flames went up into the sky. Gold was piled on the biers of
dead kings and queens; and mounds covered them, and the
stone doors were shut; and the grass grew over all. Sheep
walked for a while biting the grass, but soon the hills were
empty again. A shadow came out of dark places far away,
and the bones were stirred in the mounds. Barrow-wights
walked in the hollow places with a clink of rings on cold
fingers, and gold chains in the wind. Stone rings grinned out
of the ground like broken teeth in the moonlight.

The hobbits shuddered. Even in the Shire the rumour of
the Barrow-wights of the Barrow-downs beyond the Forest
had been heard. But it was not a tale that any hobbit liked
to listen to, even by a comfortable fireside far away. These
four now suddenly remembered what the joy of this house
had driven from their minds: the house of Tom Bombadil
nestled under the very shoulder of those dreaded hills. They
lost the thread of his tale and shifted uneasily, looking aside
at one another.

When they caught his words again they found that he had
now wandered into strange regions beyond their memory
and beyond their waking thought, into times when the world
was wider, and the seas flowed straight to the western Shore;
and still on and back Tom went singing out into ancient
starlight, when only the Elf-sires were awake. Then suddenly
he stopped, and they saw that he nodded as if he was falling
asleep. The hobbits sat still before him, enchanted; and it
seemed as if, under the spell of his words, the wind had
gone, and the clouds had dried up, and the day had been

withdrawn, and darkness had come from East and West, and all the sky was filled with the light of white stars.

Whether the morning and evening of one day or of many days had passed Frodo could not tell. He did not feel either hungry or tired, only filled with wonder. The stars shone through the window and the silence of the heavens seemed to be round him. He spoke at last out of his wonder and a sudden fear of that silence:

'Who are you, Master?' he asked.

'Eh, what?' said Tom sitting up, and his eyes glinting in the gloom. 'Don't you know my name yet? That's the only answer. Tell me, who are you, alone, yourself and nameless? But you are young and I am old. Eldest, that's what I am. Mark my words, my friends: Tom was here before the river and the trees; Tom remembers the first raindrop and the first acorn. He made paths before the Big People, and saw the little People arriving. He was here before the Kings and the graves and the Barrow-wights. When the Elves passed westward, Tom was here already, before the seas were bent. He knew the dark under the stars when it was fearless – before the Dark Lord came from Outside.'

A shadow seemed to pass by the window, and the hobbits glanced hastily through the panes. When they turned again, Goldberry stood in the door behind, framed in light. She held a candle, shielding its flame from the draught with her hand; and the light flowed through it, like sunlight through a white shell.

'The rain has ended,' she said; 'and new waters are running downhill, under the stars. Let us now laugh and be glad!'

'And let us have food and drink!' cried Tom. 'Long tales are thirsty. And long listening's hungry work, morning, noon, and evening!' With that he jumped out of his chair, and with a bound took a candle from the chimney-shelf and lit it in the flame that Goldberry held; then he danced about the table. Suddenly he hopped through the door and disappeared.

Quickly he returned, bearing a large and laden tray. Then

Tom and Goldberry set the table; and the hobbits sat half in wonder and half in laughter: so fair was the grace of Goldberry and so merry and odd the caperings of Tom. Yet in some fashion they seemed to weave a single dance, neither hindering the other, in and out of the room, and round about the table; and with great speed food and vessels and lights were set in order. The boards blazed with candles, white and yellow. Tom bowed to his guests. 'Supper is ready,' said Goldberry; and now the hobbits saw that she was clothed all in silver with a white girdle, and her shoes were like fishes' mail. But Tom was all in clean blue, blue as rain-washed forget-me-nots, and he had green stockings.

It was a supper even better than before. The hobbits under the spell of Tom's words may have missed one meal or many, but when the food was before them it seemed at least a week since they had eaten. They did not sing or even speak much for a while, and paid close attention to business. But after a time their hearts and spirits rose high again, and their voices rang out in mirth and laughter.

After they had eaten, Goldberry sang many songs for them, songs that began merrily in the hills and fell softly down into silence; and in the silences they saw in their minds pools and waters wider than any they had known, and looking into them they saw the sky below them and the stars like jewels in the depths. Then once more she wished them each good night and left them by the fireside. But Tom now seemed wide awake and plied them with questions.

He appeared already to know much about them and all their families, and indeed to know much of all the history and doings of the Shire down from days hardly remembered among the hobbits themselves. It no longer surprised them; but he made no secret that he owed his recent knowledge largely to Farmer Maggot, whom he seemed to regard as a person of more importance than they had imagined. 'There's earth under his old feet, and clay on his fingers; wisdom in his bones, and both his eyes are open,' said Tom. It was also clear that Tom had dealings with the Elves, and it seemed that in some fashion, news had reached him from Gildor concerning the flight of Frodo.

Indeed so much did Tom know, and so cunning was his questioning, that Frodo found himself telling him more about Bilbo and his own hopes and fears than he had told before even to Gandalf. Tom wagged his head up and down, and there was a glint in his eyes when he heard of the Riders.

'Show me the precious Ring!' he said suddenly in the midst of the story: and Frodo, to his own astonishment, drew out the chain from his pocket, and unfastening the Ring handed it at once to Tom.

It seemed to grow larger as it lay for a moment on his big brown-skinned hand. Then suddenly he put it to his eye and laughed. For a second the hobbits had a vision, both comical and alarming, of his bright blue eye gleaming through a circle of gold. Then Tom put the Ring round the end of his little finger and held it up to the candlelight. For a moment the hobbits noticed nothing strange about this. Then they gasped. There was no sign of Tom disappearing!

Tom laughed again, and then he spun the Ring in the air – and it vanished with a flash. Frodo gave a cry – and Tom leaned forward and handed it back to him with a smile.

Frodo looked at it closely, and rather suspiciously (like one who has lent a trinket to a juggler). It was the same Ring, or looked the same and weighed the same: for that Ring had always seemed to Frodo to weigh strangely heavy in the hand. But something prompted him to make sure. He was perhaps a trifle annoyed with Tom for seeming to make so light of what even Gandalf thought so perilously important. He waited for an opportunity, when the talk was going again, and Tom was telling an absurd story about badgers and their queer ways – then he slipped the Ring on.

Merry turned towards him to say something and gave a start, and checked an exclamation. Frodo was delighted (in a way): it was his own ring all right, for Merry was staring blankly at his chair, and obviously could not see him. He got

up and crept quietly away from the fireside towards the outer
door.

'Hey there!' cried Tom, glancing towards him with a most
seeing look in his shining eyes. 'Hey! Come Frodo, there!
Where be you a-going? Old Tom Bombadil's not as blind as
that yet. Take off your golden ring! Your hand's more fair
without it. Come back! Leave your game and sit down beside
me! We must talk a while more, and think about the morning.
Tom must teach the right road, and keep your feet from
wandering.'

Frodo laughed (trying to feel pleased), and taking off the
Ring he came and sat down again. Tom now told them that
he reckoned the Sun would shine tomorrow, and it would
be a glad morning, and setting out would be hopeful. But
they would do well to start early; for weather in that country
was a thing that even Tom could not be sure of for long,
and it would change sometimes quicker than he could change
his jacket. 'I am no weather-master,' he said; 'nor is aught
that goes on two legs.'

By his advice they decided to make nearly due North from
his house, over the western and lower slopes of the Downs:
they might hope in that way to strike the East Road in a
day's journey, and avoid the Barrows. He told them not to
be afraid – but to mind their own business.

'Keep to the green grass. Don't you go a-meddling with
old stone or cold Wights or prying in their houses, unless
you be strong folk with hearts that never falter!' He said this
more than once; and he advised them to pass barrows by on
the west-side, if they chanced to stray near one. Then he
taught them a rhyme to sing, if they should by ill-luck fall
into any danger or difficulty the next day.

> Ho! Tom Bombadil, Tom Bombadillo!
> By water, wood and hill, by the reed and willow,
> By fire, sun and moon, harken now and hear us!
> Come, Tom Bombadil, for our need is near us!

When they had sung this altogether after him, he clapped them each on the shoulder with a laugh, and taking candles led them back to their bedroom.

CHAPTER VIII

FOG ON THE BARROW-DOWNS

That night they heard no noises. But either in his dreams or out of them, he could not tell which, Frodo heard a sweet singing running in his mind: a song that seemed to come like a pale light behind a grey rain-curtain, and growing stronger to turn the veil all to glass and silver, until at last it was rolled back, and a far green country opened before him under a swift sunrise.

The vision melted into waking; and there was Tom whistling like a tree-full of birds; and the sun was already slanting down the hill and through the open window. Outside everything was green and pale gold.

After breakfast, which they again ate alone, they made ready to say farewell, as nearly heavy of heart as was possible on such a morning: cool, bright, and clean under a washed autumn sky of thin blue. The air came fresh from the North-west. Their quiet ponies were almost frisky, sniffing and moving restlessly. Tom came out of the house and waved his hat and danced upon the doorstep, bidding the hobbits to get up and be off and go with good speed.

They rode off along a path that wound away from behind the house, and went slanting up towards the north end of the hill-brow under which it sheltered. They had just dismounted to lead their ponies up the last steep slope, when suddenly Frodo stopped.

'Goldberry!' he cried. 'My fair lady, clad all in silver green! We have never said farewell to her, nor seen her since the evening!' He was so distressed that he turned back; but at that moment a clear call came rippling down. There on the hill-brow she stood beckoning to them: her hair was flying loose, and as it caught the sun it shone and shimmered. A

light like the glint of water on dewy grass flashed from under
her feet as she danced.

They hastened up the last slope, and stood breathless
beside her. They bowed, but with a wave of her arm she
bade them look round; and they looked out from the hill-top
over lands under the morning. It was now as clear and far-
seen as it had been veiled and misty when they stood upon
the knoll in the Forest, which could now be seen rising pale
and green out of the dark trees in the West. In that direction
the land rose in wooded ridges, green, yellow, russet under
the sun, beyond which lay hidden the valley of the Brandywine. To the South, over the line of the Withywindle, there
was a distant glint like pale glass where the Brandywine River
made a great loop in the lowlands and flowed away out of the
knowledge of the hobbits. Northward beyond the dwindling
downs the land ran away in flats and swellings of grey and
green and pale earth-colours, until it faded into a featureless
and shadowy distance. Eastward the Barrow-downs rose,
ridge behind ridge into the morning, and vanished out of
eyesight into a guess: it was no more than a guess of blue
and a remote white glimmer blending with the hem of the
sky, but it spoke to them, out of memory and old tales, of
the high and distant mountains.

They took a deep draught of the air, and felt that a skip and
a few stout strides would bear them wherever they wished. It
seemed fainthearted to go jogging aside over the crumpled
skirts of the downs towards the Road, when they should be
leaping, as lusty as Tom, over the stepping stones of the hills
straight towards the Mountains.

Goldberry spoke to them and recalled their eyes and
thoughts. 'Speed now, fair guests!' she said. 'And hold to
your purpose! North with the wind in the left eye and a
blessing on your footsteps! Make haste while the Sun shines!'
And to Frodo she said: 'Farewell, Elf-friend, it was a merry
meeting!'

But Frodo found no words to answer. He bowed low, and
mounted his pony, and followed by his friends jogged slowly

down the gentle slope behind the hill. Tom Bombadil's house and the valley, and the Forest were lost to view. The air grew warmer between the green walls of hillside and hillside, and the scent of turf rose strong and sweet as they breathed. Turning back, when they reached the bottom of the green hollow, they saw Goldberry, now small and slender like a sunlit flower against the sky: she was standing still watching them, and her hands were stretched out towards them. As they looked she gave a clear call, and lifting up her hand she turned and vanished behind the hill.

Their way wound along the floor of the hollow, and round the green feet of a steep hill into another deeper and broader valley, and then over the shoulder of further hills, and down their long limbs, and up their smooth sides again, up on to new hill-tops and down into new valleys. There was no tree nor any visible water: it was a country of grass and short springy turf, silent except for the whisper of the air over the edges of the land, and high lonely cries of strange birds. As they journeyed the sun mounted, and grew hot. Each time they climbed a ridge the breeze seemed to have grown less. When they caught a glimpse of the country westward the distant Forest seemed to be smoking, as if the fallen rain was steaming up again from leaf and root and mould. A shadow now lay round the edge of sight, a dark haze above which the upper sky was like a blue cap, hot and heavy.

About mid-day they came to a hill whose top was wide and flattened, like a shallow saucer with a green mounded rim. Inside there was no air stirring, and the sky seemed near their heads. They rode across and looked northwards. Then their hearts rose, for it seemed plain that they had come further already than they had expected. Certainly the distances had now all become hazy and deceptive, but there could be no doubt that the Downs were coming to an end. A long valley lay below them winding away northwards, until it came to an opening between two steep shoulders. Beyond, there seemed to be no more hills. Due north they faintly glimpsed a long dark line. 'That is a line of trees,' said Merry, 'and that must mark the Road. All along it for many leagues east of the Bridge there are trees growing. Some say they were planted in the old days.'

'Splendid!' said Frodo. 'If we make as good going this afternoon as we have done this morning, we shall have left the Downs before the Sun sets and be jogging on in search of a camping place.' But even as he spoke he turned his glance eastwards, and he saw that on that side the hills were higher and looked down upon them; and all those hills were crowned with green mounds, and on some were standing stones, pointing upwards like jagged teeth out of green gums.

That view was somehow disquieting; so they turned from the sight and went down into the hollow circle. In the midst of it there stood a single stone, standing tall under the sun above, and at this hour casting no shadow. It was shapeless and yet significant: like a landmark, or a guarding finger, or more like a warning. But they were now hungry, and the sun was still at the fearless noon; so they set their backs against the east side of the stone. It was cool, as if the sun had had no power to warm it; but at that time this seemed pleasant. There they took food and drink, and made as good a noon-meal under the open sky as anyone could wish; for the food came from 'down under Hill'. Tom had provided them with plenty for the comfort of the day. Their ponies unburdened strayed upon the grass.

Riding over the hills, and eating their fill, the warm sun and the scent of turf, lying a little too long, stretching out their legs and looking at the sky above their noses: these things are, perhaps, enough to explain what happened. However, that may be: they woke suddenly and uncomfortably from a sleep they had never meant to take. The standing stone was cold, and it cast a long pale shadow that stretched eastward over them. The sun, a pale and watery yellow, was gleaming through the mist just above the west wall of the hollow in which they lay; north, south, and east, beyond the wall the fog was thick, cold and white. The air was silent, heavy and chill. Their ponies were standing crowded together with their heads down.

The hobbits sprang to their feet in alarm, and ran to the western rim. They found that they were upon an island in the fog. Even as they looked out in dismay towards the setting sun, it sank before their eyes into a white sea, and a cold grey shadow sprang up in the East behind. The fog rolled up to the walls and rose above them, and as it mounted it bent over their heads until it became a roof: they were shut in a hall of mist whose central pillar was the standing stone.

They felt as if a trap was closing about them; but they did not quite lose heart. They still remembered the hopeful view they had had of the line of the Road ahead, and they still knew in which direction it lay. In any case, they now had so great a dislike for that hollow place about the stone that no thought of remaining there was in their minds. They packed up as quickly as their chilled fingers would work.

Soon they were leading their ponies in single file over the rim and down the long northward slope of the hill, down into a foggy sea. As they went down the mist became colder and damper, and their hair hung lank and dripping on their foreheads. When they reached the bottom it was so cold that they halted and got out cloaks and hoods, which soon became bedewed with grey drops. Then, mounting their ponies, they went slowly on again, feeling their way by the rise and fall of the ground. They were steering, as well as they could guess, for the gate-like opening at the far northward end of the long valley which they had seen in the morning. Once they were through the gap, they had only to keep on in anything like a straight line and they were bound in the end to strike the Road. Their thoughts did not go beyond that, except for a vague hope that perhaps away beyond the Downs there might be no fog.

Their going was very slow. To prevent their getting separated and wandering in different directions they went in file, with Frodo leading. Sam was behind him, and after him came Pippin, and then Merry. The valley seemed to stretch on endlessly. Suddenly Frodo saw a hopeful sign. On either side ahead a darkness began to loom through the mist; and he guessed that they were at last approaching the gap in the hills, the north-gate of the Barrow-downs. If they could pass that, they would be free.

'Come on! Follow me!' he called back over his shoulder, and he hurried forward. But his hope soon changed to bewilderment and alarm. The dark patches grew darker, but they shrank; and suddenly he saw, towering ominous before him and leaning slightly towards one another like the pillars of a headless door, two huge standing stones. He could not remember having seen any sign of these in the valley, when he looked out from the hill in the morning. He had passed between them almost before he was aware: and even as he did so darkness seemed to fall round him. His pony reared and snorted, and he fell off. When he looked back he found that he was alone: the others had not followed him.

'Sam!' he called. 'Pippin! Merry! Come along! Why don't you keep up?'

There was no answer. Fear took him, and he ran back past the stones shouting wildly: 'Sam! Sam! Merry! Pippin!' The pony bolted into the mist and vanished. From some way off, or so it seemed, he thought he heard a cry: 'Hoy! Frodo! Hoy!' It was away eastward, on his left as he stood under the great stones, staring and straining into the gloom. He plunged off in the direction of the call, and found himself going steeply uphill.

As he struggled on he called again, and kept on calling more and more frantically; but he heard no answer for some time, and then it seemed faint and far ahead and high above him. 'Frodo! Hoy!' came the thin voices out of the mist: and then a cry that sounded like *help, help!* often repeated, ending with a last *help!* that trailed off into a long wail suddenly short. He stumbled forward with all the speed he could towards the cries; but the light was now gone, and clinging night had closed about him, so that it was impossible to be sure of any direction. He seemed all the time to be climbing up and up.

Only the change in the level of the ground at his feet told him when he at last came to the top of a ridge or hill. He was weary, sweating and yet chilled. It was wholly dark.

'Where are you?' he cried out miserably.

There was no reply. He stood listening. He was suddenly aware that it was getting very cold, and that up here a wind was beginning to blow, an icy wind. A change was coming in the weather. The mist was flowing past him now in shreds and tatters. His breath was smoking, and the darkness was less near and thick. He looked up and saw with surprise that faint stars were appearing overhead amid the strands of hurrying cloud and fog. The wind began to hiss over the grass.

He imagined suddenly that he caught a muffled cry, and he made towards it; and even as he went forward the mist was rolled up and thrust aside, and the starry sky was unveiled. A glance showed him that he was now facing southwards and was on a round hill-top, which he must have climbed from the north. Out of the east the biting wind was blowing. To his right there loomed against the westward stars a dark black shape. A great barrow stood there.

'Where are you?' he cried again, both angry and afraid.

'Here!' said a voice, deep and cold, that seemed to come out of the ground. 'I am waiting for you!'

'No!' said Frodo; but he did not run away. His knees gave, and he fell on the ground. Nothing happened, and there was no sound. Trembling he looked up, in time to see a tall dark figure like a shadow against the stars. It leaned over him. He thought there were two eyes, very cold though lit with a pale light that seemed to come from some remote distance. Then a grip stronger and colder than iron seized him. The icy touch froze his bones, and he remembered no more.

*   *   *

When he came to himself again, for a moment he could recall nothing except a sense of dread. Then suddenly he knew that he was imprisoned, caught hopelessly; he was in a barrow. A Barrow-wight had taken him, and he was probably already under the dreadful spells of the Barrow-wights about which whispered tales spoke. He dared not move, but lay as he found himself: flat on his back upon a cold stone with his hands on his breast.

But though his fear was so great that it seemed to be part of the very darkness that was round him, he found himself as he lay thinking about Bilbo Baggins and his stories, of their jogging along together in the lanes of the Shire and talking about roads and adventures. There is a seed of courage hidden (often deeply, it is true) in the heart of the fattest and most timid hobbit, waiting for some final and desperate danger to make it grow. Frodo was neither very fat nor very timid; indeed, though he did not know it, Bilbo (and Gandalf) had thought him the best hobbit in the Shire. He thought he had come to the end of his adventure, and a terrible end, but the thought hardened him. He found himself stiffening, as if for a final spring; he no longer felt limp like a helpless prey.

As he lay there, thinking and getting a hold of himself, he noticed all at once that the darkness was slowly giving way: a pale greenish light was growing round him. It did not at first show him what kind of a place he was in, for the light seemed to be coming out of himself, and from the floor beside him, and had not yet reached the roof or wall. He turned, and there in the cold glow he saw lying beside him Sam, Pippin, and Merry. They were on their backs, and their faces looked deathly pale; and they were clad in white. About them lay many treasures, of gold maybe, though in that light they looked cold and unlovely. On their heads were circlets, gold chains were about their waists, and on their fingers were many rings. Swords lay by their sides, and shields were at their feet. But across their three necks lay one long naked sword.

Suddenly a song began: a cold murmur, rising and falling. The voice seemed far away and immeasurably dreary, sometimes high in the air and thin, sometimes like a low moan from the ground. Out of the formless stream of sad but horrible sounds, strings of words would now and again shape themselves: grim, hard, cold words, heartless and miserable. The night was railing against the morning of which it was bereaved, and the cold was cursing the warmth for which it hungered. Frodo was chilled to the marrow. After a while the song became clearer, and with dread in his heart he perceived that it had changed into an incantation:

> *Cold be hand and heart and bone,*
> *and cold be sleep under stone:*
> *never more to wake on stony bed,*
> *never, till the Sun fails and the Moon is dead.*
> *In the black wind the stars shall die,*
> *and still on gold here let them lie,*
> *till the dark lord lifts his hand*
> *over dead sea and withered land.*

He heard behind his head a creaking and scraping sound. Raising himself on one arm he looked, and saw now in the pale light that they were in a kind of passage which behind them turned a corner. Round the corner a long arm was groping, walking on its fingers towards Sam, who was lying nearest, and towards the hilt of the sword that lay upon him.

At first Frodo felt as if he had indeed been turned into stone by the incantation. Then a wild thought of escape came to him. He wondered if he put on the Ring, whether the Barrow-wight would miss him, and he might find some way out. He thought of himself running free over the grass, grieving for Merry, and Sam, and Pippin, but free and alive himself. Gandalf would admit that there had been nothing else he could do.

But the courage that had been awakened in him was now

too strong: he could not leave his friends so easily. He wavered, groping in his pocket, and then fought with himself again; and as he did so the arm crept nearer. Suddenly resolve hardened in him, and he seized a short sword that lay beside him, and kneeling he stooped low over the bodies of his companions. With what strength he had he hewed at the crawling arm near the wrist, and the hand broke off; but at the same moment the sword splintered up to the hilt. There was a shriek and the light vanished. In the dark there was a snarling noise.

Frodo fell forward over Merry, and Merry's face felt cold. All at once back into his mind, from which it had disappeared with the first coming of the fog, came the memory of the house down under the Hill, and of Tom singing. He remembered the rhyme that Tom had taught them. In a small desperate voice he began: *Ho! Tom Bombadil!* and with that name his voice seemed to grow strong: it had a full and lively sound, and the dark chamber echoed as if to drum and trumpet.

> *Ho! Tom Bombadil, Tom Bombadillo!*
> *By water, wood and hill, by the reed and willow,*
> *By fire, sun and moon, harken now and hear us!*
> *Come, Tom Bombadil, for our need is near us!*

There was a sudden deep silence, in which Frodo could hear his heart beating. After a long slow moment he heard plain, but far away, as if it was coming down through the ground or through thick walls, an answering voice singing:

> *Old Tom Bombadil is a merry fellow,*
> *Bright blue his jacket is, and his boots are yellow.*
> *None has ever caught him yet, for Tom, he is the master:*
> *His songs are stronger songs, and his feet are faster.*

There was a loud rumbling sound, as of stones rolling and falling, and suddenly light streamed in, real light, the plain

light of day. A low door-like opening appeared at the end of
the chamber beyond Frodo's feet; and there was Tom's head
(hat, feather, and all) framed against the light of the sun
rising red behind him. The light fell upon the floor, and upon
the faces of the three hobbits lying beside Frodo. They did
not stir, but the sickly hue had left them. They looked now
as if they were only very deeply asleep.

Tom stooped, removed his hat, and came into the dark
chamber, singing:

> Get out, you old Wight! Vanish in the sunlight!
> Shrivel like the cold mist, like the winds go wailing,
> Out into the barren lands far beyond the mountains!
> Come never here again! Leave your barrow empty!
> Lost and forgotten be, darker than the darkness,
> Where gates stand for ever shut, till the world is mended.

At these words there was a cry and part of the inner end
of the chamber fell in with a crash. Then there was a long
trailing shriek, fading away into an unguessable distance; and
after that silence.

'Come, friend Frodo!' said Tom. 'Let us get out on to
clean grass! You must help me bear them.'

Together they carried out Merry, Pippin, and Sam. As
Frodo left the barrow for the last time he thought he saw a
severed hand wriggling still, like a wounded spider, in a heap
of fallen earth. Tom went back in again, and there was a
sound of much thumping and stamping. When he came out
he was bearing in his arms a great load of treasure: things of
gold, silver, copper, and bronze; many beads and chains and
jewelled ornaments. He climbed the green barrow and laid
them all on top in the sunshine.

There he stood, with his hat in his hand and the wind in
his hair, and looked down upon the three hobbits, that had
been laid on their backs upon the grass at the west side of
the mound. Raising his right hand he said in a clear and
commanding voice:

Wake now my merry lads! Wake and hear me calling!
Warm now be heart and limb! The cold stone is fallen;
Dark door is standing wide; dead hand is broken.
Night under Night is flown, and the Gate is open!

To Frodo's great joy the hobbits stirred, stretched their arms, rubbed their eyes, and then suddenly sprang up. They looked about in amazement, first at Frodo, and then at Tom standing large as life on the barrow-top above them; and then at themselves in their thin white rags, crowned and belted with pale gold, and jingling with trinkets.

'What in the name of wonder?' began Merry, feeling the golden circlet that had slipped over one eye. Then he stopped, and a shadow came over his face, and he closed his eyes. 'Of course, I remember!' he said. 'The men of Carn Dûm came on us at night, and we were worsted. Ah! the spear in my heart!' He clutched at his breast. 'No! No!' he said, opening his eyes. 'What am I saying? I have been dreaming. Where did you get to, Frodo?'

'I thought that I was lost,' said Frodo; 'but I don't want to speak of it. Let us think of what we are to do now! Let us go on!'

'Dressed up like this, sir?' said Sam. 'Where are my clothes?' He flung his circlet, belt, and rings on the grass, and looked round helplessly, as if he expected to find his cloak, jacket, and breeches, and other hobbit-garments lying somewhere to hand.

'You won't find your clothes again,' said Tom, bounding down from the mound, and laughing as he danced round them in the sunlight. One would have thought that nothing dangerous or dreadful had happened; and indeed the horror faded out of their hearts as they looked at him, and saw the merry glint in his eyes.

'What do you mean?' asked Pippin, looking at him, half puzzled and half amused. 'Why not?'

But Tom shook his head, saying: 'You've found yourselves again, out of the deep water. Clothes are but little loss, if you escape from drowning. Be glad, my merry friends, and let the warm sunlight heat now heart and limb! Cast off these cold rags! Run naked on the grass, while Tom goes a-hunting!'

He sprang away down hill, whistling and calling. Looking down after him Frodo saw him running away southwards along the green hollow between their hill and the next, still whistling and crying:

> *Hey! now! Come hoy now! Whither do you wander?*
> *Up, down, near or far, here, there or yonder?*
> *Sharp-ears, Wise-nose, Swish-tail and Bumpkin,*
> *White-socks my little lad, and old Fatty Lumpkin!*

So he sang, running fast, tossing up his hat and catching it, until he was hidden by a fold of the ground: but for some time his *hey now! hoy now!* came floating back down the wind, which had shifted round towards the south.

The air was growing very warm again. The hobbits ran about for a while on the grass, as he told them. Then they lay basking in the sun with the delight of those that have been wafted suddenly from bitter winter to a friendly clime, or of people that, after being long ill and bedridden, wake one day to find that they are unexpectedly well and the day is again full of promise.

By the time that Tom returned they were feeling strong (and hungry). He reappeared, hat first, over the brow of the hill, and behind him came in an obedient line *six* ponies: their own five and one more. The last was plainly old Fatty Lumpkin: he was larger, stronger, fatter (and older) than their own ponies. Merry, to whom the others belonged, had not, in fact, given them any such names, but they answered to the new names that Tom had given them for the rest of their lives. Tom called them one by one and they climbed over the brow and stood in a line. Then Tom bowed to the hobbits.

'Here are your ponies, now!' he said. 'They've more sense (in some ways) than you wandering hobbits have – more sense in their noses. For they sniff danger ahead which you walk right into; and if they run to save themselves, then they run the right way. You must forgive them all; for though their hearts are faithful, to face fear of Barrow-wights is not what they were made for. See, here they come again, bringing all their burdens!'

Merry, Sam, and Pippin now clothed themselves in spare garments from their packs; and they soon felt too hot, for they were obliged to put on some of the thicker and warmer things that they had brought against the oncoming of winter.

'Where does that other old animal, that Fatty Lumpkin, come from?' asked Frodo.

'He's mine,' said Tom. 'My four-legged friend; though I seldom ride him, and he wanders often far, free upon the hillsides. When your ponies stayed with me, they got to know my Lumpkin; and they smelt him in the night, and quickly ran to meet him. I thought he'd look for them and with his words of wisdom take all their fear away. But now, my jolly Lumpkin, old Tom's going to ride. Hey! he's coming with you, just to set you on the road; so he needs a pony. For you cannot easily talk to hobbits that are riding, when you're on your own legs trying to trot beside them.'

The hobbits were delighted to hear this, and thanked Tom many times; but he laughed, and said that they were so good at losing themselves that he would not feel happy till he had seen them safe over the borders of his land. 'I've got things to do,' he said: 'my making and my singing, my talking and my walking, and my watching of the country. Tom can't be always near to open doors and willow-cracks. Tom has his house to mind, and Goldberry is waiting.'

It was still fairly early by the sun, something between nine and ten, and the hobbits turned their minds to food. Their last meal had been lunch beside the standing stone the day before. They breakfasted now off the remainder of Tom's

provisions, meant for their supper, with additions that Tom
had brought with him. It was not a large meal (considering
hobbits and the circumstances), but they felt much better for
it. While they were eating Tom went up to the mound, and
looked through the treasures. Most of these he made into a
pile that glistened and sparkled on the grass. He bade them
lie there 'free to all finders, birds, beasts, Elves or Men, and
all kindly creatures'; for so the spell of the mound should be
broken and scattered and no Wight ever come back to it. He
chose for himself from the pile a brooch set with blue stones,
many-shaded like flax-flowers or the wings of blue butterflies.
He looked long at it, as if stirred by some memory, shaking
his head, and saying at last:

'Here is a pretty toy for Tom and for his lady! Fair was
she who long ago wore this on her shoulder. Goldberry shall
wear it now, and we will not forget her!'

For each of the hobbits he chose a dagger, long, leaf-
shaped, and keen, of marvellous workmanship, damasked
with serpent-forms in red and gold. They gleamed as he
drew them from their black sheaths, wrought of some strange
metal, light and strong, and set with many fiery stones.
Whether by some virtue in these sheaths or because of the
spell that lay on the mound, the blades seemed untouched
by time, unrusted, sharp, glittering in the sun.

'Old knives are long enough as swords for hobbit-people,'
he said. 'Sharp blades are good to have, if Shire-folk go
walking, east, south, or far away into dark and danger.' Then
he told them that these blades were forged many long years
ago by Men of Westernesse: they were foes of the Dark Lord,
but they were overcome by the evil king of Carn Dûm in the
Land of Angmar.

'Few now remember them,' Tom murmured, 'yet still
some go wandering, sons of forgotten kings walking in loneliness, guarding from evil things folk that are heedless.'

The hobbits did not understand his words, but as he spoke
they had a vision as it were of a great expanse of years behind
them, like a vast shadowy plain over which there strode

shapes of Men, tall and grim with bright swords, and last
came one with a star on his brow. Then the vision faded,
and they were back in the sunlit world. It was time to start
again. They made ready, packing their bags and lading their
ponies. Their new weapons they hung on their leather belts
under their jackets, feeling them very awkward, and wondering if they would be of any use. Fighting had not before
occurred to any of them as one of the adventures in which
their flight would land them.

At last they set off. They led their ponies down the hill;
and then mounting they trotted quickly along the valley. They
looked back and saw the top of the old mound on the hill,
and from it the sunlight on the gold went up like a yellow
flame. Then they turned a shoulder of the Downs and it was
hidden from view.

Though Frodo looked about him on every side he saw no
sign of the great stones standing like a gate, and before long
they came to the northern gap and rode swiftly through, and
the land fell away before them. It was a merry journey with
Tom Bombadil trotting gaily beside them, or before them,
on Fatty Lumpkin, who could move much faster than his
girth promised. Tom sang most of the time, but it was chiefly
nonsense, or else perhaps a strange language unknown to the
hobbits, an ancient language whose words were mainly those
of wonder and delight.

They went forward steadily, but they soon saw that the
Road was further away than they had imagined. Even without
a fog, their sleep at mid-day would have prevented them
from reaching it until after nightfall on the day before. The
dark line they had seen was not a line of trees but a line of
bushes growing on the edge of a deep dike with a steep wall
on the further side. Tom said that it had once been the
boundary of a kingdom, but a very long time ago. He seemed
to remember something sad about it, and would not say
much.

They climbed down and out of the dike and through a

gap in the wall, and then Tom turned due north, for they
had been bearing somewhat to the west. The land was now
open and fairly level, and they quickened their pace, but the
sun was already sinking low when at last they saw a line of
tall trees ahead, and they knew that they had come back to
the Road after many unexpected adventures. They galloped
their ponies over the last furlongs, and halted under the long
shadows of the trees. They were on the top of a sloping bank,
and the Road, now dim as evening drew on, wound away
below them. At this point it ran nearly from South-west to
North-east, and on their right it fell quickly down into a wide
hollow. It was rutted and bore many signs of the recent heavy
rain; there were pools and pot-holes full of water.

They rode down the bank and looked up and down. There
was nothing to be seen. 'Well, here we are again at last!' said
Frodo. 'I suppose we haven't lost more than two days by my
short cut through the Forest! But perhaps the delay will prove
useful – it may have put them off our trail.'

The others looked at him. The shadow of the fear of the
Black Riders came suddenly over them again. Ever since they
had entered the Forest they had thought chiefly of getting
back to the Road; only now when it lay beneath their feet
did they remember the danger which pursued them, and was
more than likely to be lying in wait for them upon the Road
itself. They looked anxiously back towards the setting sun,
but the Road was brown and empty.

'Do you think,' asked Pippin hesitatingly, 'do you think
we may be pursued, tonight?'

'No, I hope not tonight,' answered Tom Bombadil; 'nor
perhaps the next day. But do not trust my guess; for I cannot
tell for certain. Out east my knowledge fails. Tom is not
master of Riders from the Black Land far beyond his
country.'

All the same the hobbits wished he was coming with them.
They felt that he would know how to deal with Black Riders,
if anyone did. They would soon now be going forward into
lands wholly strange to them, and beyond all but the most

vague and distant legends of the Shire, and in the gathering twilight they longed for home. A deep loneliness and sense of loss was on them. They stood silent, reluctant to make the final parting, and only slowly became aware that Tom was wishing them farewell, and telling them to have good heart and to ride on till dark without halting.

'Tom will give you good advice, till this day is over (after that your own luck must go with you and guide you): four miles along the Road you'll come upon a village, Bree under Bree-hill, with doors looking westward. There you'll find an old inn that is called *The Prancing Pony*. Barliman Butterbur is the worthy keeper. There you can stay the night, and afterwards the morning will speed you upon your way. Be bold, but wary! Keep up your merry hearts, and ride to meet your fortune!'

They begged him to come at least as far as the inn and drink once more with them; but he laughed and refused, saying:

> *Tom's country ends here: he will not pass the borders.*
> *Tom has his house to mind, and Goldberry is waiting!*

Then he turned, tossed up his hat, leaped on Lumpkin's back, and rode up over the bank and away singing into the dusk.

The hobbits climbed up and watched him until he was out of sight.

'I am sorry to take leave of Master Bombadil,' said Sam. 'He's a caution and no mistake. I reckon we may go a good deal further and see naught better, nor queerer. But I won't deny I'll be glad to see this *Prancing Pony* he spoke of. I hope it'll be like *The Green Dragon* away back home! What sort of folk are they in Bree?'

'There are hobbits in Bree,' said Merry, 'as well as Big Folk. I daresay it will be homelike enough. *The Pony* is a good inn by all accounts. My people ride out there now and again.'

'It may be all we could wish,' said Frodo; 'but it is outside the Shire all the same. Don't make yourselves too much at home! Please remember – all of you – that the name of Baggins must NOT be mentioned. I am Mr. Underhill, if any name must be given.'

They now mounted their ponies and rode off silently into the evening. Darkness came down quickly, as they plodded slowly downhill and up again, until at last they saw lights twinkling some distance ahead.

Before them rose Bree-hill barring the way, a dark mass against misty stars; and under its western flank nestled a large village. Towards it they now hurried desiring only to find a fire, and a door between them and the night.

CHAPTER IX

AT THE SIGN OF THE PRANCING PONY

Bree was the chief village of the Bree-land, a small inhabited region, like an island in the empty lands round about. Besides Bree itself, there was Staddle on the other side of the hill, Combe in a deep valley a little further eastward, and Archet on the edge of the Chetwood. Lying round Bree-hill and the villages was a small country of fields and tamed woodland only a few miles broad.

The Men of Bree were brown-haired, broad, and rather short, cheerful and independent: they belonged to nobody but themselves; but they were more friendly and familiar with Hobbits, Dwarves, Elves, and other inhabitants of the world about them than was (or is) usual with Big People. According to their own tales they were the original inhabitants and were the descendants of the first Men that ever wandered into the West of the middle-world. Few had survived the turmoils of the Elder Days; but when the Kings returned again over the Great Sea they had found the Bree-men still there, and they were still there now, when the memory of the old Kings had faded into the grass.

In those days no other Men had settled dwellings so far west, or within a hundred leagues of the Shire. But in the wild lands beyond Bree there were mysterious wanderers. The Bree-folk called them Rangers, and knew nothing of their origin. They were taller and darker than the Men of Bree and were believed to have strange powers of sight and hearing, and to understand the languages of beasts and birds. They roamed at will southwards, and eastwards even as far as the Misty Mountains; but they were now few and rarely seen. When they appeared they brought news from afar, and

told strange forgotten tales which were eagerly listened to;
but the Bree-folk did not make friends of them.

There were also many families of hobbits in the Bree-land
and *they* claimed to be the oldest settlement of Hobbits in
the world, one that was founded long before even the Brandywine was crossed and the Shire colonized. They lived mostly
in Staddle though there were some in Bree itself, especially
on the higher slopes of the hill, above the houses of the Men.
The Big Folk and the Little Folk (as they called one another)
were on friendly terms, minding their own affairs in their
own ways, but both rightly regarding themselves as necessary
parts of the Bree-folk. Nowhere else in the world was this
peculiar (but excellent) arrangement to be found.

The Bree-folk, Big and Little, did not themselves travel
much; and the affairs of the four villages were their chief
concern. Occasionally the Hobbits of Bree went as far as
Buckland, or the Eastfarthing; but though their little land was
not much further than a day's riding east of the Brandywine
Bridge, the Hobbits of the Shire now seldom visited it. An
occasional Bucklander or adventurous Took would come out
to the Inn for a night or two, but even that was becoming
less and less usual. The Shire-hobbits referred to those of
Bree, and to any others that lived beyond the borders, as
Outsiders, and took very little interest in them, considering
them dull and uncouth. There were probably many more
Outsiders scattered about in the West of the World in those
days than the people of the Shire imagined. Some, doubtless,
were no better than tramps, ready to dig a hole in any bank
and stay only as long as it suited them. But in the Bree-
land, at any rate, the hobbits were decent and prosperous,
and no more rustic than most of their distant relatives
Inside. It was not yet forgotten that there had been a time
when there was much coming and going between the Shire
and Bree. There was Bree-blood in the Brandybucks by all
accounts.

*   *   *

The village of Bree had some hundred stone houses of the Big Folk, mostly above the Road, nestling on the hillside with windows looking west. On that side, running in more than half a circle from the hill and back to it, there was a deep dike with a thick hedge on the inner side. Over this the Road crossed by a causeway; but where it pierced the hedge it was barred by a great gate. There was another gate in the southern corner where the Road ran out of the village. The gates were closed at nightfall; but just inside them were small lodges for the gatekeepers.

Down on the Road, where it swept to the right to go round the foot of the hill, there was a large inn. It had been built long ago when the traffic on the roads had been far greater. For Bree stood at an old meeting of ways; another ancient road crossed the East Road just outside the dike at the western end of the village, and in former days Men and other folk of various sorts had travelled much on it. *Strange as News from Bree* was still a saying in the Eastfarthing, descending from those days, when news from North, South, and East could be heard in the inn, and when the Shire-hobbits used to go more often to hear it. But the Northern Lands had long been desolate, and the North Road was now seldom used: it was grass-grown, and the Bree-folk called it the Greenway.

The Inn of Bree was still there, however, and the innkeeper was an important person. His house was a meeting place for the idle, talkative, and inquisitive among the inhabitants, large and small, of the four villages; and a resort of Rangers and other wanderers, and for such travellers (mostly dwarves) as still journeyed on the East Road, to and from the Mountains.

It was dark, and white stars were shining, when Frodo and his companions came at last to the Greenway-crossing and drew near the village. They came to the West-gate and found it shut, but at the door of the lodge beyond it, there was a man sitting. He jumped up and fetched a lantern and looked over the gate at them in surprise.

'What do you want, and where do you come from?' he asked gruffly.

'We are making for the inn here,' answered Frodo. 'We are journeying east and cannot go further tonight.'

'Hobbits! Four hobbits! And what's more, out of the Shire by their talk,' said the gatekeeper, softly as if speaking to himself. He stared at them darkly for a moment, and then slowly opened the gate and let them ride through.

'We don't often see Shire-folk riding on the Road at night,' he went on, as they halted a moment by his door. 'You'll pardon my wondering what business takes you away east of Bree! What may your names be, might I ask?'

'Our names and our business are our own, and this does not seem a good place to discuss them,' said Frodo, not liking the look of the man or the tone of his voice.

'Your business is your own, no doubt,' said the man; 'but it's my business to ask questions after nightfall.'

'We are hobbits from Buckland, and we have a fancy to travel and to stay at the inn here,' put in Merry. 'I am Mr. Brandybuck. Is that enough for you? The Bree-folk used to be fair-spoken to travellers, or so I had heard.'

'All right, all right!' said the man. 'I meant no offence. But you'll find maybe that more folk than old Harry at the gate will be asking you questions. There's queer folk about. If you go on to *The Pony*, you'll find you're not the only guests.'

He wished them good night, and they said no more; but Frodo could see in the lantern-light that the man was still eyeing them curiously. He was glad to hear the gate clang to behind them, as they rode forward. He wondered why the man was so suspicious, and whether any one had been asking for news of a party of hobbits. Could it have been Gandalf? He might have arrived, while they were delayed in the Forest and the Downs. But there was something in the look and the voice of the gatekeeper that made him uneasy.

The man stared after the hobbits for a moment, and then he went back to his house. As soon as his back was turned, a dark figure climbed quickly in over the gate and melted into the shadows of the village street.

*   *   *

The hobbits rode on up a gentle slope, passing a few detached houses, and drew up outside the inn. The houses looked large and strange to them. Sam stared up at the inn with its three storeys and many windows, and felt his heart sink. He had imagined himself meeting giants taller than trees, and other creatures even more terrifying, some time or other in the course of his journey; but at the moment he was finding his first sight of Men and their tall houses quite enough, indeed too much for the dark end of a tiring day. He pictured black horses standing all saddled in the shadows of the inn-yard, and Black Riders peering out of dark upper windows.

'We surely aren't going to stay here for the night, are we, sir?' he exclaimed. 'If there are hobbit-folk in these parts, why don't we look for some that would be willing to take us in? It would be more homelike.'

'What's wrong with the inn?' said Frodo. 'Tom Bombadil recommended it. I expect it's homelike enough inside.'

Even from the outside the inn looked a pleasant house to familiar eyes. It had a front on the Road, and two wings running back on land partly cut out of the lower slopes of the hill, so that at the rear the second-floor windows were level with the ground. There was a wide arch leading to a courtyard between the two wings, and on the left under the arch there was a large doorway reached by a few broad steps. The door was open and light streamed out of it. Above the arch there was a lamp, and beneath it swung a large sign-board: a fat white pony reared up on its hind legs. Over the door was painted in white letters: THE PRANCING PONY by BARLIMAN BUTTERBUR. Many of the lower windows showed lights behind thick curtains.

As they hesitated outside in the gloom, someone began singing a merry song inside, and many cheerful voices joined loudly in the chorus. They listened to this encouraging sound for a moment and then got off their ponies. The song ended and there was a burst of laughter and clapping.

They led their ponies under the arch, and leaving them

standing in the yard they climbed up the steps. Frodo went forward and nearly bumped into a short fat man with a bald head and a red face. He had a white apron on, and was bustling out of one door and in through another, carrying a tray laden with full mugs.

'Can we——' began Frodo.

'Half a minute, if you please!' shouted the man over his shoulder, and vanished into a babel of voices and a cloud of smoke. In a moment he was out again, wiping his hands on his apron.

'Good evening, little master!' he said, bending down. 'What may you be wanting?'

'Beds for four, and stabling for five ponies, if that can be managed. Are you Mr. Butterbur?'

'That's right! Barliman is my name. Barliman Butterbur at your service! You're from the Shire, eh?' he said, and then suddenly he clapped his hand to his forehead, as if trying to remember something. 'Hobbits!' he cried. 'Now what does that remind me of? Might I ask your names, sir?'

'Mr. Took and Mr. Brandybuck,' said Frodo; 'and this is Sam Gamgee. My name is Underhill.'

'There now!' said Mr. Butterbur, snapping his fingers. 'It's gone again! But it'll come back, when I have time to think. I'm run off my feet; but I'll see what I can do for you. We don't often get a party out of the Shire nowadays, and I should be sorry not to make you welcome. But there is such a crowd already in the house tonight as there hasn't been for long enough. It never rains but it pours, we say in Bree.

'Hi! Nob!' he shouted. 'Where are you, you woolly-footed slowcoach? Nob!'

'Coming, sir! Coming!' A cheery-looking hobbit bobbed out of a door, and seeing the travellers, stopped short and stared at them with great interest.

'Where's Bob?' asked the landlord. 'You don't know? Well find him! Double sharp! I haven't got six legs, nor six eyes neither! Tell Bob there's five ponies that have to be stabled.

He must find room somehow.' Nob trotted off with a grin and a wink.

'Well, now, what was I going to say?' said Mr. Butterbur, tapping his forehead. 'One thing drives out another, so to speak. I'm that busy tonight, my head is going round. There's a party that came up the Greenway from down South last night – and that was strange enough to begin with. Then there's a travelling company of dwarves going West come in this evening. And now there's you. If you weren't hobbits, I doubt if we could house you. But we've got a room or two in the north wing that were made special for hobbits, when this place was built. On the ground floor as they usually prefer; round windows and all as they like it. I hope you'll be comfortable. You'll be wanting supper, I don't doubt. As soon as may be. This way now!'

He led them a short way down a passage, and opened a door. 'Here is a nice little parlour!' he said. 'I hope it will suit. Excuse me now. I'm that busy. No time for talking. I must be trotting. It's hard work for two legs, but I don't get thinner. I'll look in again later. If you want anything, ring the hand-bell, and Nob will come. If he don't come, ring and shout!'

Off he went at last, and left them feeling rather breathless. He seemed capable of an endless stream of talk, however busy he might be. They found themselves in a small and cosy room. There was a bit of bright fire burning on the hearth, and in front of it were some low and comfortable chairs. There was a round table, already spread with a white cloth, and on it was a large hand-bell. But Nob, the hobbit servant, came bustling in long before they thought of ringing. He brought candles and a tray full of plates.

'Will you be wanting anything to drink, masters?' he asked. 'And shall I show you the bedrooms, while your supper is got ready?'

They were washed and in the middle of good deep mugs of beer when Mr. Butterbur and Nob came in again. In a twinkling the table was laid. There was hot soup, cold meats,

a blackberry tart, new loaves, slabs of butter, and half a ripe
cheese: good plain food, as good as the Shire could show,
and homelike enough to dispel the last of Sam's misgivings
(already much relieved by the excellence of the beer).

The landlord hovered round for a little, and then prepared
to leave them. 'I don't know whether you would care to join
the company, when you have supped,' he said, standing at
the door. 'Perhaps you would rather go to your beds. Still
the company would be very pleased to welcome you, if you
had a mind. We don't get Outsiders – travellers from the
Shire, I should say, begging your pardon – often; and we like
to hear a bit of news, or any story or song you may have in
mind. But as you please! Ring the bell, if you lack anything!'

So refreshed and encouraged did they feel at the end of
their supper (about three quarters of an hour's steady going,
not hindered by unnecessary talk) that Frodo, Pippin, and
Sam decided to join the company. Merry said it would be
too stuffy. 'I shall sit here quietly by the fire for a bit, and
perhaps go out later for a sniff of the air. Mind your Ps and
Qs, and don't forget that you are supposed to be escaping
in secret, and are still on the high-road and not very far from
the Shire!'

'All right!' said Pippin. 'Mind yourself! Don't get lost, and
don't forget that it is safer indoors!'

The company was in the big common-room of the inn.
The gathering was large and mixed, as Frodo discovered,
when his eyes got used to the light. This came chiefly from
a blazing log-fire, for the three lamps hanging from the beams
were dim, and half veiled in smoke. Barliman Butterbur was
standing near the fire, talking to a couple of dwarves and one
or two strange-looking men. On the benches were various
folk: men of Bree, a collection of local hobbits (sitting
chattering together), a few more dwarves, and other vague
figures difficult to make out away in the shadows and corners.

As soon as the Shire-hobbits entered, there was a chorus
of welcome from the Bree-landers. The strangers, especially

those that had come up the Greenway, stared at them curiously. The landlord introduced the newcomers to the Bree-folk, so quickly that, though they caught many names, they were seldom sure who the names belonged to. The Men of Bree seemed all to have rather botanical (and to the Shire-folk rather odd) names, like Rushlight, Goatleaf, Heathertoes, Appledore, Thistlewool and Ferny (not to mention Butterbur). Some of the hobbits had similar names. The Mugworts, for instance, seemed numerous. But most of them had natural names, such as Banks, Brockhouse, Longholes, Sandheaver, and Tunnelly, many of which were used in the Shire. There were several Underhills from Staddle, and as they could not imagine sharing a name without being related, they took Frodo to their hearts as a long-lost cousin.

The Bree-hobbits were, in fact, friendly and inquisitive, and Frodo soon found that some explanation of what he was doing would have to be given. He gave out that he was interested in history and geography (at which there was much wagging of heads, although neither of these words were much used in the Bree-dialect). He said he was thinking of writing a book (at which there was silent astonishment), and that he and his friends wanted to collect information about hobbits living outside the Shire, especially in the eastern lands.

At this a chorus of voices broke out. If Frodo had really wanted to write a book, and had had many ears, he would have learned enough for several chapters in a few minutes. And if that was not enough, he was given a whole list of names, beginning with 'Old Barliman here', to whom he could go for further information. But after a time, as Frodo did not show any sign of writing a book on the spot, the hobbits returned to their questions about doings in the Shire. Frodo did not prove very communicative, and he soon found himself sitting alone in a corner, listening and looking around.

The Men and Dwarves were mostly talking of distant events and telling news of a kind that was becoming only too familiar. There was trouble away in the South, and it seemed that the Men who had come up the Greenway were on the move, looking for lands where they could find some peace. The Bree-folk were sympathetic, but plainly not very ready to take a large number of strangers into their little land. One of the travellers, a squint-eyed ill-favoured fellow, was fore-telling that more and more people would be coming north in the near future. 'If room isn't found for them, they'll find it for themselves. They've a right to live, same as other folk,' he said loudly. The local inhabitants did not look pleased at the prospect.

The hobbits did not pay much attention to all this, and it did not at the moment seem to concern hobbits. Big Folk could hardly beg for lodgings in hobbit-holes. They were more interested in Sam and Pippin, who were now feeling quite at home, and were chatting gaily about events in the Shire. Pippin roused a good deal of laughter with an account of the collapse of the roof of the Town Hole in Michel Delv-ing: Will Whitfoot, the Mayor, and the fattest hobbit in the Westfarthing, had been buried in chalk, and came out like a floured dumpling. But there were several questions asked that made Frodo a little uneasy. One of the Bree-landers, who seemed to have been in the Shire several times, wanted to know where the Underhills lived and who they were related to.

Suddenly Frodo noticed that a strange-looking weather-beaten man, sitting in the shadows near the wall, was also listening intently to the hobbit-talk. He had a tall tankard in front of him, and was smoking a long-stemmed pipe curiously carved. His legs were stretched out before him, showing high boots of supple leather that fitted him well, but had seen much wear and were now caked with mud. A travel-stained cloak of heavy dark-green cloth was drawn close about him, and in spite of the heat of the room he wore a hood that overshadowed his face; but the gleam of his eyes could be seen as he watched the hobbits.

'Who is that?' Frodo asked, when he got a chance to whis-per to Mr. Butterbur. 'I don't think you introduced him?'

'Him?' said the landlord in an answering whisper, cocking an eye without turning his head. 'I don't rightly know. He is one of the wandering folk – Rangers we call them. He seldom talks: not but what he can tell a rare tale when he has the mind. He disappears for a month, or a year, and then he pops up again. He was in and out pretty often last spring; but I haven't seen him about lately. What his right name is I've never heard: but he's known round here as Strider. Goes about at a great pace on his long shanks; though he don't tell nobody what cause he has to hurry. But there's no accounting for East and West, as we say in Bree, meaning the Rangers and the Shire-folk, begging your pardon. Funny you should ask about him.' But at that moment Mr. Butterbur was called away by a demand for more ale and his last remark remained unexplained.

Frodo found that Strider was now looking at him, as if he had heard or guessed all that had been said. Presently, with a wave of his hand and a nod, he invited Frodo to come over and sit by him. As Frodo drew near he threw back his hood, showing a shaggy head of dark hair flecked with grey, and in a pale stern face a pair of keen grey eyes.

'I am called Strider,' he said in a low voice. 'I am very pleased to meet you, Master – Underhill, if old Butterbur got your name right.'

'He did,' said Frodo stiffly. He felt far from comfortable under the stare of those keen eyes.

'Well, Master Underhill,' said Strider, 'if I were you, I should stop your young friends from talking too much. Drink, fire, and chance-meeting are pleasant enough, but, well – this isn't the Shire. There are queer folk about. Though I say it as shouldn't, you may think,' he added with a wry smile, seeing Frodo's glance. 'And there have been even stranger travellers through Bree lately,' he went on, watching Frodo's face.

Frodo returned his gaze but said nothing; and Strider made no further sign. His attention seemed suddenly to be fixed on Pippin. To his alarm Frodo became aware that the ridiculous young Took, encouraged by his success with the fat Mayor of Michel Delving, was now actually giving a comic account of Bilbo's farewell party. He was already giving an imitation of the Speech, and was drawing near to the astonishing Disappearance.

Frodo was annoyed. It was a harmless enough tale for most of the local hobbits, no doubt: just a funny story about those funny people away beyond the River; but some (old Butterbur, for instance) knew a thing or two, and had probably heard rumours long ago about Bilbo's vanishing. It would bring the name of Baggins to their minds, especially if there had been inquiries in Bree after that name.

Frodo fidgeted, wondering what to do. Pippin was evidently much enjoying the attention he was getting, and had become quite forgetful of their danger. Frodo had a sudden fear that in his present mood he might even mention the Ring; and that might well be disastrous.

'You had better do something quick!' whispered Strider in his ear.

Frodo jumped up and stood on a table, and began to talk. The attention of Pippin's audience was disturbed. Some of the hobbits looked at Frodo and laughed and clapped, thinking that Mr. Underhill had taken as much ale as was good for him.

Frodo suddenly felt very foolish, and found himself (as was his habit when making a speech) fingering the things in his pocket. He felt the Ring on its chain, and quite unaccountably the desire came over him to slip it on and vanish out of the silly situation. It seemed to him, somehow, as if the suggestion came to him from outside, from someone or something in the room. He resisted the temptation firmly, and clasped the Ring in his hand, as if to keep a hold on it and prevent it from escaping or doing any mischief. At any rate it gave him no inspiration. He spoke 'a few suitable words', as they would have said in the Shire: *We are all very much gratified by the kindness of your reception, and I venture to hope that my brief visit will help to renew the old ties of friendship between the Shire and Bree;* and then he hesitated and coughed.

Everyone in the room was now looking at him. 'A song!' shouted one of the hobbits. 'A song! A song!' shouted all the others. 'Come on now, master, sing us something that we haven't heard before!'

For a moment Frodo stood gaping. Then in desperation he began a ridiculous song that Bilbo had been rather fond of (and indeed rather proud of, for he had made up the words himself). It was about an inn; and that is probably why it came into Frodo's mind just then. Here it is in full. Only a few words of it are now, as a rule, remembered.

> There is an inn, a merry old inn
>   beneath an old grey hill,
> And there they brew a beer so brown
> That the Man in the Moon himself came down
>   one night to drink his fill.
>
> The ostler has a tipsy cat
>   that plays a five-stringed fiddle;
> And up and down he runs his bow,
> Now squeaking high, now purring low,
>   now sawing in the middle.
>
> The landlord keeps a little dog
>   that is mighty fond of jokes;
> When there's good cheer among the guests,
> He cocks an ear at all the jests
>   and laughs until he chokes.
>
> They also keep a hornéd cow
>   as proud as any queen;
> But music turns her head like ale,
> And makes her wave her tufted tail
>   and dance upon the green.

And O! the rows of silver dishes
    and the store of silver spoons!
For Sunday* there's a special pair,
And these they polish up with care
    on Saturday afternoons.

The Man in the Moon was drinking deep,
    and the cat began to wail;
A dish and a spoon on the table danced,
The cow in the garden madly pranced,
    and the little dog chased his tail.

The Man in the Moon took another mug,
    and then rolled beneath his chair;
And there he dozed and dreamed of ale,
Till in the sky the stars were pale,
    and dawn was in the air.

Then the ostler said to his tipsy cat:
    'The white horses of the Moon,
They neigh and champ their silver bits;
But their master's been and drowned his wits,
    and the Sun'll be rising soon!'

So the cat on his fiddle played hey-diddle-diddle,
    a jig that would wake the dead:
He squeaked and sawed and quickened the tune,
While the landlord shook the Man in the Moon:
    'It's after three!' he said.

They rolled the Man slowly up the hill
    and bundled him into the Moon,
While his horses galloped up in rear,
And the cow came capering like a deer,
    and a dish ran up with the spoon.

* See note 2, VII, p. 110.

Now quicker the fiddle went deedle-dum-diddle;
*   the dog began to roar,*
The cow and the horses stood on their heads;
The guests all bounded from their beds
*   and danced upon the floor.*

With a ping and a pong the fiddle-strings broke!
*   the cow jumped over the Moon,*
And the little dog laughed to see such fun,
And the Saturday dish went off at a run
*   with the silver Sunday spoon.*

The round Moon rolled behind the hill
*   as the Sun raised up her head.*
She* hardly believed her fiery eyes;
For though it was day, to her surprise
*   they all went back to bed!*

There was loud and long applause. Frodo had a good voice, and the song tickled their fancy. 'Where's old Barley?' they cried. 'He ought to hear this. Bob ought to learn his cat the fiddle, and then we'd have a dance.' They called for more ale, and began to shout: 'Let's have it again, master! Come on now! Once more!'

They made Frodo have another drink, and then begin his song again, while many of them joined in; for the tune was well known, and they were quick at picking up words. It was now Frodo's turn to feel pleased with himself. He capered about on the table; and when he came a second time to *the cow jumped over the Moon*, he leaped in the air. Much too vigorously; for he came down, bang, into a tray full of mugs, and slipped, and rolled off the table with a crash, clatter, and bump! The audience all opened their mouths wide for laughter, and stopped short in gaping silence; for the singer

---

* Elves (and Hobbits) always refer to the Sun as She.

disappeared. He simply vanished, as if he had gone slap through the floor without leaving a hole!

The local hobbits stared in amazement, and then sprang to their feet and shouted for Barliman. All the company drew away from Pippin and Sam, who found themselves left alone in a corner, and eyed darkly and doubtfully from a distance. It was plain that many people regarded them now as the companions of a travelling magician of unknown powers and purpose. But there was one swarthy Bree-lander, who stood looking at them with a knowing and half-mocking expression that made them feel very uncomfortable. Presently he slipped out of the door, followed by the squint-eyed southerner: the two had been whispering together a good deal during the evening. Harry the gatekeeper also went out just behind them.

Frodo felt a fool. Not knowing what else to do, he crawled away under the tables to the dark corner by Strider, who sat unmoved, giving no sign of his thoughts. Frodo leaned back against the wall and took off the Ring. How it came to be on his finger he could not tell. He could only suppose that he had been handling it in his pocket while he sang, and that somehow it had slipped on when he stuck out his hand with a jerk to save his fall. For a moment he wondered if the Ring itself had not played him a trick; perhaps it had tried to reveal itself in response to some wish or command that was felt in the room. He did not like the looks of the men that had gone out.

'Well?' said Strider, when he reappeared. 'Why did you do that? Worse than anything your friends could have said! You have put your foot in it! Or should I say your finger?'

'I don't know what you mean,' said Frodo, annoyed and alarmed.

'Oh yes, you do,' answered Strider; 'but we had better wait until the uproar has died down. Then, if you please, Mr. *Baggins*, I should like a quiet word with you.'

'What about?' asked Frodo, ignoring the sudden use of his proper name.

'A matter of some importance – to us both,' answered

Strider, looking Frodo in the eye. 'You may hear something to your advantage.'

'Very well,' said Frodo, trying to appear unconcerned. 'I'll talk to you later.'

Meanwhile an argument was going on by the fireplace. Mr. Butterbur had come trotting in, and he was now trying to listen to several conflicting accounts of the event at the same time.

'I saw him, Mr. Butterbur,' said a hobbit; 'or leastways I didn't see him, if you take my meaning. He just vanished into thin air, in a manner of speaking.'

'You don't say, Mr. Mugwort!' said the landlord, looking puzzled.

'Yes I do!' replied Mugwort. 'And I mean what I say, what's more.'

'There's some mistake somewhere,' said Butterbur, shaking his head. 'There was too much of that Mr. Underhill to go vanishing into thin air; or into thick air, as is more likely in this room.'

'Well, where is he now?' cried several voices.

'How should I know? He's welcome to go where he will, so long as he pays in the morning. There's Mr. Took, now: he's not vanished.'

'Well, I saw what I saw, and I saw what I didn't,' said Mugwort obstinately.

'And I say there's some mistake,' repeated Butterbur, picking up the tray and gathering up the broken crockery.

'Of course there's a mistake!' said Frodo. 'I haven't vanished. Here I am! I've just been having a few words with Strider in the corner.'

He came forward into the firelight; but most of the company backed away, even more perturbed than before. They were not in the least satisfied by his explanation that he had crawled away quickly under the tables after he had fallen. Most of the Hobbits and the Men of Bree went off then and there in a huff, having no fancy for further entertainment that evening. One or two gave Frodo a black look and departed muttering among themselves. The Dwarves and the two or three strange Men that still remained got up and said good night to the landlord, but not to Frodo and his friends. Before long no one was left but Strider, who sat on, unnoticed, by the wall.

Mr. Butterbur did not seem much put out. He reckoned, very probably, that his house would be full again on many future nights, until the present mystery had been thoroughly discussed. 'Now what have you been doing, Mr. Underhill?' he asked. 'Frightening my customers and breaking up my crocks with your acrobatics!'

'I am very sorry to have caused any trouble,' said Frodo. 'It was quite unintentional, I assure you. A most unfortunate accident.'

'All right, Mr. Underhill! But if you're going to do any more tumbling, or conjuring, or whatever it was, you'd best warn folk beforehand – and warn *me*. We're a bit suspicious round here of anything out of the way – uncanny, if you understand me; and we don't take to it all of a sudden.'

'I shan't be doing anything of the sort again, Mr. Butterbur, I promise you. And now I think I'll be getting to bed. We shall be making an early start. Will you see that our ponies are ready by eight o'clock?'

'Very good! But before you go, I should like a word with you in private, Mr. Underhill. Something has just come back to my mind that I ought to tell you. I hope that you'll not take it amiss. When I've seen to a thing or two, I'll come along to your room, if you're willing.'

'Certainly!' said Frodo; but his heart sank. He wondered how many private talks he would have before he got to bed, and what they would reveal. Were these people all in league against him? He began to suspect even old Butterbur's fat face of concealing dark designs.

CHAPTER X

STRIDER

Frodo, Pippin, and Sam made their way back to the parlour. There was no light. Merry was not there, and the fire had burned low. It was not until they had puffed up the embers into a blaze and thrown on a couple of faggots that they discovered Strider had come with them. There he was calmly sitting in a chair by the door!

'Hallo!' said Pippin. 'Who are you, and what do you want?'

'I am called Strider,' he answered: 'and though he may have forgotten it, your friend promised to have a quiet talk with me.'

'You said I might hear something to my advantage, I believe,' said Frodo. 'What have you to say?'

'Several things,' answered Strider. 'But, of course, I have my price.'

'What do you mean?' asked Frodo sharply.

'Don't be alarmed! I mean just this: I will tell you what I know, and give you some good advice – but I shall want a reward.'

'And what will that be, pray?' said Frodo. He suspected now that he had fallen in with a rascal, and he thought uncomfortably that he had brought only a little money with him. All of it would hardly satisfy a rogue, and he could not spare any of it.

'No more than you can afford,' answered Strider with a slow smile, as if he guessed Frodo's thoughts. 'Just this: you must take me along with you, until I wish to leave you.'

'Oh, indeed!' replied Frodo, surprised, but not much relieved. 'Even if I wanted another companion, I should not agree to any such thing, until I knew a good deal more about you, and your business.'

'Excellent!' exclaimed Strider, crossing his legs and sitting back comfortably. 'You seem to be coming to your senses again, and that is all to the good. You have been much too careless so far. Very well! I will tell you what I know, and leave the reward to you. You may be glad to grant it, when you have heard me.'

'Go on then!' said Frodo. 'What do you know?'

'Too much; too many dark things,' said Strider grimly. 'But as for your business———' He got up and went to the door, opened it quickly and looked out. Then he shut it quietly and sat down again. 'I have quick ears,' he went on, lowering his voice, 'and though I cannot disappear, I have hunted many wild and wary things and I can usually avoid being seen, if I wish. Now, I was behind the hedge this evening on the Road west of Bree, when four hobbits came out of the Downlands. I need not repeat all that they said to old Bombadil or to one another, but one thing interested me. *Please remember*, said one of them, *that the name Baggins must not be mentioned. I am Mr. Underhill, if any name must be given.* That interested me so much that I followed them here. I slipped over the gate just behind them. Maybe Mr. Baggins has an honest reason for leaving his name behind; but if so, I should advise him and his friends to be more careful.'

'I don't see what interest my name has for any one in Bree,' said Frodo angrily, 'and I have still to learn why it interests you. Mr. Strider may have an honest reason for spying and eavesdropping; but if so, I should advise him to explain it.'

'Well answered!' said Strider laughing. 'But the explanation is simple: I was looking for a Hobbit called Frodo Baggins. I wanted to find him quickly. I had learned that he was carrying out of the Shire, well, a secret that concerned me and my friends.

'Now, don't mistake me!' he cried, as Frodo rose from his seat, and Sam jumped up with a scowl. 'I shall take more care of the secret than you do. And care is needed!' He leaned forward and looked at them. 'Watch every shadow!' he said in a low voice. 'Black horsemen have passed through Bree.

On Monday one came down the Greenway, they say; and
another appeared later, coming up the Greenway from the
south.'

There was a silence. At last Frodo spoke to Pippin and
Sam: 'I ought to have guessed it from the way the gatekeeper
greeted us,' he said. 'And the landlord seems to have heard
something. Why did he press us to join the company? And
why on earth did we behave so foolishly: we ought to have
stayed quiet in here.'

'It would have been better,' said Strider. 'I would have
stopped your going into the common-room, if I could; but
the innkeeper would not let me in to see you, or take a
message.'

'Do you think he——' began Frodo.

'No, I don't think any harm of old Butterbur. Only he does
not altogether like mysterious vagabonds of my sort.' Frodo
gave him a puzzled look. 'Well, I have rather a rascally look,
have I not?' said Strider with a curl of his lip and a queer
gleam in his eye. 'But I hope we shall get to know one another
better. When we do, I hope you will explain what happened
at the end of your song. For that little prank——'

'It was sheer accident!' interrupted Frodo.

'I wonder,' said Strider. 'Accident, then. That accident has
made your position dangerous.'

'Hardly more than it was already,' said Frodo. 'I knew
these horsemen were pursuing me; but now at any rate they
seem to have missed me and to have gone away.'

'You must not count on that!' said Strider sharply. 'They
will return. And more are coming. There are others. I know
their number. I know these Riders.' He paused, and his eyes
were cold and hard. 'And there are some folk in Bree who
are not to be trusted,' he went on. 'Bill Ferny, for instance.
He has an evil name in the Bree-land, and queer folk call at
his house. You must have noticed him among the company:
a swarthy sneering fellow. He was very close with one of the
Southern strangers, and they slipped out together just after

your "accident". Not all of those Southerners mean well; and as for Ferny, he would sell anything to anybody; or make mischief for amusement.'

'What will Ferny sell, and what has my accident got to do with him?' said Frodo, still determined not to understand Strider's hints.

'News of you, of course,' answered Strider. 'An account of your performance would be very interesting to certain people. After that they would hardly need to be told your real name. It seems to me only too likely that they will hear of it before this night is over. Is that enough? You can do as you like about my reward: take me as a guide or not. But I may say that I know all the lands between the Shire and the Misty Mountains, for I have wandered over them for many years. I am older than I look. I might prove useful. You will have to leave the open road after tonight; for the horsemen will watch it night and day. You may escape from Bree, and be allowed to go forward while the Sun is up; but you won't go far. They will come on you in the wild, in some dark place where there is no help. Do you wish them to find you? They are terrible!'

The hobbits looked at him, and saw with surprise that his face was drawn as if with pain, and his hands clenched the arms of his chair. The room was very quiet and still, and the light seemed to have grown dim. For a while he sat with unseeing eyes as if walking in distant memory or listening to sounds in the Night far away.

'There!' he cried after a moment, drawing his hand across his brow. 'Perhaps I know more about these pursuers than you do. You fear them, but you do not fear them enough, yet. Tomorrow you will have to escape, if you can. Strider can take you by paths that are seldom trodden. Will you have him?'

There was a heavy silence. Frodo made no answer, his mind was confused with doubt and fear. Sam frowned, and looked at his master; and at last he broke out:

'With your leave, Mr. Frodo, I'd say *no*! This Strider here, he warns and he says take care; and I say *yes* to that, and let's begin with him. He comes out of the Wild, and I never heard no good of such folk. He knows something, that's plain, and more than I like; but it's no reason why we should let him go leading us out into some dark place far from help, as he puts it.'

Pippin fidgeted and looked uncomfortable. Strider did not reply to Sam, but turned his keen eyes on Frodo. Frodo caught his glance and looked away. 'No,' he said slowly. 'I don't agree. I think, I think you are not really as you choose to look. You began to talk to me like the Bree-folk, but your voice has changed. Still Sam seems right in this: I don't see why you should warn us to take care, and yet ask us to take you on trust. Why the disguise? Who are you? What do you really know about – about my business; and how do you know it?'

'The lesson in caution has been well learned,' said Strider with a grim smile. 'But caution is one thing and wavering is another. You will never get to Rivendell now on your own, and to trust me is your only chance. You must make up your mind. I will answer some of your questions, if that will help you to do so. But why should you believe my story, if you do not trust me already? Still here it is———'

At that moment there came a knock at the door. Mr. Butterbur had arrived with candles, and behind him was Nob with cans of hot water. Strider withdrew into a dark corner.

'I've come to bid you good night,' said the landlord, putting the candles on the table. 'Nob! Take the water to the rooms!' He came in and shut the door.

'It's like this,' he began, hesitating and looking troubled. 'If I've done any harm, I'm sorry indeed. But one thing drives out another, as you'll admit; and I'm a busy man. But first one thing and then another this week have jogged my memory, as the saying goes; and not too late I hope. You see, I was asked to look out for hobbits of the Shire, and for one by the name of Baggins in particular.'

'And what has that got to do with me?' asked Frodo.

'Ah! you know best,' said the landlord, knowingly. 'I won't give you away; but I was told that this Baggins would be going by the name of Underhill, and I was given a description that fits you well enough, if I may say so.'

'Indeed! Let's have it then!' said Frodo, unwisely interrupting.

'*A stout little fellow with red cheeks*,' said Mr. Butterbur solemnly. Pippin chuckled, but Sam looked indignant. '*That won't help you much; it goes for most hobbits, Barley*, he says to me,' continued Mr. Butterbur with a glance at Pippin. '*But this one is taller than some and fairer than most, and he has a cleft in his chin: perky chap with a bright eye*. Begging your pardon, but he said it, not me.'

'*He* said it? And who was he?' asked Frodo eagerly.

'Ah! That was Gandalf, if you know who I mean. A wizard they say he is, but he's a good friend of mine, whether or no. But now I don't know what he'll have to say to me, if I see him again: turn all my ale sour or me into a block of wood, I shouldn't wonder. He's a bit hasty. Still what's done can't be undone.'

'Well, what have you done?' said Frodo, getting impatient with the slow unravelling of Butterbur's thoughts.

'Where was I?' said the landlord, pausing and snapping his fingers. 'Ah, yes! Old Gandalf. Three months back he walked right into my room without a knock. *Barley*, he says, *I'm off in the morning. Will you do something for me? You've only to name it*, I said. *I'm in a hurry*, said he, *and I've no time myself, but I want a message took to the Shire. Have you anyone you can send, and trust to go? I can find someone*, I said, *tomorrow, maybe, or the day after. Make it tomorrow*, he says, and then he gave me a letter.

'It's addressed plain enough,' said Mr. Butterbur, producing a letter from his pocket, and reading out the address slowly and proudly (he valued his reputation as a lettered man):

*Mr. FRODO BAGGINS, BAG END, HOBBITON in the
SHIRE.*

'A letter for me from Gandalf!' cried Frodo.

'Ah!' said Mr. Butterbur. 'Then your right name is
Baggins?'

'It is,' said Frodo, 'and you had better give me that letter
at once, and explain why you never sent it. That's what you
came to tell me, I suppose, though you've taken a long time
to come to the point.'

Poor Mr. Butterbur looked troubled. 'You're right, master,'
he said, 'and I beg your pardon. And I'm mortal afraid of
what Gandalf will say, if harm comes of it. But I didn't keep
it back a-purpose. I put it by safe. Then I couldn't find
nobody willing to go to the Shire next day, nor the day after,
and none of my own folk were to spare; and then one thing
after another drove it out of my mind. I'm a busy man. I'll
do what I can to set matters right, and if there's any help I
can give, you've only to name it.

'Leaving the letter aside, I promised Gandalf no less.
Barley, he says to me, *this friend of mine from the Shire, he
may be coming out this way before long, him and another. He'll
be calling himself Underhill. Mind that! But you need ask no
questions. And if I'm not with him, he may be in trouble, and
he may need help. Do whatever you can for him, and I'll be
grateful*, he says. And here you are, and trouble is not far off,
seemingly.'

'What do you mean?' asked Frodo.

'These black men,' said the landlord lowering his voice.
'They're looking for *Baggins*, and if they mean well, then I'm
a hobbit. It was on Monday, and all the dogs were yammering
and the geese screaming. Uncanny, I called it. Nob, he came
and told me that two black men were at the door asking for
a hobbit called Baggins. Nob's hair was all stood on end. I
bid the black fellows be off, and slammed the door on them;
but they've been asking the same question all the way to
Archet, I hear. And that Ranger, Strider, he's been asking

questions, too. Tried to get in here to see you, before you'd had bite or sup, he did.'

'He did!' said Strider suddenly, coming forward into the light. 'And much trouble would have been saved, if you had let him in, Barliman.'

The landlord jumped with surprise. 'You!' he cried. 'You're always popping up. What do you want now?'

'He's here with my leave,' said Frodo. 'He came to offer me his help.'

'Well, you know your own business, maybe,' said Mr. Butterbur, looking suspiciously at Strider. 'But if I was in your plight, I wouldn't take up with a Ranger.'

'Then who would you take up with?' asked Strider. 'A fat innkeeper who only remembers his own name because people shout it at him all day? They cannot stay in *The Pony* for ever, and they cannot go home. They have a long road before them. Will you go with them and keep the black men off?'

'Me? Leave Bree! I wouldn't do that for any money,' said Mr. Butterbur, looking really scared. 'But why can't you stay here quiet for a bit, Mr. Underhill? What are all these queer goings on? What are these black men after, and where do they come from, I'd like to know?'

'I'm sorry I can't explain it all,' answered Frodo. 'I am tired and very worried, and it's a long tale. But if you mean to help me, I ought to warn you that you will be in danger as long as I am in your house. These Black Riders: I am not sure, but I think, I fear they come from———'

'They come from Mordor,' said Strider in a low voice. 'From Mordor, Barliman, if that means anything to you.'

'Save us!' cried Mr. Butterbur turning pale; the name evidently was known to him. 'That is the worst news that has come to Bree in my time.'

'It is,' said Frodo. 'Are you still willing to help me?'

'I am,' said Mr. Butterbur. 'More than ever. Though I don't know what the likes of me can do against, against———' he faltered.

'Against the Shadow in the East,' said Strider quietly. 'Not much, Barliman, but every little helps. You can let Mr. Underhill stay here tonight, as Mr. Underhill, and you can forget the name of Baggins, till he is far away.'

'I'll do that,' said Butterbur. 'But they'll find out he's here without help from me, I'm afraid. It's a pity Mr. Baggins drew attention to himself this evening, to say no more. The story of that Mr. Bilbo's going off has been heard before tonight in Bree. Even our Nob has been doing some guessing in his slow pate; and there are others in Bree quicker in the uptake than he is.'

'Well, we can only hope the Riders won't come back yet,' said Frodo.

'I hope not, indeed,' said Butterbur. 'But spooks or no spooks, they won't get in *The Pony* so easy. Don't you worry till the morning. Nob'll say no word. No black man shall pass my doors, while I can stand on my legs. Me and my folk'll keep watch tonight; but you had best get some sleep, if you can.'

'In any case we must be called at dawn,' said Frodo. 'We must get off as early as possible. Breakfast at six-thirty, please.'

'Right! I'll see to the orders,' said the landlord. 'Good night, Mr. Baggins – Underhill, I should say! Good night – now, bless me! Where's your Mr. Brandybuck?'

'I don't know,' said Frodo with sudden anxiety. They had forgotten all about Merry, and it was getting late. 'I am afraid he is out. He said something about going for a breath of air.'

'Well, you do want looking after and no mistake: your party might be on a holiday!' said Butterbur. 'I must go and bar the doors quick, but I'll see your friend is let in when he comes. I'd better send Nob to look for him. Good night to you all!' At last Mr. Butterbur went out, with another doubt-ful look at Strider and a shake of his head. His footsteps retreated down the passage.

★   ★   ★

'Well?' said Strider. 'When are you going to open that letter?' Frodo looked carefully at the seal before he broke it. It seemed certainly to be Gandalf's. Inside, written in the wizard's strong but graceful script, was the following message:

THE PRANCING PONY, BREE.
Midyear's Day, Shire Year, 1418.

Dear Frodo,
    Bad news has reached me here. I must go off at once. You had better leave Bag End soon, and get out of the Shire before the end of July at latest. I will return as soon as I can; and I will follow you, if I find that you are gone. Leave a message for me here, if you pass through Bree. You can trust the landlord (Butterbur). You may meet a friend of mine on the Road: a Man, lean, dark, tall, by some called Strider. He knows our business and will help you. Make for Rivendell. There I hope we may meet again. If I do not come, Elrond will advise you.

Yours in haste
GANDALF. 🝮

    PS. Do NOT use It again, not for any reason whatever! Do not travel by night! 🝮
    PPS. Make sure that it is the real Strider. There are many strange men on the roads. His true name is Aragorn. 🝮

All that is gold does not glitter,
    Not all those who wander are lost;
The old that is strong does not wither,
    Deep roots are not reached by the frost.
From the ashes a fire shall be woken,
    A light from the shadows shall spring;
Renewed shall be blade that was broken,
    The crownless again shall be king.

    PPPS. I hope Butterbur sends this promptly. A worthy man,

but his memory is like a lumber-room:
thing wanted always buried. If he
forgets, I shall roast him.
                                    Fare Well!

Frodo read the letter to himself, and then passed it to Pippin and Sam. 'Really old Butterbur has made a mess of things!' he said. 'He deserves roasting. If I had got this at once, we might all have been safe in Rivendell by now. But what can have happened to Gandalf? He writes as if he was going into great danger.'

'He has been doing that for many years,' said Strider.

Frodo turned and looked at him thoughtfully, wondering about Gandalf's second postscript. 'Why didn't you tell me that you were Gandalf's friend at once?' he asked. 'It would have saved time.'

'Would it? Would any of you have believed me till now?' said Strider. 'I knew nothing of this letter. For all I knew I had to persuade you to trust me without proofs, if I was to help you. In any case, I did not intend to tell you all about myself at once. I had to study *you* first, and make sure of you. The Enemy has set traps for me before now. As soon as I had made up my mind, I was ready to tell you whatever you asked. But I must admit,' he added with a queer laugh, 'that I hoped you would take to me for my own sake. A hunted man sometimes wearies of distrust and longs for friendship. But there, I believe my looks are against me.'

'They are – at first sight at any rate,' laughed Pippin with sudden relief after reading Gandalf's letter. 'But handsome is as handsome does, as we say in the Shire; and I daresay we shall all look much the same after lying for days in hedges and ditches.'

'It would take more than a few days, or weeks, or years, of wandering in the Wild to make you look like Strider,' he answered. 'And you would die first, unless you are made of sterner stuff than you look to be.'

Pippin subsided; but Sam was not daunted, and he still eyed Strider dubiously. 'How do we know you are the Strider that Gandalf speaks about?' he demanded. 'You never mentioned Gandalf, till this letter came out. You might be a play-acting spy, for all I can see, trying to get us to go with you. You might have done in the real Strider and took his clothes. What have you to say to that?'

'That you are a stout fellow,' answered Strider; 'but I am afraid my only answer to you, Sam Gamgee, is this. If I had killed the real Strider, I could kill you. And I should have killed you already without so much talk. If I was after the Ring, I could have it – NOW!'

He stood up, and seemed suddenly to grow taller. In his eyes gleamed a light, keen and commanding. Throwing back his cloak, he laid his hand on the hilt of a sword that had hung concealed by his side. They did not dare to move. Sam sat wide-mouthed staring at him dumbly.

'But I *am* the real Strider, fortunately,' he said, looking down at them with his face softened by a sudden smile. 'I am Aragorn son of Arathorn; and if by life or death I can save you, I will.'

There was a long silence. At last Frodo spoke with hesitation. 'I believed that you were a friend before the letter came,' he said, 'or at least I wished to. You have frightened me several times tonight, but never in the way that servants of the Enemy would, or so I imagine. I think one of his spies would – well, seem fairer and feel fouler, if you understand.'

'I see,' laughed Strider. 'I look foul and feel fair. Is that it? *All that is gold does not glitter, not all those who wander are lost.*'

'Did the verses apply to you then?' asked Frodo. 'I could not make out what they were about. But how did you know that they were in Gandalf's letter, if you have never seen it?'

'I did not know,' he answered. 'But I am Aragorn, and those verses go with that name.' He drew out his sword, and they saw that the blade was indeed broken a foot below the hilt. 'Not much use is it, Sam?' said Strider. 'But the time is near when it shall be forged anew.'

Sam said nothing.

'Well,' said Strider, 'with Sam's permission we will call that settled. Strider shall be your guide. We shall have a rough road tomorrow. Even if we are allowed to leave Bree unhindered, we can hardly hope now to leave it unnoticed. But I shall try to get lost as soon as possible. I know one or two ways out of Bree-land other than the main road. If once we shake off the pursuit, I shall make for Weathertop.'

'Weathertop?' said Sam. 'What's that?'

'It is a hill, just to the north of the Road, about half way from here to Rivendell. It commands a wide view all round; and there we shall have a chance to look about us. Gandalf will make for that point, if he follows us. After Weathertop our journey will become more difficult, and we shall have to choose between various dangers.'

'When did you last see Gandalf?' asked Frodo. 'Do you know where he is, or what he is doing?'

Strider looked grave. 'I do not know,' he said. 'I came west with him in the spring. I have often kept watch on the borders of the Shire in the last few years, when he was busy elsewhere. He seldom left it unguarded. We last met on the first of May: at Sarn Ford down the Brandywine. He told me that his business with you had gone well, and that you would be starting for Rivendell in the last week of September. As I knew he was at your side, I went away on a journey of my own. And that has proved ill; for plainly some news reached him, and I was not at hand to help.

'I am troubled, for the first time since I have known him. We should have had messages, even if he could not come himself. When I returned, many days ago, I heard the ill news. The tidings had gone far and wide that Gandalf was missing and the horsemen had been seen. It was the Elven-folk of Gildor that told me this; and later they told me that you had left your home; but there was no news of your leaving

Buckland. I have been watching the East Road anxiously.'

'Do you think the Black Riders have anything to do with it – with Gandalf's absence, I mean?' asked Frodo.

'I do not know of anything else that could have hindered him, except the Enemy himself,' said Strider. 'But do not give up hope! Gandalf is greater than you Shire-folk know – as a rule you can only see his jokes and toys. But this business of ours will be his greatest task.'

Pippin yawned. 'I am sorry,' he said, 'but I am dead tired. In spite of all the danger and worry I must go to bed, or sleep where I sit. Where is that silly fellow, Merry? It would be the last straw, if we had to go out in the dark to look for him.'

At that moment they heard a door slam; then feet came running along the passage. Merry came in with a rush followed by Nob. He shut the door hastily, and leaned against it. He was out of breath. They stared at him in alarm for a moment before he gasped: 'I have seen them, Frodo! I have seen them! Black Riders!'

'Black Riders!' cried Frodo. 'Where?'

'Here. In the village. I stayed indoors for an hour. Then as you did not come back, I went out for a stroll. I had come back again and was standing just outside the light of the lamp looking at the stars. Suddenly I shivered and felt that something horrible was creeping near: there was a sort of deeper shade among the shadows across the road, just beyond the edge of the lamplight. It slid away at once into the dark without a sound. There was no horse.'

'Which way did it go?' asked Strider, suddenly and sharply.

Merry started, noticing the stranger for the first time. 'Go on!' said Frodo. 'This is a friend of Gandalf's. I will explain later.'

'It seemed to make off up the Road, eastward,' continued Merry. 'I tried to follow. Of course, it vanished almost at once; but I went round the corner and on as far as the last house on the Road.'

Strider looked at Merry with wonder. 'You have a stout heart,' he said; 'but it was foolish.'

'I don't know,' said Merry. 'Neither brave nor silly, I think. I could hardly help myself. I seemed to be drawn somehow. Anyway, I went, and suddenly I heard voices by the hedge. One was muttering; and the other was whispering, or hissing. I couldn't hear a word that was said. I did not creep any closer, because I began to tremble all over. Then I felt terrified, and I turned back, and was just going to bolt home, when something came behind me and I . . . I fell over.'

'I found him, sir,' put in Nob. 'Mr. Butterbur sent me out with a lantern. I went down to West-gate, and then back up towards South-gate. Just nigh Bill Ferny's house I thought I could see something in the Road. I couldn't swear to it, but it looked to me as if two men was stooping over something, lifting it. I gave a shout, but when I got up to the spot there was no signs of them, and only Mr. Brandybuck lying by the roadside. He seemed to be asleep. "I thought I had fallen into deep water," he says to me, when I shook him. Very queer he was, and as soon as I had roused him, he got up and ran back here like a hare.'

'I am afraid that's true,' said Merry, 'though I don't know what I said. I had an ugly dream, which I can't remember. I went to pieces. I don't know what came over me.'

'I do,' said Strider. 'The Black Breath. The Riders must have left their horses outside, and passed back through the South-gate in secret. They will know all the news now, for they have visited Bill Ferny; and probably that Southerner was a spy as well. Something may happen in the night, before we leave Bree.'

'What will happen?' said Merry. 'Will they attack the inn?'

'No, I think not,' said Strider. 'They are not all here yet. And in any case that is not their way. In dark and loneliness they are strongest; they will not openly attack a house where there are lights and many people – not until they are desperate, not while all the long leagues of Eriador still lie before us. But their power is in terror, and already some in Bree are in their clutch. They will drive these wretches to some evil work: Ferny, and some of the strangers, and, maybe, the gatekeeper too. They had words with Harry at West-gate on Monday. I was watching them. He was white and shaking when they left him.'

'We seem to have enemies all round,' said Frodo. 'What are we to do?'

'Stay here, and do not go to your rooms! They are sure to have found out which those are. The hobbit-rooms have windows looking north and close to the ground. We will all remain together and bar this window and the door. But first Nob and I will fetch your luggage.'

While Strider was gone, Frodo gave Merry a rapid account of all that had happened since supper. Merry was still reading and pondering Gandalf's letter when Strider and Nob returned.

'Well Masters,' said Nob, 'I've ruffled up the clothes and put in a bolster down the middle of each bed. And I made a nice imitation of your head with a brown woollen mat, Mr. Bag – Underhill, sir,' he added with a grin.

Pippin laughed. 'Very life-like!' he said. 'But what will happen when they have penetrated the disguise?'

'We shall see,' said Strider. 'Let us hope to hold the fort till morning.'

'Good night to you,' said Nob, and went off to take his part in the watch on the doors.

Their bags and gear they piled on the parlour-floor. They pushed a low chair against the door and shut the window. Peering out, Frodo saw that the night was still clear. The Sickle* was swinging bright above the shoulders of Bree-hill. He then closed and barred the heavy inside shutters and drew the curtains together. Strider built up the fire and blew out all the candles.

The hobbits lay down on their blankets with their feet towards the hearth; but Strider settled himself in the chair

---

* The Hobbits' name for the Plough or Great Bear.

against the door. They talked for a little, for Merry still had several questions to ask.

'Jumped over the Moon!' chuckled Merry as he rolled himself in his blanket. 'Very ridiculous of you, Frodo! But I wish I had been there to see. The worthies of Bree will be discussing it a hundred years hence.'

'I hope so,' said Strider. Then they all fell silent, and one by one the hobbits dropped off to sleep.

CHAPTER XI

A KNIFE IN THE DARK

As they prepared for sleep in the inn at Bree, darkness lay on Buckland; a mist strayed in the dells and along the river-bank. The house at Crickhollow stood silent. Fatty Bolger opened the door cautiously and peered out. A feeling of fear had been growing on him all day, and he was unable to rest or go to bed: there was a brooding threat in the breathless night-air. As he stared out into the gloom, a black shadow moved under the trees; the gate seemed to open of its own accord and close again without a sound. Terror seized him. He shrank back, and for a moment he stood trembling in the hall. Then he shut and locked the door.

The night deepened. There came the soft sound of horses led with stealth along the lane. Outside the gate they stopped, and three black figures entered, like shades of night creeping across the ground. One went to the door, one to the corner of the house on either side; and there they stood, as still as the shadows of stones, while night went slowly on. The house and the quiet trees seemed to be waiting breathlessly.

There was a faint stir in the leaves, and a cock crowed far away. The cold hour before dawn was passing. The figure by the door moved. In the dark without moon or stars a drawn blade gleamed, as if a chill light had been unsheathed. There was a blow, soft but heavy, and the door shuddered.

'Open, in the name of Mordor!' said a voice thin and menacing.

At a second blow the door yielded and fell back, with timbers burst and lock broken. The black figures passed swiftly in.

At that moment, among the trees nearby, a horn rang out. It rent the night like fire on a hill-top.

AWAKE! FEAR! FIRE! FOES! AWAKE!

Fatty Bolger had not been idle. As soon as he saw the dark shapes creep from the garden, he knew that he must run for it, or perish. And run he did, out of the back door, through the garden, and over the fields. When he reached the nearest house, more than a mile away, he collapsed on the doorstep. 'No, no, no!' he was crying. 'No, not me! I haven't got it!' It was some time before anyone could make out what he was babbling about. At last they got the idea that enemies were in Buckland, some strange invasion from the Old Forest. And then they lost no more time.

FEAR! FIRE! FOES!

The Brandybucks were blowing the Horn-call of Buckland, that had not been sounded for a hundred years, not since the white wolves came in the Fell Winter, when the Brandy-wine was frozen over.

AWAKE! AWAKE!

Far-away answering horns were heard. The alarm was spreading.   The black figures fled from the house. One of them let fall a hobbit-cloak on the step, as he ran. In the lane the noise of hoofs broke out, and gathering to a gallop, went hammering away into the darkness. All about Crickhollow there was the sound of horns blowing, and voices crying and feet running. But the Black Riders rode like a gale to the North-gate. Let the little people blow! Sauron would deal with them later. Meanwhile they had another errand: they knew now that the house was empty and the Ring had gone. They rode down the guards at the gate and vanished from the Shire.

In the early night Frodo woke from deep sleep, suddenly,

as if some sound or presence had disturbed him. He saw that
Strider was sitting alert in his chair: his eyes gleamed in the
light of the fire, which had been tended and was burning
brightly; but he made no sign or movement.

Frodo soon went to sleep again; but his dreams were again
troubled with the noise of wind and of galloping hoofs. The
wind seemed to be curling round the house and shaking it;
and far off he heard a horn blowing wildly. He opened his
eyes, and heard a cock crowing lustily in the inn-yard. Strider
had drawn the curtains and pushed back the shutters with a
clang. The first grey light of day was in the room, and a cold
air was coming through the open window.

As soon as Strider had roused them all, he led the way to
their bedrooms. When they saw them they were glad that
they had taken his advice: the windows had been forced open
and were swinging, and the curtains were flapping; the beds
were tossed about, and the bolsters slashed and flung upon
the floor; the brown mat was torn to pieces.

Strider immediately went to fetch the landlord. Poor Mr.
Butterbur looked sleepy and frightened. He had hardly closed
his eyes all night (so he said), but he had never heard a
sound.

'Never has such a thing happened in my time!' he cried,
raising his hands in horror. 'Guests unable to sleep in their
beds, and good bolsters ruined and all! What are we coming
to?'

'Dark times,' said Strider. 'But for the present you may be
left in peace, when you have got rid of us. We will leave at
once. Never mind about breakfast: a drink and a bite standing
will have to do. We shall be packed in a few minutes.'

Mr. Butterbur hurried off to see that their ponies were got
ready, and to fetch them a 'bite'. But very soon he came back
in dismay. The ponies had vanished! The stable-doors had
all been opened in the night, and they were gone: not only
Merry's ponies, but every other horse and beast in the place.

Frodo was crushed by the news. How could they hope to
reach Rivendell on foot, pursued by mounted enemies? They

might as well set out for the Moon. Strider sat silent for a while, looking at the hobbits, as if he was weighing up their strength and courage.

'Ponies would not help us to escape horsemen,' he said at last, thoughtfully, as if he guessed what Frodo had in mind. 'We should not go much slower on foot, not on the roads that I mean to take. I was going to walk in any case. It is the food and stores that trouble me. We cannot count on getting anything to eat between here and Rivendell, except what we take with us; and we ought to take plenty to spare; for we may be delayed, or forced to go round-about, far out of the direct way. How much are you prepared to carry on your backs?'

'As much as we must,' said Pippin with a sinking heart, but trying to show that he was tougher than he looked (or felt).

'I can carry enough for two,' said Sam defiantly.

'Can't anything be done, Mr. Butterbur?' asked Frodo. 'Can't we get a couple of ponies in the village, or even one just for the baggage? I don't suppose we could hire them, but we might be able to buy them,' he added, doubtfully, wondering if he could afford it.

'I doubt it,' said the landlord unhappily. 'The two or three riding-ponies that there were in Bree were stabled in my yard, and they're gone. As for other animals, horses or ponies for draught or what not, there are very few of them in Bree, and they won't be for sale. But I'll do what I can. I'll rout out Bob and send him round as soon as may be.'

'Yes,' said Strider reluctantly, 'you had better do that. I am afraid we shall have to try to get one pony at least. But so ends all hope of starting early, and slipping away quietly! We might as well have blown a horn to announce our departure. That was part of their plan, no doubt.'

'There is one crumb of comfort,' said Merry, 'and more than a crumb, I hope: we can have breakfast while we wait – and sit down to it. Let's get hold of Nob!'

      ★   ★   ★

In the end there was more than three hours' delay. Bob came back with the report that no horse or pony was to be got for love or money in the neighbourhood – except one: Bill Ferny had one that he might possibly sell. 'A poor old half-starved creature it is,' said Bob; 'but he won't part with it for less than thrice its worth, seeing how you're placed, not if I knows Bill Ferny.'

'Bill Ferny?' said Frodo. 'Isn't there some trick? Wouldn't the beast bolt back to him with all our stuff, or help in tracking us, or something?'

'I wonder,' said Strider. 'But I cannot imagine any animal running home to him, once it got away. I fancy this is only an afterthought of kind Master Ferny's: just a way of increasing his profits from the affair. The chief danger is that the poor beast is probably at death's door. But there does not seem any choice. What does he want for it?'

Bill Ferny's price was twelve silver pennies; and that was indeed at least three times the pony's value in those parts. It proved to be a bony, underfed, and dispirited animal; but it did not look like dying just yet. Mr. Butterbur paid for it himself, and offered Merry another eighteen pence as some compensation for the lost animals. He was an honest man, and well-off as things were reckoned in Bree; but thirty silver pennies was a sore blow to him, and being cheated by Bill Ferny made it harder to bear.

As a matter of fact he came out on the right side in the end. It turned out later that only one horse had been actually stolen. The others had been driven off, or had bolted in terror, and were found wandering in different corners of the Bree-land. Merry's ponies had escaped altogether, and eventually (having a good deal of sense) they made their way to the Downs in search of Fatty Lumpkin. So they came under the care of Tom Bombadil for a while, and were well-off. But when news of the events at Bree came to Tom's ears, he sent them to Mr. Butterbur, who thus got five good beasts at a very fair price. They had to work harder in Bree, but Bob treated them well; so on the whole they were lucky:

they missed a dark and dangerous journey. But they never came to Rivendell.

However, in the meanwhile for all Mr. Butterbur knew his money was gone for good, or for bad. And he had other troubles. For there was a great commotion as soon as the remaining guests were astir and heard news of the raid on the inn. The southern travellers had lost several horses and blamed the innkeeper loudly, until it became known that one of their own number had also disappeared in the night, none other than Bill Ferny's squint-eyed companion. Suspicion fell on him at once.

'If you pick up with a horse-thief, and bring him to my house,' said Butterbur angrily, 'you ought to pay for all the damage yourselves and not come shouting at me. Go and ask Ferny where your handsome friend is!' But it appeared that he was nobody's friend, and nobody could recollect when he had joined their party.

After their breakfast the hobbits had to re-pack, and get together further supplies for the longer journey they were now expecting. It was close on ten o'clock before they at last got off. By that time the whole of Bree was buzzing with excitement. Frodo's vanishing trick; the appearance of the black horsemen; the robbing of the stables; and not least the news that Strider the Ranger had joined the mysterious hobbits, made such a tale as would last for many uneventful years. Most of the inhabitants of Bree and Staddle, and many even from Combe and Archet, were crowded in the road to see the travellers start. The other guests in the inn were at the doors or hanging out of the windows.

Strider had changed his mind, and he decided to leave Bree by the main road. Any attempt to set off across country at once would only make matters worse: half the inhabitants would follow them, to see what they were up to, and to prevent them from trespassing.

They said farewell to Nob and Bob, and took leave of Mr. Butterbur with many thanks. 'I hope we shall meet again some day, when things are merry once more,' said Frodo. 'I should like nothing better than to stay in your house in peace for a while.'

They tramped off, anxious and downhearted, under the eyes of the crowd. Not all the faces were friendly, nor all the words that were shouted. But Strider seemed to be held in awe by most of the Bree-landers, and those that he stared at shut their mouths and drew away. He walked in front with Frodo; next came Merry and Pippin; and last came Sam leading the pony, which was laden with as much of their baggage as they had the heart to give it; but already it looked less dejected, as if it approved of the change in its fortunes. Sam was chewing an apple thoughtfully. He had a pocket full of them: a parting present from Nob and Bob. 'Apples for walking, and a pipe for sitting,' he said. 'But I reckon I'll miss them both before long.'

The hobbits took no notice of the inquisitive heads that peeped out of doors, or popped over walls and fences, as they passed. But as they drew near to the further gate, Frodo saw a dark ill-kept house behind a thick hedge: the last house in the village. In one of the windows he caught a glimpse of a sallow face with sly, slanting eyes; but it vanished at once.

'So that's where that southerner is hiding!' he thought. 'He looks more than half like a goblin.'

Over the hedge another man was staring boldly. He had heavy black brows, and dark scornful eyes; his large mouth curled in a sneer. He was smoking a short black pipe. As they approached he took it out of his mouth and spat.

'Morning, Longshanks!' he said. 'Off early? Found some friends at last?' Strider nodded, but did not answer.

'Morning, my little friends!' he said to the others. 'I suppose you know who you've taken up with? That's Stick-at-naught Strider, that is! Though I've heard other names not so pretty. Watch out tonight! And you, Sammie, don't go ill-treating my poor old pony! Pah!' He spat again.

Sam turned quickly. 'And you, Ferny,' he said, 'put your

ugly face out of sight, or it will get hurt.' With a sudden flick, quick as lightning, an apple left his hand and hit Bill square on the nose. He ducked too late, and curses came from behind the hedge. 'Waste of a good apple,' said Sam regretfully, and strode on.

At last they left the village behind. The escort of children and stragglers that had followed them got tired and turned back at the South-gate. Passing through, they kept on along the Road for some miles. It bent to the left, curving back into its eastward line as it rounded the feet of Bree-hill, and then it began to run swiftly downwards into wooded country. To their left they could see some of the houses and hobbit-holes of Staddle on the gentler south-eastern slopes of the hill; down in a deep hollow away north of the Road there were wisps of rising smoke that showed where Combe lay; Archet was hidden in the trees beyond.

After the Road had run down some way, and had left Bree-hill standing tall and brown behind, they came on a narrow track that led off towards the North. 'This is where we leave the open and take to cover,' said Strider.

'Not a "short cut", I hope,' said Pippin. 'Our last short cut through woods nearly ended in disaster.'

'Ah, but you had not got me with you then,' laughed Strider. 'My cuts, short or long, don't go wrong.' He took a look up and down the Road. No one was in sight; and he led the way quickly down towards the wooded valley.

His plan, as far as they could understand it without knowing the country, was to go towards Archet at first, but to bear right and pass it on the east, and then to steer as straight as he could over the wild lands to Weathertop Hill. In that way they would, if all went well, cut off a great loop of the Road, which further on bent southwards to avoid the Midgewater Marshes. But, of course, they would have to pass through the marshes themselves, and Strider's description of them was not encouraging.

However, in the meanwhile, walking was not unpleasant.

Indeed, if it had not been for the disturbing events of the night before, they would have enjoyed this part of the journey better than any up to that time. The sun was shining, clear but not too hot. The woods in the valley were still leafy and full of colour, and seemed peaceful and wholesome. Strider guided them confidently among the many crossing paths, although left to themselves they would soon have been at a loss. He was taking a wandering course with many turns and doublings, to put off any pursuit.

'Bill Ferny will have watched where we left the Road, for certain,' he said; 'though I don't think he will follow us himself. He knows the land round here well enough, but he knows he is not a match for me in a wood. It is what he may tell others that I am afraid of. I don't suppose they are far away. If they think we have made for Archet, so much the better.'

Whether because of Strider's skill or for some other reason, they saw no sign and heard no sound of any other living thing all that day: neither two-footed, except birds; nor four-footed, except one fox and a few squirrels. The next day they began to steer a steady course eastwards; and still all was quiet and peaceful. On the third day out from Bree they came out of the Chetwood. The land had been falling steadily, ever since they turned aside from the Road, and they now entered a wide flat expanse of country, much more difficult to manage. They were far beyond the borders of the Bree-land, out in the pathless wilderness, and drawing near to the Midgewater Marshes.

The ground now became damp, and in places boggy and here and there they came upon pools, and wide stretches of reeds and rushes filled with the warbling of little hidden birds. They had to pick their way carefully to keep both dry-footed and on their proper course. At first they made fair progress, but as they went on, their passage became slower and more dangerous. The marshes were bewildering and treacherous, and there was no permanent trail even for Rangers to find through their shifting quagmires. The flies began to torment them, and the air was full of clouds of tiny midges that crept up their sleeves and breeches and into their hair.

'I am being eaten alive!' cried Pippin. 'Midgewater! There are more midges than water!'

'What do they live on when they can't get hobbit?' asked Sam, scratching his neck.

They spent a miserable day in this lonely and unpleasant country. Their camping-place was damp, cold, and uncomfortable; and the biting insects would not let them sleep. There were also abominable creatures haunting the reeds and tussocks that from the sound of them were evil relatives of the cricket. There were thousands of them, and they squeaked all round, *neek-breek*, *breek-neek*, unceasingly all the night, until the hobbits were nearly frantic.

The next day, the fourth, was little better, and the night almost as comfortless. Though the Neekerbreekers (as Sam called them) had been left behind, the midges still pursued them.

As Frodo lay, tired but unable to close his eyes, it seemed to him that far away there came a light in the eastern sky: it flashed and faded many times. It was not the dawn, for that was still some hours off.

'What is the light?' he said to Strider, who had risen, and was standing, gazing ahead into the night.

'I do not know,' Strider answered. 'It is too distant to make out. It is like lightning that leaps up from the hill-tops.'

Frodo lay down again, but for a long while he could still see the white flashes, and against them the tall dark figure of Strider, standing silent and watchful. At last he passed into uneasy sleep.

They had not gone far on the fifth day when they left the last straggling pools and reed-beds of the marshes behind them. The land before them began steadily to rise again. Away in the distance eastward they could now see a line of hills. The highest of them was at the right of the line and a little separated from the others. It had a conical top, slightly flattened at the summit.

'That is Weathertop,' said Strider. 'The Old Road, which we have left far away on our right, runs to the south of it and passes not far from its foot. We might reach it by noon tomorrow, if we go straight towards it. I suppose we had better do so.'

'What do you mean?' asked Frodo.

'I mean: when we do get there, it is not certain what we shall find. It is close to the Road.'

'But surely we were hoping to find Gandalf there?'

'Yes; but the hope is faint. If he comes this way at all, he may not pass through Bree, and so he may not know what we are doing. And anyway, unless by luck we arrive almost together, we shall miss one another; it will not be safe for him or for us to wait there long. If the Riders fail to find us in the wilderness, they are likely to make for Weathertop themselves. It commands a wide view all round. Indeed, there are many birds and beasts in this country that could see us, as we stand here, from that hill-top. Not all the birds are to be trusted, and there are other spies more evil than they are.'

The hobbits looked anxiously at the distant hills. Sam looked up into the pale sky, fearing to see hawks or eagles hovering over them with bright unfriendly eyes. 'You do make me feel uncomfortable and lonesome, Strider!' he said.

'What do you advise us to do?' asked Frodo.

'I think,' answered Strider slowly, as if he was not quite sure, 'I think the best thing is to go as straight eastward from here as we can, to make for the line of hills, not for Weathertop. There we can strike a path I know that runs at their feet; it will bring us to Weathertop from the north and less openly. Then we shall see what we shall see.'

All that day they plodded along, until the cold and early evening came down. The land became drier and more barren; but mists and vapours lay behind them on the marshes. A few melancholy birds were piping and wailing, until the round red sun sank slowly into the western shadows; then an empty silence fell. The hobbits thought of the soft light of sunset glancing through the cheerful windows of Bag End far away.

At the day's end they came to a stream that wandered down from the hills to lose itself in the stagnant marshland, and they went up along its banks while the light lasted. It was already night when at last they halted and made their camp under some stunted alder-trees by the shores of the stream. Ahead there loomed now against the dusky sky the bleak and treeless backs of the hills. That night they set a watch, and Strider, it seemed, did not sleep at all. The moon was waxing, and in the early night-hours a cold grey light lay on the land.

Next morning they set out again soon after sunrise. There was a frost in the air, and the sky was a pale clear blue. The hobbits felt refreshed, as if they had had a night of unbroken sleep. Already they were getting used to much walking on short commons – shorter at any rate than what in the Shire they would have thought barely enough to keep them on their legs. Pippin declared that Frodo was looking twice the hobbit that he had been.

'Very odd,' said Frodo, tightening his belt, 'considering that there is actually a good deal less of me. I hope the thinning process will not go on indefinitely, or I shall become a wraith.'

'Do not speak of such things!' said Strider quickly, and with surprising earnestness.

The hills drew nearer. They made an undulating ridge, often rising almost to a thousand feet, and here and there falling again to low clefts or passes leading into the eastern land beyond. Along the crest of the ridge the hobbits could see what looked to be the remains of green-grown walls and dikes, and in the clefts there still stood the ruins of old works of stone. By night they had reached the feet of the westward slopes, and there they camped. It was the night of the fifth of October, and they were six days out from Bree.

In the morning they found, for the first time since they had left the Chetwood, a track plain to see. They turned right and followed it southwards. It ran cunningly, taking a line that seemed chosen so as to keep as much hidden as possible from the view, both of the hill-tops above and of the flats to the west. It dived into dells, and hugged steep banks; and where it passed over flatter and more open ground on either side of it there were lines of large boulders and hewn stones that screened the travellers almost like a hedge.

'I wonder who made this path, and what for,' said Merry, as they walked along one of these avenues, where the stones were unusually large and closely set. 'I am not sure that I like it: it has a – well, rather a barrow-wightish look. Is there any barrow on Weathertop?'

'No. There is no barrow on Weathertop, nor on any of these hills,' answered Strider. 'The Men of the West did not live here; though in their latter days they defended the hills for a while against the evil that came out of Angmar. This path was made to serve the forts along the walls. But long before, in the first days of the North Kingdom, they built a great watch-tower on Weathertop, Amon Sûl they called it. It was burned and broken, and nothing remains of it now but a tumbled ring, like a rough crown on the old hill's head. Yet once it was tall and fair. It is told that Elendil stood there watching for the coming of Gil-galad out of the West, in the days of the Last Alliance.'

The hobbits gazed at Strider. It seemed that he was learned in old lore, as well as in the ways of the wild. 'Who was Gil-galad?' asked Merry; but Strider did not answer, and seemed to be lost in thought. Suddenly a low voice murmured:

> *Gil-galad was an Elven-king.*
> *Of him the harpers sadly sing:*
> *the last whose realm was fair and free*
> *between the Mountains and the Sea.*

His sword was long, his lance was keen,
his shining helm afar was seen;
the countless stars of heaven's field
were mirrored in his silver shield.

But long ago he rode away,
and where he dwelleth none can say;
for into darkness fell his star
in Mordor where the shadows are.

The others turned in amazement, for the voice was Sam's.
'Don't stop!' said Merry.

'That's all I know,' stammered Sam, blushing. 'I learned it from Mr. Bilbo when I was a lad. He used to tell me tales like that, knowing how I was always one for hearing about Elves. It was Mr. Bilbo as taught me my letters. He was mighty book-learned was dear old Mr. Bilbo. And he wrote *poetry*. He wrote what I have just said.'

'He did not make it up,' said Strider. 'It is part of the lay that is called *The Fall of Gil-galad*, which is in an ancient tongue. Bilbo must have translated it. I never knew that.'

'There was a lot more,' said Sam, 'all about Mordor. I didn't learn that part, it gave me the shivers. I never thought I should be going that way myself!'

'Going to Mordor!' cried Pippin. 'I hope it won't come to that!'

'Do not speak that name so loudly!' said Strider.

It was already mid-day when they drew near the southern end of the path, and saw before them, in the pale clear light of the October sun, a grey-green bank, leading up like a bridge on to the northward slope of the hill. They decided to make for the top at once, while the daylight was broad. Concealment was no longer possible, and they could only hope that no enemy or spy was observing them. Nothing was to be seen moving on the hill. If Gandalf was anywhere about, there was no sign of him.

On the western flank of Weathertop they found a sheltered
hollow, at the bottom of which there was a bowl-shaped dell
with grassy sides. There they left Sam and Pippin with the
pony and their packs and luggage. The other three went on.
After half an hour's plodding climb Strider reached the crown
of the hill; Frodo and Merry followed, tired and breathless.
The last slope had been steep and rocky.

On the top they found, as Strider had said, a wide ring of
ancient stone-work, now crumbling or covered with age-long
grass. But in the centre a cairn of broken stones had been
piled. They were blackened as if with fire. About them the
turf was burned to the roots and all within the ring the grass
was scorched and shrivelled, as if flames had swept the hill-
top; but there was no sign of any living thing.

Standing upon the rim of the ruined circle, they saw
all round below them a wide prospect, for the most part of
lands empty and featureless, except for patches of woodland
away to the south, beyond which they caught here and
there the glint of distant water. Beneath them on this
southern side there ran like a ribbon the Old Road, coming
out of the West and winding up and down, until it faded
behind a ridge of dark land to the east. Nothing was
moving on it. Following its line eastward with their eyes
they saw the Mountains: the nearer foothills were brown
and sombre; behind them stood taller shapes of grey, and
behind those again were high white peaks glimmering among
the clouds.

'Well, here we are!' said Merry. 'And very cheerless and
uninviting it looks! There is no water and no shelter. And
no sign of Gandalf. But I don't blame him for not waiting –
if he ever came here.'

'I wonder,' said Strider, looking round thoughtfully. 'Even
if he was a day or two behind us at Bree, he could have
arrived here first. He can ride very swiftly when need presses.'
Suddenly he stooped and looked at the stone on the top of
the cairn; it was flatter than the others, and whiter, as if it
had escaped the fire. He picked it up and examined it, turning

it in his fingers. 'This has been handled recently,' he said. 'What do you think of these marks?'

On the flat under-side Frodo saw some scratches: I'·III· 'There seems to be a stroke, a dot, and three more strokes,' he said.

'The stroke on the left might be a G-rune with thin branches,' said Strider. 'It might be a sign left by Gandalf, though one cannot be sure. The scratches are fine, and they certainly look fresh. But the marks might mean something quite different, and have nothing to do with us. Rangers use runes, and they come here sometimes.'

'What could they mean, even if Gandalf made them?' asked Merry.

'I should say,' answered Strider, 'that they stood for G3, and were a sign that Gandalf was here on October the third: that is three days ago now. It would also show that he was in a hurry and danger was at hand, so that he had no time or did not dare to write anything longer or plainer. If that is so, we must be wary.'

'I wish we could feel sure that he made the marks, whatever they may mean,' said Frodo. 'It would be a great comfort to know that he was on the way, in front of us or behind us.'

'Perhaps,' said Strider. 'For myself, I believe that he was here, and was in danger. There have been scorching flames here; and now the light that we saw three nights ago in the eastern sky comes back to my mind. I guess that he was attacked on this hill-top, but with what result I cannot tell. He is here no longer, and we must now look after ourselves and make our own way to Rivendell, as best we can.'

'How far is Rivendell?' asked Merry, gazing round wearily. The world looked wild and wide from Weathertop.

'I don't know if the Road has ever been measured in miles beyond the *Forsaken Inn*, a day's journey east of Bree,' answered Strider. 'Some say it is so far, and some say other-wise. It is a strange road, and folk are glad to reach their journey's end, whether the time is long or short. But I know how long it would take me on my own feet, with fair weather

and no ill fortune: twelve days from here to the Ford of
Bruinen, where the Road crosses the Loudwater that runs
out of Rivendell. We have at least a fortnight's journey before
us, for I do not think we shall be able to use the Road.'

'A fortnight!' said Frodo. 'A lot may happen in that time.'

'It may,' said Strider.

They stood for a while silent on the hill-top, near its southward edge. In that lonely place Frodo for the first time fully
realized his homelessness and danger. He wished bitterly that
his fortune had left him in the quiet and beloved Shire. He
stared down at the hateful Road, leading back westward – to
his home. Suddenly he was aware that two black specks were
moving slowly along it, going westward; and looking again
he saw that three others were creeping eastward to meet
them. He gave a cry and clutched Strider's arm.

'Look,' he said, pointing downwards.

At once Strider flung himself on the ground behind the
ruined circle, pulling Frodo down beside him. Merry threw
himself alongside.

'What is it?' he whispered.

'I do not know, but I fear the worst,' answered Strider.

Slowly they crawled up to the edge of the ring again, and
peered through a cleft between two jagged stones. The light
was no longer bright, for the clear morning had faded, and
clouds creeping out of the East had now overtaken the sun,
as it began to go down. They could all see the black specks,
but neither Frodo nor Merry could make out their shapes
for certain; yet something told them that there, far below,
were Black Riders assembling on the Road beyond the foot
of the hill.

'Yes,' said Strider, whose keener sight left him in no doubt.
'The enemy is here!'

Hastily they crept away and slipped down the north side
of the hill to find their companions.

Sam and Peregrin had not been idle. They had explored
the small dell and the surrounding slopes. Not far away they

found a spring of clear water in the hillside, and near it footprints not more than a day or two old. In the dell itself they found recent traces of a fire, and other signs of a hasty camp. There were some fallen rocks on the edge of the dell nearest to the hill. Behind them Sam came upon a small store of firewood neatly stacked.

'I wonder if old Gandalf has been here,' he said to Pippin. 'Whoever it was put this stuff here meant to come back it seems.'

Strider was greatly interested in these discoveries. 'I wish I had waited and explored the ground down here myself,' he said, hurrying off to the spring to examine the footprints.

'It is just as I feared,' he said, when he came back. 'Sam and Pippin have trampled the soft ground, and the marks are spoilt or confused. Rangers have been here lately. It is they who left the firewood behind. But there are also several newer tracks that were not made by Rangers. At least one set was made, only a day or two ago, by heavy boots. At least one. I cannot now be certain, but I think there were many booted feet.' He paused and stood in anxious thought.

Each of the hobbits saw in his mind a vision of the cloaked and booted Riders. If the horsemen had already found the dell, the sooner Strider led them somewhere else the better. Sam viewed the hollow with great dislike, now that he had heard news of their enemies on the Road, only a few miles away.

'Hadn't we better clear out quick, Mr. Strider?' he asked impatiently. 'It is getting late, and I don't like this hole: it makes my heart sink somehow.'

'Yes, we certainly must decide what to do at once,' answered Strider, looking up and considering the time and the weather. 'Well, Sam,' he said at last, 'I do not like this place either; but I cannot think of anywhere better that we could reach before nightfall. At least we are out of sight for the moment, and if we moved we should be much more likely to be seen by spies. All we could do would be to go right out of our way back north on this side of the line of hills, where the land is all much the same as it is here. The Road is watched, but we should have to cross it, if we tried to take cover in the thickets away to the south. On the north side of the Road beyond the hills the country is bare and flat for miles.'

'Can the Riders *see*?' asked Merry. 'I mean, they seem usually to have used their noses rather than their eyes, smelling for us, if smelling is the right word, at least in the daylight. But you made us lie down flat when you saw them down below; and now you talk of being seen, if we move.'

'I was too careless on the hill-top,' answered Strider. 'I was very anxious to find some sign of Gandalf; but it was a mistake for three of us to go up and stand there so long. For the black horses can see, and the Riders can use men and other creatures as spies, as we found at Bree. They themselves do not see the world of light as we do, but our shapes cast shadows in their minds, which only the noon sun destroys; and in the dark they perceive many signs and forms that are hidden from us: then they are most to be feared. And at all times they smell the blood of living things, desiring and hating it. Senses, too, there are other than sight or smell. We can feel their presence – it troubled our hearts, as soon as we came here, and before we saw them; they feel ours more keenly. Also,' he added, and his voice sank to a whisper, 'the Ring draws them.'

'Is there no escape then?' said Frodo, looking round wildly. 'If I move I shall be seen and hunted! If I stay, I shall draw them to me!'

Strider laid his hand on his shoulder. 'There is still hope,' he said. 'You are not alone. Let us take this wood that is set ready for the fire as a sign. There is little shelter or defence here, but fire shall serve for both. Sauron can put fire to his evil uses, as he can all things, but these Riders do not love it, and fear those who wield it. Fire is our friend in the wilderness.'

'Maybe,' muttered Sam. 'It is also as good a way of saying "here we are" as I can think of, bar shouting.'

*   *   *

Down in the lowest and most sheltered corner of the dell they lit a fire, and prepared a meal. The shades of evening began to fall, and it grew cold. They were suddenly aware of great hunger, for they had not eaten anything since breakfast; but they dared not make more than a frugal supper. The lands ahead were empty of all save birds and beasts, unfriendly places deserted by all the races of the world. Rangers passed at times beyond the hills, but they were few and did not stay. Other wanderers were rare, and of evil sort: trolls might stray down at times out of the northern valleys of the Misty Mountains. Only on the Road would travellers be found, most often dwarves, hurrying along on business of their own, and with no help and few words to spare for strangers.

'I don't see how our food can be made to last,' said Frodo. 'We have been careful enough in the last few days, and this supper is no feast; but we have used more than we ought, if we have two weeks still to go, and perhaps more.'

'There is food in the wild,' said Strider; 'berry, root, and herb; and I have some skill as a hunter at need. You need not be afraid of starving before winter comes. But gathering and catching food is long and weary work, and we need haste. So tighten your belts, and think with hope of the tables of Elrond's house!'

The cold increased as darkness came on. Peering out from the edge of the dell they could see nothing but a grey land now vanishing quickly into shadow. The sky above had cleared again and was slowly filled with twinkling stars. Frodo and his companions huddled round the fire, wrapped in every garment and blanket they possessed; but Strider was content with a single cloak, and sat a little apart, drawing thoughtfully at his pipe.

As night fell and the light of the fire began to shine out brightly he began to tell them tales to keep their minds from fear. He knew many histories and legends of long ago, of Elves and Men and the good and evil deeds of the Elder

Days. They wondered how old he was, and where he had learned all this lore.

'Tell us of Gil-galad,' said Merry suddenly, when he paused at the end of a story of the Elf-Kingdoms. 'Do you know any more of that old lay that you spoke of?'

'I do indeed,' answered Strider. 'So also does Frodo, for it concerns us closely.' Merry and Pippin looked at Frodo, who was staring into the fire.

'I know only the little that Gandalf has told me,' said Frodo slowly. 'Gil-galad was the last of the great Elf-kings of Middle-earth. Gil-galad is *Starlight* in their tongue. With Elendil, the Elf-friend, he went to the land of——'

'No!' said Strider interrupting, 'I do not think that tale should be told now with the servants of the Enemy at hand. If we win through to the house of Elrond, you may hear it there, told in full.'

'Then tell us some other tale of the old days,' begged Sam; 'a tale about the Elves before the fading time. I would dearly like to hear more about Elves; the dark seems to press round so close.'

'I will tell you the tale of Tinúviel,' said Strider, 'in brief – for it is a long tale of which the end is not known; and there are none now, except Elrond, that remember it aright as it was told of old. It is a fair tale, though it is sad, as are all the tales of Middle-earth, and yet it may lift up your hearts.' He was silent for some time, and then he began not to speak but to chant softly:

> *The leaves were long, the grass was green,*
> *The hemlock-umbels tall and fair,*
> *And in the glade a light was seen*
> *Of stars in shadow shimmering.*
> *Tinúviel was dancing there*
> *To music of a pipe unseen,*
> *And light of stars was in her hair,*
> *And in her raiment glimmering.*

There Beren came from mountains cold,
*   And lost he wandered under leaves,*
And where the Elven-river rolled
*   He walked alone and sorrowing.*
He peered between the hemlock-leaves
*   And saw in wonder flowers of gold*
Upon her mantle and her sleeves,
*   And her hair like shadow following.*

Enchantment healed his weary feet
*   That over hills were doomed to roam;*
And forth he hastened, strong and fleet,
*   And grasped at moonbeams glistening.*
Through woven woods in Elvenhome
*   She lightly fled on dancing feet,*
And left him lonely still to roam
*   In the silent forest listening.*

He heard there oft the flying sound
*   Of feet as light as linden-leaves,*
Or music welling underground,
*   In hidden hollows quavering.*
Now withered lay the hemlock-sheaves,
*   And one by one with sighing sound*
Whispering fell the beechen leaves
*   In the wintry woodland wavering.*

He sought her ever, wandering far
*   Where leaves of years were thickly strewn,*
By light of moon and ray of star
*   In frosty heavens shivering.*
Her mantle glinted in the moon,
*   As on a hill-top high and far*
She danced, and at her feet was strewn
*   A mist of silver quivering.*

When winter passed, she came again,
*   And her song released the sudden spring,*
Like rising lark, and falling rain,
*   And melting water bubbling.*
He saw the elven-flowers spring
*   About her feet, and healed again*
He longed by her to dance and sing
*   Upon the grass untroubling.*

Again she fled, but swift he came.
*   Tinúviel! Tinúviel!*
He called her by her elvish name;
*   And there she halted listening.*
One moment stood she, and a spell
*   His voice laid on her: Beren came,*
And doom fell on Tinúviel
*   That in his arms lay glistening.*

As Beren looked into her eyes
*   Within the shadows of her hair,*
The trembling starlight of the skies
*   He saw there mirrored shimmering.*
Tinúviel the elven-fair,
*   Immortal maiden elven-wise,*
About him cast her shadowy hair
*   And arms like silver glimmering.*

Long was the way that fate them bore,
*   O'er stony mountains cold and grey,*
Through halls of iron and darkling door,
*   And woods of nightshade morrowless.*
The Sundering Seas between them lay,
*   And yet at last they met once more,*
And long ago they passed away
*   In the forest singing sorrowless.*

Strider sighed and paused before he spoke again. 'That is a song,' he said, 'in the mode that is called *ann-thennath* among the Elves, but is hard to render in our Common Speech, and this is but a rough echo of it. It tells of the meeting of Beren son of Barahir and Lúthien Tinúviel. Beren was a mortal man, but Lúthien was the daughter of Thingol, a King of Elves upon Middle-earth when the world was young; and she was the fairest maiden that has ever been among all the children of this world. As the stars above the mists of the Northern lands was her loveliness, and in her face was a shining light. In those days the Great Enemy, of whom Sauron of Mordor was but a servant, dwelt in Angband in the North, and the Elves of the West coming back to Middle-earth made war upon him to regain the Silmarils which he had stolen; and the fathers of Men aided the Elves. But the Enemy was victorious and Barahir was slain, and Beren escaping through great peril came over the Mountains of Terror into the hidden Kingdom of Thingol in the forest of Neldoreth. There he beheld Lúthien singing and dancing in a glade beside the enchanted river Esgalduin; and he named her Tinúviel, that is Nightingale in the language of old. Many sorrows befell them afterwards, and they were parted long. Tinúviel rescued Beren from the dungeons of Sauron, and together they passed through great dangers, and cast down even the Great Enemy from his throne, and took from his iron crown one of the three Silmarils, brightest of all jewels, to be the bride-price of Lúthien to Thingol her father. Yet at the last Beren was slain by the Wolf that came from the gates of Angband, and he died in the arms of Tinúviel. But she chose mortality, and to die from the world, so that she might follow him; and it is sung that they met again beyond the Sundering Seas, and after a brief time walking alive once more in the green woods, together they passed, long ago, beyond the confines of this world. So it is that Lúthien Tinúviel alone of the Elf-kindred has died indeed and left the world, and they have lost her whom they most loved. But from her the lineage of the Elf-lords of old

descended among Men. There live still those of whom
Lúthien was the foremother, and it is said that her line shall
never fail. Elrond of Rivendell is of that Kin. For of Beren
and Lúthien was born Dior Thingol's heir; and of him Elwing
the White whom Eärendil wedded, he that sailed his ship out
of the mists of the world into the seas of heaven with the
Silmaril upon his brow. And of Eärendil came the Kings of
Númenor, that is Westernesse.'

As Strider was speaking they watched his strange eager
face, dimly lit in the red glow of the wood-fire. His eyes
shone, and his voice was rich and deep. Above him was a
black starry sky. Suddenly a pale light appeared over the
crown of Weathertop behind him. The waxing moon was
climbing slowly above the hill that overshadowed them, and
the stars above the hill-top faded.

The story ended. The hobbits moved and stretched.
'Look!' said Merry. 'The Moon is rising: it must be getting
late.'

The others looked up. Even as they did so, they saw on
the top of the hill something small and dark against the glimmer of the moonrise. It was perhaps only a large stone or
jutting rock shown up by the pale light.

Sam and Merry got up and walked away from the fire.
Frodo and Pippin remained seated in silence. Strider was
watching the moonlight on the hill intently. All seemed quiet
and still, but Frodo felt a cold dread creeping over his heart,
now that Strider was no longer speaking. He huddled closer
to the fire. At that moment Sam came running back from
the edge of the dell.

'I don't know what it is,' he said, 'but I suddenly felt afraid.
I durstn't go outside this dell for any money; I felt that something was creeping up the slope.'

'Did you *see* anything?' asked Frodo, springing to his feet.

'No, sir. I saw nothing, but I didn't stop to look.'

'I saw something,' said Merry; 'or I thought I did – away
westwards where the moonlight was falling on the flats
beyond the shadow of the hill-tops, I *thought* there were two

or three black shapes. They seemed to be moving this way.'

'Keep close to the fire, with your faces outward!' cried Strider. 'Get some of the longer sticks ready in your hands!'

For a breathless time they sat there, silent and alert, with their backs turned to the wood-fire, each gazing into the shadows that encircled them. Nothing happened. There was no sound or movement in the night. Frodo stirred, feeling that he must break the silence: he longed to shout out aloud.

'Hush!' whispered Strider. 'What's that?' gasped Pippin at the same moment.

Over the lip of the little dell, on the side away from the hill, they felt, rather than saw, a shadow rise, one shadow or more than one. They strained their eyes, and the shadows seemed to grow. Soon there could be no doubt: three or four tall black figures were standing there on the slope, looking down on them. So black were they that they seemed like black holes in the deep shade behind them. Frodo thought that he heard a faint hiss as of venomous breath and felt a thin piercing chill. Then the shapes slowly advanced.

Terror overcame Pippin and Merry, and they threw themselves flat on the ground. Sam shrank to Frodo's side. Frodo was hardly less terrified than his companions; he was quaking as if he was bitter cold, but his terror was swallowed up in a sudden temptation to put on the Ring. The desire to do this laid hold of him, and he could think of nothing else. He did not forget the Barrow, nor the message of Gandalf; but something seemed to be compelling him to disregard all warnings, and he longed to yield. Not with the hope of escape, or of doing anything, either good or bad: he simply felt that he must take the Ring and put it on his finger. He could not speak. He felt Sam looking at him, as if he knew that his master was in some great trouble, but he could not turn towards him. He shut his eyes and struggled for a while; but resistance became unbearable, and at last he slowly drew out the chain, and slipped the Ring on the forefinger of his left hand.

Immediately, though everything else remained as before,

dim and dark, the shapes became terribly clear. He was able to see beneath their black wrappings. There were five tall figures: two standing on the lip of the dell, three advancing. In their white faces burned keen and merciless eyes; under their mantles were long grey robes; upon their grey hairs were helms of silver; in their haggard hands were swords of steel. Their eyes fell on him and pierced him, as they rushed towards him. Desperate, he drew his own sword, and it seemed to him that it flickered red, as if it was a firebrand. Two of the figures halted. The third was taller than the others: his hair was long and gleaming and on his helm was a crown. In one hand he held a long sword, and in the other a knife; both the knife and the hand that held it glowed with a pale light. He sprang forward and bore down on Frodo.

At that moment Frodo threw himself forward on the ground, and he heard himself crying aloud: *O Elbereth! Gilthoniel!* At the same time he struck at the feet of his enemy. A shrill cry rang out in the night; and he felt a pain like a dart of poisoned ice pierce his left shoulder. Even as he swooned he caught, as through a swirling mist, a glimpse of Strider leaping out of the darkness with a flaming brand of wood in either hand. With a last effort Frodo, dropping his sword, slipped the Ring from his finger and closed his right hand tight upon it.

CHAPTER XII

FLIGHT TO THE FORD

When Frodo came to himself he was still clutching the Ring desperately. He was lying by the fire, which was now piled high and burning brightly. His three companions were bending over him.

'What has happened? Where is the pale king?' he asked wildly.

They were too overjoyed to hear him speak to answer for a while; nor did they understand his question. At length he gathered from Sam that they had seen nothing but the vague shadowy shapes coming towards them. Suddenly to his horror Sam found that his master had vanished; and at that moment a black shadow rushed past him, and he fell. He heard Frodo's voice, but it seemed to come from a great distance, or from under the earth, crying out strange words. They saw nothing more, until they stumbled over the body of Frodo, lying as if dead, face downwards on the grass with his sword beneath him. Strider ordered them to pick him up and lay him near the fire, and then he disappeared. That was now a good while ago.

Sam plainly was beginning to have doubts again about Strider; but while they were talking he returned, appearing suddenly out of the shadows. They started, and Sam drew his sword and stood over Frodo; but Strider knelt down swiftly at his side.

'I am not a Black Rider, Sam,' he said gently, 'nor in league with them. I have been trying to discover something of their movements; but I have found nothing. I cannot think why they have gone and do not attack again. But there is no feeling of their presence anywhere at hand.'

When he heard what Frodo had to tell, he became full of

concern, and shook his head and sighed. Then he ordered
Pippin and Merry to heat as much water as they could in
their small kettles, and to bathe the wound with it. 'Keep the
fire going well, and keep Frodo warm!' he said. Then he
got up and walked away, and called Sam to him. 'I think I
understand things better now,' he said in a low voice. 'There
seem only to have been five of the enemy. Why they were
not all here, I don't know; but I don't think they expected to
be resisted. They have drawn off for the time being. But not
far, I fear. They will come again another night, if we cannot
escape. They are only waiting, because they think that their
purpose is almost accomplished, and that the Ring cannot
fly much further. I fear, Sam, that they believe your master
has a deadly wound that will subdue him to their will. We
shall see!'

Sam choked with tears. 'Don't despair!' said Strider. 'You
must trust me now. Your Frodo is made of sterner stuff than
I had guessed, though Gandalf hinted that it might prove so.
He is not slain, and I think he will resist the evil power of
the wound longer than his enemies expect. I will do all I can
to help and heal him. Guard him well, while I am away!' He
hurried off and disappeared again into the darkness.

Frodo dozed, though the pain of his wound was slowly
growing, and a deadly chill was spreading from his shoulder
to his arm and side. His friends watched over him, warming
him, and bathing his wound. The night passed slowly and
wearily. Dawn was growing in the sky, and the dell was filling
with grey light, when Strider at last returned.

'Look!' he cried; and stooping he lifted from the ground
a black cloak that had lain there hidden by the darkness. A
foot above the lower hem there was a slash. 'This was the
stroke of Frodo's sword,' he said. 'The only hurt that it did
to his enemy, I fear; for it is unharmed, but all blades perish
that pierce that dreadful King. More deadly to him was the
name of Elbereth.'

'And more deadly to Frodo was this!' He stooped again

and lifted up a long thin knife. There was a cold gleam in it. As Strider raised it they saw that near the end its edge was notched and the point was broken off. But even as he held it up in the growing light, they gazed in astonishment, for the blade seemed to melt, and vanished like a smoke in the air, leaving only the hilt in Strider's hand. 'Alas!' he cried. 'It was this accursed knife that gave the wound. Few now have the skill in healing to match such evil weapons. But I will do what I can.'

He sat down on the ground, and taking the dagger-hilt laid it on his knees, and he sang over it a slow song in a strange tongue. Then setting it aside, he turned to Frodo and in a soft tone spoke words the others could not catch. From the pouch at his belt he drew out the long leaves of a plant.

'These leaves,' he said, 'I have walked far to find; for this plant does not grow in the bare hills; but in the thickets away south of the Road I found it in the dark by the scent of its leaves.' He crushed a leaf in his fingers, and it gave out a sweet and pungent fragrance. 'It is fortunate that I could find it, for it is a healing plant that the Men of the West brought to Middle-earth. *Athelas* they named it, and it grows now sparsely and only near places where they dwelt or camped of old; and it is not known in the North, except to some of those who wander in the Wild. It has great virtues, but over such a wound as this its healing powers may be small.'

He threw the leaves into boiling water and bathed Frodo's shoulder. The fragrance of the steam was refreshing, and those that were unhurt felt their minds calmed and cleared. The herb had also some power over the wound, for Frodo felt the pain and also the sense of frozen cold lessen in his side; but the life did not return to his arm, and he could not raise or use his hand. He bitterly regretted his foolishness, and reproached himself for weakness of will; for he now perceived that in putting on the Ring he obeyed not his own desire but the commanding wish of his enemies. He wondered if he would remain maimed for life, and how they would now manage to continue their journey. He felt too weak to stand.

The others were discussing this very question. They quickly decided to leave Weathertop as soon as possible. 'I think now,' said Strider, 'that the enemy has been watching this place for some days. If Gandalf ever came here, then he must have been forced to ride away, and he will not return. In any case we are in great peril here after dark, since the attack of last night, and we can hardly meet greater danger wherever we go.'

As soon as the daylight was full, they had some hurried food and packed. It was impossible for Frodo to walk, so they divided the greater part of their baggage among the four of them, and put Frodo on the pony. In the last few days the poor beast had improved wonderfully; it already seemed fatter and stronger, and had begun to show an affection for its new masters, especially for Sam. Bill Ferny's treatment must have been very hard for the journey in the wild to seem so much better than its former life.

They started off in a southerly direction. This would mean crossing the Road, but it was the quickest way to more wooded country. And they needed fuel; for Strider said that Frodo must be kept warm, especially at night, while fire would be some protection for them all. It was also his plan to shorten their journey by cutting across another great loop of the Road: east beyond Weathertop it changed its course and took a wide bend northwards.

They made their way slowly and cautiously round the south-western slopes of the hill, and came in a little while to the edge of the Road. There was no sign of the Riders. But even as they were hurrying across they heard far away two cries: a cold voice calling and a cold voice answering. Trembling they sprang forward, and made for the thickets that lay ahead. The land before them sloped away southwards, but it was wild and pathless; bushes and stunted trees grew in dense patches with wide barren spaces in between. The grass was scanty, coarse, and grey; and the leaves in the thickets were faded and falling. It was a cheerless land, and their journey was slow and gloomy. They spoke little as they trudged along. Frodo's heart was grieved as he watched them walking beside him with their heads down, and their backs bowed under their burdens. Even Strider seemed tired and heavy-hearted.

Before the first day's march was over Frodo's pain began to grow again, but he did not speak of it for a long time. Four days passed, without the ground or the scene changing much, except that behind them Weathertop slowly sank, and before them the distant mountains loomed a little nearer. Yet since that far cry they had seen and heard no sign that the enemy had marked their flight or followed them. They dreaded the dark hours, and kept watch in pairs by night, expecting at any time to see black shapes stalking in the grey night, dimly lit by the cloud-veiled moon; but they saw nothing, and heard no sound but the sigh of withered leaves and grass. Not once did they feel the sense of present evil that had assailed them before the attack in the dell. It seemed too much to hope that the Riders had already lost their trail again. Perhaps they were waiting to make some ambush in a narrow place?

At the end of the fifth day the ground began once more to rise slowly out of the wide shallow valley into which they had descended. Strider now turned their course again north-eastwards, and on the sixth day they reached the top of a long slow-climbing slope, and saw far ahead a huddle of wooded hills. Away below them they could see the Road sweeping round the feet of the hills; and to their right a grey river gleamed pale in the thin sunshine. In the distance they glimpsed yet another river in a stony valley half-veiled in mist.

'I am afraid we must go back to the Road here for a while,' said Strider. 'We have now come to the River Hoarwell, that the Elves call Mitheithel. It flows down out of the Ettenmoors, the troll-fells north of Rivendell, and joins the Loudwater away in the South. Some call it the Greyflood after that. It is a great water before it finds the Sea. There is no way over it below its sources in the Ettenmoors, except by the Last Bridge on which the Road crosses.'

'What is that other river we can see far away there?' asked Merry.

'That is Loudwater, the Bruinen of Rivendell,' answered Strider. 'The Road runs along the edge of the hills for many miles from the Bridge to the Ford of Bruinen. But I have not yet thought how we shall cross that water. One river at a time! We shall be fortunate indeed if we do not find the Last Bridge held against us.'

Next day, early in the morning, they came down again to the borders of the Road. Sam and Strider went forward, but they found no sign of any travellers or riders. Here under the shadow of the hills there had been some rain. Strider judged that it had fallen two days before, and had washed away all footprints. No horseman had passed since then, as far as he could see.

They hurried along with all the speed they could make, and after a mile or two they saw the Last Bridge ahead, at the bottom of a short steep slope. They dreaded to see black figures waiting there, but they saw none. Strider made them take cover in a thicket at the side of the Road, while he went forward to explore.

Before long he came hurrying back. 'I can see no sign of the enemy,' he said, 'and I wonder very much what that means. But I have found something very strange.'

He held out his hand, and showed a single pale-green jewel. 'I found it in the mud in the middle of the Bridge,' he said. 'It is a beryl, an elf-stone. Whether it was set there, or let fall by chance, I cannot say; but it brings hope to me. I will take it as a sign that we may pass the Bridge; but beyond that I dare not keep to the Road, without some clearer token.'

★   ★   ★

At once they went on again. They crossed the Bridge in safety, hearing no sound but the water swirling against its three great arches. A mile further on they came to a narrow ravine that led away northwards through the steep lands on the left of the Road. Here Strider turned aside, and soon they were lost in a sombre country of dark trees winding among the feet of sullen hills.

The hobbits were glad to leave the cheerless lands and the perilous Road behind them; but this new country seemed threatening and unfriendly. As they went forward the hills about them steadily rose. Here and there upon heights and ridges they caught glimpses of ancient walls of stone, and the ruins of towers: they had an ominous look. Frodo, who was not walking, had time to gaze ahead and to think. He recalled Bilbo's account of his journey and the threatening towers on the hills north of the Road, in the country near the Troll's wood where his first serious adventure had happened. Frodo guessed that they were now in the same region, and wondered if by chance they would pass near the spot.

'Who lives in this land?' he asked. 'And who built these towers? Is this troll-country?'

'No!' said Strider. 'Trolls do not build. No one lives in this land. Men once dwelt here, ages ago; but none remain now. They became an evil people, as legends tell, for they fell under the shadow of Angmar. But all were destroyed in the war that brought the North Kingdom to its end. But that is now so long ago that the hills have forgotten them, though a shadow still lies on the land.'

'Where did you learn such tales, if all the land is empty and forgetful?' asked Peregrin. 'The birds and beasts do not tell tales of that sort.'

'The heirs of Elendil do not forget all things past,' said Strider; 'and many more things than I can tell are remembered in Rivendell.'

'Have you often been to Rivendell?' said Frodo.

'I have,' said Strider. 'I dwelt there once, and still I return

when I may. There my heart is; but it is not my fate to sit
in peace, even in the fair house of Elrond.'

The hills now began to shut them in. The Road behind
held on its way to the River Bruinen, but both were now
hidden from view. The travellers came into a long valley;
narrow, deeply cloven, dark and silent. Trees with old and
twisted roots hung over cliffs, and piled up behind into
mounting slopes of pine-wood.

The hobbits grew very weary. They advanced slowly, for
they had to pick their way through a pathless country, encum-
bered by fallen trees and tumbled rocks. As long as they
could they avoided climbing for Frodo's sake, and because
it was in fact difficult to find any way up out of the narrow
dales. They had been two days in this country when the
weather turned wet. The wind began to blow steadily out of
the West and pour the water of the distant seas on the dark
heads of the hills in fine drenching rain. By nightfall they
were all soaked, and their camp was cheerless, for they could
not get any fire to burn. The next day the hills rose still
higher and steeper before them, and they were forced to turn
away northwards out of their course. Strider seemed to be
getting anxious: they were nearly ten days out from
Weathertop, and their stock of provisions was beginning to
run low. It went on raining.

That night they camped on a stony shelf with a rock-wall
behind them, in which there was a shallow cave, a mere scoop
in the cliff. Frodo was restless. The cold and wet had made
his wound more painful than ever, and the ache and sense
of deadly chill took away all sleep. He lay tossing and turning
and listening fearfully to the stealthy night-noises: wind in
chinks of rock, water dripping, a crack, the sudden rattling
fall of a loosened stone. He felt that black shapes were advancing to smother him; but when he sat up he saw nothing but
the back of Strider sitting hunched up, smoking his pipe, and
watching. He lay down again and passed into an uneasy
dream, in which he walked on the grass in his garden in the

Shire, but it seemed faint and dim, less clear than the tall black shadows that stood looking over the hedge.

In the morning he woke to find that the rain had stopped. The clouds were still thick, but they were breaking, and pale strips of blue appeared between them. The wind was shifting again. They did not start early. Immediately after their cold and comfortless breakfast Strider went off alone, telling the others to remain under the shelter of the cliff, until he came back. He was going to climb up, if he could, and get a look at the lie of the land.

When he returned he was not reassuring. 'We have come too far to the north,' he said, 'and we must find some way to turn back southwards again. If we keep on as we are going we shall get up into the Ettendales far north of Rivendell. That is troll-country, and little known to me. We could perhaps find our way through and come round to Rivendell from the north; but it would take too long, for I do not know the way, and our food would not last. So somehow or other we must find the Ford of Bruinen.'

The rest of that day they spent scrambling over rocky ground. They found a passage between two hills that led them into a valley running south-east, the direction that they wished to take; but towards the end of the day they found their road again barred by a ridge of high land; its dark edge against the sky was broken into many bare points like teeth of a blunted saw. They had a choice between going back or climbing over it.

They decided to attempt the climb, but it proved very difficult. Before long Frodo was obliged to dismount and struggle along on foot. Even so they often despaired of getting their pony up, or indeed of finding a path for themselves, burdened as they were. The light was nearly gone, and they were all exhausted, when at last they reached the top. They had climbed on to a narrow saddle between two higher points, and the land fell steeply away again, only a short distance ahead. Frodo threw himself down, and lay on the ground shivering. His left arm was lifeless, and his side and shoulder felt as if icy claws were laid upon them. The trees and rocks about him seemed shadowy and dim.

'We cannot go any further,' said Merry to Strider. 'I am afraid this has been too much for Frodo. I am dreadfully anxious about him. What are we to do? Do you think they will be able to cure him in Rivendell, if we ever get there?'

'We shall see,' answered Strider. 'There is nothing more that I can do in the wilderness; and it is chiefly because of his wound that I am so anxious to press on. But I agree that we can go no further tonight.'

'What is the matter with my master?' asked Sam in a low voice, looking appealingly at Strider. 'His wound was small, and it is already closed. There's nothing to be seen but a cold white mark on his shoulder.'

'Frodo has been touched by the weapons of the Enemy,' said Strider, 'and there is some poison or evil at work that is beyond my skill to drive out. But do not give up hope, Sam!'

Night was cold up on the high ridge. They lit a small fire down under the gnarled roots of an old pine, that hung over a shallow pit: it looked as if stone had once been quarried there. They sat huddled together. The wind blew chill through the pass, and they heard the tree-tops lower down moaning and sighing. Frodo lay half in a dream, imagining that endless dark wings were sweeping by above him, and that on the wings rode pursuers that sought him in all the hollows of the hills.

The morning dawned bright and fair; the air was clean, and the light pale and clear in a rain-washed sky. Their hearts were encouraged, but they longed for the sun to warm their cold stiff limbs. As soon as it was light, Strider took Merry with him and went to survey the country from the height to the east of the pass. The sun had risen and was shining brightly when he returned with more comforting news. They were now going more or less in the right direction. If they went on, down the further side of the ridge, they would have the Mountains on their left. Some way ahead Strider had caught a glimpse of the Loudwater again, and he knew that, though it was hidden from view, the Road to the Ford was not far from the River and lay on the side nearest to them.

'We must make for the Road again,' he said. 'We cannot hope to find a path through these hills. Whatever danger may beset it, the Road is our only way to the Ford.'

As soon as they had eaten they set out again. They climbed slowly down the southern side of the ridge; but the way was much easier than they had expected, for the slope was far less steep on this side, and before long Frodo was able to ride again. Bill Ferny's poor old pony was developing an unexpected talent for picking out a path, and for sparing its rider as many jolts as possible. The spirits of the party rose again. Even Frodo felt better in the morning light, but every now and again a mist seemed to obscure his sight, and he passed his hands over his eyes.

Pippin was a little ahead of the others. Suddenly he turned round and called to them. 'There is a path here!' he cried.

When they came up with him, they saw that he had made no mistake: there were clearly the beginnings of a path, that climbed with many windings out of the woods below and faded away on the hill-top behind. In places it was now faint and overgrown, or choked with fallen stones and trees; but at one time it seemed to have been much used. It was a path made by strong arms and heavy feet. Here and there old trees had been cut or broken down, and large rocks cloven or heaved aside to make a way.

They followed the track for some while, for it offered much the easiest way down, but they went cautiously, and their anxiety increased as they came into the dark woods, and the path grew plainer and broader. Suddenly coming out of a belt of fir-trees it ran steeply down a slope, and turned sharply to the left round the corner of a rocky shoulder of the hill.

When they came to the corner they looked round and saw
that the path ran on over a level strip under the face of a low
cliff overhung with trees. In the stony wall there was a door
hanging crookedly ajar upon one great hinge.

Outside the door they all halted. There was a cave or
rock-chamber behind, but in the gloom inside nothing could
be seen. Strider, Sam, and Merry pushing with all their
strength managed to open the door a little wider, and then
Strider and Merry went in. They did not go far, for on the
floor lay many old bones, and nothing else was to be seen
near the entrance except some great empty jars and broken
pots.

'Surely this is a troll-hole, if ever there was one!' said Pippin. 'Come out, you two, and let us get away. Now we know
who made the path – and we had better get off it quick.'

'There is no need, I think,' said Strider, coming out. 'It is
certainly a troll-hole, but it seems to have been long forsaken.
I don't think we need be afraid. But let us go on down warily,
and we shall see.'

The path went on again from the door, and turning to the
right again across the level space plunged down a thick
wooded slope. Pippin, not liking to show Strider that he was
still afraid, went on ahead with Merry. Sam and Strider came
behind, one on each side of Frodo's pony, for the path was
now broad enough for four or five hobbits to walk abreast.
But they had not gone very far before Pippin came running
back, followed by Merry. They both looked terrified.

'There *are* trolls!' Pippin panted. 'Down in a clearing in
the woods not far below. We got a sight of them through the
tree-trunks. They are very large!'

'We will come and look at them,' said Strider, picking up
a stick. Frodo said nothing, but Sam looked scared.

The sun was now high, and it shone down through the
half-stripped branches of the trees, and lit the clearing with
bright patches of light. They halted suddenly on the edge,
and peered through the tree-trunks, holding their breath.

There stood the trolls: three large trolls. One was stooping, and the other two stood staring at him.

Strider walked forward unconcernedly. 'Get up, old stone!' he said, and broke his stick upon the stooping troll.

Nothing happened. There was a gasp of astonishment from the hobbits, and then even Frodo laughed. 'Well!' he said. 'We are forgetting our family history! These must be the very three that were caught by Gandalf, quarrelling over the right way to cook thirteen dwarves and one hobbit.'

'I had no idea we were anywhere near the place!' said Pippin. He knew the story well. Bilbo and Frodo had told it often; but as a matter of fact he had never more than half believed it. Even now he looked at the stone trolls with suspicion, wondering if some magic might not suddenly bring them to life again.

'You are forgetting not only your family history, but all you ever knew about trolls,' said Strider. 'It is broad daylight with a bright sun, and yet you come back trying to scare me with a tale of live trolls waiting for us in this glade! In any case you might have noticed that one of them has an old bird's nest behind his ear. That would be a most unusual ornament for a live troll!'

They all laughed. Frodo felt his spirits reviving: the reminder of Bilbo's first successful adventure was heartening. The sun, too, was warm and comforting, and the mist before his eyes seemed to be lifting a little. They rested for some time in the glade, and took their mid-day meal right under the shadow of the trolls' large legs.

'Won't somebody give us a bit of a song, while the sun is high?' said Merry, when they had finished. 'We haven't had a song or a tale for days.'

'Not since Weathertop,' said Frodo. The others looked at him. 'Don't worry about me!' he added. 'I feel much better, but I don't think I could sing. Perhaps Sam could dig something out of his memory.'

'Come on, Sam!' said Merry. 'There's more stored in your head than you let on about.'

'I don't know about that,' said Sam. 'But how would this
suit? It ain't what I call proper poetry, if you understand me:
just a bit of nonsense. But these old images here brought it
to my mind.' Standing up, with his hands behind his back,
as if he was at school, he began to sing to an old tune.

> Troll sat alone on his seat of stone,
> And munched and mumbled a bare old bone;
>   For many a year he had gnawed it near,
>   For meat was hard to come by.
>   Done by! Gum by!
>   In a cave in the hills he dwelt alone,
>   And meat was hard to come by.

> Up came Tom with his big boots on.
> Said he to Troll: 'Pray, what is yon?
>   For it looks like the shin o' my nuncle Tim,
>   As should be a-lyin' in graveyard.
>   Caveyard! Paveyard!
>   This many a year has Tim been gone,
>   And I thought he were lyin' in graveyard.'

> 'My lad,' said Troll, 'this bone I stole.
> But what be bones that lie in a hole?
>   Thy nuncle was dead as a lump o' lead,
>   Afore I found his shinbone.
>   Tinbone! Thinbone!
>   He can spare a share for a poor old troll,
>   For he don't need his shinbone.'

> Said Tom: 'I don't see why the likes o' thee
> Without axin' leave should go makin' free
>   With the shank or the shin o' my father's kin;
>   So hand the old bone over!
>   Rover! Trover!
>   Though dead he be, it belongs to he;
>   So hand the old bone over!'

'For a couple o' pins,' says Troll, and grins,
'I'll eat thee too, and gnaw thy shins.
    A bit o' fresh meat will go down sweet!
      I'll try my teeth on thee now.
        Hee now! See now!
    I'm tired o' gnawing old bones and skins;
      I've a mind to dine on thee now.'

But just as he thought his dinner was caught,
He found his hands had hold of naught.
    Before he could mind, Tom slipped behind
      And gave him the boot to larn him.
        Warn him! Darn him!
    A bump o' the boot on the seat, Tom thought,
      Would be the way to larn him.

But harder than stone is the flesh and bone
Of a troll that sits in the hills alone.
    As well set your boot to the mountain's root,
      For the seat of a troll don't feel it.
        Peel it! Heal it!
    Old Troll laughed, when he heard Tom groan,
      And he knew his toes could feel it.

Tom's leg is game, since home he came,
And his bootless foot is lasting lame;
    But Troll don't care, and he's still there
      With the bone he boned from its owner.
        Doner! Boner!
    Troll's old seat is still the same,
      And the bone he boned from its owner!

'Well, that's a warning to us all!' laughed Merry. 'It is as well you used a stick, and not your hand, Strider!'

'Where did you come by that, Sam?' asked Pippin. 'I've never heard those words before.'

Sam muttered something inaudible. 'It's out of his own

head, of course,' said Frodo. 'I am learning a lot about Sam
Gamgee on this journey. First he was a conspirator, now
he's a jester. He'll end up by becoming a wizard – or a
warrior!'

'I hope not,' said Sam. 'I don't want to be neither!'

In the afternoon they went on down the woods. They were
probably following the very track that Gandalf, Bilbo, and
the dwarves had used many years before. After a few miles
they came out on the top of a high bank above the Road. At
this point the Road had left the Hoarwell far behind in its
narrow valley, and now clung close to the feet of the hills,
rolling and winding eastward among woods and heather-
covered slopes towards the Ford and the Mountains. Not far
down the bank Strider pointed out a stone in the grass. On
it roughly cut and now much weathered could still be seen
dwarf-runes and secret marks.

'There!' said Merry. 'That must be the stone that marked
the place where the trolls' gold was hidden. How much is
left of Bilbo's share, I wonder, Frodo?'

Frodo looked at the stone, and wished that Bilbo had
brought home no treasure more perilous, nor less easy to
part with. 'None at all,' he said. 'Bilbo gave it all away. He
told me he did not feel it was really his, as it came from
robbers.'

The Road lay quiet under the long shadows of early
evening. There was no sign of any other travellers to be seen.
As there was now no other possible course for them to take,
they climbed down the bank, and turning left went off as fast
as they could. Soon a shoulder of the hills cut off the light
of the fast westering sun. A cold wind flowed down to meet
them from the mountains ahead.

They were beginning to look out for a place off the Road,
where they could camp for the night, when they heard a
sound that brought sudden fear back into their hearts: the
noise of hoofs behind them. They looked back, but they

could not see far because of the many windings and rollings of the Road. As quickly as they could they scrambled off the beaten way and up into the deep heather and bilberry brushwood on the slopes above, until they came to a small patch of thick-growing hazels. As they peered out from among the bushes, they could see the Road, faint and grey in the failing light, some thirty feet below them. The sound of hoofs drew nearer. They were going fast, with a light *clippety-clippety-clip*. Then faintly, as if it was blown away from them by the breeze, they seemed to catch a dim ringing, as of small bells tinkling.

'That does not sound like a Black Rider's horse!' said Frodo, listening intently. The other hobbits agreed hopefully that it did not, but they all remained full of suspicion. They had been in fear of pursuit for so long that any sound from behind seemed ominous and unfriendly. But Strider was now leaning forward, stooped to the ground, with a hand to his ear, and a look of joy on his face.

The light faded, and the leaves on the bushes rustled softly. Clearer and nearer now the bells jingled, and *clippety-clip* came the quick trotting feet. Suddenly into view below came a white horse, gleaming in the shadows, running swiftly. In the dusk its headstall flickered and flashed, as if it were studded with gems like living stars. The rider's cloak streamed behind him, and his hood was thrown back; his golden hair flowed shimmering in the wind of his speed. To Frodo it appeared that a white light was shining through the form and raiment of the rider, as if through a thin veil.

Strider sprang from hiding and dashed down towards the Road, leaping with a cry through the heather; but even before he had moved or called, the rider had reined in his horse and halted, looking up towards the thicket where they stood. When he saw Strider, he dismounted and ran to meet him calling out: *Ai na vedui Dúnadan! Mae govannen!* His speech and clear ringing voice left no doubt in their hearts: the rider was of the Elven-folk. No others that dwelt in the wide world had voices so fair to hear. But there seemed to be a note of haste or fear in his call, and they saw that he was now speaking quickly and urgently to Strider.

Soon Strider beckoned to them, and the hobbits left the bushes and hurried down to the Road. 'This is Glorfindel, who dwells in the house of Elrond,' said Strider.

'Hail, and well met at last!' said the Elf-lord to Frodo. 'I was sent from Rivendell to look for you. We feared that you were in danger upon the road.'

'Then Gandalf has reached Rivendell?' cried Frodo joyfully.

'No. He had not when I departed; but that was nine days ago,' answered Glorfindel. 'Elrond received news that troubled him. Some of my kindred, journeying in your land beyond the Baranduin,* learned that things were amiss, and sent messages as swiftly as they could. They said that the Nine were abroad, and that you were astray bearing a great burden without guidance, for Gandalf had not returned. There are few even in Rivendell that can ride openly against the Nine; but such as there were, Elrond sent out north, west, and south. It was thought that you might turn far aside to avoid pursuit, and become lost in the Wilderness.

'It was my lot to take the Road, and I came to the Bridge of Mitheithel, and left a token there, nigh on seven days ago. Three of the servants of Sauron were upon the Bridge, but they withdrew and I pursued them westward. I came also upon two others, but they turned away southward. Since then I have searched for your trail. Two days ago I found it, and followed it over the Bridge; and today I marked where you descended from the hills again. But come! There is no time for further news. Since you are here we must risk the peril of the Road and go. There are five behind us, and when they find your trail upon the Road they will ride after us like the wind. And they are not all. Where the other four may be, I do not know. I fear that we may find the Ford is already held against us.'

* The Brandywine River.

While Glorfindel was speaking the shades of evening deepened. Frodo felt a great weariness come over him. Ever since the sun began to sink the mist before his eyes had darkened, and he felt that a shadow was coming between him and the faces of his friends. Now pain assailed him, and he felt cold. He swayed, clutching at Sam's arm.

'My master is sick and wounded,' said Sam angrily. 'He can't go on riding after nightfall. He needs rest.'

Glorfindel caught Frodo as he sank to the ground, and taking him gently in his arms he looked in his face with grave anxiety.

Briefly Strider told of the attack on their camp under Weathertop, and of the deadly knife. He drew out the hilt, which he had kept, and handed it to the Elf. Glorfindel shuddered as he took it, but he looked intently at it.

'There are evil things written on this hilt,' he said; 'though maybe your eyes cannot see them. Keep it, Aragorn, till we reach the house of Elrond! But be wary, and handle it as little as you may! Alas! the wounds of this weapon are beyond my skill to heal. I will do what I can – but all the more do I urge you now to go on without rest.'

He searched the wound on Frodo's shoulder with his fingers, and his face grew graver, as if what he learned disquieted him. But Frodo felt the chill lessen in his side and arm; a little warmth crept down from his shoulder to his hand, and the pain grew easier. The dusk of evening seemed to grow lighter about him, as if a cloud had been withdrawn. He saw his friends' faces more clearly again, and a measure of new hope and strength returned.

'You shall ride my horse,' said Glorfindel. 'I will shorten the stirrups up to the saddle-skirts, and you must sit as tight as you can. But you need not fear: my horse will not let any rider fall that I command him to bear. His pace is light and smooth; and if danger presses too near, he will bear you away with a speed that even the black steeds of the enemy cannot rival.'

'No, he will not!' said Frodo. 'I shall not ride him, if I am to be carried off to Rivendell or anywhere else, leaving my friends behind in danger.'

Glorfindel smiled. 'I doubt very much,' he said, 'if your friends would be in danger if you were not with them! The pursuit would follow you and leave us in peace, I think. It is you, Frodo, and that which you bear that brings us all in peril.'

To that Frodo had no answer, and he was persuaded to mount Glorfindel's white horse. The pony was laden instead with a great part of the others' burdens, so that they now marched lighter, and for a time made good speed; but the hobbits began to find it hard to keep up with the swift tireless feet of the Elf. On he led them, into the mouth of darkness, and still on under the deep clouded night. There was neither star nor moon. Not until the grey of dawn did he allow them to halt. Pippin, Merry, and Sam were by that time nearly asleep on their stumbling legs; and even Strider seemed by the sag of his shoulders to be weary. Frodo sat upon the horse in a dark dream.

They cast themselves down in the heather a few yards from the road-side, and fell asleep immediately. They seemed hardly to have closed their eyes when Glorfindel, who had set himself to watch while they slept, awoke them again. The sun had now climbed far into the morning, and the clouds and mists of the night were gone.

'Drink this!' said Glorfindel to them, pouring for each in turn a little liquor from his silver-studded flask of leather. It was clear as spring water and had no taste, and it did not feel either cool or warm in the mouth; but strength and vigour seemed to flow into all their limbs as they drank it. Eaten after that draught the stale bread and dried fruit (which was now all that they had left) seemed to satisfy their hunger better than many a good breakfast in the Shire had done.

They had rested rather less than five hours when they took to the Road again. Glorfindel still urged them on, and only

allowed two brief halts during the day's march. In this way
they covered almost twenty miles before nightfall, and came
to a point where the Road bent right and ran down towards
the bottom of the valley, now making straight for the Bruinen.
So far there had been no sign or sound of pursuit that the
hobbits could see or hear; but often Glorfindel would halt
and listen for a moment, if they lagged behind, and a look
of anxiety clouded his face. Once or twice he spoke to Strider
in the elf-tongue.

But however anxious their guides might be, it was plain
that the hobbits could go no further that night. They were
stumbling along dizzy with weariness, and unable to think of
anything but their feet and legs. Frodo's pain had redoubled,
and during the day things about him faded to shadows of
ghostly grey. He almost welcomed the coming of night, for
then the world seemed less pale and empty.

The hobbits were still weary, when they set out again early
next morning. There were many miles yet to go between
them and the Ford, and they hobbled forward at the best
pace they could manage.

'Our peril will be greatest just ere we reach the river,' said
Glorfindel; 'for my heart warns me that the pursuit is now
swift behind us, and other danger may be waiting by the
Ford.'

The Road was still running steadily downhill, and there
was now in places much grass at either side, in which the
hobbits walked when they could, to ease their tired feet. In
the late afternoon they came to a place where the Road went
suddenly under the dark shadow of tall pine-trees, and then
plunged into a deep cutting with steep moist walls of red
stone. Echoes ran along as they hurried forward; and there
seemed to be a sound of many footfalls following their own.
All at once, as if through a gate of light, the Road ran out
again from the end of the tunnel into the open. There at the
bottom of a sharp incline they saw before them a long flat
mile, and beyond that the Ford of Rivendell. On the further

side was a steep brown bank, threaded by a winding path; and behind that the tall mountains climbed, shoulder above shoulder, and peak beyond peak, into the fading sky.

There was still an echo as of following feet in the cutting behind them; a rushing noise as if a wind were rising and pouring through the branches of the pines. One moment Glorfindel turned and listened, then he sprang forward with a loud cry.

'Fly!' he called. 'Fly! The enemy is upon us!'

The white horse leaped forward. The hobbits ran down the slope. Glorfindel and Strider followed as rear-guard. They were only half way across the flat, when suddenly there was a noise of horses galloping. Out of the gate in the trees that they had just left rode a Black Rider. He reined his horse in, and halted, swaying in his saddle. Another followed him, and then another; then again two more.

'Ride forward! Ride!' cried Glorfindel to Frodo.

He did not obey at once, for a strange reluctance seized him. Checking the horse to a walk, he turned and looked back. The Riders seemed to sit upon their great steeds like threatening statues upon a hill, dark and solid, while all the woods and land about them receded as if into a mist. Suddenly he knew in his heart that they were silently commanding him to wait. Then at once fear and hatred awoke in him. His hand left the bridle and gripped the hilt of his sword, and with a red flash he drew it.

'Ride on! Ride on!' cried Glorfindel, and then loud and clear he called to the horse in the elf-tongue: *noro lim, noro lim, Asfaloth!*

At once the white horse sprang away and sped like the wind along the last lap of the Road. At the same moment the black horses leaped down the hill in pursuit, and from the Riders came a terrible cry, such as Frodo had heard filling the woods with horror in the Eastfarthing far away. It was answered; and to the dismay of Frodo and his friends out from the trees and rocks away on the left four other Riders came flying. Two rode towards Frodo: two galloped madly towards the Ford to cut off his escape. They seemed to him to run like the wind and to grow swiftly larger and darker, as their courses converged with his.

Frodo looked back for a moment over his shoulder. He could no longer see his friends. The Riders behind were falling back: even their great steeds were no match in speed for the white elf-horse of Glorfindel. He looked forward again, and hope faded. There seemed no chance of reaching the Ford before he was cut off by the others that had lain in ambush. He could see them clearly now: they appeared to have cast aside their hoods and black cloaks, and they were robed in white and grey. Swords were naked in their pale hands; helms were on their heads. Their cold eyes glittered, and they called to him with fell voices.

Fear now filled all Frodo's mind. He thought no longer of his sword. No cry came from him. He shut his eyes and clung to the horse's mane. The wind whistled in his ears, and the bells upon the harness rang wild and shrill. A breath of deadly cold pierced him like a spear, as with a last spurt, like a flash of white fire, the elf-horse speeding as if on wings, passed right before the face of the foremost Rider.

Frodo heard the splash of water. It foamed about his feet. He felt the quick heave and surge as the horse left the river and struggled up the stony path. He was climbing the steep bank. He was across the Ford.

But the pursuers were close behind. At the top of the bank the horse halted and turned about neighing fiercely. There were Nine Riders at the water's edge below, and Frodo's spirit quailed before the threat of their uplifted faces. He knew of nothing that would prevent them from crossing as easily as he had done; and he felt that it was useless to try to escape over the long uncertain path from the Ford to the edge of Rivendell, if once the Riders crossed. In any case he felt that he was commanded urgently to halt. Hatred again stirred in him, but he had no longer the strength to refuse.

Suddenly the foremost Rider spurred his horse forward.

It checked at the water and reared up. With a great effort Frodo sat upright and brandished his sword.

'Go back!' he cried. 'Go back to the Land of Mordor, and follow me no more!' His voice sounded thin and shrill in his own ears. The Riders halted, but Frodo had not the power of Bombadil. His enemies laughed at him with a harsh and chilling laughter. 'Come back! Come back!' they called. 'To Mordor we will take you!'

'Go back!' he whispered.

'The Ring! The Ring!' they cried with deadly voices; and immediately their leader urged his horse forward into the water, followed closely by two others.

'By Elbereth and Lúthien the Fair,' said Frodo with a last effort, lifting up his sword, 'you shall have neither the Ring nor me!'

Then the leader, who was now half across the Ford, stood up menacing in his stirrups, and raised up his hand. Frodo was stricken dumb. He felt his tongue cleave to his mouth, and his heart labouring. His sword broke and fell out of his shaking hand. The elf-horse reared and snorted. The foremost of the black horses had almost set foot upon the shore.

At that moment there came a roaring and a rushing: a noise of loud waters rolling many stones. Dimly Frodo saw the river below him rise, and down along its course there came a plumed cavalry of waves. White flames seemed to Frodo to flicker on their crests and he half fancied that he saw amid the water white riders upon white horses with frothing manes. The three Riders that were still in the midst of the Ford were overwhelmed: they disappeared, buried suddenly under angry foam. Those that were behind drew back in dismay.

With his last failing senses Frodo heard cries, and it seemed to him that he saw, beyond the Riders that hesitated on the shore, a shining figure of white light; and behind it ran small shadowy forms waving flames, that flared red in the grey mist that was falling over the world.

The black horses were filled with madness, and leaping

forward in terror they bore their riders into the rushing flood. Their piercing cries were drowned in the roaring of the river as it carried them away. Then Frodo felt himself falling, and the roaring and confusion seemed to rise and engulf him together with his enemies. He heard and saw no more.